THE SMALL MUSEUM

THE SMALL MUSEUM

Jody Cooksley

Allison & Busby Limited
11 Wardour Mews
London W1F 8AN
allisonandbusby.com

First published in Great Britain by Allison & Busby in 2024.

First Edition

HB ISBN 978-0-7490-3152-7
TPB ISBN 978-0-7490-3157-2

Typeset in 11/16pt Adobe Garamond Pro by
Allison & Busby Ltd.

By choosing this product, you help take care of the world's forests.
Learn more: www.fsc.org

FSC
www.fsc.org
MIX
Paper | Supporting
responsible forestry
FSC® C171272

Printed and bound by
CPI Group (UK) Ltd, Croydon, CR0 4YY

For my sister, Jacqui

Dear you should not stay so late
Twilight is not good for maidens;
Should not loiter in the glen
In the haunts of goblin men.

'Goblin Market', Christina Rosetti

Exhibit 1

Grey stone female figurine. Hellenic.
Catalogued 1873.

Our wedding was cold and silent, unmarked by flowers or hymns. Pity no choir drowned the noise of my sister. Isabel had no right to cry. She'd done nothing to save me and now her weeping echoed round the chapel and tore at my nerves. I gripped Father's arm, feeling the darned patch in his suit, and watched the congregation through watery eyes. In the left pews sat as many family shreds as Mother could gather at short notice, overdressed in country finery. On Dr Everley's side was a group of suited men, and a woman in a beautiful emerald dress with mourning bands. She couldn't help those, but surely everyone knew green brought brides bad luck? A wide-brimmed hat hid her face from view; a fox stole clawed across her shoulders.

Mother beamed so brightly I felt ashamed. She had no need to pretend we were happy, everyone in the church knew my duty – a respectable marriage to heal our past. Isabel was quick enough to explain. *What chance of escape, for either of us, if you refuse?* So why was she crying? Not for me. Mother ignored her, turning to wave at the aunts like a duchess at a coronation, and Isabel snivelled into her handkerchief, throwing sideways looks at my shoes. Pale blue kid with two rows of buttons and heels that clicked when I walked. They were all that felt beautiful. *Shoes for a lady,* Mother had sighed as the cobblers boxed them up and Isabel sulked for a day. She was welcome to walk in them now.

My veil was the 'something old'. A gift from Grandmother, delivered in a package of waxed paper stretched thin as her lips.

An heirloom meant for three sisters, was all she said but I knew she blamed Mother for Rebecca's disgrace. She blamed her for this too, saying things about Dr Everley that made me anxious. Hinting at darkness. Father's friendship with Dr Everley was shrouded in stage smoke, yet now I must promise to honour him, and all Mother said was that I should be glad he wasn't ugly. He was tall, sword-slim, with just a streak of grey hair at his temple.

Through Grandmother's fine lace I saw high cheekbones, eyes dark as tombs and deep lines around his mouth as though everything displeased him. Would marriage make him happy? He had certainly seemed keen, arranging things so quickly we'd barely had time to talk. I swallowed hard. As Mother said, I was to be wed, and I should make the best of it.

Paintings flanked the altar, crowding the wall. Gilded frames around the lives of saints. Symeon in his cave, Sebastian shot with arrows. The artist seemed especially to relish the sufferance of holy women. Devoted Agatha on fire; Felicity torn to pieces by wild animals; and Perpetua herself, so great a woman she could not be slain unless she herself willed it. When the service ended, Dr Everley took my hand and I recoiled at his icy touch. He didn't lift the veil to kiss me. All along the aisle, one arm in the crook of his, the other aching from the weight of my bouquet, I imagined Perpetua and willed myself not to be slain.

* * *

At least there would be music at the reception. We came directly from the church, in two coaches which, to Mother's delight, both bore the Everley crest.

'Will there be dancing?' Isabel indicated the string quartet setting up in the corner.

I shook my head, embarrassed. Who could imagine Dr Everley dancing? He was a man of letters, too clever for amusements. Father said his research was gaining attention, perhaps notoriety, and I always pictured him in a library. 'Dr Everley's a serious man.'

'But he's a gentleman. You'll do alright here.' Isabel surveyed the room, devouring details for Mother when they returned home and left me. 'Those colours!'

'This isn't his house.' I would not give her the satisfaction of admitting it was beautiful. Watered silk dressed the walls in shimmering tangerine and the furniture was covered to match, low ottomans and broad-backed chairs in intimate groups. Small dark-wood tables waited to hold drinks and cigars. 'He may live in a perfect hovel for all we know. I'm sure Mother forgot to request the details in her haste to see me off.' I should have been trying to lift Isabel's spirits, but I had no patience for such foolish talk. What did orange walls matter? My life was ripped apart.

'Father's been to his house.'

'His clinic.' I couldn't imagine them as equals. Father had barely a fee-paying patient left. 'You know Brewsters aren't welcome in respectable places.' I turned away too late to avoid the hurt in her face.

'Don't you want to be happy? You'll want for nothing now.'

'I wanted nothing before.' Why should everyone's fate rest in *my* hands? Isabel and the boys could look forward to the summer at Lynton and I would have enjoyed it more than any of them. It was never me who resented the creeping shame after Rebecca left,

9

the lack of invitations, all the parties and picnics we missed. Lynton would have been enough for me. Walking the dogs in the coppice, taking my sketchbook, or setting my easel in the orchards. The scent of long grass and ripe apples. No-one to watch or admonish. No responsibilities. Before Dr Everley came, I was free as the swifts that returned in spring. As free as my brothers to sketch and draw all day. Afterwards I was made to wear dresses that caught on branches, hair dressed and fussed until my scalp ached. Mother closed my sketchbooks and balanced them on my head, training me to stand tall and walk without them falling. She dismissed my careful notes and drawings as 'showing off', and I bit my lip until it bled.

Isabel sighed. 'You'll have a house. A London address! And people to call. Your husband will be respected. You can stop worrying that you'll die before you live.'

'I've never worried about that.' I frowned. Mother threw a sharp look from the buffet table and my heart sank as she bore down on us, a full plate in one hand, the other pulling at her too-tight gown.

'For heaven's sake, Madeleine, stop looking so miserable. You're as far from a blushing bride as it's possible to be! You don't want Dr Everley changing his mind.'

'It would be a little late if he did.'

'You think he will like sarcasm? You're lucky to be taken at all.'

I tried to smile before she moved off to seize Aunt Honour. No use parting on bad terms; I would miss them soon enough. I turned to Isabel. 'You'll come to stay, won't you? As soon as you can.' I could not imagine life without them.

'You'll need to ask permission for that now.' Isabel looked across at Dr Everley, deep in conversation with an elaborately whiskered man. She sighed again. 'Perhaps your new husband will want you all to himself.'

'Lucius is not such a selfish man.' The woman in the wide-veiled hat extended her hand and I pressed it, hit by an overpowering scent of roses and something sickly that I couldn't place. My cheeks burnt to think what she'd overheard. Such striking looks, with amber eyes and deep-red hair set off by the green of her gown. The fox on her shoulders bared sharp white teeth.

'Delighted to meet you, dear sister. Lucius has told me so little about you that I feared I would guess all wrong. But you're perfect. So young. So pretty.' Said with the confidence of one who knows her own appearance is unrivalled. 'I'll visit as soon as you're settled. Do you like children? I *could* bring them, ghastly as they are. But we might better get to know each other if I leave them with Nurse.' She paused, throwing her hair back over one shoulder. 'But I mustn't put you off. Lucius *adores* children.'

Dr Everley – I must try to call him Lucius – had told me very little. We had only walked together once, talking mostly of his work. I learnt about his expertise in bone-setting and the method by which his father cured a royal child of club foot. Yet I knew nothing of his family.

Isabel dropped an awkward curtsey and the woman turned, clasping her hands together in a dramatic gesture.

'You must be dear Madeleine's true sister; you look so very alike. I am Lucius's sister, Grace. I hope you don't mind me stealing her? I only had Lucius, and I have always longed for a sister of my own.'

'We have brothers too. We know very well how they can be,' I said, trying to cover my surprise. A new sister, just as beautiful as Rebecca.

'Are they also doctors?' She looked around as though trying to identify them, her lip curling slightly at the sight of Mother clinking glasses. 'I hope not, for your sake. So dreary always being called to watch Lucius's scientific experiments. Frogs and fireworks.' She raised her hand as if to brush their childhood away, but her eyes shone. They must be very close.

'They're still in school. Younger than us, but even younger brothers can be demanding. James would like to travel; he's keen on India. I think he'll make a fine businessman one day.' I pointed at my brother who was trying to balance one more cake on an overloaded plate. I felt a surge of love and sympathy. Perhaps it would now be in my power to help him make his way in the world.

'He's remarkably young, but then you,' she looked me up and down, 'are remarkably young also. Don't expect too much of my brother and perhaps you'll be happy together.' She continued to hold me in her steady gaze.

I nodded, unsure what she meant. What was too much to expect? I felt silly; a child dressed up as a bride. We waited warily until Isabel blurted out, 'Your gown is so beautiful.'

Grace turned her attention. 'I did worry that its colour might offend you. I know that country folk can sometimes be . . . *superstitious* in believing that green will bring bad luck to a wedding, but it's new and I *so* wanted to wear it and I can see that you two, at least, are not the type.'

Isabel opened her mouth, and I threw her a warning glance.

'Perhaps a cup of tea?' Grace perched on the edge of a small love seat and smoothed her dress, watching Isabel rush to obey. She was clearly used to people doing as she asked.

'Sweet thing,' she said. 'And you have another sister, I believe? But she . . . can't be here?'

I nodded, turning my head so my face would not betray me, though I could feel the way she watched.

'Perhaps that is why the rest of your family came? I understood Lucius asked for a quiet ceremony.'

'Mother is fond of a gathering.'

'So I see. And how do you like our little part of London?' She leant in, expectant. The fox's eyes glinted orange.

What I'd seen from the carriage couldn't have been more different to the market towns and villages of Cheshire. So many tall buildings, so many strangers. 'The streets are very wide,' I said, instantly wishing I'd thought of something clever.

'You've never visited before?'

She must think me naïve. Isabel's return interrupted the need for an answer. If my hand shook slightly as I accepted the teacup, if her fingers gripped the saucer a little too fiercely, then both of us worked hard not to show it.

By the time our party left, the sky was darkening to black. Rain drizzled down. Gas lamps blurred in the mist, so the street seemed viewed through tears. Yet London was alive as day, thick with walking couples and costers in bright coats, gentlemen calling from their carriage to be let down at the very door we were leaving through to go home. Lucius grabbed my arm and steered me away, almost pushing me inside the carriage.

'I'm sorry they took so long.' I leant against the window, tired from attention and long farewells, and rubbed my sleeve where his fingers had pressed too firmly.

'You'd think they'd want to get home. It's a long enough drive.'

'James said if Thursday's weather was good there'd be a picnic by the pack bridge.'

'Indeed,' Lucius replied.

His disinterest in my family was plain. Why would he care? But the thought of them all together dried my throat and I found nothing else to say. Mother had probably organised the picnic to campaign her social return. James planned to try painting the bridge, he promised to send me the picture, though he was a boy and would forget. They would all carry on just as well without me. I could write and remind him, ask him to post my paints. I wish I'd thought to pack them, though I wasn't sure there'd be enough grey to paint London. Perhaps it would seem less miserable in daylight.

We travelled in silence until the carriage rolled to a halt at the centre of a long, curved street. Houses all pushed together with no room to breathe. Arlington Crescent had grey-brick buildings, patterned with sandstone, and lidded with slate tiles that gathered like frowns over the eaves. Lucius took my arm to help me down and led me to a flight of worn stone steps, railed with iron. Number five had huge windows and white shutters, a shiny black front door. *Elegant*, Mother would declare. It looked unfriendly and I longed for the thatched roof and sprawling lawns of Lynton. Two more rows of windows glared under the low hanging roof. How many servants could a single man need? How many would I have to manage? There was only Ellen at home.

'Good evening, sir.' The sudden deep voice was startling. 'Good evening, madam.' Standing in the darkness was an old man, his back slightly crooked, the tails of his black coat hanging to his knees. A strange smell emanated through the open doorway. Sweet and rotten, like forgotten flowers long dead in their urn.

'Evening, Barker. Take the bags, would you? And have Mrs Barker show my wife to her rooms, make sure she's comfortable.' He turned to me with his sister's air of assurance. 'It's been a long day and I'm sure you'll wish to retire. I rise early for work, but the Barkers will see that you have what you need.' Holding out his hand, he reached towards me and then seemed to think better of it. 'I'll take my brandy in the study.'

I wanted to keep him there, to apologise for the guests, the noise of the wedding. He was a quiet man, and I would have liked him to realise that I understood him. But he didn't wait, and Mrs Barker was already sailing down the passage, her black dress scratching against the walls.

Half the night I waited for steps in the corridor. They all told me – Mother, my cousins, even Grandmother – that he would come whatever happened, that men would always come. They described things I only half believed. Cradled in the stiff four-poster bed I waited, at first with the curtains tightly drawn and then, when I couldn't stand wondering if he'd come in unseen, with them hanging half open again. I sat upright as a statue, a stone figure, stiff with waiting, until I drifted in and out of fitful sleep, dreaming of some unknown thing that followed close behind me, only to disappear as I turned.

2

Great Marlborough Street Public Office

'Am I to understand that she killed her own child?' The magistrate sounded bored, as though he dealt with such things every day and they never troubled his sleep. He spoke slowly, precisely, his head resting delicately on his left arm, while the right smoothed a sheaf of papers on his desk.

'Yes. Sir.' Mrs Atherton added the title as though she would rather not, and patted her hat. I'd never seen her in daylight, and she looked different without jewels. She was still beautiful. More so, perhaps, her colouring enhanced by the simplicity of her grey dress.

'Was there anything in Mrs Everley's behaviour, or manner, prior to this that might lead you to believe she was capable of such a thing?'

The magistrate motioned to a scribe and handed over the papers before turning his full attention to the witness stand. Court life had given him an ashen complexion and pouches of skin gathered beneath his eyes. How many horrors had he judged?

'There were several . . . incidents.'

Silence hung in the waiting room.

'Continue, Mrs Atherton.' The magistrate waved his hand. 'This office must take everything into consideration before deciding how to proceed.'

16

'My sister-in-law was awkward with my children. She behaved strangely around them, as though she couldn't bear to have them near her.'

'What age are your children, Mrs Atherton?'

'Six and ten years. A girl and two boys. Twins.'

'Did Mrs Everley have a good relationship with them?'

Grace bowed her head demurely and her lashes threw long shadows across her cheeks. She appeared to be a perfect society mother.

'She's the wife of my brother. When he married, I brought my babies to visit, of course, so that they would know their only aunt. I had hoped they would love one another.' She glanced up at the viewing gallery and, for a brief moment, our eyes locked. I hoped she could see what I thought of her act. Maddie always suspected she had something to hide. If poor Maddie had asked for my help, we might never have ended up here. I wished she had trusted my friendship more and I willed Mrs Atherton to falter, but she was perfectly calm. 'I'm sorry to say that she didn't take to them. She seemed almost afraid to be close to them. I remember one incident where she deliberately knocked Eloise from her chair and then tried to blame Edmond. Poor girl was quite hurt. Madeleine showed no concern at all.'

'Was Mrs Everley ever alone with the children?'

Grace looked horror-struck. Her right arm hovered across her heart. What an actress.

'I would never have left Madeleine alone with them. Goodness knows what might have happened. Another time she pushed Edmond, quite violently, in front of an open window. I'm sure she meant harm.'

'Do you have anything further to add?'

'She wandered. All the time. Up and down the corridors in the night. And she slept at strange hours of the day too, often going to bed in the afternoon. My brother said she sleepwalked. But she always seemed awake when we encountered her. It was as though she used restlessness as an excuse for being all over the house.'

Why did she *need* an excuse for being all over her own house? Why didn't the magistrate ask that? And where was Lucius? His own wife sat motionless in the wooden dock, hands chained, weals clearly visible on her arms, below the short sleeves of her prison dress. Her face was hidden by guards, though I could see her hair was filthy and matted. Her beautiful hair. I could weep at the sight of it. How much had she borne alone? I should have been a better friend. If I'd listened more carefully, I could have seen this coming.

'My brother is the victim here. And his poor child.'

'Thank you, Mrs Atherton, no further questions.' The magistrate waved at the court hand, who stepped forward and opened the gate with a sweeping gesture. Grace nodded, raised her head to the viewing gallery and paused just long enough to show how she both needed and trusted them. She might as well have taken a bow for such a performance.

'Bring the accused to the stand.'

The guards on either side of Maddie drew her roughly to her feet and she stumbled, shaking her head wildly. I had to stop myself crying out that I was here, her Caro. I wanted her to look up. The magistrate waited a few moments before raising his hands and ushering the guards impatiently.

'Very well. Give her some time. A glass of water. Bring the next witness.'

A stout woman took the stand, her bombazine rustling as she heaved herself inside. Part of her face was slightly puckered, giving her left eye an odd squint. Disconcerting. It was as though she looked past you and straight through you at once.

'Name?'

'Mrs Henrietta Ermentrude Barker.'

'What is your relationship to the accused?'

'Housekeeper to Dr and Mrs Everley.'

'Thank you.' The magistrate leant over to one of his court hands, who whispered something and handed him another sheet of paper. He read through it slowly before turning his attention back to Mrs Barker, who hadn't moved a muscle. 'And in your role as housekeeper you must have seen a good deal of Mrs Everley?'

'No, sir. Mrs Everley was a very private person. She didn't like to spend time with others.'

Why did they all insist on speaking as though Maddie were deceased? She was right there, in the same room, listening to their condemnation. No wonder she watched the floor. I wanted to wave and shout, show her that someone was there for her. But I couldn't risk being thrown out.

'She didn't talk to you about the household management?'

'She never came to the kitchen, sir. Mrs Atherton was more interested in the management of the house than Mrs Everley.'

'Mrs Everley's sister-in-law?'

'Yes. She visited often. Always made a point of checking on me in the kitchen, too. And she was never anything but good to Mrs Everley. She treated her like a sister.'

Grace had stayed to listen, smiling as though she'd won a prize. She was straight from a faerytale – a wicked sister intent on harm. I watched the magistrate carefully to see if he was fooled, but his face was impassive.

'Did you not meet with Mrs Everley at mealtimes, for example?'

'Not to speak to. She complained, sometimes, about the food.' Mrs Barker heaved her arms across her chest and folded them together, defensive. 'A lot of the time, actually. She didn't eat much, that's certain, though she liked wine. Most nights she

19

asked for wine. Lunchtimes too . . . if Dr Everley wasn't there. Didn't have much of an appetite, as I said. I put it down to the laudanum.'

The magistrate stopped writing notes and looked towards the accused's box. Maddie sat with her shoulders hunched forward and I saw that she was painfully thin. Her hands were reddened with cold, and her fingers plucked repeatedly at her skirts. I had never seen her take more than a glass of wine. It went to her head and she disliked the feeling of dizziness, the loss of control. I had heard her say it on more than one occasion. So why would she take laudanum? It made no sense.

'Mrs Everley took laudanum?'

'Yes. Most days.'

'Did you administer it at her request?'

Mrs Barker hitched her folded arms across her ample chest and pursed her lips. 'No. I did not. But when I went to clean the cups I could smell it there. I believe she added it herself to the cocoa she asked us to bring.'

'Where do you think Mrs Everley procured this laudanum?'

'I don't know. Like I said, she wasn't downstairs often.'

'Downstairs?'

'The kitchen. Where I spend most of my time. That's why it was odd when I saw her creep through with the bundle. Because she never went there, or to the garden. That's when I followed her.'

Maddie's prison dress was faded to the colour of a charcoal smudge, patched at the neckline and elbows. What kind of women had worn it before? Had they died in it? Was Maddie wondering the same? She wouldn't get the chance to speak today, the magistrate was already checking his watch. Mrs Barker unfolded her arms and slowly raised her right hand to point at Maddie. 'She knows what she did. She should be sentenced at the Assizes.'

Exhibit 3

Carved bone doll. Egyptian Coptic.
c.200 A.D.

D r Everley spared no expense on my trousseau, and my closet
harboured fine lace collars, satin and silk in pale blue and
grey like shades of winter skies. More new clothes than our family
had seen in years. Isabel would be envious, but shouldn't married
women choose their own gowns? Like Rebecca, I favoured brighter
colours. Her own closet was a rainbow to set off her dark curls,
though much fortune such finery had brought her.

Part of me had hoped she might appear at the wedding.
Ridiculous, of course; how would she know? But life was unsettled,
and my thoughts turned to her often. Poor Rebecca. The oldest
and best of us, beautiful in ways I barely understood. She would
have known exactly how to charm Dr Everley, Mrs Atherton,
all of them. She could have helped me. Although, if she hadn't
abandoned us, I might not be here at all.

On the night Rebecca disappeared, Mother explained through
noisy sobs that she had married badly enough to curse our
family. She screamed that we were never to speak of it and later
it transpired that my sister never married at all. I must have been
the last to know. All I understood was that the house became
quiet, people stopped coming – my friends, Mother's circle,

Isabel's admirers. In a matter of months, we'd dropped from the height of Doctor's Family to Unwelcome in Polite Society. Father lost his patients slowly, until Dr Pearson was called from town so often that he took a house in the village and our fate was sealed. By the time Father met Dr Everley, Isabel and I were tainted goods, bound to turn out badly, and would have to take someone from far away or not at all. It mattered little to me, but Mother jumped at the chance to introduce Isabel to our first house guest, the man Father had met in London years before on 'family business', insisting on our smartest dresses, hair washed and brushed, cheeks pinched red. Isabel bit at her lips to bring out their colour and borrowed Mother's powder, caking her face until she looked ill. She capered and chattered like a squirrel, while I sat in the corner with my sketchbooks, and everyone was furious when he chose me. Father said he liked my calmness, but I would like my husband to look at me properly. My husband! When would I get used to that? Selecting a blue gown, I held it against myself and spun round before the glass, screaming in fright as I noticed a small woman standing by the end of the bed. She was painfully thin, and her starched apron and dark blue dress gave her the look of a carved wooden doll.

'Good morning . . .'

'Annie, ma'am.' The poor thing looked terrified. Purple smudges below her eyes showed I wasn't the only one who slept badly.

'Annie. I'm sorry if I startled you. I wasn't expecting . . . call me Maddie. Could you help with my hair?' Ellen always did it at home. Annie stared fixedly at the floor, ignoring the brush I held out. 'Do you know how to dress hair?'

'No ma'am.' She turned and began to set the grate. 'I'm just here to do the fire.'

Why would I need a fire in my room in the morning? Was I expected to stay there all day? Before I could ask, she gave a shallow curtsey and left, closing the door as silently as it had opened. A quiet ghost moving through rooms. Something else I would have to get used to.

With badly pinned hair and a stiff blue dress, I stepped out into my new home, quickly confused by the corridors. The house was as tall as it was wide, and at each end the stairwells spiralled like steps to the underworld. Heavy curtains blocked the windows and rows of portraits watched me lose my way, bright eyes following as I tracked back and forth. The sweet-rotten scent of dead flowers was everywhere. From a long window at the top of the central staircase I looked out to the small garden, wondering if there would be fresh flowers to cut and bring inside, but the borders looked empty. A plinth on the lawn held a statue of a woman with both arms outstretched, pleading, looking sadly at the raven perched on its hand. Three more ravens pecked at clods of earth on the gravel path, slick feathers shiny black. Already I missed the countryside around Lynton. What would be happening at home? Mother wouldn't keep the news to herself for long. She'd be at the baker's in her muslin and wedding hat, talking up Dr Everley as though he were royalty while Isabel reeled off descriptions of the hotel. I missed them. As soon as it was seemly, I would invite them to stay. There must be some things a wife was permitted to arrange for herself.

In a room to the left of the entrance was a breakfast table laid for one. A dead mouse curled by the chair, one eye open like a bright black bead, the other missing – a gift from the house cat. Outside, maids called across to one another while they scrubbed the steps, and I envied their sense of purpose. I sat at the small table, smoothing my skirt, and Mrs Barker bustled in so quickly that she must have been watching. She held a tall china pot of what smelt like coffee.

'Morning, Mrs Everley. Late sleeper.'

'Good morning, Mrs Barker. Call me Maddie. Is it terribly late? I was so tired after the journey and I slept badly in a strange bed.'

'It's a quarter past ten.' She moved the cup and bent the pot forward, flinching perceptibly when I stayed her hand.

'Thank you, I don't drink coffee.'

'I can pour you a glass of milk if you like?' It was hard to tell if she mocked me. One side of her face was slightly puckered, as though she'd suffered a bout of palsy, and it gave her a devious look. I would have liked a glass of milk, but I must learn adult habits. I must hold my nerve.

'We can order some tea when we go through the grocery lists.'

She raised an eyebrow. 'Whyever would we be doing that, Mrs Everley?'

Mother had told me what I'd need to do as Mistress: ordering the food and arranging the dinners. I wanted to tell this woman that it was my household now, to run as I pleased, but I couldn't find the words. 'How many will we be for dinner?'

'Dr Everley doesn't take to entertaining. I wouldn't expect much in the way of that sort of thing.'

An uncomfortable silence spread while Mrs Barker occupied herself with lifting lids off dishes and slapping chunks of butter onto floury bread. The lines on her face were deep and set, her flesh sagged and greyish against the white of her cap. I didn't want her to believe she had won.

'Perhaps you could give me a tour of the house?'

'I'll ask Barker to show you around tomorrow, Mrs Everley. I hope you have everything you need.'

'Please, call me Maddie.'

'I'm sorry, Mrs Everley,' she answered, her mouth a firm line. 'It doesn't seem right.'

I retreated to my room and wasted time trying to entice some sparrows onto my windowsill with crumbs from the box of biscuits Ellen had placed in my trunk. They were bold, quite unlike the birds at home, which flew off at the slightest noise when I tried to sketch them. I managed to get two to feed together for several moments, until Mrs Barker arrived with a bundle of linen.

'If those things come into the house, you'll be cleaning up their mess yourself.'

I opened my mouth to apologise, then changed my mind. If I wanted the company of birds, it was my business. Mother had a pretty cage in the garden room at Lynton, white-painted and strewn with ribbons, which housed a pair of lovebirds.

'Could you show me the library? I have nothing to read and I'm not sure when Lucius will return.' Dr Everley's given name felt unfamiliar, but I used it to show that I could, to remind her of my station. And hers. Wordlessly she led me there and opened the door before leaving, her stiff gown rustling as she turned.

The library was even gloomier than the rest of the house but it contained more books than I'd imagined could exist, beautiful editions and leather-bound volumes shelved in walnut and glass. I craned my neck to read the titles. Anatomy, medical dictionaries and scores of bound scientific papers on subjects I barely recognised – phrenology, geology, the lives of surgical pioneers and adventurers. Toxicology occupied an entire shelf. Was poisoning so common in London? I wanted to read something comforting, just for the sound of the words. But there was nothing by Rosetti, and the only copies of Shelley's works were three thin pamphlets on the use of electric currency to raise the dead. The idea made me shiver. Why had I listened to Mother's insistence that I bring no books of my own? *You will read whatever your husband wishes, Madeleine.* Would Dr Everley want me to learn about poisons? Or raising the dead? Tucked in a corner I found a volume of Tennyson, melancholy poems full of nature's teeth and claws, that made me feel keenly what I didn't know. How dull a man of science would find my conversation!

At exactly eight o'clock, I took the east stairs down to dinner and was surprised to find Dr Everley standing in the hallway, wearing a long frock coat with emerald button slips and a silk choker the colour of a beetle's wing. We exchanged polite 'good evenings' and I waited for him to lead me in to dine but he remained, gloves clasped loosely in his right hand.

'I trust you're comfortable?' He tilted his head to one side like a raven. I sensed bad news.

'You have a lovely home.' I was about to add 'and I am grateful for it', hoping to begin a conversation that might allow me to assess his feelings, when I saw Barker standing just behind him, in the shadows by the hallstand, brushing down a tall hat.

'It's all Grace's doing. She's always looked after us, Father and me. Of course, it's your house now and yours to change. If you so desire.' He didn't sound as though he meant it. 'She sent word to say that she'll visit tomorrow, she's keen to get to know you. I hope you'll grow to like each other.'

Why did *he* not wish to know me? 'I'm certain I will. And what of her family?'

His face clouded. 'Her husband . . . is abroad with his company, in India. A hard journey and one he undertakes seldom.'

Then the black bands were not for Grace's husband. She must

still mourn her father. 'She must miss him.'

'I doubt it. And Grace is kept busy enough.'

I was shocked to hear such intense dislike. What had the man done? I was sure Grace had told me his name, but I couldn't remember. 'She mentioned children?'

'Twin sons, and a daughter.'

'It's rare to have healthy twins. They're blessed.'

'They're not,' he said shortly. 'Only one is what you'd call healthy, and he remains at best a delicate child. At birth the cord was wrapped around his brother's neck, starving his oxygen. I delivered them myself and there was nothing to be done. They may have dwelt in the womb that way. Edmond, the stronger twin, determined to survive at all costs. He left Daniel without breath, a damaged brain. He survived, but only just and he does not like company, or trust strangers. He stays mostly in his room.'

So bluntly professional. Doctors must have their bedside manner, but this was family, his nephew. And to deliver babies, his own sister's babies! I struggled to stay composed.

'How terribly sad. Poor Grace.'

'That is life, Madeleine. Nature doesn't favour weakness. At certain points in our history, he would have been thrown to lions.'

We fell silent. Expectation hung in the air.

'Should we go to table? Mrs Barker said eight and it's already quarter past.'

Barker coughed and handed over the hat with a silver-topped cane, giving the rosewood a slight polish. Dr Everley made a show of examining his pocket watch and then turned to me apologetically, as though helpless before time.

'I'm afraid you must dine alone. It's the Collector Society's monthly meeting and I'm presenting something quite new to what I hope will be a generous audience. I mustn't keep them waiting.'

I examined the rug's floral pattern. 'Of course. You must go. Please, don't wait on my account. I'm tired and will retire early.'

'Soon you won't have time for me.' He stroked my cheek with his gloved hand. What did he mean? I had nothing to fill the lonely days that stretched before me. Barker opened the door and Dr Everley ran smartly down the steps. Carriage wheels echoed and the ghost of his touch burnt my cheek.

The dining room was laid with heavy plate in multiple settings, as though guests were expected, and polished like glass so that everything had to be picked up and replaced slowly. I barely managed to eat a mouthful of soup before Annie whisked my bowl away, almost dropping the spoon in her haste. I determined to talk to her when she brought the next course, but it was Barker who entered with the trolley and its single salver containing beans, potatoes and a small pie with a thick crust of suet decorated with a row of tiny beaks, yellowed with egg yolk. I stifled a cry of horror and my stomach turned at the thought of the bright eyes and dirty feathers of my sparrows.

'I'll take some wine.' I tried hard to sound like a mistress who would do as she pleased, but I'd rarely been offered wine at home. In fact, I'd only been eating at the same time as the adults for a year and Barker looked at me as though he knew that. Slowly he pulled a long chain from his belt and opened the wooden wine box with a small key, slipping it back into his pocket once he set the glass on the table, as if he was the only one to be trusted.

'Everything in order, Mrs Everley?'

'Is there to be pudding?' My stomach ached for palatable food.

'Old Dr Everley didn't agree with it. I could bring in some Stilton?'

I shook my head, hoping he saw, and cared, that I was cross.

Absurd to obey the authority of a deceased man. The whole dinner took barely half an hour and, exhausted and hungry, I retired to the drawing room, falling heavily on the small sofa. I had no energy for sewing and neat stitches would be impossible after wine. I would happily draw – if only I'd thought to bring my things. Mother always hated me sketching from nature, she thought it attracted the wrong sort of attention. *Frogs and beetles are not ladylike, Madeleine. Don't be such a tomboy or you'll end up unmarried.* She got that wrong. And I liked to draw. I was good at it.

I lay back against the cushions, close to tears with homesickness, and almost jumped from my skin when Mrs Barker entered with a loud cough, holding a bag of mending. She pulled her chair next to the lamp and began to darn a patch on an apron so small it must belong to Annie. I took up my own sewing in an attempt to cover my surprise.

'Dr Everley said to make sure you weren't lonely.'

She seemed to work without a single glance downward, her needle flying in and out of the worn fabric. The crossed hairpins in her bun cast long shadows, creeping up the wall behind her like spider legs.

Exhibit 4

Opium bowl.
Carved rosewood in primitive bird shape.
Persian. c. 300 B.C.

R ain had fallen heavily for days, steam shrouding the windows
and preventing all thoughts of excursions. Barker, unable to
work in the garden, was finally persuaded into the grand tour, and
I found that Dr Everley's house was far bigger than I'd thought
possible. Wings stretched out on either side, covering two or three
of what used to be neighbouring properties, and decorated with
Grace's exquisite taste. Shuttered windows stretched to the ground,
draped with muslin and corded velvet, and the ground floors were
dressed in green silk; rooms filled with so much furniture it was
hard to navigate a way through. Places for visits and afternoon
teas, though I had no idea when such things might happen. Did
people just call? Would Lucius tell me? How badly I needed a
friend to ask.

Upstairs were bedrooms with jewel-coloured spreads and
patterned rugs that looked as though they might fly if I wished
hard enough. There were nine, perhaps ten, not counting the
nursery near the servant's floor; more than we could possibly need
and easily enough for Mother and Isabel to be comfortable if
they wished to stay. Another of the bedrooms on my floor looked

occupied. Photographs on the dresser, a pile of books by the bed and shoes on stretching racks before a mirrored wardrobe. Freshly brushed evening clothes hung over a stand, papers and ink waited on the writing desk.

'Do we have a guest, Barker?' I never saw my husband leaving, so perhaps others came and went too.

'Not at present.'

'Then this is Dr Everley's room?' I thought his rooms were on the floor above.

'*Old* Dr Everley's room. Mrs Atherton laid out his things, so he'd still be in our thoughts. Door's always kept open, things ready to use.'

'He must have been a remarkable man.' What an odd thing for Grace to have done. Was he loved or feared? I stepped over to the portrait on the opposite wall. 'His wife?' In the painting a pale woman with a high pile of auburn hair and an elegant neck sat upright on a throne-like chair, her right hand crossed over her chest. Standing behind her, hands on her shoulders, was a tall man with cold eyes and fierce whiskers. By their feet sat a pretty girl in a froth of white frills, amber eyes staring straight from the canvas.

'And Dr Everley's mother. Not that he knew her as such. Passed away in her confinement. Very hard on them.'

Knowing he was the cause of her death must be even harder to bear. Poor Lucius. Grace, too, must have grieved, though she looked barely five years old in the painting. I asked why he didn't remarry to give them a mother, but Barker seemed not to hear. We continued our tour, alternating heavy silence with stilted conversation, and I discovered that Barker had served the family for more than forty years, since joining as footman. The term itself suited him, old-fashioned and slightly ridiculous.

Barker hesitated at the handle of the next door. 'Dr Everley's room.'

'We won't disturb him, Barker, he's not here.' Perhaps there would be clues to my husband's personality. Barker stood to one side and held the door open with a look of mistrust.

Moss-green walls and dark brown paint reminded me of a cave, filled with musky cologne that masked the sweet-rotten flower smell. A bear's cave. Two crossed swords hung on the wall above the dressing stand, which held a dark photograph of a much younger Lucius and Grace, and a pair of white kid gloves in stretchers like a floating pair of hands. No cushions, counterpane or rugs. Such a deeply masculine room that I felt heat rise to my cheeks and I could not stay long inside.

'And these?' Barker clearly intended to pass the last two doors.

'They're locked.'

'But you have keys?'

'Dr Everley keeps the keys to his workshop. And his cabinets. Some of the things in his collection are very old and need to be kept safe.'

'I'd like to see them.' Father had a small glass-fronted cupboard of things he found interesting, a few stuffed creatures, bird eggs and shells. I'd sketched some of them. Imagine a room full! 'There must be a key for cleaning?'

'Dr Everley cleans the rooms himself.'

A shiver thrilled my spine at the thought of what might be contained in collections to be kept away from ordinary eyes. 'I'm sure he'll entrust me to assist him.' I drew myself upright, pleased to see I was taller than Barker, and reached out to push against the door. It gave. Lucius did not strike me as a man who might forget to lock doors. Perhaps Barker was being untruthful about the keys. A smell of chemicals and something like decay made me pause momentarily, and Barker seized his chance to push between me and the open doorway. His grip was surprisingly strong, enough to wrestle me from the handle, but not before I caught a glimpse of the inside. A carcass the size of a female deer appeared to have been partially skinned, hind quarters stripped so that shocking white bones stuck from the flesh. Grisly butchery for a suite of gentleman's rooms. And Barker so keen to keep things secret that all my questions died on my tongue. I knew what he would answer: *Dr Everley is a surgeon, he works in ways you would not understand.* But I needed to understand, or I would never sleep. When Lucius returned, I would ask him.

I cleared my throat. 'What time does Dr Everley usually come home?'

Barker raised his eyebrows with some effort, as though they were too heavy for his face. 'He might be late if his patient's ailing, or not come home at all if they take bad. And if it's late it also depends on whether he goes to his club. Or straight to a lecture or meeting. Or a friend's house to borrow books and papers.' He spoke as slowly and carefully as someone explaining life to a child, making my question sound ridiculous. Why should I feel I had any claim on my husband's time?

'Dr Everley's a private man.' Barker's thick eyebrows sank back down, and he peered through them like a creature in leaves. 'He's had his own way for a long time.'

Grace arrived as we reached the front hall, as though her visit was timed, and ushered me into the sitting room. Soon she was entirely at home, reclining along the sofa, Edmond hiding in the folds of her dress. Eloise ran busily back and forth, fetching balls of tapestry wool and picture books to show her brother, who studiously ignored her, staring straight up at me instead. He had a sallow, peevish face and long legs that stuck out in front of him, his feet repeatedly knocking against the leg of my chair, unnoticed or unheeded by Grace. His presence made me nervous, though I tried to forget what Dr Everley had told me. The boy couldn't help the way he was born.

Grace leant back with a weary expression as though I were in *her* home, having overstayed my welcome. 'I do hope Lucius is looking after you, he can be tedious when something bothers him.'

What could be bothering him? Most evenings he went to his club and to all the lectures and society meetings he could wish. He had his research and his patients. Being married affected him very little. But with my new name and ring, I was left by myself, waiting all night for a visit that never came. And when I awoke, late, curtains thick against the daylight, my husband had already left for work.

'I haven't seen much of him.'

Grace's eyes glittered. 'He hardly has time for any of us. I haven't seen him in *days*, but I hear his talk went down well with the Society. He is quite the celebrity. Davenport's dinner was awash with him.'

I smiled as though I knew all about research and dinners and Davenports. I hadn't spoken more than a handful of words to Dr Everley since I caught him on his way out. Perhaps that was the talk he mentioned. Had such success placed demands on him? He'd made a few courteous visits to the drawing room and then disappeared to his work, his patients, his fellow men of science.

'He seems content.'

'You mustn't feel jealous of his research – for all we know he really is uncovering the great mysteries of life. Personally, I find it slightly terrifying. I would much rather believe that we were the product of Adam and Eve, but there we are.' She stared at me hard, as though trying to find me out in some way. 'He hasn't told you? Well, it *is* difficult work. I've watched him for so long. Father too. They shared it all with me. I'm sure he'll tell you when he's ready.' Grace wore an expression of triumph.

'We're to attend a lecture together soon.' A complete untruth, but it was enough to stop her gloating. I was unable to venture anywhere alone and, it seemed, I wasn't wanted with him.

She narrowed her eyes as though considering the lie and then tossed her hair back, relaxing again. 'And have you met the Grays? Or the Barringtons? Lucinda Barrington is adorable.'

I shook my head. Although he'd promised a drive, and a trip to his bookshop, Lucius hadn't taken me anywhere. Grace was the first visitor I'd entertained, and I hadn't left the house. Barker had even prevented me from sitting in the garden, claiming the borders had just been dug and my clothes would spoil.

'I've been quite solitary until today. I think perhaps Lucius is letting me get used to London rather gently.' I tried a knowing smile. 'You may have to be my saviour. I would so like to find a bookshop. I've quite exhausted the books I might enjoy in your brother's library.'

'If you're looking for stories, then you won't find any here. Neither Lucius nor I is fond of stories.'

Such continual reminders that I was out of my depth. If she wasn't his sister, I'd say she was jealous, but he paid me no attention anyway. What did either of them want from me? And why had Dr Everley been so quick to force a marriage he did not appear to want?

Grace watched Eloise push Edmond's leg away so that she could clamber up on the high-backed chair next to her mother. Edmond waited until she reached the seat and then slowly moved against the chair's leg until it wobbled and sent her crashing to the floor in a tangle of petticoats and tears. Grace stayed me as I rose to comfort her, and turned to Edmond.

'Apologise to your sister at once,' she said in a level voice.

'I'm sorry that you fell,' he intoned.

Grace picked up the child, still howling, and sat her on the other side of the room.

I waited for some sort of explanation or apology, Mother would never have allowed such behaviour, but she simply said: 'I will leave the children with Nurse next time. They're rarely with me during the day.'

The little girl lifted her pinafore to hide her face. What kept her from the children? I felt deeply sorry for Eloise being left to the mercy of such an unpleasant brother. 'You must be busy.'

Grace fanned a hand in front of her face. 'Aside from the charity work, there are always people to call on, dinners to plan, reading to do so I can keep up with events. And Lucius's work, of course. It's so important to be interested.'

I *would* be interested. And I would know more than her before long. 'What is your charity work?'

'My *fallen* women, Matthew called them.'

Why speak as though her husband was dead and not abroad? Did she never expect him home? I would ask Dr Everley if I found the chance.

'They are delinquents really, women who've disgraced themselves in . . . various ways. Unmarried mothers, drinkers, those who live for pleasure.'

Poor Rebecca could be any of those things by now, according to the talk at home. Heat flushed my neck and I turned to look at Eloise, who covered her face with her pinafore again.

Grace leant forward eagerly, as though enjoying my

discomfort. 'London is full of squalor and poverty, Madeleine; none of us is able to judge another's life. There's little we can do to change some of them, but we clothe and feed them. We listen to their stories and try to help them. They live at Evergreen House, a mission our dear father started, and I'm pleased to continue his work.'

Their visit left me low in spirits and I went at once to my room, almost tripping on a small bowl on the rug. Who had dropped it there? The rosewood handles were roughly carved into the head and tail of a bird and the bowl was dirty, smeared with white. A strange object, but probably antique, and I took it carefully into my room, set it on the dresser. I would ask Annie when she next appeared. A mug of cocoa sat on the bedside table, covered with a cloth and still warm, fragrant with cinnamon. Someone knew I'd be here. There must be spyholes all over the house. Though a fire was laid in the grate I had no means to light it and the room was so cold, worsened by the damp air, that I climbed beneath the covers.

Suffocation woke me in a panic, the sensation of something knelt on my chest. When I lit the candle and my vision focused, I was quite alone, though voices could be heard outside the room. My head filled with a strange rushing as I tried to rise, and I leant heavily on the nightstand, managing to pour a few inches of water into the bowl and scoop it up to my face in a shock of cold.

The voices grew loud as an argument and I began to make my way towards the stairs, following the sound. Darkness had fallen while I slept, and the hallways were difficult to navigate in dim light. I walked slowly, feeling along the wall, hearing more as I drew closer. A woman's voice carried.

'For heaven's sake, people are starting to talk!'

I struggled to hear the response.

'Don't draw attention to yourself. Take her out, anywhere, just let them see you together. She can take my place tomorrow evening.'

'She'll be bored to tears.'

'Just act as though you are in love, then it won't be hard to profess yourself heartbroken.'

'It is hardly fair.'

'You *are* too weak for medicine. Father was right. He would never have stalled this long.'

I stumbled on the crumpled edge of the rug, losing my footing, and I threw out my hands to steady myself against the wall. The door flew open, and Dr Everley appeared, holding a low-burnt candle stub.

'What are you doing wandering around the corridors at this time of night? You look as though you've seen a ghost!'

'I heard voices, a woman's voice . . .'

'Mrs Barker has just brought me tea.'

'It didn't sound like Mrs Barker.'

'Perhaps earlier? Grace was here before – she was concerned about you after her visit, she came back to see that you were well. She went home some hours ago.'

'But I heard . . .'

'Would you like to sit down? Barker said you slept through dinner.'

'Earlier I felt unwell. But I *did* hear people talking.'

He affected a bright, cheerful tone as though reassuring a child with unreasonable fears. 'You see I am quite alone. You don't think I have begun to talk to myself? I do spend a lot of time in here, but I can assure you I'm not mad yet.'

Perhaps *I* looked mad with my hair still loose and wild. A

sleepwalker. Could I really be sure of what I'd heard? I'd slept so deeply it could have been a dream or nightmare, a conversation imagined from my own worries. That was probably it: all the thinking about him and Grace, being unsettled before sleep, imagining the worst. I'd invented it all.

Behind Dr Everley the room was dim with flickering tongues of candlelight. Internal doors leant open. Ways into the locked rooms. Through the gap I saw shelves and open drawers filled with surgical implements, silver and glinting. Tiny, vicious blades and hooks. I thought of the butchered remains I'd glimpsed on the tour and my stomach lurched, but my need to understand his secrets was more powerful than my fear of violence. I stepped forward and Dr Everley took my hand in a courteous gesture, as though we were about to dance, then closed the door behind him.

5

The Marlborough Assizes

'Have you need of the book?' Different magistrate, same manners. Small this time and thin, with a beaked nose and narrowed eyes peering over a pair of lorgnettes that he constantly raised. Why not just wear spectacles? For effect, perhaps, or to give him time to prepare a question. Imperative for him to hold the only air of authority. It must be tiring.

'Indeed. I pledge to honour with this book as I have pledged my life for the same service. In His name. And in His name, I promise to tell only the truth as I have witnessed with my own eyes.'

A deep, sonorous voice that he clearly liked the sound of, but what could he prove? Not Maddie's story. As far as I knew she'd barely been allowed to church.

'Name?'

'Reverend Isambard Bewley. At your service. And God's.'

'And you are the reverend of St Nicholas's Church, Kensington?'

'For seventeen years.' The vicar smoothed his grey muttonchops and drew himself straighter.

'The parish church of the Everleys?'

'I believe that is correct.'

'Then you will know the family from your congregation?'

Reverend Bewley shook his head sadly. 'I barely knew them. The Everleys attended my church only on two occasions to my knowledge. One of which was their wedding.'

A shocked gasp from the public gallery drew a smirk to his lips. 'Did they, then, attend a different church?'

'I believe that Dr Everley and his sister attend the Holy Trinity Church in Putney. They run a charitable house there and it seems that their philanthropic work in the parish binds them to the church, as it did their father. The family has achieved much among the poor, and it would naturally be expected that they school those in their care by accompanying them to church nearby.'

'How might we check this information?' the magistrate asked his clerk in the same voice he used for the witness. The clerk was paper-pale from a life spent copying letters in dusty rooms. He rose as though the question was a call to arms, spilling his notes.

'A visitation, sir. Someone would need to visit the Holy Trinity Church. I could be the visitation . . . the visitor . . .'

The magistrate scribbled a note on the paper in front of him. 'Very well, see it is done.' He turned back to the witness box. 'So, Dr Everley and his sister. And what of the accused?'

'I don't believe she attended the Holy Trinity. And I've only ever seen her twice before. Once, as I said, at her wedding.' He shook his head from side to side as though the knowledge made him sorry. I clenched my hands until the nails dug half-moons into my skin. Where was Maddie? I couldn't see her anywhere. She should be fighting her corner. I should be. I could tell them she was practically a *prisoner* in that house. I wouldn't mind betting she had no idea her husband went to that church with his sister. *If* he did. But supporting witnesses couldn't testify until they were formally invited by the accused, or her lawyer. So far, she'd refused both.

'As I am to understand things, it was a godless house. Members of my congregation, people I trust, have hinted at unnatural research.' The vicar paused, then dropped his voice. 'The Everleys are said to own a large collection of craven effects.'

'Have you witnessed this collection?' asked the magistrate.

'I've never set foot in the house.' He gripped the edge of the box and drew himself up again.

'Did your . . . informants believe that these "craven effects" were the property of Dr Everley or the accused?'

'I could not tell you.'

I could tell him! Or Ambrose or Father; they'd both been to the house, both spoken of the collection. Why would she not invite us to help her? His part finished, the vicar made a show of gathering his robes and lifting them up while he walked, showing the richly embroidered hem of the gown beneath his surplice. The court was silent for a few moments, then whispering turned to excited conversation. A woman behind me let out a sudden peal of laughter. Treating it like a show. An entertainment. My beautiful friend could be hanged, and no-one seemed in the slightest bit concerned. The magistrate rose, waited for the court to follow suit, and then left by the right-hand door. On the benches around me, the spectators were pulling out wax-wrapped pies and cakes. A savoury aroma filled the room and my stomach growled in anticipation. A stout woman to my left tore off a chunk of bread and handed it over without turning to look at me. I took it meekly. What would Ambrose say if he knew I was here? Was this what Maddie felt? Terrified to be herself? Was that what she'd always felt?

Exhibit 6

Ichthyosaur snout. Mesozoic Age of reptiles
c. 200m years B.C.

Relentless rain coloured everything miserable, from the shuttered houses to the slick road with its bare trees. As I stared at the wet garden, a raven shook out its wings and resettled on a bench, tucking its head down into its body. The misty weather seemed to cloud my mind. How hard could it be to choose something to wear? I was nervous of meeting Dr Everley's friends and colleagues. What if I displeased them? No doubt their wives were all as clever as they. Perhaps, if I knew more about his work, he wouldn't treat me like a child. When he'd held my hand in the doorway of his bedroom, I was so sure something would happen. Anything was better than being ignored. But he led me back along the corridor and left me in the doorway of my own room. I half thought he might lock me in. For a long time I listened, though I heard nothing further and not a word since. It wasn't real, of course. Nervous dreams caused by an unfamiliar house, a strange new way of life. My letters home didn't mention it. Why worry them? It would only sound as though I couldn't cope.

Finally, I settled on pale green silk, shot through with threads of violet that shimmered under the lamplight like the wings of a faery or a mermaid's tail. Things that men of science would ridicule. I pinned my hair badly, wishing Annie would help. It was awkward to reach, and as I twisted before the glass, I noticed a small ivory box on the dresser. A gift from my husband? Initials were carved on the underside – *A.N.E* – his mother's? She was never mentioned, though Old Dr Everley filled the house like a curse. Paintings and portraits hung everywhere. Upright and imperious in surgical dress or morning suits, a haughty expression and a cruel mouth. The air was thick with him. Had he frightened his children? Hurt them? Lucius barely spoke of his upbringing.

Nestled inside the box was a locket, on a short gold chain, inlaid with fine-cut amethyst that glittered in the lamplight. Pale purple that perfectly matched the cross-threads of my dress. Had Lucius anticipated what I would choose? Unable to shake the feeling that someone was watching, I opened the locket carefully, hoping not to find private tokens. It was empty. The same initials were engraved on the back, decorated with tiny vines.

I fastened the clasp, admiring the way the locket sat between my collarbones, and left my hair loose at the back. Mother would be delighted to see me take such care. She always wanted me like Isabel, dressed for the drawing room, though I found it irritating to be fussed and frilled. Countryside surrounded Lynton and I was far more interested in running with the boys, hems and boots caked in mud, chasing frogs and damselflies. Lynton was never boring, whatever Isabel said. When I wasn't helping Father with his tinctures there was always something to discover. My studies of plants and animals quickly grew better than the boys', good enough to sell once times got hard. Why had I forgotten to pack any paints or paper? Some sketching would at least help pass the dark hours of winter at Arlington Crescent. Father always said my understanding of anatomy was better than his own. But if Dr

Everley wouldn't spend any time with me, then how was I to show my talent?

He was already waiting when I walked downstairs, dressed in evening coat and gloves, and his eye was immediately drawn to the necklace.

'Where did you find that?' He seemed angry.

Instinctively I touched the locket. 'In my room. I thought it was . . .' I shouldn't presume it was a gift, even if he had left it. 'I thought you'd put it there.'

'It was Mother's.'

'I did wonder. What was her name?'

'Amelia.'

'A pretty name. And a pretty locket. I can take it off, if you don't want me to wear it?' He continued to stare at it, lips pursed as though struggling for the words he wanted. 'Shall I take it off?'

'It was in a drawer in my study. A locked drawer. I haven't seen it in years.'

Surely he didn't think I'd stolen it? 'It was in an ivory box, on my dresser.' I lifted my arms to unfasten it, lip trembling.

Lucius stayed my hand. 'You're wearing it now. Keep it on. But I expect you to look after it.'

'Of course I will. I . . . don't have to keep it. But it was there, I promise.' Had Grace placed it there? It didn't seem like the sort of thing she'd do. But things changed in my room; the little wooden bowl was missing from the dresser. 'There are . . . things do come and go sometimes.'

Lucius stopped staring at the locket and gave me a sharp look. 'What things?'

'My belongings disappear, small items. And sometimes there are different things on the dresser. A bud vase a few days ago, and a thimble enamelled with daisies. I found a little wooden bowl, in

45

the corridor outside, and I put that in my room too, but it's gone. I didn't think it worth mentioning before but . . .'

'They were all Mother's,' he interrupted, and a chill ran the length of my spine.

We travelled in silence to the dinner and were parted as soon as the doorman took our cloaks, before I'd had the chance to ask what to expect of the evening. My skin was uncomfortably wet where Lord Barrington's lips had pressed too keenly and I surreptitiously wiped the back of my hand against my dress. He slapped Lucius on the back before pushing him towards the fire where several men were raising toasts. If he seemed drunk at such an early hour, it didn't bother his wife. She carried on welcoming her guests with the same air of far-away indifference as she greeted me.

Lady Barrington wore her hair in an elaborate girlish style, looped with thin braids that framed her angular face and unnaturally pink cheeks. A necklace of huge emeralds set off her wrinkled décolletage and matching bracelets scratched my arms as she led me to the window seats where the women were gathered, dresses pressed together in a colourful sea of silk. Grapes and sliced peaches floated in a punch bowl. The woman on my right half rose and bowed her head as though honoured, to the entertainment of the others. 'Lorna Marethwaite. I assume you must be the lucky bride of Lucius Everley?'

'Madeleine.' I inclined my head and tried to smile. Lady Barrington passed me a small silver cup and I took it, feeling awkward and on show. The locket felt heavy as skeletal fingers around my neck. Lucius's words still stung. Had he really meant to suggest Amelia's spirit brought it to my room? The only other jewellery I wore was a diamond ring framed with a plait of hair, presented to me on the day I was told to accept his proposal. Stiff brown hair from his grandmother, who'd owned the ring before Amelia. More ghosts. Grace had shown great interest in it on our wedding day, and I still felt as though it wasn't mine to wear, like the wedding band itself – a fine thick rose gold, only slightly worn at the back.

'So glad you're feeling better, we've all been dying to meet you.' Lorna leant towards me, eyes bright as a rat's. 'We missed you at the Society Ball. I do hope you're quite recovered?'

Had Lucius turned down invitations on my behalf? Had he told them I was ill?

'Perhaps it's the change in air?' she continued. 'You're not a London family?'

'Cheshire, near to Cheadle.'

'Fine countryside if we're to believe the stories of Mrs Gaskell. I'm fonder of Italy myself. I didn't think country maids to be so delicate.' She sipped her drink, maintaining steady eye contact. 'I did wonder whether you were . . . confined in some way, but I see you're still as slender as a reed.'

A gasp of delighted shock rippled across the benches. So everyone assumed that Lucius was obliged to marry me. Why else would he have done so? I wondered often enough myself. What would she say if I told her he'd never even touched me?

'I'd no idea that London society would be so starved of conversation,' I murmured. 'I do hope we'll find more interesting topics over dinner.' Attempting sophistication, I took a larger gulp of punch than intended. The fiery liquid burnt my throat, causing me to splutter, and a young woman jumped up to pass me her own glass of water.

'Conversation will be interesting enough without gossip this evening,' she said firmly. 'Aside from my father and husband, and yours of course, there are two other scientists and a tolerable poet, along with Dr Lewis, whose latest book has caused something of a scandal. The rest of us,' she looked pointedly at Lorna, 'you will simply have to take as you find.'

'I'm not used to . . .' I didn't want to appear childish, and since the others partook easily in the punch, I decided to play along with my supposed illness. It wouldn't harm. 'I should have taken more rest. But I so wanted to meet Lucius's friends.' I was grateful when a gong sounded and attention shifted to the table.

Paintings of birds and blossom trees spread across the walls and on the legs of the lacquered furniture. Huge ginger jars stood almost as high as the men who lined up along facing walls, ready to pull or push chairs and spread napkins. Sandalwood and jasmine mixed with a rich food smell, and I began to feel faint. When I found my name card, I stood behind the chair and leant hard for support, surveying the table. Lucius sat diagonally from me, next to Lorna, too far away for free conversation, so when the woman who'd helped me to water took the chair opposite, I was delighted to see her. She told me her name was Caroline and pulled a face.

'It's a pretty name,' I said. It suited her. 'And your husband?'

'Ambrose. Much prettier.'

'Which is your father? You said he and my husband were colleagues?'

'Fellow men of science, I think they would say. Dr Stepwood is my father.' She leant forward to point him out: a thin, pale man with greying sandy hair, older than Lucius and with looks quite unlike Caroline's vivacious features. As he spoke, Dr Stepwood shifted the condiments around the table in order to explain something to the woman on his left, making excited little movements with his hands. Caroline rolled her eyes, though I could tell she was fond of him. 'Though usually at pains to explain their different disciplines. "Not real medicine unless you are sawing at limbs or cadavers", that's what Father says Dr Everley thinks anyway.'

A sudden image of Lucius carving flesh to shocking white bones with his vicious miniature implements came to mind. It brought a wave of nausea and I placed my cutlery carefully together on the plate. 'Do you live in this part of town?'

'Wetherby Street, above Ambrose's clinic. Dull and respectable. How do you like your new house?'

'It's very beautiful.' And felt neither dull nor respectable. Just lonely. 'I miss having space outside. There's no light in our garden and it's not the same as having a place to walk through trees, or sit and listen to the birds.'

'Such freedom in the countryside!'

'I'm not used to spending so many hours indoors.'

'Have you been to the parks? If you take a path from the top of Baker Street you can . . .'

Listening was pleasant and I let my thoughts drift to the sound of her voice as we made plans to take outings together, feeling comforted by having things to anticipate. Could this be a friend at last? An easy companionship that I'd missed.

Aside from Caroline and her husband, all the guests were older than Lucius. Perhaps he mainly knew them through his father. With a sudden wish to understand him better, enhanced by the convivial mood of the table, I glanced to where he sat and was shocked to register the look he threw in my direction. It couldn't be plainer that he disapproved of Caroline. A look so harsh that for a moment I wondered whether she had spurned him.

'It seems the more we know the less we understand with certainty.' Lucius spoke as though he read my thoughts.

'Human knowledge is not a great tidal wave of understanding, sent to sweep away the knowledge of the generations before. We are all contributing to the discourse, every one of us here,' said a stout man with the wary placatory air of one who had met these words before and understood the need to keep them in their place.

'Every *man*, he means,' whispered Caroline. 'Try joining in and see who listens to *your* ideas.' I wasn't sure I had any. I would willingly listen to hers.

'I don't have anything to say.'

Caroline rolled her eyes. 'Of course you do, you've just been stopped from saying it. We're not supposed to have ideas. Or do anything useful.'

Mother's words came to mind. *It's not for you to draw attention like that, trying to compete with men. No good will come of it.*

'Mother never liked me helping Father with his clinic.'

'Why?' Caroline looked incredulous.

She wanted the boys to help him because Isabel and I were only good for marriage. 'I don't know. In case I saw something unpleasant, maybe. It wasn't ladylike to be mixing tinctures and counting pills.' I felt a stab of fondness for Father as he used to be, carefree, absorbed in his cases. We hadn't spoken much lately. 'I used to really enjoy it.'

'Of course you did. Because you were *useful.*' Caroline glanced to the end of the table where Ambrose held court. 'It's nice to feel useful. I'm working on being allowed to manage his clinic.'

Would Lucius ever allow me the same trust? Caroline was right, it *was* nice to feel useful. I would think of some things I could do to help. He was so busy, always working, there must be something. Impossible for me to work as a doctor, of course, but an artist, perhaps, or an assistant? Imagine the help it could be for a collector to have someone document his finds.

Smaller pockets of conversation petered out around the table until only one set of voices was heard, four men with equally confident tones.

'We have reached the point at which only tangible proof will allow us to progress,' said Lucius, leaning back in his chair.

'And your research, this digging into the base mud you call *creation* itself . . .' the stout man began.

'Creation is no longer sacred,' interrupted Lucius tersely, 'we're all, now, in some way, God, a series of gods, each incarnation superior to the last. I'm simply interested in the parts of our physical bodies that changed, and from what. Evidence that will give us certainty, and ensure time is not wasted on speculation.'

'Your last paper seemed to intimate that you're certain now of this proof?'

'Indeed?' Dr Stepwood, who seemed to have been making polite small talk with Lorna Marethwaite throughout most of the conversation, suddenly sat upright and attentive. 'Is this what you presented at the last meeting?'

'Shame you missed it,' said the stout man. 'A fine talk. Almost convincing.'

'I assume the paper concludes your assumptions about missing links?' Dr Stepwood's face was taut. Caroline watched him with an anxious expression. I felt myself tense.

'To set yourself against God is not a battle you will wish to win, Dr Everley,' said the stout man sadly.

'I dare say it may suit some to convince themselves that God is not watching their every move,' said Dr Stepwood, his eyes narrowed.

I glanced at Caroline who lowered her gaze and replaced her cutlery, folded her napkin. It seemed I wasn't the only one whose appetite was spoiling.

'Is he ever really watching?' countered Lucius. 'The ichthyosaur found on the Jurassic coast show the beginnings of structures that would become like ours. Bones that jut like shoulders. Snouts that are capable of breathing air. Fins with joints at the point of elbows. A neck with three vertebrae.'

'But no fish with feet, or, indeed, humans with tails.' Dr Stepwood's comment brought laughter from the table, though his face was serious.

'Words alone may not be convincing.' Lucius flattened his napkin with an air of finality. 'But who's qualified to say that something they've never seen – a mermaid, or a human soul – does not exist?'

A mermaid? Or a water baby, like the story. Weren't they the same things as souls? The story was once my favourite and I suddenly longed to read it again. In *The Water Babies* the underwater creatures were lost souls turned into river children, mer-people as Lucius described. Did he believe in such things? Did he have proof of their existence? Mermaids and souls. His small museum must contain marvels I could scarcely imagine.

Exhibit 7

Small surgeon's bonesaw with rosewood handle.
German. c. 1800s.

Listless and bored, I tried everything to persuade Mrs Barker to allow me the run of my own household – firmness, wheedling, pleas. But she was set in her ways, unwilling to allow even the smallest task to be taken over by someone she considered a child. A nuisance. I picked at the heavy food and stopped challenging her, and for a while it seemed that she stopped watching me. Annie was sent in her place for almost everything, though I often heard others moving through the house. Walking up and down the back stairs before dawn and in the evening dusk. Venturing like foxes outside daylight hours. But I felt them.

'Beautiful morning, Annie.'

'I dare say, madam.' She answered without lifting her head, as though the day had nothing to do with her. She must know I only watched through windows too. It wouldn't hurt her to speak to me. I tried again.

'You're a hard worker, Annie. It's as though you do the chores of the whole staff.'

'It is just me. Mrs Barker doesn't like a big house.'

'Oh, but I . . .' I heard people in the attic quarters. Footsteps, voices. I could feel them.

Annie glanced up at me and quickly looked back to the floor, as though embarrassed.

'I wondered if you might find time to go through my wardrobe.'

'I can take your mending down.'

'That's not what I meant.' The blue kid shoes so admired by Isabel were still tide-marked with dirt from the wet pavement, the green dress stained with punch from Lady Barrington's party. That was all. But some time spent going through everything would be nice, talking to her about which wraps would match which dresses. There was no pleasure in such tasks without company. 'I'd rather like some advice.'

Annie finished polishing the table and stood by the door with her trug as though waiting to escape. Couldn't she just leave the corridors undusted for once? Her eyes were still bruised and tired, and there were red weals on her right arm, as though she'd reached into a hot oven or been held by strong fingers.

'Are you happy, Annie?'

'I'm very happy with my work, madam.'

She was impossible to draw. Either she'd been told to avoid me, or she was simpler than she looked. A small metal cross on a chain hung half over her collar and I reached over to tuck it back in. 'I'm not sure Mrs Barker would like to see that.' I smiled but she shrank back as though I was about to take it. Perhaps it was given by a boyfriend? The one with strong fingers? More likely she felt it protected her in some way. Before I could ask, she turned and left the room.

'Wait!' I was sure she needed a friend as much as I did. I pushed my feet back into my slippers and picked up my wrap from the back of the chair, following her. The corridor was empty. 'Annie?' My own voice echoed in reply.

* * *

54

Annie was nowhere to be seen, and I stopped searching for her on the third floor, where the door to Lucius's study stood ajar. No-one answered my call, and with a soft push I opened it further and stepped inside, supporting it closed behind me like a thief. The scent of hair oil mixed with spiced cologne, and my pulse quickened, eyes slowly adjusting to the gloom.

A thick journal and several piles of paper covered a huge desk and most of the rug beside it. My chance to read his words and understand his work, his thoughts. Listening, I held my breath. The house seemed quiet. A Tuesday, so Mrs Barker would be managing the laundry, and I'd seen Barker in the garden earlier. Every time I tried to venture outside, he was working there, busily smoothing and raking back and forth, scraping with such fierce concentration he could have been trying to summon something from the earth. Perhaps he was simply avoiding Mrs Barker, no-one could blame him, but the garden couldn't possibly need so much of his time. It wasn't large; not by country standards anyway, and as far as I could see the only plants that grew there were hellebores. Shade lovers. Probably Old Dr Everley's favourites.

I sat down and drew the chair towards the desk, trying not to feel guilty for the intrusion. He was my husband and I should know about his work. Sketching paper covered in drawings was weighted down by a small saw with a rosewood handle, worn to a fine patina with use and age. Its teeth bit sharp as I tested them on the back of my hand. Old Dr Everley's, perhaps? If Lucius still used such a tool, he would surely not keep it so carelessly, though it was still keen enough to saw through flesh and bone. The drawings were anatomical, neat lines of ink in thin pen strokes and crosshatch, and my heart soared to realise that his talent for sketching fell far below mine. I should show him my artwork at the very first opportunity. He would be only too pleased with my help.

Repetitions of elbows and ankles, human joints with fins protruding. What were his sketches supposed to show? Threads of the conversation at the Barringtons' surfaced. Was Lucius drawing what he hoped to find? Underneath the drawings was a journal, thick pages edged with marbled paper in brown and yellow swirls that reminded me of our family Bible. I pushed away the thought. What would Mother say to know I hadn't been to church in weeks? Lucius had promised we'd start soon and I believed him; he'd been busy and the rhythm of our life was yet to settle. Still, it troubled me to wait so long. The journal was full of purposeful copper script, so fine that it was hard to decipher without straining my eyes – but it seemed to be an account of personal discovery. I would have to find a time to return so I could read it properly.

Below the journal was a large book, bound in black vellum and embossed with the Everley coat of arms. A family history? The cover was smooth and cold, the Everley crest imperious – two ravens and a pair of crossed swords, longer than standard heraldic weapons, one gold and one silver-coloured. It seemed aggressive, warlike. A relic of battling knights. Isabel was taken with it, especially after seeing it painted on the doors of our carriage. She'd asked James to translate the matching motto in his schoolboy Latin – *spectemur agendo*, 'let us be viewed by our actions'.

I ran my hand across the crest, wondering when it would feel like mine, and opened the book carefully. The flyleaf was dated May of the previous year and inscribed with a signature I couldn't read. On the first page was a picture of a group of girls, wearing long robes like stage costumes – naiads or water nymphs, perhaps? They stood together in a Greek pose with robes almost thin enough to see through and long hair tumbling across their shoulders. So risqué, and so softly focused, that at first I thought it was a painting and was shocked to realise that, in fact, it was a slightly blurred photograph. I peered more closely. One of the women was beautiful, with big dark eyes and a neat, pointed chin, curls half covering her naked shoulders. Who would pose for such a thing?

For a moment, I hesitated, remembering something our old governess had told Isabel: *spies rarely find good news*. It was true in that instance, when Isabel followed her out of the garden and caught her meeting with the curate behind the church wall. She was the only governess we'd ever liked, and she wasn't replaced because Father's practice was already declining. What would she think of me now? She'd probably tell me to mind my own business and leave my husband to his. But I could not stop looking. Page after page of portraits, women dressed in similar sheer robes, the fabric pulled across their chests so it was clear they wore nothing underneath. Standing in a high-walled garden filled with columns. By their side were two huge stone greyhounds with haughty expressions, one sitting upright and the other crouched down, paws crossed. One of the women looked cold and uncomfortable, eyes lowered and hands over her chest as though she wished to hide. On the next page, the same woman was completely nude, hair loose down her back, leaning over her shoulder to stare at the photographer. Her body was beautiful in long lines and curves. The only naked flesh I'd ever seen was my own and even then I had never looked full-length in the glass. I wanted to now, to see if I was half as lovely. Could a man's body ever look so perfect? At once I wanted, and did not want, to see more. In Father's drawers at home, Isabel had found some sketches of naked women and we giggled over them together. But those were drawings, artistic; the model would have shared herself only with the artist and anyone viewing it afterwards would have to imagine life from the brush strokes. Photographs were not the same. Some of them even showed two women, naked together with no shame.

When Grace arrived, I was still trembling, and Edmond asked his mother in a loud voice what was the matter with me. I was terrified I'd left something out of place, that my prying would be discovered and punished, and I found it impossible to regain my composure while he stared at me. Grace pounced on my weakness like a cat with a bird.

'You're very pale, would you like me to ask Mrs Barker for something?' Grace leant over my chair in a show of concern.

I needed to clear my head, to put what I'd seen in perspective. All men had pictures, I told myself, even Father. 'I've had so little fresh air. Couldn't we go outside? A walk, perhaps?'

'Not today. The children are weary. Besides, I haven't brought their rainwear.' Grace glanced across to Eloise, humming to herself as she stacked a pile of wooden blocks into a castle shape. Edmond watched silently.

'It's not raining. It would be fun for them to walk out.' I jumped up and went over to the window. 'There are chestnut sellers on the corner.' Warm chestnuts popping from their skins, wrapped in little twists of paper, brought a stab of homesickness. James's favourite treat on our trips to town. The lane at home was full of chestnut trees but when we tried to cook them on the fire ourselves, they always burnt black. Mrs Barker would probably tell me off if I tried here and poor Annie would be sent to scrape the grates.

'It doesn't do for children to have too much fresh air and

excitement.' Grace threw me a sly look. 'You'll be having your own soon, and then you'll understand.'

My cheeks burnt with virginity. She knew, too, I was certain of it. I must change the conversation before she began to pry.

'We dined at the Barringtons'.' Hopefully the scent of social gossip would be distracting.

'I do hope Lucius passed on my regards to Lucinda?' she asked.

I nodded, though he hadn't in my earshot.

'I expect the conversation was dull for you? They usually draw quite a group from the Society. Doctors rambling on.'

'It was very interesting. I feel I understand Lucius's research better.'

'Remarkably complex work to be learnt in one dinner.'

'Of course, I have more to understand.' I hesitated. Should I tell her I had found a friend? 'I met some nice people.'

'Lorna Marethwaite, I assume? She's usually to be found there. Great company if you please her.'

Then I had evidently not. 'Yes. And Dr Stepwood with his daughter and son-in-law.'

Grace drew her face into a sneer as disapproving as Lucius's own over dinner. 'I wouldn't count Stepwood as fit company, or Caroline. Who did she end up finding to marry her?'

'Her husband's name is Ambrose Fairly. They seem happy.'

'No doubt they're continuing the family tradition of dragging others into the mud?'

What did she mean? They were good company. 'Caroline has promised to call.'

Grace's eyes became mean. 'You are to refuse her. In any case Lucius would not have her here.'

Must I take orders from my husband's sister? I liked Caroline, and badly needed friendship. A sudden crash sent the bricks tumbling to the ground. They scattered noisily all over the floor, and Eloise began to cry. Edmond smiled. He must have been waiting a long time to knock them over.

'Both of you leave the room this instant!' Grace's voice was dangerously low. 'You may kneel on the floor in the corridor until you are sorry. Face the wall.' She glared at them until they shuffled from the room, Eloise sobbing as Edmond pushed her roughly in the small of the back.

'Why may I not see Caroline Fairly?'

Grace rounded on me, using the same voice she had for the children. 'Because she is Stepwood's daughter.'

'And what of him?' Both of them had been kind to me; Stepwood had spoken at length to Lucius. Why was I to be denied a friend?

'He's a dangerous man. He ruined my father, our name. Almost cost us everything.'

I waited. From the corridor, a thudding sound. Eloise's wails grew louder.

'He told the Society that Father was . . . a resurrectionist. That his research didn't count. All the lectures and demonstrations, all the techniques he taught them. He was the best surgeon in London, but after that it counted for nothing. Even Matthew . . .' A flash of anger hardened her mouth. Whatever she was about to tell me regarding her husband, she thought better of it. 'Lucius still strives to regain our standing and he is almost there. Be careful not to stand in his way.'

Resurrectionist. I'd never heard the word before, but I sensed it wasn't the time to ask. Did he bring dead things to life? Like Shelley's frogs? Caroline's father and my husband were adults, men of science. They shouldn't be squabbling like children. I kept the words on my tongue, but I promised nothing.

My Dearest Isabel

London is dreary in the autumn, with little for a newcomer that's cheering against the constant rain. I would like to take afternoon tea and I find I must wait for a friend. When will you come to stay? You may have a room for as long as you wish.

I screwed the letter into a ball and threw it into my wastepaper basket. Begging my sister to save me. It wasn't what she or Mother would wish to hear. It was up to me to make the most of things. Was I not mistress in my own house? Why must I ignore Caroline when we had struck up such a good friendship? Ashamed by my weakness, unable to start another letter in such a mood, I rang Annie and asked for tea in the library. It was time to educate myself.

Four copies of *The Origin of Species* sat on the neatly ordered shelves, making it necessary to take each down to check the edition so I could read the latest one. Whatever Lucius had found in here was clearly fascinating enough for him to order each updated volume. A large library desk was flanked by two wing-backed chairs, and I settled in one with the book on my lap, propping my feet on a stool to take its weight. Lucius had underlined several sections.

Geology assuredly does not reveal any such finely graduated organic chain; and this, perhaps, is the most obvious and gravest objection which can be urged against my theory . . .

Was he trying to find fault? In the margin a scribbled note, but his handwriting was hard to read: *must species appear in rock?*; *transitional forms?* It was what he'd discussed over dinner, fish evolving into land creatures. Great sections of this edition had been scored through with a sharp nib, though whether in disagreement or frustration it was hard to tell. What were transitional forms? Lucius had spoken of ankles forming in fins, of souls and mermaids. What did he have to prove?

'Come in, Annie,' I answered the knock. But it was Mrs Barker who sailed inside, carrying a heavy wooden tray. She set out cups and a plate of small cakes, the kind I hadn't seen since the wedding, and I was touched that she had brought them to please me. Such fancies were generally viewed as weakness. I thought I heard a cry through the open door, shrill like the wail of a baby. But before I could ask what it was, she had disappeared, closing the door behind her, and the sound became muffled and faint. The cocoa tasted bitter, but it was well meant on such a dreary day and I drank it all.

When I awoke, curled in the chair, it was late and dark and my cheek stuck to the leather wing-back. In the quiet I was sure I heard a baby's cry again, mewling and pitiful, but when I held my breath to listen, it disappeared. The lamp had died, and I didn't know where candles or matches were kept. I would have to feel my way along the corridor to bed. Although the tray still lay on the table and the fire was out, someone had taken the heavy book from my lap and replaced it on the shelf. They'd also removed my shoes and left them neatly paired, facing backwards from the door, like a charm to stop me running away.

8

The Marlborough Assizes

After half an hour the magistrate returned and called another witness to the box. A tall man I vaguely recognised. A colleague of Lucius, perhaps? He gave his name as Venables and when he took the stand he leant against the side, slightly perched as though sitting. Quite at home. He was, apparently, the Everleys' own physician.

'Apologies for the lateness of my attendance. One doesn't hurry a royal visit.'

'Is the patient quite well?'

'That would not be my place to divulge.' Venables gave a thin-lipped, sneer possibly intended as a smile.

'Let us start, then, and try to make up the time.' The magistrate stared until his witness began to shift uncomfortably before he continued. 'In your relationship with the Everleys, had you ever cause to be concerned for the accused?'

Now things were moving. How could he fail to be concerned for her well-being? The woman with the bread tried to hand me another piece, but I didn't want to miss a word.

'I was struck by her interest in pursuing her husband's work. She read widely, scientific works and medical volumes, as though attempting to understand them. She seemed to want to join the discussions. It's my professional belief that such reading wasn't good for her delicate constitution. It can prove . . . too much . . . for the female brain.'

I failed to stifle a snort of derision and the magistrate's head turned sharply towards the sound. Bread lady dug me in the ribs. 'They'll throw you out,' she said in a stage whisper, 'seen it last week.' An expert. There must be dozens of women like her in here, enjoying the spectacle. Probably hoping for a hanging too. It was Maddie's life at stake, and they were taking the word of this ridiculous man who never knew her at all. She understood those books very well. One had merely to look at her sketches to see she was a natural scientist. The only thing stopping me from calling out was the risk that I'd be banned. I'd be no help from the outside.

'Continue.'

The doctor smoothed his coat. His blue waistcoat shone with silver thread. A frivolous look on such a serious man. A vanity. And he was the very type that would sneer at a woman's hat ribbons.

'There was much in Mrs Everley's manner that was worrying. For some reason she was fascinated by medical surgery, always asking questions about it. Especially the work of her husband's father. I remember Lucius becoming quite frustrated about it. He would find her with his father's volumes all spread out over the library as though she hoped to discover something there. She was, I am told, obsessed by the idea of resurrectionists.'

The word sent a shiver of excitement and mutterings around the viewing gallery. As if they were willing things to turn dark. The doctor paused. Waited for silence.

'The work of the resurrectionists held some sort of compulsion. She did, I believe, try to order papers on the matter and was prevented by Lucius who worried for her mind. It wasn't healthy, he felt, and we all agreed. It wasn't healthy or natural for a woman to be so *preoccupied* with such dark thoughts.'

'*We all* agreed? With whom did you and Dr Everley discuss his wife's concerns?'

Dr Venables flinched slightly, and his eyes began to dart around the room. Had he spoken out of turn? If he was looking for Lucius, he wouldn't find him in court. I'd been to every session, and he hadn't appeared yet.

'I only discussed her with Lucius himself. What I meant was that I did, on occasion, have recourse to discuss her frame of mind with colleagues. We were concerned. For Lucius and for her. It was a professional matter, you understand, rather than common gossip.'

'I think I *do* understand,' said the magistrate in a way that made me warm to him. I understood too. If they were talking about Maddie like that, then it was only because Lucius wanted them to. He'd seeded those thoughts about her, he must have. From what I knew of medical men they were, otherwise, very unlikely to be discussing one another's private lives. A struggling wife would not be a cause for concern.

'Is it your *professional* opinion that Mrs Madeleine Everley was not in her right mind?'

'It is.'

'And how long would this have been the case?'

'I couldn't rightly say. Her morbid fascinations had, I believe, been ongoing for some considerable amount of time. But Lucius only really began to share his concerns after the child . . . well . . . after that time. Her state of mind had begun to slide, and he was greatly concerned that he was unable to manage alone. To manage her ill health.'

'Had he tried to do so?'

'I understand that he took her to recuperate in the sea air.'

'An effective therapy.'

'In this case I believe not. Indeed, she seemed worse on their return.'

Not true at all. In many ways she was calmer. Why had I not brought a means to take notes? I would do so next time. I wanted to make sure that, if I had the chance to speak for Maddie, I could put things right. Would the magistrate listen so well to a woman? Unqualified? Before my marriage I'd been proud to work as a governess, enjoyed the relative status conferred by the position. A woman who'd made her own path on the strength of her brain. Where would it get me in this court? I wanted to believe that the magistrate was working to uncover the truth, but these questions were leading; they seemed only to make things look worse for Maddie.

'How so?'

'Agitated. Secretive. She could not seem to keep still.'

'Are these medical signs?'

'Perhaps. Mental distress will make people restless, as will the keeping of secrets. Women's minds are prone to hysteria and weakness. I have seen it many times, especially in new mothers. Or, rather . . . I'm not a psychiatrist. My assessment is that of a general physician. But, yes, those could be medical signs of mental problems.'

'Dr Everley seems to have shown some concern for his wife. Was she, to your knowledge, ever seen by a psychiatrist?' The magistrate considered Dr Venables as though he could see into his soul.

'Not to my knowledge. As I said, Lucius found her condition rather . . . embarrassing to discuss with his peers.'

He didn't consider psychiatrists his peers. *Mind meddlers,* he called Ambrose and Father. He was happy to have her restrained though. Tied down as though he were breaking a horse. She tried to cover the marks, but I'd seen them. Twisted red patches on her wrists where the bits had rubbed. I'd seen similar on Ambrose's recovery clients. They were all women too.

Exhibit 9

Ornate stiletto dagger, with silver handle.
Stained on blade. Italian. c. 1600s.

When I finally slept in my own bed, I dreamt of human souls and mermaids. In my visions, they were the same – breaths of life that slipped from people and found form beneath the sea. My rest was haunted by high keening cries that dragged me awake only to disappear as I strained to hear them, returning again to taunt me as I dozed. Such human cries. But there were no babies, there couldn't be. A cat, perhaps, or a fox howling outside. The foxes that roamed Lynton looking for stray chickens made similar noises, eerie and wild.

In the morning my nerves were jarred, my head heavy with strange dreams and the cries that echoed in my mind. I dressed carelessly. Lucius would already be out and there was no need to make effort for the Barkers, who would probably send me to my room after breakfast. As I started to brush my hair, sudden raised voices carried to the window, and I peered out to see Mrs Barker turning a visitor away from the front door. Could it be Caroline? My heart leapt. No-one else was likely to call. As she stepped backwards, I recognised her immediately. A friend! Pleasant company to stop me thinking about phantom babies and servants that crept out of reach.

I didn't care if they told Lucius. Throwing open the window, I called down in a brazen voice. 'Wait! I'll be down in a moment.'

Caroline looked up and waved. Mrs Barker stood grimly, hands on hips, but she couldn't stop me while someone watched. I pulled a shawl around my dress and picked up the shoes, their charm broken. I was running after all. I had a friend, she had come to me and nothing could spoil that.

Taking the stairs two at a time, I beat Barker to the front door and sidestepped his wife. 'My apologies, Caroline.' Slightly breathless, I grasped her hand. 'I'm so very pleased to see you.' Her face was just as pretty as by candlelight. She had a welcome look of permanent amusement, as though refusing to take life seriously.

'You've been so naughty in not answering my cards, I thought I would come to see whether you were ill again.' She did not let go of my hands. 'Have you been unwell?'

'No.' I jerked my head towards the Barkers, but she didn't guess my meaning. Why should she? Her staff were unlikely to concern themselves with limiting her freedoms or hiding visitors' cards. 'Let's walk. Fresh air is exactly what I need.'

'My carriage is here. I remember you saying you needed books, so I thought I would take you to Hatchards. We can walk in the park afterwards.'

Without a backward glance I half ran down the steps to the carriage. If she thought me strange, hatless with half-dressed hair and wearing an indoor shawl, my boots unbuttoned, then she didn't say. I could not have loved her more.

Hatchards' huge, curved windows glittered with promise and I hesitated by the entrance, unsure how to navigate a bookshop the size of a village. A man in a white apron ran out to the pavement with a pile of paper-wrapped books.

'We'll start at the top.' Caroline took charge, batting away the assistant that moved to help. 'Poetry and novels. If your husband is anything like mine, his library will be full of dreary papers.'

Was he like mine? I longed to ask questions. 'What's your favourite book?' I wanted to read it, to be more like her in any way I could.

'I'm fond of anything by Mr Hardy.' She removed her gloves and ran a finger along the spines. Elegant hands, with nails like sugared almonds. A cabochon ruby sat above her wedding band. It looked new. Perhaps she and Ambrose had designed it together.

'I haven't read them.' Mother thought his novels too daring. She destroyed Isabel's copy of *Desperate Remedies*, as though its words might ignite the household.

'My favourite is *The Water Babies* . . . I know it's a children's book but . . .'

'I love it too!'

'I'd like to read it again. Something about the discussion at the Barringtons' made me think of it.'

'Mer-people! Ambrose says Lucius is obsessed. Fish with feet, he calls them. Do you think they're real?'

'He feels close to a discovery that will . . .' I dropped my voice, 'prove how we came from the sea.'

'I wish him luck. And you. Tell me, how did you meet?'

'He's a friend of my father's.'

She gave me a searching look. 'Did he sweep you off your feet?'

'It was all very quick. I met him only once before the arrangements were made.' I paused, torn between pride and the need for a friend. 'It was agreed by my family.'

'Then he's a lucky man,' she said softly.

'We thought he'd prefer Isabel.'

'You're a charming young woman, who would not choose you?'

I felt a secret smile at the thought she found me charming. 'He seems very disinterested now.'

'Men are single-minded when they have the bit between their teeth. Once he proves this research, things will be different. You must help him to find his fish with feet.'

Where would I start? I thought of the papers in his room, the sketches and scribbles that covered his floor. I *could* help him. If I drew what he desired, perhaps it would bring us closer. I told Caroline about my sketchbooks, and my fingers itched to practice.

'Downstairs at once!' A circular staircase ran between the floors, its spindles painted in gold leaf like the subject signs that lined the shelves. Caroline pointed to the sign for artists' materials and we were halfway down before I realised, with dismay, that I had no means to pay for anything I'd chosen. There was little point in looking at materials I couldn't buy.

'Lucius will have an account here, I can't think where else he would shop. Just add them to that.'

Could I? Perhaps just this once. With the number of books in his library, a few more would not be noticed. But I needed money of my own. I would write to Father and ask him to send some. No, I would write to Isabel. Finally, I had a friendship to report, and she could appeal to Father for me; after everything I'd done for her, it wasn't much to ask.

After loading the carriage with parcels, we drove around the edge of the park, happily leaning against each other as if no-one else mattered. All the while I worried that I wouldn't get another chance to see her. My new friend. If Lucius forbade me, I'd have no choice. Should I say something? Would she know about their feud? And how would I ask? I couldn't risk our friendship before it had begun.

'This is where Ambrose asked for my hand.' Caroline pointed to the row of chairs by the bandstand.

'Did you already know him well?'

'I was governess to his brother's children. He visited so often they actually began to believe he was interested in their education.'

A good marriage. She looked comfortable ordering the carriage and driver, suited to such a life. Though she must regret her independence.

'Do you miss being a governess?'

She wrinkled her nose. 'The children were sweet. I liked being with them. And it was better than waiting around at home for Father to finish work. It was always just the two of us. And books, of course, lots of books for company.'

'You must be very clever.'

Caroline's smile left a dimple in her right cheek. 'I've read a lot of books, which isn't always the same thing.'

I'd heard Father say it about Dr Pearson with all his new ideas. Even if I did manage to read through Dr Everley's library, there was no guarantee I could understand his work. But I must try. If I didn't, I would never feel at home. A young couple wandered past, heads bent low in earnest conversation. A spray of violets wilted on her hat brim. His scarf caught on her shoulder.

'It seems to be the place for lovers to walk.'

'It is. Lovers of all kinds,' she added, as a woman in a scarlet dress and hat walked past on the arm of an older man. Bright dress, dark curls unruly under her bonnet, something in the way she moved. A glimpse of Rebecca. The woman leant across her companion, one hand cupped to his ear as she whispered something that made him roar with laughter. Would Rebecca still be so free? Given Grace's descriptions of girls who made such choices, it was unlikely. No, my sister had been much in my thoughts and I was imagining her, as I had imagined her in the book of photographs. I *wanted* to see her, and the more I remembered, the more I missed her. Lately I'd had far too much time to think, and it seemed not to suit me. My mind was weakening.

Mrs Barker must have been waiting, because the very moment we returned she threw open the front door and held out her arms for my parcels. I'd hoped to see Annie. Now I'd have to carry them myself or bear her questions. I felt suddenly weary.

'No need, Mrs Barker, thank you, I can manage.' I struggled awkwardly to the stairs and began to climb, unable to hold the handrail and fearful that I may lose my footing.

'Mrs Atherton called.'

I halted and replied without turning my head. 'Did she leave any message?'

'I told her who you'd gone with.'

'Thank you.' I wouldn't give her the satisfaction of seeing me flustered.

'She'll be calling tomorrow.'

'Marvellous. I shall look forward to it.' I began to walk up the stairs, concentrating on not falling until I reached the top. If she said anything further, then I didn't hear. Caroline's friendship had made me bold. And if Dr Everley was worried, then perhaps it would make him spend some time at home. He seemed to have forgotten where he was supposed to live.

My room had been tidied again, objects on the dressing table moved. The thimble and bud vase had disappeared, as had the locket in its case. I felt sure Annie wouldn't move things. Did Mrs Barker come in when I was out? I pushed aside the memory of Lucius's face when he saw the locket. Foolish to think of ghosts.

Though reminders of Lucius's parents were everywhere, my room filled with Amelia's things. I put my parcels down on the chair and picked up what looked like a letter opener, or a thin dagger, made of sharp narrowed metal, with a little silver bee on the handle, thin, like a wasp. The bee's slight body decorated everything in the Everley house but the letter opener itself was unfamiliar. An uneven rust stain marked the blade. Someone had placed it there deliberately. But why? I rarely received letters. I couldn't decide if it was worse to ask Lucius and risk his shock, or Mrs Barker and feel her contempt.

Two birds landed on the windowsill, already trained to visit for crumbs. I placed some pieces of biscuit for them and began to unwrap my materials, excited to use them. Familiar scents of chalk dust rose from the packet as I selected a thin wand of charcoal and began to outline the shape of the birds, the fold of their wings. If I captured some quickly, I could work on detailed drawings later and leave them out for Lucius to see. But as soon as the crumbs disappeared, they flew away. Lucky things. Pale blue feathers showed in small patches below the brown. Young birds. Still trusting. They'd probably be back tomorrow. I kept sketching absent-mindedly, imagining how it must feel to open your arms and find feathered wings, to stretch them wide and swoop across the earth like an angel. When I looked down at the paper, I'd drawn the sketch into a water baby. A kind of angel. But its face looked like Rebecca's.

Exhibit 10

Brass facial clamp with magnifiers. c. 1813.

'You will have to get used to it, Madeleine. The Barkers have been with us for ever, I'm not about to tell them they must work differently.' Lucius's pen was still poised in his hand, raised above the paper. He didn't move from the library desk, and I stood in front of it like a punished child.

'I just wanted to know who it was.' I couldn't shake the feeling that someone had touched me whilst I slept, moved my things. They'd removed my shoes and I hadn't stirred. Why would they do that and just leave me there?

'The Barkers look after all of us. They often take my pen from my hand and send me off to bed.' His left hand began to rifle through a box of slides. 'They're just looking after us,' he repeated.

'They didn't send *me* to bed.'

'Mrs Barker said you were out cold. Probably thought you'd be comfortable enough in the chair.'

Freezing and stiff, feeling my way along the corridors without a candle. 'It was frightening to wake there.'

Lucius threw his pen onto the desk and pushed at the box of slides. He wasn't used to being interrupted, or sharing his time. 'How can your own home frighten you?'

'I couldn't see anything without a candle. The fire was out.'

'Yet you often wander at night.'

Something else for him to disapprove of. I did wander. But only when I heard noises I couldn't explain.

'Can't you just try to fit in, Madeleine?'

'I heard . . . I keep thinking I can hear . . . it's like a baby's cry. Not all the time but sometimes. Sometimes I hear people going up and down.'

Lucius frowned, showing deep lines across his forehead, and sprang from the chair to my side of his desk. For a moment I thought he would strike me, then just as suddenly he changed his expression to one of concern and ushered me into a high wing-backed chair. 'How long have you been hearing things that aren't there?'

I hesitated. The things I heard *were* there. Weren't they? I'd never experienced such a feeling before arriving in this house. Now I heard things constantly, although nothing was evident whenever I looked.

Instinctively, I replied with caution. 'Once or twice. I've heard the cries a handful of times.'

Lucius went to his desk and reached for a leather bag that rested against the wall, half open, returning with a handful of silver instruments. My heart quickened. He unfastened a clamp and held it to my face, pushing against the skin around my left eye, holding it open. 'Don't blink.' He leant closer, examining, and I caught the scent of hair oil, cologne, something sour beneath. He moved to my right eye, pulling the skin. I felt gathered tears washing away his touch. 'Nothing obvious for hallucinations.' He grabbed my hand, turned it over and felt for a pulse, checking his pocket watch. 'You seem panicked, nervous. How is your breathing?' Without waiting for an answer, he stood with one hand flat on my back and asked me to breathe in and out deeply.

'Shallow. Very shallow indeed. I think it would do you some good to see Dr Venables. He's more experienced than I in such matters of nervousness. I'll ask him to come by tomorrow. Meanwhile . . . get plenty of rest.'

'I feel . . .' I was about to say that I felt quite well, but I wasn't really sure. I *was* growing nervous. More than the gloom and strangeness should cause. Perhaps it wouldn't hurt to be seen. My eyes stung and I rubbed at them, which seemed only to make them worse.

'Is there something else?' I was being dismissed.

There were very few chances to converse with Lucius so intimately and I took the opportunity to speak out. I wanted routine. Even after Rebecca, when the fun disappeared, Lynton held a busy family life. London was lonely and I missed company. 'I would like to attend church.'

Lucius contemplated. 'It can be overstimulating for those of a nervous disposition. But we could try.'

Our agreement was interrupted by a scream so long and shrill that even Lucius looked startled. The noise stopped and then started again almost immediately. A woman screaming. Following the noise downstairs, I found Mrs Barker holding Annie, her arms tight behind her back. 'What's the meaning of this? Release her at once!'

'This doesn't concern you, Mrs Everley.'

She didn't loosen her grip. Annie's eyes were wild and frightened. I felt my own fear return. 'What's the matter, Annie?'

Mrs Barker shook her. 'Nothing but a foolish little girl's imagination.'

'I saw it!' Annie set her jaw. There were red marks on her skin where Mrs Barker's fingers pinched.

'There's no need to hold her quite so tightly. You're hurting her.'

'And let the little thief escape?'

Thief? Annie held nothing, I couldn't see anything out of place. 'Will someone please explain what's happening?' It was hard to show authority when Mrs Barker refused to listen. 'Where is Dr . . . Lucius?' I had thought he followed me.

Annie began whimpering at the mention of his name and Mrs Barker shook her roughly. 'We can deal with this. It's not the first time we've caught a housemaid stealing.'

'Do let her go, Mrs Barker!' I closed the door behind me. 'There, she cannot leave now.'

Reluctantly she released Annie, who came to stand near me, rubbing at her arms.

'Did you take something?'

'From Dr Everley's workshop,' interrupted Mrs Barker.

'Let her answer, please.' I looked expectantly at Annie, who shook her head violently.

'I caught her red-handed, touching his things. She knows very well she's not allowed in those rooms.'

'Could you show me?' A chance to see the rooms for myself.

'That won't be necessary. It's righted now.'

'Two of the little things joined together! It's the devil's work, that's what it is!' Annie burst out. Mrs Barker raised her hand and brought it sharply across her face. A loud crack and the girl was silenced. What did she mean by it? Two what? Before I had the chance to ask, Lucius and Barker arrived together. I felt an overwhelming urge to be held, but Lucius didn't move to comfort me. Instead he considered Annie, who seemed unable to look at him, until Barker seized her arm and marched her from the room.

'He'll take her straight to the workhouse, save the bother of the magistrate.' Mrs Barker wore a grim look of satisfaction.

'There's no need for magistrates,' said Lucius. 'Was anything taken?'

'No. But only because I found her. Poking through the things in your workshop.'

'Barker might wish to take her to St Margary's instead, they will be better equipped to manage such hysteria. I'll send word to the Master.' He nodded, his decision final, and I was dismayed to see him turn to leave. How could he be so calm? His housemaid had accused him of working with the devil and he didn't seem surprised. What was she scared of?

'She was screaming.' I spoke loudly, clearly. 'Why would she scream?'

'Probably because I caught hold of her. Didn't want to be found out. I've seen the type before.' Mrs Barker folded her arms across her chest. Her face was flushed and mottled. How long had she been fighting Annie?

Lucius went to his patients, and with a renewed fear of the Barkers I hid myself in the library with a book I had borrowed from Caroline. Faerytales, though they did little to calm my nerves. As a child I hadn't seen the dark threats in such magical worlds. *It's the devil's work.* The phrase would not leave my mind. Poor Annie. She was tired and sullen, but she hadn't seemed like a *nervous* girl. To work for the Barkers must require a strong constitution. Those marks on her arms – I'd imagined a man friend, now I wondered whether the Barkers had found reason to restrain her before. I couldn't be sure, but I felt it. And despite my position I knew I wasn't safe from such treatment. Though I was desperate to understand, there was danger afoot and I must be careful what I shared of my fears. Questions must wait.

'I see you're acquainting yourself with my brother's work.' Grace strode in and I looked up, startled, losing my place as I slammed the book shut and placed it beneath my chair. I'd been lost in stories, despite my good intentions to read the volumes she recommended. I indicated the pile on the low table, worthy scientific treatises, and she nodded her approval. Light caught on the combs in her hair, decorated with thin silver bees. Were they Amelia's too?

'What have you discovered today?' She began to pick up the books and read their spines. I willed her not to ask about the book I'd closed.

'I've been rediscovering the works of Mr Darwin.' I'd only read his words the other day, they would be easy enough to remember. As I spoke, I racked my brain for questions to ask that would deflect attention. 'I hadn't read the later editions that Lucius has marked.'

'One day someone will prove what he only suggests, and those weak musings will be forgotten.'

None of Mr Darwin's words had struck me as weak or musing and, judging by the number of editions in his library, Lucius didn't think so either. Why couldn't she read in her own house if she was so interested? I wished she wouldn't keep arriving unannounced, especially at such a late hour. Feeling she may appear at any moment made me feel watched, so that, despite my loneliness, I was always looking over my shoulder. My thoughts stayed with the book under my chair, wanting to return to the story of the little mermaid. Sad and terrible, a warning tale of heart's desire, and I yearned to know how it finished. How could it end well for the poor heroine? Dark woodcut plates showed an evil witch peering from a cave, the mermaid wobbling on strange long legs, each step like knives piercing her body. She could never return. Even if she managed to make the prince love her, she'd be changed for ever.

'Madeleine? Did you hear me? You seem far away.'

I snapped to attention. 'I'm a little distracted.' Did she know about Annie? Something told me that may be why she was here, though I would not give her the satisfaction of asking.

'Perhaps an early night would be in order. Are you drinking Mrs Barker's cocoa? Lucius always finds it helps him to rest.'

I nodded. How did she know about that?

'I was asking how Lucius's paper was received on Friday? He promised to be here so we could discuss it.'

Something else I was supposed to understand? He'd not mentioned a paper at all, though I knew he'd been at the Society. Why was it so important to tell Grace?

'I believe one of his patients is unwell. He was needed suddenly, just before dinner.'

'Then I'll stay until he returns. Did you ask Mrs Barker to wait supper?'

There was no need. The Barkers seemed to know far more about his movements than I did. She must have read my thoughts.

'You mustn't expect to lead a normal life here, Madeleine.' Her voice was cold as ice. 'My brother's work is *important*. One day he'll make a great discovery that's worthy of Father's legacy.'

It sounded like a warning. I opened my mouth to ask what she meant, just as Barker opened the door, handing a glass of brandy to Lucius as he walked in.

'I'll take one of those,' called Grace.

'Mrs Everley?' he enquired.

'No,' Grace replied for me. 'She's feeling unsettled. Bring some cocoa.'

'Good evening, Lucius,' I said. 'How is your patient?'

'She is comfortable, but may not be for long. A very delicate constitution.'

'How sad. And how tiresome for you just as dinner was served. I had hoped we'd have the evening together.'

Our eyes met, and for a moment I thought I saw a glimmer of understanding.

'Consumption will always take the weak,' said Grace with an air of boredom. 'A waste of your time.'

'Since my time is paid for, we should not consider it a waste.' Lucius drank half the glass of brandy in one gulp. Was I to be included in his 'we', or would it always refer only to the two of them?

'Do sit down, Lucius, and tell us about your paper,' I asked, before Grace could whisk him off for another private conversation.

He pulled the upright chair from behind the door and sat heavily, nursing his glass, looking as though weights hung from his shoulders. Father looked the same after difficult visits, the ones he knew he couldn't save. He would try to shrug it off and pretend he had no choice but to be an instrument of divine will. Still, it hurt him that he couldn't save everyone. Perhaps all medics were the same.

'It was well received. The men approved its publication in the journal. Maycott has agreed to peer review . . . among others.'

Grace clapped her hands in a girlish way that didn't suit her. 'And they agreed with you?'

'They seemed to. But you know they must have proof now. If I can't provide it soon then the moment will be lost.'

Grace's eyes flicked to where I sat, just for a second. What could it have to do with me? Perhaps she wished me to leave so they could speak freely. It made me determined to stay.

'Who were the others, who supported your paper?' asked Grace.

'I said they agreed to review it. The level of support remains to be seen. Fairly, of course, trying to make a name for himself on the back of others' work, Pelling, and Stepwood.'

'And you agreed?'

'I could hardly refuse.'

My heart soared. If he was working with Caroline's husband and father, then surely Lucius couldn't continue to prohibit my friendship with the Fairlys?

'You're as bad as Madeleine, consorting with the enemy.' Grace bore a look of malice as she accepted the brandy Barker had brought. He bowed, retreating with his back still bent. 'Mrs Barker tells me she was out with Caroline this week.'

'Is this true?' Lucius confronted me. His lace cuff was stained with a ring of rust-red. I felt a sudden chill as I realised it was the same colour as the mark on the letter opener. A bloodstain. Natural on a doctor's linen, but on a paperknife? Whoever had put it in my room must have known. Unless they were not human.

'She took me to buy books. It was good of her to remember me, and it would have been rude to refuse.' The conversation I wanted would have to wait. 'I thought perhaps we could invite the Fairlys to supper? Caroline has been kind to me.'

'That family must not set foot in this house!' Grace jumped up, stamping her foot, and Lucius raised a warning hand. His index finger was stained purple with iodine around a deep thin cut that looked as though a knife had slipped. 'Father would turn in his resting place.'

'Madeleine makes a point. If I'm to get anywhere I must work with Stepwood. And change his mind. Their friendship won't hurt.'

Grace muttered something under her breath. I thought I caught the word 'weak' but I could have been mistaken. She seemed to consider weakness the worst fault of all. I wondered how many times she'd used it to describe me.

'How are the children?' asked Lucius. Just as quickly as before, her demeanour turned, and I saw something of Edmond in her face as she spoke sweetly.

'Quite well, thank you, and as fond of their uncle as ever. Soon I'll be asking after your own. It will do Madeleine good to have something else to occupy her.'

Shame rose in my throat and made me nauseous. What did she hope to achieve by such comments, other than to irritate us both? How could I become a mother, in this strange house, with a husband who didn't touch me? Children could not be further from his mind.

'I'm tired. Forgive me, it's been a long day. I'll carry on my reading upstairs, if I may be excused.'

'I see I've touched a nerve.' Grace sounded delighted at the idea.

'That is enough,' Lucius growled, and I took the opportunity of discord to slip the book from under my chair and push it under my arm with the spine hidden.

'Goodnight.'

'Goodnight, Madeleine.'

Raised voices followed me up the stairs. Why was Grace so determined to clear her father's name? She pushed Lucius so relentlessly that arguments brewed always just below the surface, and I couldn't help thinking he would be a nicer person without such pressure. Before permission was withdrawn, I determined to visit Caroline and ask her opinion. She knew more than she'd let on, I was sure of it.

As I prepared for bed, the heavens opened, and I moved to the window to watch a growing storm. Slashes of lightning scarred the sky and rain lashed against the windowpanes. Grace would be soaked, could catch a chill. She was hard to like but I bore her no ill feeling. When Mrs Barker brought my tray, I asked if Grace's coach could be brought to the front of the house so she wouldn't be drenched.

'No-one expects her to travel in this,' she replied curtly, 'I'm preparing the red room.'

Lucius would doubtless leave early for work, and I would be faced with an exhausting breakfast with his sister. I pulled the curtains closed around my bed as though I could shut out more than the cold and, picking up my book, found 'The Little Mermaid' and began to read. Rain drummed at the windows and rattled the shutters. A high-pitched wind moaned through the rooms in the attic. The cocoa's bitter warmth made me drowsy and I slipped in and out of a doze, dreaming of knife wounds and consumptive women fading to their deaths. After a while I thought I heard voices, raised and fast in heated discussion, though what they said was unclear.

Wrapped up in blankets, I imagined myself as the mermaid. Underwater she was free and loved. She swapped it for a life of unknown pain. If Lucius were right and merfolk existed, could I swap this life for theirs? A crashing sound and a thin, high cry from one of the rooms along the corridor caused me to sit upright and draw the covers around my knees, listening keenly for the cause.

'No-one need know.' I heard that plainly enough, a woman's voice, though whether Mrs Barker or Grace was hard to tell. It was conceivable that either should wish me harm, or even plot to kill me. Look what had happened to Annie. I might end that way myself. Oh but I was foolish, fanciful! I shouldn't read faerytales in this creaking house; such thoughts could send me mad. Mother and Isabel would tell me to think myself lucky for everything the Everleys had given me. I should be grateful for my clothes, my soft bed, my respectable husband. Look where wanting to be free got Rebecca.

Exhibit 11

Dried Hippocampus erectus. Cambodia.
Discovered 1873.

I awoke late, and when I opened my curtains I saw that the storm had given way to a calm morning. Puffs of cloud hung in a pale grey sky, thin fingers of sunlight trying to claw through. I threw a shawl over my nightclothes, pushed my feet into slippers and ran to the red room to check on Grace. The handle gave, swinging open to show a fresh-made bed and tidy room. If she had stayed the night, she was long gone.

It was early enough for Lucius to be at home and I went to find him at breakfast, determined to discover what Annie had seen. It was a new day, and without Grace's presence it would be safer to ask questions of my husband. Mrs Barker could not come between us twice. I hardly knew what to imagine; thoughts jumbled and sank in my mind, but I could not spend another day without knowing. *It's the devil's work.*

My husband stood by the table, speaking with Mrs Barker. Both seemed surprised to see me. I levelled my gaze at Lucius and asked after Annie.

'She said it was the work of . . .' My tongue refused to speak the name. 'What did she mean?'

'Hysterical!' snorted Mrs Barker.

Lucius looked thoughtful. 'Not everyone understands the needs of science,' he said slowly. 'There are things we must do to understand the natural world, or the human body, that might seem shocking.'

'What things?' I whispered. Without answering he walked to the door and gestured for me to go first. His signet ring banged against the wood, and he twisted it round on his finger to check it wasn't scratched. The family crest was paramount, even at such a time. Was I invited to the locked rooms? I could not show fear. I did not want the offer withdrawn.

I followed him up the stairs and along the corridor, hardly daring to breathe lest the spell was broken and he changed his mind. Lucius pushed open the furthest door, the one Barker called his workshop, holding it open behind him in silent invitation.

No light came through the shuttered windows. Lucius took up a box of matches, catching the lamp on the third. I stood away from the edges of the room and clasped my hands together, fearful of touching evil in the darkness. My heart beat faster. The lamp began to sputter and flicker. The sweet-rotten smell grew stronger. I held my breath.

As my eyes slowly adjusted to the gloom, I saw a long wooden bench, covered in thick leather and stained with rust-red rings. The colour of dried blood. Something furred was pinned out across the bench. A squirrel with eyes like funeral beads. Its underbelly – yellow-white against its red tail – opened in a long slit, showing a rounded stomach and the embryo of its baby. Another squirrel lay limp beside it, little clawed hands clasped together in supplication. My stomach lurched but I forced myself not to turn away. This was my chance to persuade him that I wasn't nervous, or easily shocked.

'I'm sorry if it appears brutal.'

He mustn't think me *weak* or I would lose my place entirely. 'I grew up in a doctor's house, surrounded by wildlife,' I replied. But Annie had been a country girl too. Would this have shocked her? She would surely have seen rabbits skinned, deer staked out to bleed or hung from ropes to season.

One of the bench drawers was partially open. Nestled on green baize, like silver spoons, were row upon row of thin, sharp dissection tools. Cold metal implements for cutting and slicing through tissue. A saw smaller than the one on his papers. I reached out, but Lucius stayed my hand.

'You'll hurt yourself. There's an art to holding some of those that cannot be quickly taught.' He picked up a pair of open, dissected wings, with layers of white feathers like painted angels. I would have dearly liked to draw them.

'Beautiful.' I stroked the wings. 'What bird is this?'

'A ptarmigan, wearing its winter plumage.' He stretched the wings flat to demonstrate how they folded to close. 'Similar to arms, in a way. See how the top attaches like a shoulder blade, moving backwards where the tendons grip bone.'

I did see. If I could learn to sketch the sections of things, then my drawings would come to life. I ran my fingers across them, pushing and spreading the joints. I'd never seen anatomy in such detail, and I was fascinated. Surely Annie would have been too? Did something hide in the shadows or was this all she saw? It was hardly the devil's work.

'How do you expose the bones like this?'

Lucius gave me a curious look, as though he hadn't expected such eagerness to understand his research. It would do him good to share. I pushed aside the memory of the voices I'd heard. Foolish fancies. There was no room in here for another to work with him, and the meticulous hours he spent must be lonely. Studies in melancholy. There was no need for us to spend such hours apart in this house. I nodded encouragement and he picked up another wing, devoid of feathers, the tiny socket joints exposed.

'You must strip the feathers carefully, individually, so as not to upset the structure or push it out of place.' He indicated a sack full of snowy white. 'Once all the feathers are removed the bones are dipped into lime, here – it strips the flesh and makes them clean. Whitens the bone so the joints are visible. Leave it in too long and the parts dissolve completely. But if you dip it quickly, only the skin dissolves and the tendons remain intact.'

'How?' I leant over the vat of lime.

'They're made of tougher tissue.' He pushed me back. 'It's caustic, it could burn you, or your clothes.'

My nightclothes. In the excitement of the locked room, I'd forgotten how I was dressed. My neck and ankles were quite bare, my legs unclothed beneath thin cotton. As exposed as the women in his photographs. Had he even noticed? I pushed my hands into the sack of feathers. Snowy puffs escaped, landing gently on my skin. 'They would make soft pillows,' I said. But Lucius was folding and replacing the wings. 'I'd like to bring my sketchbooks here, to draw these things,' I said. I would practise first, trying ways to show the precision of what lay beneath these animals, as much as how they looked when they were alive. If I could prove myself useful, he might see me differently and, perhaps, I might begin to feel more at home.

Lucius pulled out his watch as though he hadn't heard. Was I about to be dismissed? I'd barely looked at the rest of the workshop, or been inside the small museum. What had frightened Annie? So many objects to examine. A long row of narrow shelves, full of treasures, ran down the wall by the door.

Jars containing bloated white shapes, giant shells, long claws like severed chickens' feet, several sets of teeth. I pointed to a shrivelled husk, like a curled leaf with a tiny spiral pattern and what looked like the face of a dragon. 'What's this?'

'*Hippocampus erectus.*' He took it carefully from the shelf and placed it into my open hand. 'Some call it a seahorse.'

'A faery creature.' Its body was one fluid curve, the fins atop its head like a spiked crown. A faery king. My fingers itched to draw him.

'No. But proof of the strangeness of things beneath the sea. So many discoveries to be made.'

'What's it like?' I asked.

'Have you never seen the sea?'

'Never.' I imagined it as wild and dangerous.

'We'll go, one day.'

I looked down at the tiny, curled seahorse king. 'I would like that,' I said and meant it. If such things were what he hoped to find, then his was not the devil's work at all. It was something magical.

12

The Marlborough Assizes

It was impossible to find a seat in the public gallery. I pulled my skirts free and tried to jostle as others were doing. Why didn't I leave earlier? I should have known it would be packed. It was exactly the type of case that people enjoyed. Dark histories dredged up with the added scandal of a murderess. All combined with the chance to watch a wealthy family toppled from its perch. Within weeks of the trial ending the story would appear in the penny dreadfuls, thinly veiled with different details, but everyone would know what was intended. It would make fortunes for someone. Him, perhaps? I glared at the one man brazen enough to keep his seat while women stood, calfskin notebook on his lap, massaging his fingers. I hoped his words were poison to him. Or could it be her? The woman dressed in scarlet with black velvet trim, a huge hat blocking her face from view. She had a notebook too. I'd always assumed men wrote the dreadfuls, but I could be wrong. A woman's mind could be dark just the same.

Murmured whispers threaded the crowd, sudden and violent, and I craned my neck to see. One of the taller men in front of me ushered me forward and I moved just in time to see Maddie take the stand. Pale as winter, with shadowed eyes and wearing the same patched prison dress as before. Her hair looked dull and matted. Did they even allow her to wash? She clasped her hands together like a saint, at once ancient and childlike. Too young to be so sad. Presumably her family had stayed in Cheshire. How could they bear it, waiting for news? If I'd been refused admission, I would have battered down the doors.

Everyone rose as the magistrate entered, grimly serious in his mothy wig. He settled himself for several minutes before motioning us to sit and turning his attention to the stand.

'Mrs Madeleine Everley. Do you understand the charges made against you?'

She lowered her head further, which he took as agreement.

'Do you understand the seriousness of the charges made against you? Murder is a crime that rightly carries the gravest penalty. You must understand that this means death. If this court finds you guilty, you will be hung by the neck until you are dead.' An excited gasp passed through the crowd and the magistrate paused, as though allowing the horror of his words to sink in. 'Do you understand?'

This time she nodded, several times, without raising her head.

'Failure to speak the truth will also result in serious penalties. Take the holy book in your left hand and place your right hand upon it before you pledge to tell only the truth.' A court hand passed a Bible, bound in plain black leather, and Maddie took it carefully, as if it were a newborn child. She whispered her pledge, handing it back almost reluctantly.

'Doesn't look capable of killing a mouse,' said one of the men behind me, causing a low ripple of laughter. I clenched my fists. No point in turning on them. And he was right, she didn't. Her frame was now so thin that her shoulder blades were clearly visible through the grey serge.

'Miss Annie Hawton left your service earlier this year. Miss

Hawton was, I believe, *your* personal maid?' He continued without waiting for an answer, already weary of pushing Maddie to speak. 'Can I ask you to tell the court what caused your maid to leave your employment?'

'I don't know.'

'Miss Hawton is at St Margary's, unfit to take the stand as a witness. But we have been informed by her nurse that her illness was brought on by something she had seen in your house, that she became frightened to stay. Her statement claims that "it was full of unnatural behaviours". What sort of behaviour is she describing?' Maddie stayed silent. I thought Tizzy was her maid? She was always loyal to Maddie, so where was she now?

'What work did Miss Hawton carry out for you?'

'She cleaned my room. But I didn't see her often and she didn't speak to me.'

'Why didn't she speak to you? Had you frightened her in some way, as she alleges?'

'I don't know how.'

Someone tapped the shoulder of the woman in the scarlet dress and she stopped writing to remove her hat, which must have been blocking his view. Black curls tumbled across her shoulders and she retied her ribbon, pushing her hat awkwardly beneath her seat before taking up her pen again. She was too thin, and her shoulders hunched forward as though she felt the cold, but there was something about her that held the gaze. Huge dark eyes and glowing skin, a slight curve to the mouth like a secret smile. Every man in the room had turned to watch her, including the magistrate. He paused before beginning again.

'What do you think Miss Hawton meant by "unnatural behaviours"?'

'I don't know.'

'As a housemaid, Miss Hawton would have had free run of the house?'

'I suppose so. Except for Dr Everley's rooms, which stay locked.'

'She didn't clean those rooms?'

'Dr Everley cleans them himself.'

This time I'd remembered my notepaper, but with nothing to rest it on I was unable to make notes. Every fibre of my body strained to hear and remember. Maddie seemed so desperately alone. I couldn't imagine calling Ambrose 'Dr Fairly'. They weren't married at all. She had no-one but me and she wouldn't let me help her.

'Did you ever have the opportunity to observe Miss Hawton at her work? Or speak to her about her duties?'

'She spent most of her time with the Barkers, below stairs.'

'Mrs Barker being your housekeeper?'

'Yes.'

'Who managed the household?'

Maddie opened her mouth to speak and then closed it again, as though reconsidering what she'd been about to say. 'Yes.'

'What might Miss Hawton have found to frighten her into leaving your employment? A good job. At a time when good jobs are not easy to find for those of Miss Hawton's background.'

What was her background? The question seemed to throw Maddie. There was a long pause before she replied. 'Perhaps Dr Everley's work. His research. He collects medical curios.'

'What kind of curios?'

'Unusual things. I suppose they could upset someone who didn't know what they were. He has samples of . . . birth defects, animals born with too many limbs, that sort of thing. He studies them. To find out what caused the abnormalities.'

'Only one thing causes that sort of evil,' muttered a woman sitting in front of me, to no-one in particular. The others tutted and clucked, condemning. They weren't seeing Maddie at all.

'Yet you have just told us that your husband's rooms were locked? How might she have been frightened by something she was prevented from seeing?'

Maddie shook her head miserably. 'I don't know.'

'Blaming everyone but herself,' the woman judged. She'd already decided on Maddie's guilt. Perhaps everyone had. 'No smoke without fire' seemed to be the general principle of the system. The man with the notebook was sitting next to her and he shrugged, lifting his pencil for a moment. I saw that he wasn't writing but sketching. A haunting portrait of Maddie was drawn on the page, full of misery and pain. Perhaps the artist's mind, at least, was open. He shrouded her face with a sheer blotting sheet, turned the page and pressed it down, prepared to start a new one.

'Unnatural behaviour,' said the magistrate, 'can be difficult to discuss. But it's not uncommon in your family is it, Mrs Everley?'

Finally, they were going to bring up Lucius's father. Ambrose had told me everything about the story, things I should have hidden from Maddie before. He'd scolded me for telling her, thinking she'd be frightened. I should have listened. What must it have been like for her there in that house? Medical murder. He said the Society cared little for where the bodies were procured until the wrong ones were brought. Too much attention caused and a stop to all of it.

'I don't understand. My husband . . .'

'Your *own* family, Mrs Everley. Your sister, I believe, is a delinquent.'

The woman in the scarlet dress dropped her notebook and a lead pencil went clattering below the chairs. She was white as a winding sheet. The sketch artist hastened to pass one of his own pencils along the row towards her and she took it without meeting anyone's eye.

'We are informed that your own sister eloped with a man whom she did not, subsequently, marry. That she is an unmarried mother.'

Maddie said nothing.

'I'll try again. What happened to your sister, Mrs Everley?'

'I was a child.'

'You were old enough to understand.'

'I was twelve years old.' Maddie raised her head and regarded the magistrate with something like defiance. It was the first sign of fight and I willed her to continue. 'A child. Nothing was discussed in my hearing. I missed her. I missed her so badly. And no-one told me where she was, or who she was with, or what she was doing. I thought she'd run away from us. I thought it was *my* fault.'

A scrape of chairs. The scarlet woman stood, fumbled to grab her hat, and pushed her way through the gathered crowd to the door at the back of the court. The door swung back behind her and the chattering started. Did they suspect, as I did, that the woman was Rebecca? Maddie hadn't even turned her head so I couldn't check for signs of recognition, but even before she left the court I'd had my suspicion – she was so like Maddie's description. Too much of a coincidence that she should be at this trial by chance. While Maddie remained in the dock, I couldn't follow her, as much as I wanted to. I couldn't bear to miss any of Maddie's words. The way things were going, it could be the only time we'd hear from her. If it was really Rebecca, then she'd be back over the next days of the trial.

'Quiet in the stands, or you'll be removed.' Loud shouting from the stick-thin clerk with the voice of a fishwife, who clearly relished that part of his job. The magistrate winced and turned back to Maddie, whose knuckles were raised up, white against the bluish skin of her hands as she held herself steady on the edge of the box.

'The loss of your sister affected you, then. Would you say it made you nervous?'

Maddie's eyes were wide; she looked scared to speak and who could blame her. It seemed as though everyone tried to put words into her mouth. *Made her nervous*. Didn't everything make women nervous? Isn't that what they wanted to hear? That she'd caved in to all the things that could make her lose her mind? Even if she *was* nervous, it didn't make her a murderer.

'Let me put it another way, did you worry about your sister?'

'Yes.'

'You worried that she wasn't safe?'

'Yes. I worried that she wasn't happy.'

'When did you find out that Mrs Atherton and your husband were helping your sister?'

'I didn't know that.'

'You knew she was at Evergreen House.'

'I guessed. But I didn't know they were helping her.'

The magistrate paused. 'What did you *think* happened at Evergreen House?'

Maddie was silent. What was she thinking? Embarrassed to admit to strange fantasies or too scared to tell the truth?

'Did you know that Rebecca had left Evergreen House?'

Maddie ran her tongue along her lips. They looked dry. Though the magistrate and witnesses had water, no-one had offered her anything. As though, by ending up accused, she had somehow ceased to be human.

'No.' Could she be lying? She didn't register surprise.

'If you know where she is, you'd be best advised to say so. The proprietors are, naturally, keen to know and it goes without saying that cooperation would be in the best interests of your case.' He sighed. 'It would be best for Rebecca too.'

'I don't know,' said Maddie quietly. The skinny clerk made a show of checking his watch, then held up five fingers. The magistrate nodded. Maddie's time was running out. Though I was glad I'd heard the rest of her interview, I realised that if the woman who left was actually Rebecca, then she'd never risk coming back to the trial. Lucius and Grace were looking for her. Why? If I could find her first, I may be able to help Maddie. The problem was where to start.

Exhibit 13

Phrenology head, female features. Scottish pottery.
Inscribed 'Man Know Thyself'. c. 1835.

Though I had no wish to subject myself to more prodding, by agreeing to see Dr Venables I persuaded Lucius to attend church, which was as cold as on our wedding day. My husband was still a stranger and, though I felt ten years older, I remained bewildered by our relationship. If Lucius was also thinking of our vows, he didn't say. His expression was unreadable.

He'd dressed beautifully, as always, his waistcoat burnished with copper that set off the lights in his hair. Nut-brown leather gloved his elegant surgeon's hands. They rested calmly together on his cane, but his features were hard as stone. Of what, or whom, was he thinking? Dressed in my new clothes, I felt pale and invisible. If only I had Rebecca's charm. When I wrote to Mother, I couldn't find the words to ask why I seemed to disappoint my husband. Several drafts were thrown into the fire because I didn't want her pity. Better they should all think I was happy. I filled the letter with news of Caroline and my outing instead, sealing it up tightly with navy wax in a little bead like a rodent's eye.

The church was almost full. Ordinary families in smart suits and new hat ribbons. Children in pinafores, clutching parents' hands.

Though I watched him carefully, Lucius acknowledged no-one. Not a dip of the head, a raised hand, a smile of recognition. My heart sank. Church should be a community, a chance to meet others and talk or to walk home together discussing the sermon. There'd be none of that here.

A family hurried in at the last moment and, finding nowhere else to sit, pushed themselves onto the end of our pew, squeezing up against us. Lucius stiffened and threw disapproving looks at the children.

'Sorry.' The mother was plump and friendly-looking. 'Never enough space. Haven't seen you before?'

'Just moved.' I smiled and the youngest child poked out his tongue at me.

'Stop that, William. You're watched in here.'

He grimaced at his mother who turned to me and whispered, 'Don't have any for as long as you can manage, that's my advice, little blighters.' She didn't look as though she meant it. Her hands were constantly stroking their hair, smoothing down their clothes. 'Harriet Fanshaw, this is Albie.' A pleasant-looking man leant forward, as tall and thin as his wife was short and round. 'We can't afford names for this horrible lot, we call them one, two, three and four.' She roared with laughter.

'Madeleine B—Everley.' I'd nearly said Brewster. It was, I realised, the first time I'd spoken my new name aloud. It didn't sit easily on my tongue.

'Ah, newlyweds. Lovebirds, eh? Enjoy it while it lasts.' She exchanged a look with Albie and I felt my face flush.

'Lucius, my husband,' I indicated but he barely acknowledged them. Harriet raised her eyebrows. We all stood as the reverend walked in and, flustered, I dropped my hymnbook to the floor. Lucius passed me his and I was grateful, though later I realised it was because he did not sing. I wondered whether his voice was poor, but he didn't even mouth the words. Everything seemed to displease him. Throughout the sermon his foot tapped the floor impatiently. His ill will made me anxious as I listened to the service, especially as the reading was from Genesis.

'Without Creation there is no creator, no kindly hand to guide our actions and save us from the very worst of ourselves. Brother killing brother, child fighting child, without Creation and divine love, humanity would be brutalised, our divine race would be sunk . . .' The rector seemed to stare straight at us as he spoke. Gold embroidery shone on his surplice. Such words struck me with terror.

'It's what you were talking about at the Barringtons',' I whispered, pulling at his jacket.

'What?' he hissed.

'Don't you worry?'

Lucius gave a sudden barking laugh that made me jump in fright. Harriet and Albie turned to stare at us.

'Absolute rubbish,' he muttered. 'I won't let you drag me here again. And you're not to attend alone, having your head filled with nonsense. Leave it to parlourmaids.'

Harriet stared straight ahead, as though in rapt attention to the sermon. I thought again about the painting of Perpetua, hidden to me now behind a plaster pillar. To have her unshakeable faith in anything would be wonderful. I thought we had understood each other in the small museum. His discoveries were magical, wonderful, they showed the goodness and hand of a benign creator. Science and medicine were the saviours of mankind, and yet they must marry with faith and love or surely such discoveries were meaningless? Here was a stark reminder that my husband felt otherwise.

Dear Sister,

It seems a lifetime since we delivered you to your new life and you have been cruelly sparing with your news. Who are you meeting? What are you wearing? We are starved of parties here. If we could but read of how you enjoy yourself, then we would not feel so bereft.

You will be pleased to know that Father's practice goes well. He was called to see to Sir Aylett in a frightful rush and cured his fever. Father says it was breaking anyway but that's not how people are talking. He has picked up a dozen more patients since, good families, all smiles and forgiveness. He says they ask after you now, and not Rebecca, and that is the difference. It means that James can stay at school after all – he studies so hard, you would hardly recognise him. Mother has formed another music group, her visits keep her busy, and we have taken on a maid to help out Ellen. So you see things do not stand still!

My life is also changing, in the most exciting way. I believe I, too, am to be married! Arnold Hillen is the new rector, widowed with three children. He hasn't yet asked but I'm sure he will soon. He visits twice a week and is most particular to be polite to Mother. We always walk together in the garden. His children are so small, they do so need a mother. Arnold is the most fascinating man, I would love for you to meet him before the wedding. I have asked Grandmother to teach me to make lace, in case he asks soon, but her eyesight is not so good on these dark evenings. She asks after you too, and says she still likes to receive letters even though she can't write them any more.

We would so like to see you. And I dare say Father would like to see Lucius again. There would be little to interest you here, after London, but you could introduce us to your circles, and we could shop for my trousseau. When may we come?

Your loving sister,
Isabel

Such news from home left me restless. She would be good with children but Isabel, a rector's wife? There could be few less suitable. Imagine her in a plain dress, with a spotless apron, bringing food parcels and comfort to the poor. A beacon of respectability. Perhaps, after everything, it was what she craved. Arnold had come along at the right time, with our family's standing restored, but Isabel would still wish to seal the arrangement with as much haste as was seemly.

With the letter in my pocket, I left the house and hailed a hansom on Langham Place. It would do me good to see Caroline and she'd told me, several times, how she enjoyed surprise visits. I spent the journey in pleasant anticipation of a warm welcome, but we had driven all the way to Grosvenor Square when I realised I'd forgotten the number of the Fairlys' house and was forced to ask to be let down at the side of the road. I paid from my dwindling coins. Isabel hadn't mentioned the allowance I asked her to seek from Father. If they were to visit, they would wish to go shopping and I would have to ask again. Somehow I could not find the words to ask my husband about money.

As I was wondering where to knock, a door opened, close to the end of the row of houses, and a tall man ran down the steps. Ambrose, with his distinctive height and long thin legs. When he reached the bottom he turned, laughed and flew back, taking the steps two at a time to meet Caroline standing at the door and seize her in a long embrace. Such affection between husband and wife made a stark contrast to our own formal exchanges. Had these two always been the same? Or did love grow as people began to understand one another? It wasn't something I felt able to ask. I had to hope it was true.

I waited until Ambrose's carriage had left before walking to the door and ringing the bell. The housemaid answered, starched as a tablecloth. Knuckles red against her pale hands. I felt suddenly shy.

'Is Mrs Fairly at home?' It was a long time since I'd called on anyone and I twisted the fringe of my shawl tightly between my fingers, feeling out of place. If the girl noticed, she was too well trained to show it. A broad smile spread across her face, and she welcomed me in without calling her mistress, asking me to wait in the warm while she went to see.

Flowers filled the hallway, huge vases brimming with arrangements like bridal bouquets – pink roses, lilies and hothouse iris, flowers for love and remembrance. They were the only ostentation. Behind them the decor was simple, pale green walls and two chairs clad in eau-de-Nil silk, a grand curved oak bannister. Light poured in from the double windows that flanked the door. A happy house.

'Maddie!' My heart warmed to hear my true name.

'Forgive my intrusion.' I held out my hands. 'I don't make a habit of arriving unannounced.'

'It means you were thinking of me, and for that I am grateful.' Caroline beamed. 'You don't intrude at all. Would you like some tea?'

My back was stiff with cold. Warm tea and a fire would be wonderful. 'Thank you. Your flowers are beautiful.'

She laughed. 'Ambrose sent an entire carriage full yesterday, for our anniversary. It's like living in a hothouse. We had to use pails for some of them.'

'How long have you been married?'

'Six months, still a novelty. I wonder if he'll do the same in another six?'

'You seem very happy.'

'I believe we are. As are you and Lucius, I'm sure.'

I tried to imagine my husband rushing back to kiss me goodbye, holding me at the waist, and said nothing as I followed her into the drawing room.

'You weren't exaggerating about the flowers!' Four huge stone urns, like garden statuary, flanked the hearth. They brimmed with boughs of blossom, ivy and baby's breath.

'He's quite mad,' she said cheerfully. 'They could have lasted a year. Though I rather like living among them. I feel like an actress.' She struck a pose next to one of the urns.

'These are beautiful.' I pulled out a large white flower, a delicate ball formed of dozens of smaller joined balls of petals. 'What are they?'

'Hydrangea. We have several in the garden. I can send some for you to plant if you like?'

'I'd like to draw them.' Such delicate strands of petals and yet so strong. Individually fragile, but grouped together they could not be crushed.

'Then we shall draw!'

Caroline disappeared and returned with a small wooden easel that folded up on the top of a paintbox, along with sketching paper, charcoals and paints. She spread them across the table. 'So much more fun than sewing. I can barely stitch a thing without creating knots and lumps that stick through the fabric.'

Unfazed, the housemaid placed the tea things down and went to fetch some sheets of newspaper, which she placed around us on the floor and table 'to catch the worst of the mess'. It was the happiest afternoon. We covered sheets of paper with botanical drawings, sketched out and painted in light watercolours. Caroline's sketching was neither so skilful nor so precise as mine, but she possessed a fine talent for painting the delicate colours of petals. Her pictures were as pretty as mine were accurate.

'You have a scientific eye.' Caroline held up my drawing of the hydrangea. 'Have you tried anatomical drawing?'

'I'd like to do more.'

'The collectors, and their publishers, pay handsomely for the right style.'

A chance to receive money without asking my husband or father. The option to take a cab or buy a book when I pleased. Where would I begin to find such work? And how without insulting Dr Everley? 'I was hoping to help Lucius with his collections, but we haven't found much time to discuss it. He's careful. And much involved with his latest research.'

'Don't allow him to neglect you, Maddie.' Her voice turned serious when she saw my face. 'Does he neglect you?'

'He's not much at home. His work keeps him busy.'

'Don't make too many excuses for him, a husband should know his place.'

I laughed, to show I wasn't worried, but it was out there now. And a part of me liked that. I had a friend for whom my happiness mattered, and that was better than pretending my marriage was perfect.

'I can show you some of those collector books, if you like?'

I began to gather up the art things, but Caroline stayed my hand. 'Maud will do that, she's used to my mess.'

Imagine Mrs Barker if I left the drawing room like that! Perhaps I should try. It would certainly catch some attention for my work.

There were no flowers in the library, where Ambrose worked,

but it housed more than books. Strange objects were stuffed onto every shelf, making it hard to read the spines. Something told me Lucius would be pleased to see the muddle. He could be scathing about others and would probably call it a sign of intellectual confusion.

'Sorry, bit of a mess. I keep asking if I can organise it, but you know what they're like with their special things.' Caroline rifled through one of the shelves, pulling out a large folio book with loosely bound pages decorated with detailed botanical drawings. 'These sorts of pictures. I know the woman who did these and she's turning work away.'

I set the folio down on the reading desk and began to turn the pages. The prints were skilful, but I knew they weren't as good as mine. 'Who is she?'

'Alice. The governess I replaced at Juliette's – Ambrose's sister. She earns enough to support herself this way. Though Juliette's children are quite a handful, and she was more than a little cross at needing to find two new staff in as many years.'

Enough to support herself. It was good to know. 'I should like to meet her. These are excellent.'

'She lives in Hamblin Mews. You would like her.'

'A stable?'

'It was. Now a group of artists live there. Her new life has encouraged her to be a little bohemian, but she's excellent company.'

I closed the book and replaced it on the shelf, trying not to upset a line of strange wooden carvings. It was heavy and the corner caught one of the figures, sent it clattering across the floor. Curious, I bent to retrieve it, turning it between my fingers. A squatting man, with a rough-hewn face, a large forehead protruding over closed eyes, a flat wide mouth.

'From the Americas, I think, some sort of god.'

It didn't look like any god I'd imagine. More like a demon. *The devil's work.* I felt a sudden urge to tell Caroline about Annie and what she thought she saw in the lime room, but it was too much to test our new friendship. The unspoken words hung between us and I stayed bent for a moment, feigning interest in the reading matter. On the bottom shelf was a line of fat books bound in oxblood leather and embossed in gold leaf with the name of Augustine Everley. So our families had not always been enemies. I pointed to them. 'Lucius's father?'

'Father was very fond of Old Dr Everley, once. He was often at home with us.'

'Something happened to change that.' I stood upright, replacing the figure on the shelf with the others. 'Grace has hinted but Lucius tells me little. I know he's keen to work with Ambrose and your father on the work he has in hand.'

'I don't really know what caused the rift. I don't think Lucius is blamed, I know Father sets great store by his work, as he did Old Mr Everley.' Caroline twisted the ruby around her finger, setting it straight. She looked as though she wanted to say more.

'Yet he is blamed for something. Grace has hinted at it. If you know, I'd be pleased to hear.'

'Father wouldn't tell me, he always thinks I'm more delicate than is the case. But Ambrose has mentioned something about his methods. It's hard to find the right teaching material for medical lectures.'

'What do you mean?'

'Flesh must be found to cut. To demonstrate the correct surgical procedures. Usually the flesh is dead but it mustn't be . . . too dead. For lectures, I am told, people can be paid to take bodies from graves.' Caroline bit her lip and looked down at her hands.

I had heard Father talk of the same thing. Is that what Grace meant by resurrectionists? Old Dr Everley could surely not have been the only surgeon to resort to such a thing? There must be something more. Why would no-one tell me? Before I could ask, a sudden crash caused me to jump from my skin and Caroline burst out laughing.

'That can only be Ambrose. He's like a bull at a wedding and always in the most fearful hurry. I despair of the doors.'

'I should go. It's been such a wonderful afternoon, but he won't thank me for keeping you.'

'You can't possibly rush off in this weather.'

I looked up, surprised to see rain running down the windows. The streets would be deep with water. If I walked home, I would ruin my dress and catch a chill.

'Besides, you should meet him properly. He's quite nice.' She gave a smile that told me everything. I was pleased for them, really, but my heart ached for such happiness.

Ambrose burst through the door and flung his jacket onto the chair before he noticed that his wife was not alone. It didn't stop him seizing her in a long embrace. I studied the wooden carvings again.

'Madeleine Everley, charming to see you. I knew Caroline wouldn't be in here of her own volition. She seems to have left studying behind with her old life. Are you looking for something in particular?' He beamed at us both, eyes twinkling. Lucius never came in like that. He was always fuming over his meetings, or exhausted from patients. How lucky to have such pleasant company.

'We were looking at Alice's flowers.'

'Ah, the lovely Alice. Only just escaped from me but you will have to do.'

I busied myself with examining the shelves, an uncomfortable witness to their teasing. A life-size ceramic head perched precariously, and I traced along the painted lines that scored it into sections. *Caution, sublimity, veneration.* There was a section for *destructiveness* next to the parts that read *acquisition* and *secrecy*. It could be a description of Lucius.

'Phrenology,' said Ambrose, lifting it down. 'A map of character. These are the areas that control both our primal and civilised urges. You can tell everything about a man from these.'

'Ambrose specialised in the brain,' Caroline explained. 'He's working with several institutions at the moment, trying to understand madness.'

'Madness and the so-called "ordered brain". The spheres criss-cross all the time. As do the patients. Come, you must have seen such things at home?'

I shook my head. 'Father is a country doctor, and Lucius . . . is more concerned with the physical body.'

'You don't have to be polite. I know very well what Lucius thinks of "mind meddlers". I see you have some knowledge yourself. And talent too if those pictures downstairs are yours?' Ambrose threw his arms open wide. 'This little collection is very modest in comparison with your husband's. I would like to see it one day.'

So would I. 'He's very private with his collection.'

'I'm sure. But we're working together now, perhaps he has mentioned? Interesting hypothesis and of course if he can find the transitional form, he'll convince us all.' Ambrose put an arm around Caroline and drew her towards him, as though he spoke for them both. 'He sees it as a challenge that we don't believe it exists.'

Exhibit 14

*Mummified crocodile with linen wrappings and
inlaid glass eyes. Grave offering to the deity Sobek.
Egyptian. c. 395 A.D.*

D ear Caroline was as good as her word and the hydrangea
arrived the next day, planted in deep stone troughs so heavy
it took three men to lift them from the carriage. It wouldn't be
appropriate to tip the Fairlys' staff, thankfully, as I'd hardly any
coins left and nothing from Father yet, but we should at least be
hospitable. I asked them to use the side gate, called for Mrs Barker
and waited in the garden.

Autumnal rot spread a rich, sickly stench, though the leaves
had been swept away and the lawn was neatly trimmed. Damp
and decay rose from the mounds of earth collected in the borders,
looking as though plants had been dug up. Had they been cleared
in anticipation of my gift? I couldn't recall speaking about the
plants. No-one was much interested in anything I did. Crumbs
of earth trailed across the lawn to the corner, freshly raked behind
a clump of hellebores. In the centre of the grass was the statue
I'd seen through the stairwell window. A stone nymph, lithe and
willowy, a carved crown of flowers on her flowing hair. One hand
covered her modesty, the other was flung across her eyes as though
blocking the sight of something terrible. Echo perhaps, broken by

Narcissus's self-love? It belonged with a water feature, really, and the more I looked the more I became convinced it was different. Hadn't the arms been outstretched before? The first time I saw it, a raven sat on the open hand. I pushed the nymph lightly. She was set firm in the ground and didn't move. But no frond of grass grew up around her base, no curling trails of ivy. The gardener must be meticulous with his work. Or the statue was new.

Mrs Barker arrived with a face like thunderclouds. I had the men leave the troughs on the gravel path by the rowan tree and asked her to bring them some tea.

'It's laundry day, Mrs Everley. If you want to treat delivery men like royalty, then I'm afraid you'll have to make it yourself.'

The men stifled smirks. Hardly my fault the house was busy; if she hadn't sent Annie off, we might have someone else to help. How long could it take to find another housemaid? 'Then you'll need to allow me into your kitchen.'

Mrs Barker turned smartly on her heel and headed back to the house. I bid the men to wait, embarrassed, and followed her in.

'They're not delivery men, they're the Fairlys' household staff. It's kind of them to bring the plants, and very kind of Caroline to provide them. It's the least we can do.' I wanted to remind her of my authority but my voice wavered, sounding more like pleading.

'We're short-staffed.' She did not turn around to answer me or break her stride. Her breath came in cross huffs.

'That is not my fault.'

'Well, it isn't mine.'

She could hardly think I had something to do with Annie's departure. Could she?

'What do we need to do to get another maid?'

She gave me a look of disgust. Would it hurt her to be kind? She knew my lack of experience.

'Mrs Atherton is finding someone.'

Why should Grace choose my housemaids? She had already chosen my wallpaper, my clothes. I wanted a maid like Ellen, someone to share stories with while she brushed my hair. Someone like a friend. I didn't expect Grace to share that view of domestic staff any more than I expected Mrs Barker to understand.

'When do the gardeners work? I'd like to tell Caroline when the plants will be dug in.' She would appreciate an invitation to view the plants in their new home; I could send word back with the men.

'Barker does the garden. He'll get round to it.'

'It looks as though he's already been busy this week. The statue . . . has it . . . changed at all? I thought it looked different the other day, something about the arms. They were stretched out before.'

'I've no idea what you're talking about, Mrs Everley. How could a statue move?'

We stopped at the kitchen door and Mrs Barker turned to face me.

'I'll make the tea, but I haven't got time to take it out. Wait here.'

Prohibited from entering my own kitchen. I made a move to enter but she barred the way.

'It's a mess in there. Laundry day, like I said.'

Why on earth would the kitchen be used for laundry when the scullery was just as large, with two vast stone sinks and a mangle? It didn't smell like laundry either. A rotten odour emanated to the hallway, like leaf mould or some plucked fowl hung a little too long. It reminded me of the lime room. What sort of soak was she using? She shut the door behind her, and I waited, foolish, unable to complain. Even if I mentioned it to Lucius, I knew he'd be disinterested, or take her side. He would certainly disapprove of my being below stairs.

The tray, when it arrived, was too heavy for me to manage. Mrs Barker watched me struggle for a while then, sighing, she seized it back and carried it outside, knocking against me on her way.

I determined to ask Lucius about the statue, though I knew he'd try to examine me again. More nervous imaginings for him to talk down. But, when he finally came home, he appeared so weary that I wanted to look after him. If I were allowed the keys to the cabinet, I could pour him a drink, though his breath indicated that he'd already partaken. If there was anything I could do to give him ease or comfort, he would ask. At least he'd remembered where he lived.

'You look tired.'

'It was a difficult call, made worse by the circumstances. The fifth child doesn't necessarily make things easier. And there were so many nursemaids fussing in the room, it's a wonder the child survived at all.'

'But it did. And the mother?'

'Lost a lot of blood. I'll return tomorrow.'

Lucius must feel his own pain – a mother lost at birth. Did he work so hard at saving others to make up for it? Did he leave me untouched because he couldn't bear to try bringing his own child into the world? He rubbed at the skin around his temples and, remembering the ceramic head at the Fairlys', I tried to see if his skull showed any distinctive lumps. It might help me to understand him. Strong bones protruded just above his brow. Although I could picture the shape of the model, I couldn't recall what that part of the head was labelled, what characteristics it ruled. What was the use of trying to learn if I remembered nothing? Together with his sharp cheekbones, the protruding temples gave him the permanent look of straining to hold his tongue, as though the world and everything in it displeased him greatly.

'Where were you yesterday?' he asked suddenly. 'Grace came to visit. And no-one was here.'

'The Barkers were here.'

'She didn't come to see the Barkers.'

'She doesn't really come to see me.' I looked at him until he turned his head towards me. I was ready for the conversation. I'd been kept in the dark for long enough. 'I was at the Fairlys'. The weather prevented me from leaving as early as I might, it's true, but I wasn't expecting Grace. If she wishes to visit, it's better if she lets me know.'

'It isn't always easy for her to get away, with the children . . . as they are.'

'More reason to plan.' Did he really believe I should wait in on the off-chance his sister may call? Without waiting for a response, I began to talk about the Fairlys' house, the extravagance of Ambrose's flowers. 'They were extraordinary, we spent the afternoon drawing them.' I pushed my sketchbook across the table, amazed at my own confidence. 'It's what I like to do.' Pushing it further towards him, I willed him to open it. Something told me I might not get another chance to catch his attention in this way, whilst he was weary and listening. If he didn't begin to see me as a person, we'd miss the chance to understand each other, and I would become lost in this house.

'Very pretty.' Lucius turned the pages of flowers quickly, with disinterest, until a drawing caught his attention. A sketch of the birds on my windowsill, from several angles, one with the wings outstretched as though they'd been plucked from the bench in the lime room.

'Those are the ones I'm most interested in,' I said. 'I prefer that kind of drawing.' I held my breath. Let him see my talent.

'Remarkable.' He spoke slowly, tracing the lines of charcoal with his elegant finger. His signet ring shone as though it had been polished. Did he remove it when he saw patients, or clean it afterwards? 'Who taught you to draw like this?'

'No-one.' I shrugged. 'At home I used to sketch the wildlife. And the things in Father's study.'

'You have a very careful eye. Accurate. Detailed as well as artistic . . . these are very good.'

Lucius looked up from the sketchbook as though seeing me for the first time. It was a chance to change the way things were between us. If he valued me more, then the Barkers would have to respect me.

'I'd like to do more, to draw the . . . the things you showed me the other day.' I took his silence for reluctance. What would persuade him? 'I could help with your research, draw what you want to find. If you tell me how it should look, I could help others to picture it.' He closed the sketchbook and leant back, one hand over his eyes. I was losing him. 'I know they don't believe you. I want to help you convince them. I believe you.'

He was silent for so long I began to lose hope. 'If you're to help me, you need to understand what I seek,' he said at last.

'I'm willing to learn.' He sighed. Perhaps flattery would work. 'Ambrose says your collections are the best in London. Show me. And let me help.'

'It's late, Madeleine. And some of the cabinets are in disarray.' Just as I thought my hopes were dashed, he continued. 'Let me see to them tonight. You may view them tomorrow morning, before my calls.'

* * *

117

Something in the house prevented me from enjoying a restful sleep or rising early, and I couldn't miss my chance to see the locked room properly. Just in case, I settled down for the night on my bedroom chair with a blanket wrapped round me for warmth. Clock chimes woke me, stiff and cold, having dreamt that some menacing part-animal chased me across water. Several times it caught me, pushing my head below the surface, but it couldn't keep hold and I struggled away, only to be caught again and dragged under, clammy fins tugging at my arms, too slippery to grip. A chill hung in the air, so damp it felt wet, and I dressed as warmly as I could, layering petticoats under my gown and adding another bodice before wrapping a shawl across my shoulders. It took a long time to fasten my buttons and stays with trembling fingers and light a candle for the dark stairs.

Lucius was already waiting, perfectly dressed in white linen and grey wool. Everley crests shone on the buttons of his waistcoat. His eyes were weary, pouched and drooping. Had he suffered a fitful night or stayed up late tidying the rooms? I felt anxious at what he might hide. Could he wish me harm? He held out an arm to steady my step into the cabinet room, and it was reassuringly solid and warm after the clammy fins of my dreams.

'Our small museum,' he announced, with a tinge of pride. For a moment I really thought he meant *ours*, but this collection would have begun years before. He must mean Old Dr Everley and himself. Lining the walls from floor to ceiling were cabinets, made of polished rosewood and glass-fronted like real museum cases. Below the doors were narrow drawers, rows of them, neatly labelled in Lucius's perfect script. He nodded as I moved to open one, revealing trays of preserved insects and smaller mammals and birds, their wings pinned out in coloured fans and beaks painted yellow, like pie-baked heads. Rows of delicate butterflies, all the colours of the rainbow. To lay out and pin a butterfly and not lose the dusty colour from its wings would take patience and tenderness – a side to him I'd never seen.

'Are these all your work?'

'Not all. A lot of them. Father taught me when I was small. Some are his, though he always favoured working on human anatomy. I found it interesting to learn the delicacy these required.'

How many little bodies were littered behind him as he pulled and pinned these creatures? How long could it take a child to learn such skills? I tried to imagine James with scalpel and pincers. Hard enough to persuade him to sit still to join me for an hour's sketching in the meadows; he could never be such a doctor. Father had none of this at home either, had probably never mastered delicate surgical skill. Treatment with tinctures and compress were the tools of his trade. I felt a sudden rush of shame and affection for his provincial methods.

Immediately inside the door stood an open cabinet full of remains. Incomplete human bodies with souls that could not be at rest. So many skulls and bones, some beautifully carved, and some strange bundles that looked exhumed. Yellow-grey strips of cotton cloth, like bandages, wrapped around lumpen shapes.

'What are these?'

'A mummified crocodile and snake. From Egypt. A present to Father from a colleague, though I've tried the procedure myself.'

'Procedure?'

'Like everything, it begins with the right tool.' He held aloft a long thin piece of metal, like one of the curved hooks Grandmother used to make lace, and began to describe the process in gory detail. 'A way to keep flesh from decay, in the heat of the desert. Under the bandages it looks like old leather. Expensive, only used for the wealthy.'

'Wealthy snakes and crocodiles?'

Lucius actually smiled and immediately I wanted to make him smile again. It changed his face completely.

'*Sacred* snakes and crocodiles. They were gods on earth to the Egyptians, among other animals.'

If they were right, then crocodiles had souls too. Fish with feet. What would Caroline make of these ones? I reached into the next cabinet and picked up a lump of what looked like rock.

'Mammoth,' said Lucius. I had no idea what he meant until he pulled out an illustrated book of fossils and pointed to a painting. His nails were very white, as though he'd scrubbed them with lime, and the skin of his hands looked rough.

'Extraordinary creature! Like something imagined.'

'Maybe it is. But *something* has left us this tooth. And this is what they think it looked like.'

They? Artists not scientists imagined these things. What good was a fossilised animal part without someone to imagine the rest? A tooth certainly, striated with deep ridges, but longer than my own spread hand. Not unlike the hard molars of sheep, the kind we found in skulls in the fields at home. Could I imagine a sheep from a jawbone? Perhaps, if I'd seen other similar animals. But would I know to draw its woolly coat, or the shape of its feet? The tooth was heavy in my palm, cold to the touch.

'How was it found? Surely this would look like a lump of rock against other stone and earth?'

'Not to a trained eye. Fossil hunters spend years researching the right places and ground conditions for such things to be found. It's not a science of chance finds.' His brows knitted together, making him look more like the portrait of his father. 'There's too much written about it now. People think they can just walk along the beach and pick these things up, but that's not how it works.'

Palm flat, I lifted the tooth up to the picture of the mammoth and held it there for a moment. 'Who painted the creature?'

Lucius tilted his head to read the curled signature. 'William Clift. He's well known for such drawings. An amateur finder but an artist first and foremost.'

'Of course. Because artists are needed to imagine such things.' I stopped myself from saying more. He needed my sketching, he must know that. Lucius took the tooth to replace on the baize-covered shelf, pushing the open drawer with a nudge of his hip. Had he understood? His face was impassive as he moved me on to face the last cabinet. Displayed inside were four gruesome and compelling tableaux, like depictions of hell in chapel paintings. Animal skeletons dressed in elaborate costumes and pinned around with dried flowers, butterflies and taxidermy. They were clever works of art, of which Lucius seemed particularly proud.

'These are all Father's, his hobby. He spent so long hacking at bones in the lecture theatre that he wanted to create something delicate, for once. A beautiful reminder that death walks among us.'

They must have taken many hours to complete. 'They are, really, quite beautiful.' I meant it. The whole display was so delicately rendered. With extraordinary tenderness Lucius opened each door to remove the tableau inside and turn it round for me to view. I saw something close to happiness in his expression and I sensed that my amazement had pleased him. Such a secret room, a private obsession. Yet he must sometimes want to show it off, to reveal his talents. And those of his father.

'I'm grateful you've chosen to share it with me.'

A shadow crossed his face, and I shrank back. Had I crossed a line? So badly did I want to be involved, that I was terrified to say the wrong thing and be shut out of this room for ever. 'It's a wonderful museum. Like a mirror to the world.'

'I hope one day all this will help me to reveal what I'm beginning to understand.'

'Our world is so full of these miracles of nature, it must be hard to know where to begin.'

'Nature has not, so far, defied categorisation. It's simply necessary to observe more closely. As you know very well from your sketches. A pattern of marks on the skin of a reptile, a similar eye structure, the number of feathers in a wing, these can be matched and grouped together to create seemingly ad infinitum types. The same can also be said of the human animal, of course.'

Not a collection, or a hoard of treasures. A small museum. There was method here, a clinical collection of oddities curated in a way that revealed connections to nobody but Lucius now. I wanted to ask so much more. Where did he find them? What happened to human souls when their bodies were studied in this way? A sudden scraping noise broke the strange tenderness and alerted my attention to a door at the far end of the room.

'It's where I prepare my other samples.' Lucius's eyes had followed mine towards the sound.

'May I see?' The noise was unmistakably made by a scrabbling creature. Did he keep live specimens for research?

Lucius shook his head slowly and began to close the cabinets, preparing to leave. 'I'm obliged to keep it locked at all times. There are chemicals inside that it would not do for laymen to touch, and the methods I use for skeletonising may look a little shocking to some. I don't wish to lose any more housemaids.'

Exhibit 15

Ebony carving with circular head.
Unnamed fertility goddess. African. Date unknown.

The first thing Lucius had asked me to draw, and I was finding it almost impossible. A creature carved from ebony, with a large disc-shaped head, and small eyes half-closed in what looked like an ecstasy of malice. A fertility goddess, apparently. Lucius wanted to have it valued and needed an accurate image to post before deciding where to take the real thing. It was ancient. Older than the name of Everley. The more I stared at it the less comfortable I felt.

At least he'd listened, and he'd already asked me to help. Something in my sketchbooks must have caught his attention. But all the tenderness I'd felt when he showed me his museum disappeared as soon as the door closed behind us. I'd been certain such closeness would lead to something and for several days had waited for him to visit. But he didn't come. And in the subsequent days he'd been just as remote and absent as before. How could he put it from his mind? He'd delighted in showing me the museum. I knew he'd enjoyed my reaction and I thought he'd enjoyed my company. As for myself, I couldn't stop thinking about what I'd seen, the strangeness and difference of the natural world. Did nature really change itself over time? If only Lucius would talk to me, our conversation might just spark the thoughts he needed.

In a bid to understand, I read most of his father's papers. They were all in the library, bound in leather, identical to the set at the Fairlys'. His research on the brain came recommended by Ambrose but all I found in it was cruelty. Papers detailing the administration of small jolts of pain to various animals, registering the lights in their eyes and the frequencies of their cries. He claimed to have discovered the places where feelings were registered and controlled, not in the heart but the brain. Such papers made me concerned over whether he'd ever hurt Lucius, or Grace. It would not surprise me. Their coldness was something more than arrogance over their ancient crest.

I pulled my feet up onto the padded window seat and stared out to the garden. Caroline's stone troughs were still on the path and the lovely hydrangea blooms were drooping, turning brown at the edges, dropping snowy puddles on the gravel. They hadn't been watered. I would have to go down and do it myself. I could see Barker in the corner, raking at the earth in the borders. Was he still preparing for planting? I'd ask him, and about the statue too. Something about it had definitely changed, even if Mrs Barker hadn't noticed.

'Observing the staff?' Grace's voice made me jump as though a cold hand was placed on my neck. I'd heard nothing as she came in.

'Caroline sent some hydrangea.' I rose to greet her. 'I was considering where they would look best.'

She wrinkled her nose, disapproving. 'Leave the gardening to the experts. Barker's fussy about his little patch.'

'I noticed. Hard to understand what occupies his time in such a small garden.'

'Beautifully kept though, wouldn't you agree?' Grace leant over to look. 'Those things look almost dead. Why don't I send you some shrubs?'

'They'll be fine, they just need watering.'

Grace noticed the carving and picked it up. 'Where did this come from?'

'Africa, I believe.'

'Yes.' Her tone was icy. 'But it's Father's.'

Was your father's. No need to explain why I was drawing it – Lucius must have his reasons and if she didn't know then it was because he didn't want her to. It felt good to have a secret between us.

'If you don't mind me saying, you don't look yourself.' Her hair was damp and frizzed, escaping from its pins. Mud caked the hem of her dress, leaving smears on the rug. 'Did you walk from Evergreen House?'

'Mrs Barker prefers to walk. It isn't far, but I wasn't expecting the rain today.'

Why was Mrs Barker there? Surely she had her work cut out with no housemaid? As if she read my mind, Grace explained. 'She often comes to help, teaching the women about keeping house and so on, or training them for jobs in service. Most of them disgraced themselves very young, before they had a chance to learn, and are grateful for her advice.'

Had she been to choose another maid? The thought of her bringing a delinquent woman into the house made me anxious. 'I thought she'd be occupied. We lost our maid, and she doesn't let me do anything downstairs.'

Grace looked at me as though I'd taken leave of my senses. 'Why would she? She's managed the house for years. Lucius told me about Annie. She was always the same, frightening the other girls with her superstitions.'

Annie had come from Evergreen. It made sense now, her sullen demeanour, the resentful looks. She'd been poorly treated by life. And then by the Barkers.

'Is she back there now?'

'At Evergreen? Goodness, no, we couldn't have her there like that. They'd all fall like dominoes. We work hard to keep such behaviour from the house. I'm only sorry we didn't take the early signs seriously. She's being cared for at St Margary's.' Confusion must have been plain on my face. Grace gave one of the irritable sighs she usually kept for her children. 'It's an insane asylum. Madhouse. Mrs Barker tells me she was quite hysterical.'

An asylum! Poor Annie, to be dispatched so quickly. I would need to take care not to share my own fears, or to mention the voices I heard when I couldn't sleep. 'She was frightened of something she saw.' Grace knew more about the house than I did, she might know what scared Annie. I watched her closely for signs.

'Maybe an odd number of starlings? They're all superstitious.' Grace walked across to the chairs and began shaking the cushions. 'They drive us mad. Some of them won't walk any further if they see a black cat crossing the street. She was probably the same. You need someone a bit more stable. We have a couple who might suit but they'll need another session or two with Mrs Barker first.'

'Where do they come from?'

'Superstitions? The parents usually. Might be more useful if they taught them to be more suspicious of men who promise too much.' Grace sank into the chair and draped an arm across the back. 'Would you mind fetching some wine? It's been rather a long day.'

I rang the bell. It wouldn't cross my mind to refuse her. 'I meant the women. Where do they come from?'

'Girls usually when they arrive. They don't always want to tell us. Some are in hiding from the terrible choices they have made in life, others are brought by their families. Quite a lot from London, but other places too. If they need us, they find us eventually.'

What family would do such a thing? It was hard to imagine. Hard to picture Evergreen properly too, though it sounded a better life than the workhouse or St Margary's. Barker arrived bearing wine I hadn't asked for yet. Perhaps Mrs Barker had explained about Grace's bad day.

Grace thanked him and continued. 'Some have escaped the very men they ran off with, the ones they rejected their families for.' Maybe Rebecca was already without the man she'd eloped with, living at a place like Evergreen. At the mercy of someone like Grace. I hoped she wasn't. Grace took a long drink from her glass. My own sat untouched.

'Why was today so difficult?'

'Sometimes the regimen doesn't work. They seem not to care about bettering themselves.'

'I'm sure they're awfully upset.'

'Then you'd think they'd want to clear their names – their families' names! – rather than drown themselves in gin.'

'Families can be sad places.' I only wanted to open the conversation enough to ask about Old Mr Everley, but she gave me a curious look.

'Rebecca was unhappy before she absconded?'

'No! I didn't mean . . . she was always the happiest.' She was, too. When she left it felt as though someone had stolen all the laughter from the house. 'Was . . . it must have been hard for you and Lucius, with no mother.'

'Father was both parents to us. He worked hard to give us a good life, whatever you've heard from the Fairlys.'

'They spoke highly of his research. In fact, I was reading some myself on their recommendations. His pain research.' I watched her closely for any sign that this brought back memories she'd rather forget, but she smiled.

'He was a genius. A brilliant man and an exceptional surgeon.'

'I'm sure he was.'

'So much jealousy when men achieve great things. He was the first medic to demonstrate the removal of internal organs. The most famous surgical lecture of all. Other doctors are so jealous of his fame that they still claim he came by it through foul means.'

The infamous lecture. His friendship with bodysnatchers. No wonder they felt the need to clear his name. I thought about his skill with mummified beasts, the practice he would have had. Just as I was about to ask whether he'd ever removed an organ from a live patient, Grace stood up to leave.

'That sounds like Lucius returning. Don't get up, I'll see myself down. I have something I wish to speak to my brother about. I'll send him up to you when we're done.'

She had seemed on the verge of telling me something. Now I'd have to wait until they'd finished their private conversation, *if* they finished. I put the wooden carving as far from me as I could, picked up my book and the undrunk wine and settled myself into the window seat. After a couple of pages, I lost concentration and began to look out of the window, going over our conversation, trying to work out what was troubling me. And then I realised. She knew Rebecca's name. I'd never used it in her presence and she had used it easily, as though she knew it well, not having just plucked it from memory after a chance mention from Lucius.

After Grace, I thought maybe Lucius had another visitor. Raised voices could be heard coming from his study, but when I ventured into the corridor all became silent. I don't know how long she stayed or whether the argument was with someone else, but they often spoke to each other like that, despite Grace's claims that they were close.

For a while I read my Blake, cocooned in the tapestry bed curtains and unwilling to snuff the lights in case the voices returned. Just as I was about to turn in, I heard a gentle knock at my bedroom door. The Barkers retired early, Annie was gone; who else could it be but Lucius? The knock was so soft he must have believed I was already asleep. 'Who is it?' The door opened with a low creak, the iron handle rattling as it closed. Nobody spoke, though I heard steps on the floorboards, the slow tap of hard-soled shoes. My heart beat faster. I drew my legs up under the covers and closed my book, raising it above my head. It was a small book, but the element of surprise and the sharp corners might stay an intruder long enough for me to dart through the curtains on the other side and run round to the door before they gathered their senses. Why didn't they speak?

'Who's there?' My voice wavered.

A hand appeared around the bed curtains and drew them back slowly. Unmistakably Lucius's hand with its elegant fingers, the signet ring with the Everley crest. Was he trying to frighten me? He'd never been into my room before and I was afraid of what it might mean.

'Lucius! You scared me.' His face was flushed and his eyes bright. I remembered Mother's words. *Don't try to stop him, wait until it's over.*

'I wasn't sure if I'd be waking you. It's late. But I wanted to . . .'

'I just didn't know it was you.' Whatever he wanted, I didn't want to hear him say it. Taking the book from my hand, he threw it to the floor and drew me towards him. He still wore his dress coat and the rough wool pressed against my cheek. Cigars and brandy wafted in the air. His evening scent, but stronger this time. Had he fortified himself, or been drowning their argument? 'The lamp.' I pulled away to move the lamp and placed it on the floor outside the curtains, noticing a page had fallen from the book. I tucked it back inside. Suddenly I felt Lucius's arms around my back, pulling up my nightdress. His hands held my waist and I braced myself.

As he entered me, I bit my lip so hard it bled, gripping against the bedpost, my hands in the pleading shape of prayer. His coat brushed my skin. The sounds he made were animal. Images from the book in his study swam before my eyes and then he slumped against my back for a brief moment before pulling his clothes together, leaving as silently as he'd arrived.

Smoothing down my nightdress, I knelt on the floor beside the torn book, put my hand to my lip. It felt swollen, strange. A metallic taste filled my mouth. Had I pleased him? Though I was, in some ways, relieved that the long-awaited first visit was finished, his silence was confusing after the tenderness we'd shared in the small museum. I'd expected more. Lucius hadn't even undressed, as though his night visit was an irritation, something to be finished quickly and then ignored.

My legs were sore, the space between them empty and bruised. A wound. It was hard to imagine why anyone would find such a thing enjoyable. Harder still to concentrate on poetry. The book was broken, all the pages of *Songs of Experience* now loose and difficult to hold together. What immortal hand did frame the tyger? What hand made anything? Could what just happened between Lucius and me really make a baby, and would a baby make a family of us? It could take many visits, or he may not come back at all, and it was clear that we were not to speak of it. I was as powerless to change things as a tyger in the hands of the great creator.

All those things I was shown in his museum, all the changes that happened in nature over time, slow and subtle but deliberate changes. Evolution. Could a man change? I wanted to change him. I wanted the tenderness he showed to his collection, but affection was something I could barely remember. I had been promised a husband and a life, and I wanted them.

16

The Marlborough Assizes

Maddie was there. Staring straight ahead to the patch of wall at the left of the witness box. A scarf covered her head this time and I was glad. Yesterday the slow crawl of lice in her matted hair had made me weep with uselessness. She still refused my visits. Refused Ambrose too, telling the guards to warn us to stay away.

'Could you describe the nature of your professional relationship?' The magistrate addressed a young man who claimed to be her doctor. He didn't look long out of Oxford. The type of gentleman who seems generally bewildered by life outside the club. Floppy hair, too long, fell over one eye and gave him a coquettish look. He was handsome enough, to those who enjoyed the look. Dandyish in dress, silk bows and long leather boots. Evidently pleasing to some of the women in the viewing gallery, nudging each other and giggling. He'd be used to the attention.

'I'm an alienist.'

The magistrate curled his lip as though he wanted to spit on the floor. I was as shocked as the rest of the gallery. Men as foppish as Threlfall rarely worked for a living, though the magistrate clearly did not consider his a useful profession.

'For the benefit of the court – an alienist is a mind doctor employed by such assizes as these to determine the state of mind of the accused in criminal cases. Murder charges usually. Crimes of the most serious nature.'

Alienists were a new breed. Hard-working, intelligent, according to Ambrose, who was keenly following the adoption of such modern psychological practices. I half thought he wanted to undertake such work himself, though like all public services it was poorly paid. He'd be interested in this development. *Edward Threlfall, alienist, dandy*, I scribbled in my notebook. Was his persona just an act?

'I will ask again, what was the nature of your relationship with Mrs Everley?'

'I was asked to assess Mrs Everley's mental state. In a professional capacity.'

Why would someone need an alienist *before* a crime had been committed?

'You were asked by her husband to assess her mental state? Because you are friends? Colleagues?' The magistrate's eyes took in the silk shirt, the long satin neckscarf. He didn't trust him any more than I did.

'Yes. No . . . Dr Everley and I share a club. We were introduced by a mutual acquaintance. Dr Everley is . . . not known for his tolerance of physicians who treat ailments of the mind. I was surprised by his interest in my work. Flattered, too, naturally. Who doesn't like to talk of their own work?'

'Please stick to answering the questions asked and don't waste the court's time.'

'My sincerest apologies. It seemed pertinent to explain. I did not know Dr Everley, other than by reputation. And his father's, of course. As I said, we spoke of my work and he was interested. He asked a lot of questions. We dined together, with our friend

Dr Venables, and later took brandy in the library. When we were alone, he began to talk about his wife.' His blue eyes darted to the accused cage and quickly away again. 'He was worried about Mrs Everley. He thought that she had some symptoms of hysteria, and he was looking for someone who could assess her condition without emotional involvement.'

Hysteria. Highly convenient considering all doctors were men. Permission to mistreat, dose and restrain a woman all in one diagnosis. Useful for removing any inconvenient relatives, if it came to it.

'And you agreed?'

'Not at first. It's not really my work. I prefer clients to come to me at my practice.'

'Not your criminal clients?' The magistrate affected shock.

'No. Those I see in buildings such as these.' He turned his elegant wrist and swept his arm across the room as though he were dancing. 'But they are not, strictly speaking, my clients. My criminal work is for the court.'

'Your practice then?'

'I have a clinic at home, like most psychologists. My patients visit at their convenience.'

I'd seen such women in Ambrose's clinic, usually brought in at their husband's request. Cowed and submissive or shrieking in anger. Sometimes I wondered if there was much middle ground for any woman.

'What is your speciality, Dr . . . I assume you are still a doctor . . . Threlfall.'

'Female hysteria.'

'You told him this that night at your club?' He waited briefly for Threlfall to affirm. 'And when did you visit?'

'The next day.'

'Did you see Mrs Everley that day?'

'No. She was indisposed.'

'Presumably indisposed with the very malady you had come to see?'

'She was in bed with a headache.'

'Did she often suffer with headaches?'

'I don't know.'

'Yet you looked after her head.' The magistrate delivered his lines in his customary deadpan manner. I was beginning to like him, trust him a little. Was he keen enough to see through this mess?

'I monitored her thoughts, her nervous disposition. I returned the next day and spoke with her then. The headache did not strike me as a serious matter.'

'What was your impression of Mrs Everley?'

'She was certainly distressed. At first, I did not think her hysterical. We spoke of her loneliness away from her family in the country.' Maddie had barely shown any interest in her trial so far but the terrible looks she threw at Threlfall showed me how much she disliked him. 'It was understandable of course, the loneliness. Everley was away so much and to be left with servants . . .'

She'd never told me about Threlfall's visits – did he frighten her? She could have seen Ambrose. He would have been kind.

Threlfall continued, 'Loneliness doesn't help with a predisposition to melancholy, I'm afraid. It is easy for things to deteriorate quickly. The slide of the mind is so much faster when left unchecked.'

'Was there anything in particular that caused you to be concerned for her mind?'

'Everley was worried because she was seeing things that weren't there. She was obsessed with the statues in the garden and kept insisting that they were moving. You don't need to be an expert to understand how troubling that is.'

Something that would have been clear to Lucius. Did he ask Threlfall in because he knew he was a charlatan? Suggestible? Someone who wouldn't dig too deep? Had Lucius seen this courtroom coming all along? It made no sense.

'Indeed, Dr Threlfall. And what were these statues doing when they were moving?'

'She never caught them moving, she said, but they were changing, their limbs moving, things like that. I was wholly unable to reassure her that they were not. She seemed to think they were somehow alive and threatening. Everything in the house made her nervous. Including the staff.'

'Please explain.'

'The housekeeper . . . forgive me but I don't remember her name . . . yes, Mrs Barker, she felt Mrs Barker was intent on causing her harm. And Barker too. She didn't trust either of them, though they've been in the family for years, "part of the furniture", Lucius said. That was another reason for his concern, she'd become hysterical and asked him to get them out of the house, for no reason other than that she'd taken against them. An overactive imagination. No doubt influenced by reading. Mrs Atherton was adamant that novels should be removed from the house. Overstimulating, I think she called them. I'd agree actually. Most of my patients are too taken with things they read. It can be dangerous for women to read too much.'

More dangerous for them not to read at all. Why was it Grace's business anyway? I always thought Lucius was scared of his sister. Perhaps I was right.

'Were you in the habit of discussing Mrs Everley's case with her husband's sister?'

Threlfall flushed a deep and unflattering pink. Embarrassed at his lack of professional integrity, or something more? Grace was a very attractive woman. Persuasive too, and possibly lonely. Her husband had been abroad for many years without a return visit and Ambrose was convinced that he'd abandoned her after Old Dr Everley's undoing. He must still send money though. She always looked immaculately dressed.

'Mrs Atherton was also concerned. She was . . . is . . . very fond of her new sister. On occasion she happened to be there when I visited.'

'Did you ever see anything that caused you to believe that Mrs Everley's fears about the house, or the staff, had any basis in truth?'

'None whatsoever,' he said, firm for once. He'd been hired for this very reason, I could see that clearly. I only hoped the magistrate could too. 'Once we were talking in the library and Mrs Barker had brought some tea, was it? No, some cocoa, specifically for Mrs Everley. A touching kindness on a cold day. Mrs Everley waited until she had left and then begged me to drink it first in case it contained poison. Delusions, we call it, when a patient is convinced people are plotting bad things for them, trying to kill them. No-one was trying to kill her.'

'Have you anything to add?'

'She was mad, in my opinion, quite mad. She wasn't in her right mind when she hurt that child. That's why she doesn't deserve to die for it.'

'Mr Threlfall, you are not invited to speak as an alienist but as Mrs Everley's doctor. You are not practising your court psychology here.'

'She should plead insanity.' Long poet's fingers interlaced and held out in a gesture of supplication. He was winning the crowd.

The magistrate banged his gavel onto the wooden desk.

'In my court that is not an answer. We are here to decide if the baby was murdered by Mrs Everley, or by someone else. Whoever murdered the baby is, by very definition of the crime, not in their right mind.'

Exhibit 17

Spiked metal collar. Spanish. c. 1400s.

I didn't see Lucius for several days and the night's events played over in my mind. Should I have behaved differently? Should he? I imagined it wasn't his first time, Mother said the rules were different for men. Several times I thought to ask Caroline, but felt ashamed at the memory of her with Ambrose. Our behaviour contrasted so starkly with their sweet displays of affection, and there were bruises where he'd held me that were difficult to hide. It wasn't something I could write about either, the thought made me wince. Isabel and Mother were due to visit soon, so anything I felt able to discuss would have to wait until then.

Small, shrill cries could be heard at odd times of day, puncturing the silence. Once the bruises faded and my lip returned to normal size, I set out to investigate. The noises grew louder the lower I walked and clearly emanated from the basement floor. I waited near the kitchen, reluctant to disturb Mrs Barker, wondering if she was harbouring a baby in there. Did it belong to one of the Evergreen women? I'd just raised my hand to knock on the outer door when it was flung open and a young woman flew out, knocking straight into me and scattering the things she was carrying all over the flagstones.

'What a racket! Mrs Everley, I suppose? Hattie Tisman. Some

people call me Tizzy. I don't mind either. Which do you prefer? Sorry, here's me rattling on . . . did you want to get in there?'

She can't have been much older than me. A pretty girl with a fresh, pleasant face, wide smile and unruly curls poking out from under her cap. Her eyes were the most extraordinary shade of blue. The colour of happiness, like skies on picnic days or a bright river. Looking at her made me feel warmer. Could someone so charming have come from Evergreen?

'No . . . well . . . yes, but let me help you.' We both bent down at the same time, knocking our knees together, and she staggered back onto her heels, laughing. 'I like Tizzy, I think. It suits you.' I gathered up the dustpan, brush and dusters and handed them to her. 'Do you work here now?'

She nodded eagerly and dropped the dusters again. I covered a smile. She was clearly not too experienced. 'General maid of work.'

'Well, Tizzy, welcome to the house. I hope we'll be friends.' She beamed. Definitely a fresh one. Most maids would shrink from the idea. Still, a friend was what I needed, and Tizzy would light up this dreary house. I remembered the reason I'd ventured downstairs. 'I don't suppose you know anything about a baby?'

Her face fell and she jerked back as though I'd reached out to strike her.

'I was sure I could hear one crying. It sounded as though it was coming from down here.'

Just as suddenly her smile returned. Whatever did she think I'd meant?

'That's the puppy. It's yours! Dr Everley brought it in to us yesterday.'

But I'd been hearing the cries for days. Hadn't I? 'Yesterday?'

'Come and see.'

Crawling up out of a deep basket with its little legs on the rung of a kitchen chair was the most adorable Spaniel, with long curled ears and liquid-brown eyes. Someone had docked its tail, as though intending it for work, though it seemed very small. From the back of the chair hung a horrible metal collar, studded with short spikes and rusted with age, a short chain attached to one end and a lock at the other.

'What is that?' I pointed at the collar and Mrs Barker's eyes followed. She let out a puff of annoyance.

'Dr Everley brought it from upstairs. Far too big for that little thing. Meant for humans, I shouldn't wonder.'

I shuddered at the thought. I hadn't noticed it in Lucius's rooms, but before I could ask further the Spaniel gave a squeaky bark and launched itself across the floor. When it tried to wag where its tail should have been, its entire back end wriggled from side to side delightfully.

'Is it really mine?'

Mrs Barker pushed the basket along the floor with her foot. 'Get it out of my sight. Dirty little thing. No place in a kitchen. Don't know what possessed him.' She stopped to look at the dog for a moment. 'Just like the ones his mother used to love. Loads of them she had, all over the place.' She threw a thick wad of cotton at me. 'That's to train it on. I don't want to see anything on the rugs up there.'

Without waiting for a response, she turned on her heel and flounced back into the kitchen, knocking Tizzy slightly off balance as she pushed past. After a moment our eyes met and we both stifled giggles. My heart soared. To have someone in that house who understood me, someone young and fun, would change everything. What did it matter that she was a maid? All the more time to spend together.

* * *

'Ariadne. It's a pretty name. It suits her.' I nuzzled into the puppy's face, and she bounced on her front paws, nipping at my collar. The name had come to me immediately because she was such a sweet dog and so different to the hounds Father kept at Lynton. In *The Water Babies*, Ariadne was the good fairy, the one that helped Tom and the others adjust to life underwater. 'It's from Kingsley.'

'From the Greek myths, actually.' Lucius removed his jacket. A sign that he might stay a little longer. He'd visited every night for a week and it was always the same, rough and perfunctory, as though he couldn't wait for it to finish, but this time he stayed afterwards, to make sure I was pleased with his gift. If I couldn't have affection, then conversation would do.

'Ariadne helps Theseus to find his way back out of the labyrinth. She gives him a ball of thread and he unrolls it all the way to the middle. When he has found and slain the minotaur, he simply walks back along the string, rolling it up until he's out of the maze.' He considered the puppy, rolling on its back with legs waving in the air. 'It's not a name for a silly dog.'

'She's not silly!' I covered her ears as though she might take offence. 'She's adorable.'

'It suits you better.'

'You think so? I could be a good fairy.' Could I save him from himself? There was human feeling in there, I knew it, a fleeting tenderness.

'Or a practical helper. Your drawing of the fertility god was excellent, thank you. I've sent it already.'

Grace must have given it to him, unless he found it on the pad? We certainly hadn't discussed it.

'I look forward to sketching more for you.' A sure sign that we would work together in the museum. Things were improving since

Tizzy arrived; perhaps she had brought us luck.

'Have you met Tizzy yet?' He gave me a puzzled look. 'Harriet, the new maid.'

'At Evergreen, and I brought her here. Is she settling well with Mrs Barker? Grace said she might need some training. She certainly seems lively.'

I wouldn't mention our friendship. Something told me that he wouldn't approve. 'I think she'll do very well.'

'She is bolder than Annie, at least. Hopefully we will keep her longer.'

Poor Annie. I felt a flash of fear that we might lose Tizzy too. I would have to keep her from the locked rooms.

'Is there news of Annie?'

'You're aware of where she is?'

'Grace told me. I wondered if I might be allowed to visit.'

Lucius threw me a sharp look. 'I don't think that's advisable for you at all. St Margary's is no place for someone of your disposition.'

I shifted uncomfortably, unsure of what he meant by my *disposition*. 'Why?'

'Mrs Barker agrees that you're becoming nervous.'

They were discussing me together like one of his patients. *She agreed with him.* Did that mean he made the suggestion? He never had time for me, yet he could gossip with his housekeeper. 'I see. And did she say why?'

'She tells me you think the statues in the garden are moving. Is this true?'

'No. I said I thought it was a different statue. It looks as though it has been replaced.'

Lucius shook his head slowly. 'That statue was put in by Father. It's been there for years.'

'Then I was mistaken.'

'And your wanderings, the voices you hear . . . It's not healthy. You need to take more rest and you certainly need to worry less about people like Annie.'

Was I becoming nervous? His list of wrong behaviours made me sound foolish. Victim of an overactive imagination. I should stop reading faerytales, start working properly. Too much time to think could be bad for anyone. If I became hysterical, they would have no choice but to send me to join Annie. A fear that, in itself, was enough to loosen my reason.

'Would you like to talk to someone? About your terrors?'

'I don't have *terrors*. Things are very different for me here. I'm getting used to it.' I vowed never to speak to Mrs Barker again, because everything came straight back to Lucius with a nasty twist. I would be more careful.

'I'll send someone to speak with you. I think the episode with Annie has upset you.'

'I'm fine. Really.' Ariadne gave a short little bark as though it were playtime. I put her back in her basket and she nipped my finger with teeth as sharp as pins. 'What happened to Ariadne? In your story.'

'In *my* story? There are two different endings to her fate, depending on which version you read. In one of them, she escapes.'

Caroline visited the next day, turning to thank Mrs Barker so profusely that it must have been for her own amusement. The old woman's face was pure loathing. There was no need to bring Caroline through herself, she could have asked Tizzy, but she must have wished to make a point. As she left, she did not fully close the door to the drawing room and I couldn't be sure she wasn't still outside, listening.

'I can't stay long, Maddie, but I have the most wonderful news and I had to rush straight here to share it with you.' Caroline sat down and stood up again quickly, as though her secret fizzed inside her.

I laughed, warm with friendship. She had chosen to come here first, to share her news with me above others. Fingertips to my lips, I walked to the door and looked up and down the corridor before closing it. 'In case you don't wish to be overheard.'

'I don't mind who hears this. Mrs Barker's not too friendly though, is she? Oh look!' Ariadne, who adored attention, was already rolling on her back to show off her tummy for scratching. 'She's getting bigger already.'

'I think she is. Do tell me your news! I can hardly bear it.'

'It's two things really. Ambrose and I are to be parents! Isn't it wonderful?' She grabbed my hand and placed it on her belly. It felt hard, gently rounded.

'Wonderful, wonderful news.' It was all I could manage to say as I blinked back tears of joy. They'd be such good parents. Kind and caring, a family. 'I'm so very pleased for you both.'

'Ambrose is beside himself. He's already insisting I rest constantly. You must talk to him for me, or he'll never let me out at all.'

'He won't listen to me! But if he won't let you out, I shall come to you and bring cakes to your couch.'

'Dear Maddie. You can read to me and mop my brow. You shall be godparents! Do you think it's a boy or a girl? I shan't at all mind which, though I do think it's nice to have a boy for the eldest.'

I listened to her for a while, Ariadne on my lap, feeling as content as I could remember feeling. A friend was all I needed. Someone to plan with, to look forward. Here, with Caroline, there was nothing for me to fear.

A knock at the door sent Ariadne bouncing over, barking and

dashing back to my side. Tizzy peeped in. 'I wasn't sure if you were still here. Mrs Barker said the dusting needed doing, but I can come back.'

'Come in. Tizzy, meet my dear friend, Caroline.'

Tizzy dropped a flustered curtsey, curls flying, and Caroline smiled. 'Pleased to meet you, Tizzy. And you won't disturb us. I was just leaving.' She turned to me. 'Ambrose wants me to attend a dinner this evening. I know he's going to tell everyone, he's too excited, so I wanted you to hear it from me first. Will you come soon? Not tomorrow, we'll be late tonight, but Friday morning?'

'I would love to.'

'We can paint. Oh, I almost forgot, the other news. Alice is visiting next week, the artist that I told you about. You must meet her, you'll adore her.'

Caroline left in a flurry, insisting she saw herself out, and I beamed at Tizzy. A friend, good news, social plans, the possibility of work and a maid I liked more every time I saw her. Life was improving daily.

'She seems nice,' said Tizzy.

'She is,' I agreed. 'She's a very dear friend and I'm sure you'll get to know her. How have you been getting on?'

'It's a nice house, thank you, Mrs Everley, but . . . am I allowed to get on? It's just that she'll be up to check and if it's not done . . .'

'Mrs Barker answers to me.' I sounded as though I was convincing myself. 'We can talk while you dust. What was the "but"? You were about to say something about the house?'

'Nothing really, just a smell I can't place. I looked everywhere for an old vase of flowers, that's what it's like, water with rotten stems in it. I can't work out where it's coming from.'

'I've noticed it, too. It comes and goes.' Did it come and go?

Or did it bother me less? I was getting used to it. 'Perhaps there's damp on the lower floors.'

'Maybe.' Tizzy looked doubtful. It gave her an endearing look, like a child working out a difficult problem.

'But you're comfortable here? You will let me know if there's anything you need?'

'My room is very nice, thank you.'

'You're in one of the attic rooms at the top? They have big windows under the eaves, I hope they're light . . . are you . . . it's just you up there?' Tizzy's eyes were so remarkably blue, her hair so unruly. I wanted her friendship so badly that I had to fight the urge to reach out and touch her. Why was I asking such questions? I didn't want her to think I was going mad too. 'It's just that we sometimes . . . sometimes there are others.'

'I don't think there are any others. No-one that shares the work anyway.' She grinned and her face lit up, showing the carefree girl she must have been before Evergreen. I wanted to listen while she told her story from the start. It was suddenly important that I should really understand her, get to know everything about her. But, before I could ask even one question, Grace arrived with both of the children and stared fixedly at Tizzy.

'Good afternoon, Harriet. I do hope you are remembering your place?'

Exhibit 18

Arm of Salmacis carved in alabaster.
Missing thumb. Hellenic. c. 450 B.C.

'You seem quite on edge.' Tizzy watched me fussing over the jar of hothouse lilies I was arranging for Mother's room, ordered from the flower stand to mask the smell of the house. Their scent was overpowering by the bed, and they didn't look so pretty on the dresser. 'You've moved that thing half a dozen times now.'

'Don't you think they look a bit lost there?'

'How can a vase look lost?' Tizzy laughed and I relaxed a little. She was right, I was agitated about the visit, wanting things to be perfect so I could prove to Mother I was in control of my life.

'You're right. I'm fussing. But I want it to be nice for them.'

We'd put Isabel in the red room, the 'best' guest room usually reserved for Grace. Knowing Isabel would find it dark, I'd bought a cheerful new patchwork counterpane and added rag rugs from my own room. While we were cleaning and setting it straight, we found two small lace caps and a swaddling band in the bottom drawer of the wardrobe. They must have been left when Eloise was a baby. As far as I knew, no-one but Grace ever slept there.

Mother was in the blue room, my favourite of the guest rooms. It was painted a lovely deep indigo and the glazed tiles on the fireplace were patterned with irises. I'd brought up some pretty cushions from the drawing room and added them to the low chair by the dresser. Everything looked as comfortable as Mother could expect. I moved the lilies back to the bedside table and pollen dropped from the petals, smearing the floorboards in rust-red rings. Tizzy rolled her eyes and flicked a cloth across the marks.

'Leave them there now or you'll mess it all up again.' She smiled to show me she was joking but I already knew. Tizzy was always joking. She warmed the house like sunshine. 'Why's it so important anyway, this visit?'

'It's their first visit. They wanted a good life for me . . . it was . . .' How could I begin to explain when I wasn't sure myself how it all made me feel? Sometimes I forgave them for trying to do their best for the family, sometimes I hated being the scapegoat. I'd never shared their need for parties and clothes, or for social acceptance, but I understood it now. Living almost alone and friendless for so long; I hadn't realised how hard it was until I had Caroline and Tizzy. Now I'd never want to go back. In some ways it made me feel closer to Mother and Isabel, but I couldn't explain to them either and for some inexplicable reason I was also eager for them to see that I had thrived. I wanted them to approve of my status, of *me*; to know I was no longer a child. 'It's just family,' I shrugged, 'you know how it is.'

'I do,' said Tizzy, 'I've two sisters. Haven't spoken to either of them since I got into trouble, but I'd like them to know I was alright now.'

She'd read my thoughts so well that it was all I could do not to reach out and embrace her. We were not so different underneath our social positions. If only she wasn't so fearful of upsetting the Barkers we could spend more time together. I was sure she would understand me perfectly.

'That is exactly it, Tizzy. But you should write, and visit too if you can? You must be allowed some time off work?'

'I don't know about that. Anyway, Sunday afternoon's all I get, not long enough to get to Charmouth and back.'

Where had I heard that name before? 'Then we must see about a holiday. In the meantime, you must write and let them know how well you're doing. You can use my paper whenever you like.' I had a sudden terrible thought that perhaps she couldn't read and write, and kicked myself for the assumption. I knew so little about her and I wanted to know so much. 'Are your sisters older?'

She nodded. 'Both married with children. They thought that'd be me too. Still. Wasn't ever what I wanted. So things have turned out for the best.'

'I'm glad to have you here.' I would have dearly liked to tell her how grateful I was for her friendship. 'How did you meet Grace?'

'I met Dr Everley first, just after I'd been turned out. He brought me back to Evergreen, where I could be looked after.' She pulled a face.

'Of course, Charmouth's where he looks for fossils.' What was he really looking for? Evidence, he said, of the link between fish and humans. Mer-people. But he'd found Tizzy instead. 'I'd like to see it one day. Is it very beautiful?'

'It is. I miss the sound of the sea. River's not the same.'

'I've never seen the sea. What's it like?'

Tizzy looked at me, incredulous, and then paused for a while, thinking. Sun caught the window and threaded her hair with red lights, showed the line of pale freckles that studded her nose. I wanted to trace them gently with my finger. 'Bigger than everything. Sometimes still, blue and beautiful, sprinkled with diamonds as the sun catches the foam. Sometimes grey and stormy, wild enough to draw you towards it. Sometimes green and full of seaweed that you can gather to make bread.'

'It must have been hard for you to leave.' She sounded so wistful. I hoped she didn't regret it.

Footsteps sounded on the stairs and Tizzy snapped to attention. 'We can't sit here all day chattering like starlings. Mrs B reports back everything I don't do.'

'Reports to who? You work for me and Mr Everley.'

'To Mrs Atherton. They think I talk too much.'

What did it matter to Grace? What secrets did she want Tizzy to keep? 'Well I like you just as you are, Tizzy. You can leave those two to me.'

When Mother and Isabel finally arrived, I was in the garden with Ariadne, throwing a soft leather ball for her to fetch. Tizzy had suggested I try to train her with it because she wasn't living up to her good faery name. During the night she cried until I lifted her onto my bed and snuggled her down, but I could never do that until I was sure Lucius wasn't coming, however much I needed the comfort of her silky fur. *Dogs are not children, Madeleine.* When he found her in the covers, he'd thrown her down as roughly as he threw the book, and I was forced to listen to her whimpering. I remembered the papers by Old Dr Everley, the jolts of pain he gave. What kind of dogs had he used? His wife's, perhaps, once she'd gone.

Tizzy shouted in excitement, carriage wheels ground to a halt and I called out to Ariadne to fetch the ball so we could go inside to greet them. 'Naughty dog. Ari, do come along. You're to meet my family.' Rustling sounds from the shrubs in the far corner. A furious scratching. Sometimes she failed to get the ball without digging underneath it. 'Don't get yourself all muddy, Ari, or I won't be able to pick you up!' I called again but something more important had captured her attention. I hitched up my skirts and walked over to the shrubs, hoping it wasn't a rat. Nasty things. If she poked her nose into a rat's hole, it might bite her. 'Come along!'

What had she found? Her back end wriggled from side to side, feathered legs jumping. She was certainly pleased with herself. I gave her a smart tap and she hopped back with a little excited bark, then pushed her nose under the leaves again. Foolish dog! What a time to be naughty. I was going to have to fetch her myself. Walking gingerly on the slick mess, I lifted the leaves at the bottom. Decay wafted up, the smell of rotten earth, and I covered my nose with my sleeve before bending to lift up more leaves so I could look underneath. Ariadne's claws scrabbled on something smooth, and paler than moonlight. It looked horribly like fingers. Was it human? Long, white fingers, an arm bent into an unnatural position. I let out a cry of horror, stumbling backwards, and Ariadne scampered about my legs in concern, jumping up and barking. What had I just seen? Whose arm could it be? A woman's arm. Annie. Is that what the Barkers meant when they said they would deal with her? She wasn't at St Margary's at all. The smell filled my senses and bile rose to my throat. Dizziness almost overwhelmed me, but I thought of Perpetua and willed myself not to faint. If I didn't discover the truth now, they would hide things from me again. This was my house, my garden.

'Mrs Everley, they're here.' Tizzy tapped me on the shoulder, and I screamed. She jumped back in fright. 'I didn't mean to startle you. Seen a ghost?' She giggled as Mrs Barker hurried down the steps.

'What is all this noise? Your mother and sister are here, I've put them in the drawing room for now but I've the rooms to see to and you two are out here playing silly devils.' Her face changed as she looked at me. 'What's the matter?'

My whole arm trembled as I pointed to the corner where the body lay, feeling as though my legs would give way beneath me. Mrs Barker seized Ariadne by the scruff of her neck to get her out of the way. She thrust her roughly at me and I held her, still scrabbling to get down, shedding mud and leaves all over my dress. Tizzy put her hand on Ariadne's back, stroking her fur to calm her. Bending low over the shrubbery, Mrs Barker lifted up the leaves and pulled. Ariadne gave a high-pitched bark. I recoiled as Mrs Barker turned and held aloft the arm, but Tizzy burst out laughing.

'Oh, my goodness, did you think . . . ?'

I didn't know what to think. Why would someone hide the broken arm of a statue like that? I tried to bury my face in Ariadne's fur, but she spied the ball as it rolled out and jumped from my arms to catch it, wagging her body furiously. I brushed at the mud on my dress, ashamed for Mother to see me in such disarray. Hardly the sight of a woman in control of her household, or even herself. Taking the arm from Mrs Barker, I tried to see if it matched the one I thought was in the garden before, that might have been replaced in the centre of the lawn. This could prove I was right. It was heavy stone. What had happened to the rest of it?

Tizzy examined the stone fingers. 'I suppose, in the darkness, poking out of the mud, it might have looked lifelike.'

She was trying to be nice. And I was just a foolish girl.

Neither Mother nor Isabel asked how I was, or why I looked so dishevelled. They appeared greatly excited to have travelled by train and were happy to be taken off by Tizzy to have the soot brushed from their clothes while I went to change. Mother examined everything on the way and Isabel talked of nothing but her rector. It took some time for my hands to stop shaking enough to undress. It was just a stone arm, but it had unsettled me. Why could no-one tell me the reason it was broken up like that, or why it had been moved when everyone had insisted it hadn't? And Mrs Barker wasn't in the least bit surprised that I'd instantly assumed there was a body in the garden. Had I really become so nervous here? Was that what they thought of me? Or were my suspicions founded in something worse? By the time I was dressed, it was early evening and music drifted upstairs. Isabel had evidently been practising.

It was good to hear the piano played well. My fingers weren't so nimble, and I'd almost forgotten how cosy it was to have evening concerts. I never wanted to play alone, and Lucius never seemed to want to listen. It annoyed me more than it should to see him sitting on the sofa with Mother, head bent in apparent rapt attention to the piece that Isabel played. Glasses of sherry were gathered around a half-empty decanter.

'Very nice, Isabel. You've been working hard.'

'It's a useful skill for a rector's wife. In case the organist falls ill, or we have lots of visitors to entertain.'

'I don't think rectors generally go in much for entertaining. You'll more likely be sorting old clothes for sending round to the poor, or darning his socks.'

Mother threw me a warning look. She was right. I should try to be nice. I walked behind the piano stool and placed my hand on Isabel's bare shoulder. 'It sounded lovely. Thank you.' Perhaps we should try one of our duets. Lucius had never heard me play. As I was considering whether I could remember enough of the notes not to embarrass myself, Lucius rose and bowed to Mother.

'Charming, Mrs Brewster. A very pleasant musical evening.'

'Surely you're not going out before dinner? Are London patients so demanding?' Those ringlets didn't suit Mother, and neither did the simpering. She knew very well he wasn't treating a patient.

'Lucius is at a critical juncture in his current research,' I said. Isabel pulled a face. 'His Society meets twice a week and, so far as I have heard, they will talk of little else. One must be present when one is the cause of debate.' Could I read gratitude in his eyes? In showing off to my family I was equally trying to convince myself. It sounded impressive. I was the wife of an important man.

'What research?' Mother asked.

Why didn't he just leave? Mother would barely understand. But he paused in the doorway and smiled. 'Investigating tangible proof of our descent from the animal kingdom. I'm close. Close enough to have people waiting for the next steps.'

Isabel gasped and threw a hand across her chest as though she'd been struck. 'You are a non-believer, Dr Everley?'

She could drop the pious act away from her rector. But Lucius should have known better than to be so frank before them. They were country people, after all. Unlikely to understand. A chasm of life stood between us in the months I'd been away.

'I am not. There must be a divinity that shapes us. But time also shapes us. I'm afraid that I don't believe we are God's image, or that the world was created exactly like this in seven days.'

'What does your rector believe, Isabel?' The sherry had made me bold.

'What a question, Maddie! The Reverend Hillen is a man of God. He delivered a wonderful sermon on the Creation last Sunday, didn't he?'

Mother nodded, looking anxiously from one daughter to the other. She disliked disagreement, or any kind of what she called 'clever talk'.

'I'm quite sure I do not know what to think. But if Lucius is right then the Church will need to provide proof too.' I wished I could stop then. Trying to prove myself as his wife was pushing me from my family just when I needed them. And I did need them.

'We will see.' Lucius walked across and raised my hand to his lips. He was playing too. The dutiful husband.

'We don't wish to keep you, Lucius,' I said. 'If we're lucky we'll see you when you return.'

'You two are quite the happy couple,' said Isabel after he left. 'I want to hear everything!'

I cursed my pride. How could I ask the questions that burnt in me after that display? I wanted to ask Mother if marriages always started like ours, if she'd ever felt so lonely she'd have done anything to keep Father with her. I wanted to know if it was normal to be scared of your husband, or your new family. But it was too late. They both thought Lucius was charming and that he shared his life and research with me. We'd shown them what they wanted to believe.

'You'll find out soon enough,' I said, 'and you'll make your own story. You don't want to live someone else's. Have you set a date?'

'He hasn't asked me yet.'

'He will though, dear. He's quite besotted with you.' Mother patted Isabel's arm and reached over to top up her sherry. I'd never seen Barker leave wine unattended before, but I was glad he wasn't waiting on us. He'd been so strange earlier, after we found the statue. Furious that we'd all been in his domain. I overheard him telling Tizzy I was not to be allowed in the garden, especially with *that dog*. I pulled Ariadne onto my lap and fondled the curls of her ears.

'You'll baby that animal,' said Mother. Though she began to stroke her too.

'She's good company when Lucius is away.'

'And he's away often?'

I nodded.

'That's doctors for you. Everyone else always needs them more. Now what about your circle? We want to hear everything. We're still quite starved of parties. Aren't we, Isabel?'

'I've only been to two dinners. Both at Lord Barrington's.'

'Oh! Lord and Lady. Listen to her.'

What would they want to know? That I'd felt underdressed and out of place, a child in someone else's clothes? I could barely remember enough to give them details.

'I met a friend. The one I wrote about. Caroline Fairly, you would like her.'

'The governess?' A note of snobbery crept into Mother's voice. She was finding her feet again.

'Not any more. Her husband's a doctor too, he specialises in the mind. You'd like them both. They're very well read.'

'Will they be throwing any parties?' Isabel sounded wistful, as though she needed a taste of society before becoming a country rector's wife. Perhaps we should entertain. Mrs Barker wouldn't dare refuse in front of Mother.

'I don't know, perhaps – invitations are often late in London.' I put on an airy voice. 'But we'll certainly be holding a dinner in your honour.'

Mother clapped her hands and Isabel beamed. I should have thought to organise it before. Suddenly I realised the hour. I must not keep dinner waiting if I wanted favours from Mrs Barker, and it wouldn't hurt to put some distance between Mother and the sherry. 'Come, you must be hungry after such a long journey.' I looked around for Ariadne, who had to be shut in my bedroom while we ate in case she stole food. She was nowhere to be seen. 'I'll just fetch Ari and put her away.'

Calling her name, I walked upstairs. Such a naughty little

thing. Mother was right to warn me not to baby her. A puppy should be shown its place and I was not good at discipline. I heard a scuffling sound in the corridor above and tracked it down to Lucius's bedroom where the door was slightly ajar. 'Ari!' She came running but immediately ran back inside. What had she found this time? I dreaded to think. Following, I saw she had something in her mouth and scolded her crossly, holding her head so I could take it.

A stiff animal, a kitten probably, with fur tufted wet from Ariadne's bite. Stuffed and hard, with four legs in the normal places and four more withered little legs sticking up from its back. It was horrible. What was it Lucius had said? *Freaks of nature are as vital to us as healthy specimens in understanding our world.* He had plenty of natural freaks on display in the small museum, but why was this in here? What a blessing that Mother and Isabel hadn't seen it. A muddle of papers lay on the dressing table. He must have been researching late.

'Where did you get this?' Ariadne wagged her tail then sat to attention, as though I would throw the hideous thing for her to catch like a ball. I wagged my finger, but it was hard to stay cross with her for long and I placed the kitten right side up on the pile of papers, beside a book that was half open, pages down on the table. It made me cross to see the spine so damaged; books were expensive and they should be treated properly. I wasn't quite used to having such a number of them all over the house. Father's collection was modest and Mother preferred newspapers – until we featured in them.

Lucius's book was bound in deep-blue leather, tooled in gilt. A beautiful edition. I held it gently, careful not to lose the marked page. It looked interesting. The brief English translation on the inside cover described it as the story of a fisherman who turns into a half-man, half-fish creature and goes to live in the sea. But the rest was in another tongue, Latin perhaps, not something I could read. Several of the pages were underscored with lines, the margins covered in tiny handwritten notes.

There were two large boxes at the side of the room, draped in velvet like magicians' chests. Lifting the edge of the cloth, I realised they were cameras. Quite beautiful. Polished wood and brass, with artfully folded leather at one end and mirrored lenses at the other. Was Lucius keen on photography? I pushed the images in his book from my mind. I was sure the cameras hadn't been there before, but I'd learnt not to mention what I found strange.

Exhibit 19

Leather belt with buckle made from the hind leg of a hare.
Irish. c. 1750.

What was I thinking to plan a dinner for Mother? Throwing the invitation in such a casual manner? I knew only two people to ask and nothing of what food might be needed. Worry crept in that the Barkers would try to serve songbirds, but I knew that if I mentioned it they would concoct something worse. My head spun with lists and arrangements. In the end I appealed to Lucius and, keen to keep Mother quiet, he told Mrs Barker himself that we were to entertain. In my presence, so she was unable to fuss. Caroline helped me to plan the menu, and lent me a low-cut, midnight blue dress that she insisted was appropriate. *It will draw everyone's eye and your husband's jealousy. A hostess should be the centre of the room.* Mother and Isabel decorated, adding huge fans of hothouse flowers that brought to mind my afternoon at the Fairlys'. Lucius invited impressively titled guests. Along with Drs Stepwood, Pelling and Maycott came Lord and Lady Barrington, the Duke of Wiltshire and his fragile wife, the Chancellor of the Exchequer, society portraitist George Frederic Watts and the Dowager Duchess of Essex. My own choice, the Fairlys, came so late I began to worry they'd forgotten.

Caroline swept me aside. 'I'm sorry we took so long. I've been quite unwell today, but I wouldn't have missed it for the world.' She took my arm. Pretty opal drops hung from her ears and she was already ripe as a peach in snug satin. It wouldn't be long before she was too busy for me.

Ambrose hovered protectively. 'She should really be resting.' He brushed my cheek with a kiss.

'I can hardly lie down for months on end! Time enough to hide myself when I'm forced to wear strange clothes.' Caroline flashed him a brilliant smile. 'Now run along and say hello to Father, we have womanly matters to discuss.'

Dutifully he turned tail and headed for the drawing room. Caroline drew me closer. 'The dress looks wonderful on you. Is it working?'

'He's certainly playing the perfect host.' Lucius brought drinks to Mother and the Duke, and Mother looked as though she might burst. She'd never listen to my worries now, would consider the house and his circle to be worth anything.

'I've something to tell you, more about the questions you were asking before.' Caroline looked so serious that I felt a flush of panic.

'What is it? You look wonderful, by the way. As though something lights you from inside.'

'Glowing, isn't that what they say?' Though she still smelt of the cold evening air, her skin was warm and soft as she took my arm. 'You will know soon. I'm sure of it. We'll learn to be mothers together.'

Perhaps we would. Lucius had been visiting most evenings. Before I could reply, we were interrupted.

'Do you have some news you're not sharing, Madeleine?' Grace appeared so suddenly she must have been in a side room.

'You startled me.' I tried to laugh it off, but everyone had noticed me cry out. Grace made such an unpleasant habit of creeping up on people. Lucius must have invited her because I certainly hadn't. Scent from the flowers caught in my throat.

'So nervous! No need at all. You're among friends. I've been right there, talking to Caroline's father.' She patted my arm. 'Good evening, Caroline. I understand that congratulations are in order?'

'Thank you. We're very happy.'

'Do let us know if you need a doctor, I can vouch for Lucius's care.'

How dare she speak to my friend like that? In my own house! Struggling to remain composed, I tried to steer Caroline towards the sofa, but Grace grabbed my wrist and held it tightly.

'Have you taken on too much with this evening? You seem terribly nervous. There are some important people here. If you need me to take charge, just say so.' She relaxed her grip a little. 'Lucius has asked me to look out for you.'

'How kind of him to worry,' I said, my voice catching. Isabel walked towards us and instinctively I surveyed the room for Mother. She was deep in conversation with the Dowager, ringlets bouncing as her head bobbed. The ancient Duchess looked as though her eyes might close at any moment.

'Isabel, how wonderful to see you again. You *have* been busy in the shops! What a very intriguing neckline, is this quite the thing? You must enlighten an old lady, behind on fashion.' Grace looked far from old in a black taffeta gown covered in jet beads that glittered in the lamplight, giving her bare arms a statue's pale sheen.

'You look very nice, Isabel,' said Caroline quietly. 'Grace, would you be so kind as to get me some water? It's so hot in here.'

Grace inclined her head graciously and swished away to find someone, but our moment was lost, and Caroline's news would have to wait. It was almost time to seat people and I hadn't had the chance to speak with Lucius about how the evening would work. A new girl had appeared that afternoon, to help with the preparations, and was serving glasses of claret from a tray that looked much too heavy for her. I would guess her age at about thirteen, too young, surely, to have come from Evergreen?

The sound of the gong made me jump again, and I noticed Lucius and Grace exchanging pointed looks. Throughout the meal I was too nervous to eat much; the food stuck in my throat and the claret went straight to my head. I barely remembered what was said. The evening fractured. Jewels glinted on wrists and fingers, flickering candles made faces look hard and shadowed. Cutlery clattered and glasses clinked. Mother and Isabel seemed to enjoy themselves, especially after dinner when Isabel played her repertoire. Ambrose recited a moving poem and Caroline asked to see my latest sketchbook.

'No-one wants to look at morbid drawings on such a nice evening.' Mother held out a bowl of sugared almonds and gave me a warning look. I sat down again.

'I'll bring them when I come to visit Alice,' I said.

'Who would like dancing?' Lucius jumped up and brought Stepwood to the piano, who protested weakly as he rubbed his fingers to warm them for the keys. Isabel clapped her hands, Tizzy and the young girl rolled up the rugs and stood them upright in the corners like sentries. Someone spilt claret in a deep-red wound on the sofa cushion. The heady smell of wine mixed with overblown florals and food from the dinner being cleared on the floor below. Gowns swished and shoes pattered a beat on the floorboards. I leant against one of the rolled rugs to watch my party unfold, not noticing when Lucius slipped away.

* * *

'You don't try hard enough to make yourself pleasant.' Mother spoke freely the next morning, despite others being in earshot. Isabel was used to it, but I minded for Tizzy, who was trying to clean the panelling on the far side of the room. She was treated like a piece of furniture. Embarrassing for me too; Tizzy's good opinion mattered to me far more than it should. I didn't want her to hear me being lectured. 'Lucius is an important man. He requires an amiable and social wife.'

What Lucius seemed to require was a wife who didn't mind him disappearing. How could I explain that? 'I thought it was a nice evening.' I was too tired to argue.

'Shrinking against the wall all night! I didn't even *see* you with the Duchess.'

Mother had so monopolised her that I wouldn't have managed a word anyway. 'You seemed to like her.'

'*And* Lady Barrington. I hear she throws parties constantly. You would have done well to sit with her for longer.'

'She was more than occupied with keeping her husband's hands from the claret jugs.' Mother gasped but I didn't care. They were awful people, and I had no wish to spend more time in their company. I glanced over to Tizzy, catching her eye for a moment, and she covered a smile. Good. At least someone understood me.

'Don't you want to be accepted, Maddie?' Isabel pulled a pitying expression but, for all her talk, she didn't really know how it worked. Lucius's standing was all that determined my social worth. It didn't matter to any of them if I went to the parties or stayed in bed with my nerves. Whether we found anything in common. Whether they called on me or not. Either way, I'd be accepted. It didn't mean any of us had to like one another.

'I'd rather be understood.' I drew my sketchbooks from the shelf and placed them on the table in front of us. 'And I'm useful to Lucius. See.' I opened the first book onto sketches of a hare's hind leg, stretched and bent into various shapes. Bone and tendon separated from flesh. Quite beautiful. Mother turned the page quickly and uncovered a page of rat's feet, splayed and pushed apart, long claws like elegant fingers.

'I thought you'd left all this behind you, Madeleine. These are worse than the things you used to draw at home.' She screwed up her eyes as she peered, showing her teeth like a rodent.

'I'm helping Lucius to look at movement in creatures. It's his research.'

'How horrid. It's not suitable for ladies to go about drawing dead things. Not seemly. You're his wife, not his assistant.'

'Why may I not be both?'

'It's not a woman's place,' Mother replied sharply. 'Enough of this nonsense. Leave him to his work and just make sure you're here when he needs you.' Before I could reply she closed the book and rose to her feet. 'I'm going to dress. We have a fitting in less than an hour and I suggest we add in something for you.'

After they swished out, I heard low whispers in the hallway. Probably planning some sort of intervention. I groaned and placed my head in my hands.

'Don't be too hard on them, Mrs Everley. They're just excited to be here. I'd have been the same once.' Tizzy wrung out her cloth and hung it on the side of the bucket. A flash of sunlight caught the water inside as it moved.

'You're right. Isabel anyway. Mother just enjoys a good lecture.'

'Don't they all? Mine was always warning me about something or other, something dreadful I'd get myself into if I wasn't careful.' She gave a sad sideways smile. 'Don't know if she'd have been glad to be proved right. Good job she never lived to see it.'

'Mother doesn't need to wait to be proved right. She's always

165

right!' I began to pack away the sketchbooks and place them back on the shelf. 'I've never matched her idea of the perfect daughter. She'd rather I played piano and sang pretty tunes, or made beautiful embroidery, like Isabel.'

'Your pictures *are* beautiful. She just can't see it. But why try to make her? You'll only argue. Isn't it more important that Dr Everley likes them?'

Why did it please me so much to hear that Tizzy had looked at my drawings? She called them beautiful. She understood. 'How did you get so wise, Tizzy? You can't be much older than me.'

'Somewhere along the line you learn what you can change and what you can't, and what you have to be happy with. No point in fretting about the rest of it.' She picked up her bucket. I didn't want her to go.

'When did you lose your mother?'

'Four years, almost to the week. My sisters were already gone, so it was just me then. I missed her: she had a wicked tongue and she used it too, but after she went it was so quiet. No-one to put me right and tell me off.' She jutted out her chin. I couldn't imagine anyone telling her off.

'Why don't you come with us?' I could persuade her to afternoon tea. The idea was delightful.

'I've got work to do, Mrs Everley.'

'Of course.' Foolish of me to think she'd enjoy it anyway; she'd have her own things to do, with her own friends, on her Sunday afternoons off. The thought made me suddenly sad, like a child left out of a party.

'We never got to the bootmakers on Regent Street and it's our last chance. I do so want white kid boots for the Winter Ball.' Isabel pouted. The ball was the highlight of the country calendar. An invitation would complete their social return.

'White kid boots in the country! They would mark as soon as you left the carriage. They would here, too, in the winter months.'

'She's determined to have the best of things.' Mother patted her arm with an indulgent smile.

'They won't be wasted, they can go with my wedding dress.'

Isabel must feel conflicted. Torn between the life of a successful doctor's daughter and that of a rector's wife, forced to dress plainly. Whatever would a rector's wife want with white kid boots?

'Then you'll need to hurry about getting him to ask. Lucius didn't hang about that long, did he Madeleine?' Mother fiddled with the ribbons of her bonnet, pulling them free and straightening them on her lap.

'I didn't *get* him to ask, Mother.' In fact, I'd always harboured my suspicions that she'd done so herself. 'I'm sure Arnold won't need much persuading when he sees you looking so wonderful in your new finery. He'll have missed you too.'

Isabel scowled. 'It's only that he always has his children there, otherwise he would have asked by now, I'm sure of it.'

'Don't they go to school?'

'They're too small, Maddie. All of them under five years old.'

No wonder his poor wife hadn't survived. Three children so close together. It was a miracle anyone got through it. I thought of the jars in Lucius's study and felt my stomach knot. A sudden wave of nausea rose and I sat down heavily.

'I think *someone* will be finding out all about children quite soon.' Mother narrowed her eyes. Could it be true? It wasn't the first time I'd felt strange in the last couple of weeks, but I'd put it down to the excitement of guests. My belly pushed against the stays that Tizzy had failed to lace tightly that morning. Heat crept across my face. Too late now to ask Mother about Lucius's night visits, to find out if men were always the same. I'd been trying to find courage to speak of it but if she was right, and I suspected she was, then none of it would matter. Everyone would care only for the baby.

'I'm right, aren't I? Your skin looks so fresh, that's always the first sign. And I saw you at dinner too, you couldn't touch the heavy food. You need to speak with your cook about some different menus. I can share the ones I had if you like?'

'Thank you, I would like that.' Such touching concern from Mother made me feel closer to her, briefly, until I remembered everything I was hiding. I'd never dream of speaking to Mrs Barker in such a fashion. Did I dare ask Mother to do so on my behalf? 'I do feel a little tired, don't wait for me. Enjoy your last shop.'

The moment they'd gone I burst into tears. Lately, everything made me weep. Was that another sign? I knew nothing of what to expect. How could one even be sure? Lucius could probably check but I didn't want to ask him until I was certain. At least I could talk to Caroline. It might be her first, but she was further along, and happy. She would have asked Ambrose everything already. And he would have told her. They would be planning things together. Maybe spending time with them would help me understand how to tell Lucius. I determined to visit whilst my family were out and walked to my room to change. It wouldn't do to arrive dishevelled.

Through a blur of tears, I noticed that the library door was open, and a fire was lit. Could I start by reading about it? Try to find answers to my questions in Lucius's medical books? Better than appearing entirely ignorant. In all the shelves there must be something useful. Pathology, diseases, then human anatomy – that would be it. The book was heavy and I lifted it carefully, newly aware of the movement of muscles in my stomach. Illustrations showed how my body would change shape to stretch and mould itself around the new life inside. I would need to let out my dresses, or make new ones. Ellen had worn two dresses as she neared her confinement, one slit entirely at the back, the other at the front. She put her arms in both and wore them like a sandwiched gown, but then she always cared little what others thought. I could certainly not do the same. Tizzy would be the one to ask, she must have known lots of women at Evergreen House who needed help with clothes. Perhaps even herself; I hadn't forgotten her reaction to my question about babies when I discovered Ariadne in the kitchen.

One of the drawings showed cross sections of the body in neat, unnatural lines, all carefully hatched in ink. So many layers of skin. How did the artist know? Had Old Dr Everley cut it through to show him? I thought of the squirrel pegged out on Lucius's bench, her own young still inside her, and the nausea returned. The picture showed muscle and skin stretched taut around a tiny life, floating in fluid. A little underwater creature swimming. A seahorse. A water baby. Something strange to be loved.

'Lace caps, swaddling blankets, tiny stockings and ten smocks!' Caroline beamed as she laid out the baby's things. Lucky child. Its nursery was newly papered with hand-painted sailing boats and smiling suns. A deep wooden cot in the centre of the room was padded with white lace and soft blankets. Sheepskins covered the floor. The nursery near the servant's floor was bare, its walls plain plaster. I wondered if I'd be able to choose my own things for the baby or whether I'd be forced to ask Grace. I had the feeling she wouldn't allow much choice.

'Ten? Why ever will it need so many?' The tiny smocks were made in layers of gathered cotton, beautifully embroidered and edged in fine spiderwebs of lace. They must have taken someone hours to make.

'Babies are messy.' Caroline held one out, smoothed its frills. 'You'll find out for yourself soon enough.'

Sooner than she thought. We could be sharing this excitement. Would she be pleased for me? I hesitated slightly too long before speaking. She grabbed my arm with an air of excitement.

'But I almost forgot!'

The news she hadn't wanted to tell me at dinner. I could only think it must be something that Lucius wouldn't like. A promotion for Ambrose, or even a royal appointment? They deserved happiness.

'Old Dr Everley. I've found out why our families began to feud, because Father turned his back on their friendship.'

I'd rather talk about babies. 'You mean what Grace said about resurrectionists? Lucius says all surgeons are, or at least were, the same. More interested in demonstrating their skill than worrying about where their samples came from.' He'd mentioned Dr Stepwood's name in the same sentence, but I left that out. Caroline and her father were close.

'It was more than that. I beat it out of Ambrose. It wasn't something Father would share with me.'

My heart sank. For something to do I began to fold the smocks and place them back into the drawer.

'Don't worry about that, Maud or I will do it later.'

'They'll get dirty. And you should be resting.'

'I like having them out. I can't wait to see them on. And I will rest. We'll take some tea in the drawing room.' Caroline waited. 'Do stop fussing with those and listen.'

I turned to face her and lowered my eyes.

'He was accused of murdering two young men. The very week he had a gathered audience of new medical students, he was first on the scene to get the bodies from the morgue. When the Thames boatmen fished them out and took them there, he was already waiting.'

'Was anything proven?' Lucius had never mentioned a case, a trial. Caroline shook her head.

'Nothing. But Ambrose says they'd both been killed by blows to the back of the head. Dead before they were pushed into the water.'

Had he struck lucky and capitalised on some fighting men's misfortune, or was there a darker side to the house of Everley? Much as I loathed to believe it, I could hardly say it felt like a surprise. The feelings I had constantly, the atmosphere in the house, Lucius's fierce need to prove himself and Grace's drive to clear the family name. It was all over something unspoken.

Shock made my voice cold. 'I'm sure it was coincidence. Lucius speaks highly of his father. I can't imagine my husband knowing such a thing.'

Caroline seemed taken aback. 'I'm sorry, Maddie, I didn't mean anything by it. It's just that you're always talking about his hold on the house, hinting at things. I thought you might want to know. Ambrose doesn't entirely believe it.'

That meant Dr Stepwood *did* think Lucius's father capable of murder. I could hardly tell her my news now. The moment had passed. 'I fear it isn't something for amusement.'

'I realised as soon as I said it. Now I've spoilt our afternoon. Ambrose says I always talk too much. Shall we take our charcoals to the park? It's a beautiful afternoon.' She looked crestfallen.

'Ambrose is right.' It did look like a beautiful afternoon. Pale sunlight bathed the windowsill. How much nicer to walk through the park and do some sketching than be dragged from milliner to cobbler with Mother and Isabel. My anxiety diminished. Why worry about Old Dr Everley? He could hardly harm me now.

'And so are you. It's a perfect sketching day.'

Caroline seized me into a warm hug, and I felt the hard swell of her belly against my side. I almost blurted out my own news, but she bundled me out of the room and down the stairs, calling for shawls and picnics and sketching things all at once.

Eventually we left, wrapped warmly, Caroline holding a bag of cakes and I juggling a pack of materials with Ariadne's lead. She disliked walking tethered and made a big show of jumping round to try to bite the leather. It made walking difficult, and I had trouble keeping up. Caroline was still a fast walker, despite her growing size. Lagging behind, I watched as a woman, dressed in the brightest yellow, ran out of a side street and collided with her, almost knocking her over. The woman put one arm around her, showing concern and, I would hope, apologising. Flowers and ribbons covered her huge bonnet, black curls fell down her back. A harsh look, too bright and bold for the pale colours of the afternoon. As I neared, my view became clearer and I saw that it was Rebecca. Older and tired-looking, but unmistakably my sister. She turned and hurried away, crossing into the opposite streets, and I called after.

Caroline looked worried. 'I'm fine, she said sorry,' I said. She pulled at my sleeve and I shook myself free. All the years I'd wondered what happened, why Rebecca left us, who he was. I couldn't let her go now. Thrusting over my parcel and Ariadne's lead, I followed the direction she had taken. It should be easy to spot someone dressed in yellow. But as I turned the corner, I was faced with a busy street market, covered barrows pushed together, topped with bright umbrellas. Dozens of people milled between them. I'd lost her again.

Ariadne had pulled away and chased over to find me. I picked up her lead and hurried back across the street.

'Why did you chase her? Poor Ariadne was upset.'

How could I explain and risk our friendship? 'I just . . . I thought I recognised her. Someone from home.'

'I doubt very much you would know someone like that. You must be mistaken.'

Bright colours and showy finery; Rebecca had always loved pretty things. Whatever she appeared to be, she wouldn't have cheapened herself through choice. We walked to the park in silence. I could focus on little else. I was sure now that my first glimpse as we drove in the carriage had been Rebecca too, laughing and walking with a gentleman. And if I'd seen Rebecca twice in almost the same place, then she must be staying close to here. It was only a matter of time before I caught her.

20

The Marlborough Assizes

'Let me in, Maddie.' I tapped against the metal grid of the door, straining to hear a response. The cell looked empty. Hard to see through the small hatch, but I assumed she was in a corner. Number seven. Definitely the number I was given by the guards. Keen moaning from the room next door filled the corridor. Someone called out for God to help him. How long before Maddie crumbled in this place? Why would she not take my help?

'Maddie.' I tapped again and the moaning rose in pitch. 'They'll only allow a half-hour visit before they throw me out again. Talk to me, please.' Sour smells of sweat and excrement came through the grilles. Unwashed clothes and unemptied buckets. I couldn't stand to think of her alone for hours on end, wondering if she'd be condemned to die. No wonder it was taking her fight.

'It's not afternoon tea.' The guard stomped back along the corridor, opened the door roughly and gestured for me to go inside. Purple-red blotches covered the lower part of his face. 'You don't need to ask permission to visit.' He gave the next door a vicious kick and the moaning stopped suddenly. Then he dropped back to the doorway and scratched at his neck. 'Go on then. I've better things to do than stand here.'

I stumbled, put out a hand to steady myself. The wall was

slimy with damp that seemed to stay on my hands. Rubbing them together, I walked inside, blinking in the gloom. It smelt the same as the corridor. Maddie was curled on a hard straw pad, bound in cloth the colour of her dress and just as dirty. I crouched beside her and touched her as gently as I could in case she was sleeping. She wasn't. But she didn't move or turn.

'I want to help you, Maddie. I've been there, every day, have you seen me? Can you see in the gallery?' What a stupid thing to say. Of course she didn't want to look there. All those people gawping at her pain. 'I can't talk for you unless you ask them. You have to ask them.'

Tears ran dirt streaks down her cheeks. She didn't move or speak. I put my arm around her shoulders.

'You only have a few days left. Don't let them decide this without you.'

Maddie stirred and sat upright, hugged her arms around her knees. 'I don't want you and Ambrose mixed up in my trouble.' Her head rested on her arms, muffling her voice, and I strained to hear. 'It's what started it all. Lucius, his father, their reputations. They think it's worth more than anything. More than life.'

'Ambrose isn't . . .' What was I going to say? That he didn't care about his reputation? Of course he did, they all did. But I was pretty sure he didn't care about it more than life. I thought of him with our child. He loved him, of course he did. But would he put him first, before name and reputation? I shook my head. Ridiculous to doubt him. How could anyone hurt such a helpless thing? And how could we possibly let Maddie be blamed. She'd suffered enough. I couldn't imagine how it would feel to lose a baby that way. 'Ambrose wouldn't want you to suffer.'

'It's too late for me,' she said sadly. 'And I don't want you to suffer either.'

175

'The only suffering I endure is to be pushed away from a dear friend when she needs me most. When I can be of help. Let me speak for you.'

Maddie buried her face and my heart sank. Was I wrong about her? Mrs Barker had been convincing in the stand. Didn't she think every noise was a baby crying? She treated her own dog like a baby. She was obsessed, her mind unhinged. Could Maddie harm a baby? It was unthinkable. Yet her resolute silence brought doubt.

The guard peered round the door and jerked his thumb at me. 'Off you go. She's not the only one in here, you know.'

I stood, trying not to think of what brushed against my hem. 'I think I saw your sister, Rebecca. She's been here too.'

'Wait! How do you . . . is she safe?' Maddie suddenly stood.

'I said time's up, save it for next time.'

'I'll come tomorrow,' I called over my shoulder.

'Can you prove that you wanted the child?'

Maddie looked up to the viewing gallery, searching. Looking for me? Or maybe Rebecca.

'I did want my child.'

'Yet we have heard that you did not prepare baby things, or the room for its arrival. Such tasks that should be pleasing to mothers.'

'I wasn't allowed.'

'Who didn't allow you?'

'My husband's sister always chose the things for the house.'

'You were mistress of the house, did you not want to choose for yourself? Did you show no interest? It is odd, Mrs Everley, to show no pleasure in such preparation.'

'I was never allowed the choice.'

'Imagine the things you could buy if you had that sort of

money!' said a woman in the row behind me. 'Little mite'd want for nothing. Still, doesn't do no good does it? Can't buy yourself happiness.'

I turned to give her what I hoped was a cold look. Wealth, or the appearance of it, was no indication that a woman would equally share. Maddie had never been allowed money, had always been forced to borrow and beg. She hated to ask. Another way of limiting her freedom.

'You hid your pregnancy, did you not?'

'I did not.'

My heart sank, because she did hide it. All the time she listened to my excitement over being with child, she must have known that she carried her own. To keep it secret and fret about telling people. It must have meant that she was scared, not that she didn't care. She always said that something meant her child harm, and now they were using that against her. Why would Ambrose not come with me? He was trained. He could tell just by looking who was lying. A professional should be able to tell who had something to hide. But then a professional would also be able to hide it.

Exhibit 21

Punchinello figure with hunched back and stick.
Painted porcelain. Italian. c. 1780.

Mother was so concerned they would miss the return train to Dallam that we arrived at the station a full hour before it left. They chose seats in the ladies' carriage and Isabel carried her new white boots like a lapdog, settling them on the rack under a blanket. Mother shook her head crossly at a man in a battered hat who waved a news-sheet from the top of his stack. Penny bloods. I craned my neck to read the title – *True Life Stories* – a crude etching of an anguished woman beneath. There must be a living to be made illustrating those, with the added benefit of annoying Mother twice, though I'd have to read them, and such gruesome stories would do me no good in the lonely evenings.

'We have time, don't we, Maddie?' Isabel pointed to the puppet show being unveiled on the concourse.

Mother made a show of checking the station clock.

'Of course,' I said, 'your trunks are stowed and there's nothing to do now but wait.' I was glad of an amusement to cover my distraction. Rebecca was everywhere, in the shapes of strangers, in dreams where I chased her through twisting streets. I worried I wouldn't find her again, and then I worried that I would. Because how could I help? Unlikely that Mother would take her home, or Lucius welcome her to ours.

'You're both a bit old for puppets.' Mother unfastened her travelling cloak and drew a lace shawl around her shoulders. Isabel was already changed, and I suspected that her eagerness to join the crowd was mainly driven by the chance to show off her new clothes. A vicar's wife would have to watch such pride.

'Look, there's Toby Dog!' said Isabel, pulling at Ariadne's lead. 'Come on.'

A small crowd gathered before the theatre in the main hall. Several wooden seats were empty towards the back, but Isabel refused to sit with Mother and pulled us straight to the front row as though we were still children.

'Ladies and gentlemen, knaves and princesses.' The Professor gave a deep bow; Isabel giggled and turned to look at Mother who sat upright in her new dress, regarding the audience with disdain. How could I talk to her about Rebecca? She'd only just recovered. If she had to go back, try to make sense of what Rebecca might have become, she may never be happy again.

Isabel nudged me with a sharp elbow. 'What are you mooning about?' she whispered.

'Where are you, you naughty man?' The swazzle had changed the Professor's voice to the high puppet squeal that set my nerves on edge. A crocodile clattered into the stage window, roughly painted, eyes leering closed. It had a ragged cloth body like the mummified animal in Lucius's small museum. An arm could be seen under the material, moving it along.

'I don't know where he is. You can come back later. Oh, what am I to do?' Mrs Punch raced from one side of the stage to the other, watched by the crocodile. It gave a final snap of its jaws and sank below the curtain. I flinched, startled by the noise of the wooden teeth.

'At least try to enjoy it,' hissed Isabel.

I couldn't follow what happened on the little stage. Clowns and skeletons came and went. Another puppet, with yellow ringlets and red cheeks, came looking for Punch. Eventually he returned with Toby and started smacking his wife with a stick that banged against her plaster head and the wall of the theatre box. The crowd roared with laughter and the more they laughed, the more the slapstick swung. Punch grabbed the baby as it started wailing and began to hit that, too. The baby stopped crying but he swung at it again and again, until it lay limp on the stage and was seized off by a wailing Mrs Punch. I winced with every slap.

'Don't be silly, Maddie. The policeman will come – or Jack Ketch – Mr Punch will say sorry and it will all be over.'

'Did someone call for a doctor?' The puppet wore a purple tailcoat and a white lace shirt, its body stuffed to look corpulent. 'You need to take one of these three times a day.' The doctor hit Punch hard on the head. The crowd stayed quiet. Why were they so keen for this horrible puppet to win? He had killed a baby while they cheered. Punch played dead, only to rise up and kick the doctor before swinging him round on his stick. The crowd roared. Isabel clapped. Ariadne bared her teeth, and I stroked her ears to calm her.

'She doesn't like the noise. I'm going to take her back to the platform.'

As we stood to leave, an elderly man, with long strings of grey hair hanging from the sides of his head, grabbed Isabel's arm and shook a leather bottle. Narrow at the top for coins to pass through, but impossible for him to shake them out again without his employer hearing from behind the stage. 'Professor can't put on a good show if he's hungry.' Two teeth were missing and gobs of spit flew as he spoke. Mother appeared beside us and dropped in a few small coins. With an expression of distaste, she watched the bottler slink off. 'Train's not long now, we should go.'

I would have to travel home alone. By the time I saw them again I'd probably already be a mother myself. In the meantime, I would look for Rebecca and try to uncover the Everley family secrets. Moving statues and medical corpses – a tale for the penny bloods. If I got closer to Lucius, I could ask him more. But first I must reveal my own secret, and I had no idea how he would react.

When I returned, Lucius was in the library, leaning over the desk with his feet propped up on a footstool. My news burnt inside me. 'Will you be dining here this evening?'

His eyes remained fixed on the pen he turned in his hands as carefully as if it were a dagger. 'I'm needed at the Society.'

Lucius was dressed so beautifully that I'd known the answer before I asked. A large bundle of papers sat by his glass of wine, clearly prepared for transit. Pages tied together in a wide yellow ribbon, the colour of Rebecca's dress.

'I have something to tell you.' Would he be displeased? Or did he want a family? He didn't seem to like Grace's children; at least, he never put himself out to be there when they visited.

'I should be leaving. Can it wait?'

The nib of the pen pointed towards me, silver-sharp. I inhaled deeply, feeling on the edge of something that must radically change our lives. I thought of Punch's baby in its ragged gown, then Caroline's neat row of embroidered smocks. If I were not brave now, I'd never be able to bring a child into the world. A mother must be brave.

'No. It can't wait.' He looked up and I held his gaze. 'You're to be a father. I thought you would wish to know.' Silence for a few moments and then a rare, slow smile spread across his face.

'Wonderful!' Lucius leapt from the desk, seized my hand and kissed it. The pen rolled across the floor and caught by the wall. He wore a genuine look of delight. Perhaps it was all we needed, a family to put right whatever darkness existed in the house before. The rooms would be filled with the laughter of children, and we would live. We smiled at each other for a few moments, and I thought he would change his plans and stay home, so that we could talk. But then he drew back again, took up the bundle of papers. 'Do let Grace know as soon as you can, so that she can help you with all the . . . arrangements. She will be just as pleased as I am.'

If she was pleased, she didn't show it. Instead, Grace seemed to take delight in stoking my fears about motherhood with her tales of the slums, neighbourhoods of hovels and gin shops, children pouring out of them like farm kittens. 'I've seen what happens to women who keep working, as though carrying a baby isn't difficult enough.' I couldn't imagine Grace on those streets, finding women for Evergreen House. Yet every time we spoke, she told me how such poverty ruined lives. Perhaps she was warning me that one slip and I would end up there. Like my sister. Before I'd seen Rebecca, it hadn't worried me so much, but now I couldn't stop thinking about her, and what her life must be like.

'You should take better care of yourself. Barker would have taken your family to the train station.'

'I wanted to say goodbye. And to see it all. I've only travelled by train once.'

'Nasty, dirty things.'

It was hard to tell if she spoke of the trains or my family. 'There were lots of street entertainers. Isabel made us watch a Punch show.'

Grace wrinkled her nose. 'All that shrieking and wailing. I can't understand why it's so popular with the lower classes.'

Did my family count as such with her? It seemed that most people did. No wonder she was so keen to clear her father's name and claim her rightful place in society. It must have killed her to be ostracised in such a way, to be pushed from the top of the tree.

'You like Punch.' Edmond spoke clearly. 'You took us to see it in the park.'

'You're thinking of Nanny.' She spoke without turning to look at him.

'No. It was you. You left us under the tree while you went off with those women.'

'He gets confused.' She gave me a gracious smile.

'No, I don't.' Edmond drew his legs up and kicked out. Nails in his hard leather soles clattered against the floorboards. 'You said the show would be fun and you laughed while we watched it. And then you left us for ages. And it wasn't fun. It was cold.'

'Stop showing off, Edmond. Your Aunt Madeleine doesn't wish to hear your lies.' She threw him an icy look and he pushed out his lip.

'I didn't care that you'd gone. She did though, big baby.' A sudden, violent shove and Eloise toppled backwards, banging her head.

Grace gave a sharp intake of breath and walked over to where they sat. I expected her to comfort her daughter but instead she gave Edmond a hard slap and another warning look, before pulling Eloise up and sitting her down hard on the chair next to me. I smiled and patted her hand. She stared back at me, eyes streaming. Mother, who met the children briefly, had insisted they looked like Lucius. Though I hadn't seen it before, I saw it then. Something about the eyes and temples that were more like Lucius than his sister. Would my baby be so wild? Did darkness really streak the Everley family? There was a coldness to them that was frightening.

'Would you like to play with Ariadne? You could throw her ball in the garden. She's getting to know how to fetch it back.' I smiled encouragingly at Eloise.

'I want to go too,' said Edmond.

I hesitated, fearful of them together out of sight. Would fresh air be better for them? Grace made the decision for me.

'No-one is to go into the garden. Barker is planting today.'

He hadn't mentioned it to me, though I'd generally been made to feel unwelcome in the garden since finding the broken statue.

'A story then.' I picked up my copy of *The Water Babies* and opened it at the first page. *And so there may be faeries in the world and they may be just what makes the world go round.* What did make the world go round? I used to think it was love and kindness. I would do everything in my reach to ensure my own child had an abundance of both.

'What's a faery?' asked Eloise.

Grace snorted. Edmond gave a strange laugh and Ariadne jumped to attention. Ignoring them, I passed over the book. Beautiful, winged faeries decorated the cover.

'Like this. Little magical things that we can't see, that help us. These ones live in flowers.' I turned a few pages over. 'And these are faeries too, good ones. They live under the water, so they don't have wings. They help the children in the book that fall in the river, the water babies. It's where Ariadne's name comes from.'

Eloise patted the dog. 'Which one is she?'

I pointed to the drawing of Ariadne, and she smiled, cheeks smeared with dirty tear tracks. Perhaps I could teach her to draw them.

'A foolish name for a character that's supposed to be good.'

Grace pulled a face that showed she also thought it was a silly name for a dog. 'You know the story of Theseus and Ariadne?'

'Yes. Lucius told me. She saved his life in the labyrinth.'

'He abandoned her in the end. After everything she did for him. Some say she hanged herself. Some say she ended up with Dionysus.'

'Who is Dionysus?' I asked quietly, stroking Eloise's hair.

'The god of wine and debauchery.' Grace smiled. 'Isn't that a typical faerytale ending? It's what happens to most fooled women.'

I held my tongue. Grace seemed irritated.

'You look tired, Madeleine. We'll leave you now. And don't worry about your arrangements, you mustn't exert yourself. I will organise everything.'

'That's very kind, but I'm looking forward to furnishing the nursery. Perhaps Eloise would like to help me choose things?'

Edmond began to throw toy soldiers across the floor. One of them caught Ariadne's leg and she gave a little yelp of pain that made him smile.

'There'll be no need for that. All the nursery things are still in the attic. Lucius has already asked Barker to fetch them down. And I've ordered some new cotton, for the crib. In yellow. It will suit a boy or a girl.' Her eyes travelled slowly down the length of me. 'Though I think you'll have a boy.'

There was no arguing with Grace in such a mood. Best to play along and then change things later, if I could, though it was deeply disappointing to hear. I pictured Caroline's room, with its pretty wallpaper and little drawers of swaddling. It would have been such fun to get things ready with a friend. Grace swept from the room with Edmond, and Eloise ran after them. Halfway to the door she stopped, ran back and gave me a kiss on the cheek. 'More story?' she asked.

'Next time. I'll read it to you next time you visit.' I handed her the long-legged rabbit she carried everywhere. 'What's his name? Or is she a girl bunny?'

Eloise cuddled the rabbit to her chest. 'Name's 'Becca.'

Just coincidence, I told myself as I watched them leave. But Grace had spoken Rebecca's name before. Did she know what happened to her? Caroline's park wasn't so far from Putney. Perhaps she was, after all, at Evergreen House. Rain streaked the windows, and I looked out to make sure they could manage the carriage. Grace helped both children up first, a surprising maternal gesture. As she swung herself up onto the footplate a figure pulled at her skirts, stopping her from climbing in. A woman, wet and bedraggled. It was hard to see her face. Her wet hair hung straight. Grace looked left and right, as though checking for observers, then pulled the woman into the carriage beside her before they drove off.

Exhibit 22

Belemnite. Cretaceous. c. 70m years B.C.

My body changed. Not just my belly, I was expecting that. Tizzy helped me alter two of my dresses to accommodate its growth and I was grateful to loosen my stays. But I hadn't known that my face would look bloated and puffy, that my heart would burn after every meal. No-one told me that my ankles would swell to twice their size after an hour of being up in the morning. Tears came at the slightest provocation – a raised voice, a sad poem – and most nights I found myself weeping into the pillow before drifting into fitful dreams. My sleep was poor, punctuated by nightmares of water creatures and lifeless babies, and I tossed and turned in the bed, too uncomfortable to sleep on my side and too heavy to rest on my back. The child was strong, kicking and wrestling against the muscle that held him as though he wished to emerge any day.

Encouraged by Grace, I began to take naps in the afternoon, retiring to my room after lunch and lying on the bed, propped up on cushions with Ariadne at my feet. Lucius had not made a night visit since I shared my news, and she saw it as her rightful place again. Mrs Barker often brought cocoa to help me rest. I knew, by then, that she laced it with something but I drank it anyway. At least sleep passed the time.

Lucius had taken to spending the hour before dinner at home and usually I found myself looking forward to our conversation. The time between afternoon sleep and a solitary dinner had become the best part of a lonely day.

'Fast today. Did you rest properly?' He let go of my wrist and I settled my hands in my lap. If my pulse was racing it was not from overexcitement.

'I'm resting too much.' Aside from letters from Isabel, which were full of her rector, and others from Caroline, who was suffering from sickness, I was alone in my thoughts. Whenever Tizzy stayed too long, she was called back downstairs. Even Grace would have been welcome. Why was she staying away just when I had questions? I couldn't stop thinking about the woman I'd seen climb into her carriage. Who was she? So very like Rebecca. But, as Lucius said, I couldn't trust my mind. Each day left me doubtful and craving his approval. He put away his pocket watch.

'I finished the birds.' My sketchbook lay open on the table and I pushed it towards him. Stretched wings, like arms with multiple feathered fingers, covered the pages. Studies of the magpie wings he'd handed me, newly sectioned, fresh enough to shine in the sunlight. Against dark hatching I'd used coloured inks to show the brightness of the blue line, the flash of white. 'Are they what you wanted?'

He examined them carefully, tracing the lines with a finger. I imagined those elegant hands dissecting animals, forcing blades through sinew and bone. 'They're very skilful.' He indicated the line at the top of the wing. 'This is the part I need in detail. The feathers you've drawn are beautiful . . . like Blake's angels.' He looked up and gave me one of his rare dazzling smiles, which I returned, though I was unsure what he meant. Wasn't Blake driven mad in the end? His drawings were hallucinatory visions. 'But quite useless.' My heart sank. 'It's the joints I need to understand. They have the same type of bones as humans – see here, the ulna and radius are the same, the join at the scapula is different, more fixed. But in the last piece of bone, the metacarpus, what I need to understand is how the buds of the phalanx end. Could they have been anything else?'

It was hard to keep up with his mood swings. One moment critical, the next encouraging. 'I thought your research was on water life?'

'It is. But I believe all limbs evolved the same way.'

'Wings are limbs?'

'Of course. See how the tips stretch out like fingers? The way the bones fold?' Lucius walked around to the back of my chair and held out my right arm, running his hand along the length of it. Gentle, as usual, when demonstrating anatomy. If only his touch was always so tender.

'I'd never thought of birds being like us.'

'All creatures are like us. Torsos, limbs, eyes. We're the same.'

'Not many creatures have two legs.'

'Picture them on their hind legs and you'll see the similarities. Even the great lizards.'

Ariadne lifted her head at some unseen noise, wary as always with Lucius in the room. She'd run to curl up in her basket at the sound of his voice, her huge brown eyes fixed on my face. She looked towards me, showed willing to come to my aid, and then settled back down.

'Do you believe the great lizards existed?'

'We've seen their giant bones uncovered many times. What more proof do you need?'

More than imagination. The idea that such things walked the earth so long before us made me shudder. They were faerytale monsters. How could God have made them?

'I haven't seen proof. Just drawings.'

Lucius patted his pockets as though looking for something, finally drawing out a curled shape, flat on one side and ridged in a spiral shape on the other. Cold like stone but jointed like a creature. 'What is it?'

'An ammonite. Prehistoric. A kind of squid, I suppose. Smaller of course, though it's possible to uncover bigger ones if you know which rocks to split. You can find these all over the beaches in Dorset.'

I stroked the cold dead thing, trying to imagine it once alive. So ancient. What would it have looked like? I'd tried to draw centipedes in the garden at home, though they moved too quickly to copy properly until James killed some and proudly dropped them on my lap. This thing would never shrivel like their husks. It was immortalised.

'Keep it. I've dozens. When you're well I'll take you to see Sloane's collection. An extraordinary amount of things, how he ever had time to treat his patients I will never know. It would fascinate you.'

Why could we not go now? 'I'm not unwell. I'm with child.'

Lucius returned to his seat and leant over, patting me on the knee. 'But you won't want to be on your feet for hours. Nor would I let you. You need rest, as I keep telling you.'

Boredom would end me as quickly as effort. I was losing his attention. Soon he'd forget I could help him. 'What does this have to do with your water creatures?' I pointed to the uppermost part of the magpie's wing. 'Did the limbs grow on fish like this?'

'I think so. I have some work to do on some of the bigger sea creatures.'

'Do you have one? I can't remember what they called them, something beginning with i . . .'

190

'Ichthyosaurs? No! If only. That would make things rather easier. There are only one or two and they're all with the palaeontologists. I have a delivery of large fish coming though, I'll show you when they're done. I just need to prevent them smelling while I work on them, or the Barkers will turn out my workshop.'

Why did he always talk as if it were their house? He wasn't a boy any longer. It was up to him what he did, though between the damp decay and his lime room the house couldn't smell much worse.

'I think you can use alum.' Father had a friend who made glass cases for fishing trophies. Albert Netters. Another of Rebecca's conquests. We didn't see him much after she left. Mother hated anything dead, but I was fascinated by the displays he made for our dining room. Perch and rod in fabric weeds, reproachful eyes glinting in candlelight. 'Father knew a taxidermist, I'm sure that's what he used.'

'That's what the apothecary recommended.' Lucius looked at me closely. 'You really *are* interested.'

'Will you strip the fish limbs in the same way?'

'With fish, or even seals, it's more difficult to see the way they extrude. Those with pectoral as well as dorsal fins might well hold clues.'

'And you need to see the tops of these wings to see if they form in the same way?'

'Exactly!'

'I'd need to strip the feathers to see more clearly.'

'I've some already limed, I'll bring them to you before I leave.'

I could picture him clearly, bent over the lime pot, sleeves rolled to the elbow and cloth wrapped over his hands as protection against the caustic chemicals. A serious look on his face as he dipped in the body parts, slowly, carefully, and withdrew them again. Thin, white objects that he seemed to love more than living creatures. If I didn't agree, then at least I understood.

After he left, I dozed again before a loud cracking sound woke me with a jolt that jarred my side, causing me to cry out in pain. Immediately the baby started kicking, hammering with the sharp nubs of its heels. My heart pounded. Rebecca's lovers used to rain stones against our bedrooms. A sound I hadn't heard in years. One associated with trouble. Who would throw stones at my window? Were the Barkers refusing Caroline again? Or could Rebecca know where I lived? All the time I was looking for her, maybe she already knew about me.

Holding my hands under my bump to relieve the dragging weight, I moved slowly over to the window. The curtains were open, the afternoon already overcast. Ink-blue clouds, like magpie feathers, threatened more rain. The crescent was unusually quiet. Two men hurried past. A starched nurse pushed a bassinet with two small children hanging from the sides, stopping briefly to straighten their hats. Ravens bickered on the square of grass by the plane tree. But no-one waited on the street below, looking up.

A door slammed along the corridor. The unmistakable icy vowels of Grace could be heard. Who was she talking to? Heart hammering, I was on my way to investigate when Tizzy burst into the room, a duster in each hand.

'It's like Bedlam downstairs. Mrs B is living up to her name and barking orders left, right and centre, you'd think the Queen was coming when Mrs Atherton's here and . . .' She peered at me. 'You look queer. Sit down.' Tizzy helped me into the chair by the window, a delicate dressing chair too narrow for me now, its thin spindled legs bowed beneath my weight. I kept one hand on the wooden shutter for balance.

'I thought someone was throwing stones at the window and I sat up too quickly, jarred myself.' I glanced up at the pane and saw a chip in the glass. 'Look, there's a mark.'

Tizzy put her dusters on the table where Lucius had left several wing joints. She pulled a face. 'No wonder you're faint. You might like to remind him that ladies prefer flowers.'

'He asked me to draw them. I wanted to.' I'd been hoping to make a start that afternoon, but now I wasn't sure if I'd be able to get comfortable enough. The pain in my side made it hard for me to breathe properly.

'Well they don't belong in your chamber, dirty things. I'll take them down to the library, you can admire them in there. Enough to give you nightmares.'

Plenty worse things to give me nightmares than a few pairs of featherless wings. 'They're just bones.'

Tizzy picked up the ammonite, frowning as though she was trying to call something to mind. 'I've seen these before. Snake-stones they call them at home. Those and the longer ones, like cones, what were they called? Devil's fingers, something like that.'

'Of course. Your home is Dorset. Lucius has been telling me about the fossils.' Perhaps she knew his beach.

A wistful look crossed her face. 'Used to be. Now it's here.' She turned the ammonite over in her hands. Almond nails, like Caro's, and such soft white skin. She wasn't made to black grates, and I wondered how different her life was here with us. Did she want to go back? I couldn't bear to lose her. But if she asked me to let her go, I would. Her happiness would win.

'See this mark? I think someone *was* throwing stones.'

'Be a good aim, wouldn't they? Three stories up.' She rolled her eyes. 'Let's have a look.'

Tizzy gave the ammonite a little polish with her apron, wiped her hands, then pulled up the sash and leant out so far I had to hold her feet to stop her falling. 'Do be careful!'

'Crow,' she called, jumping back in, a black-feathered bird in her left hand.

'Don't let it loose in here!' Mother was terrified of crows, of the misfortune they were said to bring. The last thing I needed was a bird loose in the room. Ariadne uncurled from her basket and stretched, shuffled over to give it a half-hearted sniff.

'It's not going anywhere. Dead as a doornail.' She held out the lifeless bird for me to touch. It was soft and warm. 'I'd say it bashed into the window and dropped down dead. It was on the parapet of the second-floor window. Chip was probably its beak. Poor thing. Dr Everley might want it for his collection.'

'I think Dr Everley can do better than that for his museum, don't you, Harriet?'

Tizzy jumped as though she'd been slapped. I blinked hard to disperse my tears. What was Grace doing here? Did social convention just disappear with pregnancy? It seemed that everyone felt it was their privilege to visit me at rest.

'I'll be down directly. Tizzy was just helping me to rescue a bird.'

'I don't think your rescue has worked. Don't hurry, I'll make myself at home. Would you like tea?' Grace sailed from the room in a cloud of violet scent. Tizzy grimaced and followed her out, still clutching the crow. Mother would call it an omen of death. But whose? I mustn't think of it.

The pain in my stomach worsened. Doing anything seemed to strain it. When I finally managed to pull on my dress and walk downstairs, Grace had finished afternoon tea and rung for sherry. She was barefoot, her boots and stockings in a heap beside her, and her unpinned hair flowed like fire across the sofa.

'Have some. It'll do you good.'

I took a sip, surprised by the warmth of the liquid. Grace's cheeks were flushed, her eyes glassy. How much sherry had she already taken? A third glass, empty, sat on the tray. Was Lucius expected? I couldn't bear her delight in my ignorance if I enquired.

'How are the children?'

'Ghastly, darling. You'll see. They never leave you alone.'

'Haven't seen you in a while.'

'Evergreen's been busy.'

'There was someone else with you last time. In the carriage.' It slipped out before I had time to think. Grace's eyes narrowed like those of a cat caught in daylight. 'Who was that? She joined you just as you left.'

'I don't recall.' Her voice was ice.

'It was awfully wet that day. Kind of you to offer a lift.'

Grace leant forward and poured herself another sherry from the heavy decanter with a steady hand, though her mouth was a thin line, her nostrils flared in secret anger. She didn't like my questions. It made me more determined.

'Just someone I knew from Evergreen. As you say, it was wet. And I'm not heartless.' She threw her hair over one shoulder and leant against the sofa, one hand draped along the back.

'She looked familiar. I thought it was someone I knew.'

'I'm afraid those girls do all come "after a type" and many look similar. Pretty. Bright. Garish. The kind that draw the eye for a moment, before boredom sets in and they are discarded. Some of them will change their names, too.' Grace drained her glass and rested it on the tray. She wouldn't like feeling cornered; I should have held my tongue. 'I do *like* your interest in my fallen women. I'll take you there when you're stronger. In your condition it wouldn't do to be exposed to such things. Your mind must be calm.'

Exhibit 23

Skeleton of conjoined baby with double skull.
Siam. c. 1800s.

Lucius was pleased with the wings. 'Somehow more beautiful without feathers.' I couldn't agree, but I liked the look on his face as he held up the sketchbook to admire the drawings. A new style for me, mixing fat stripes of brown and red sealing wax with delicate ink pen nibs. Showing the difference in bone and sinew more effectively. I enjoyed experimenting, seeing how such technique gave the pitiful skeletons life. Ribbons of coloured wax, sharpened to new points with my penknife between every stroke, showed the puffed sinews folded and then stretched out taut, as they would be under flesh when birds took flight.

While I watched he labelled one of the sketches, in painstaking detail.

'You seem happy. I'm glad to have been the cause.' Maybe this would lead to us working together, side by side in his workroom, me drawing the threads of his imagination together with my pens. A dream I hoped he shared.

Finally he finished, replaced the pen in his waistcoat pocket, and looked up as though he'd forgotten I was there.

'What's next?' I asked.

Lucius wore his pocket watch upturned on its chain. He glanced down. It was inscribed with Old Dr Everley's initials, as though his father still owned his time. 'I've to be in Kensington at eight. Linnean Society. Just as interested as the collectors, probably more so.'

But what was next for me? 'I'm much at leisure, as you know. I could draw some more?' He waited. I searched for the right words to make him see that I understood. That I wanted to help. As his wife. 'I can draw fins. I could draw them together with these, to show how the limb buds grow.' And we could study them together. You could look as me as Ambrose does Caroline. Write my name on your papers.

'It might help. I have some dogfish in saline in the workroom. Sharks really, I suppose. They've been there for a day or two but I'm hoping the water will keep the fins supple. If they dry they'll become stiff, shrivelled. Though they're large fish and their fins should be easy enough to fan away from the body to draw.'

'I'd like to see them.' Sepia ink would work for sharkskin. Yellow-brown wash for the rough body and fine brown strokes for the thin feathers of webbing on the fins. I would need to buy new materials to make the sketches perfect.

'Five fins, that's the thing. Two on the back for balance and speed, and the caudal fin of course, for steering. But they've two separate clumps of fin underneath, spaced apart. It's those that interest me.'

'Fish with feet,' I said quietly.

'No.' Lucius drew his eyebrows together as he did when he wanted to make himself clear. It gave him the look of a vengeful god. 'Not a mixture of creatures. I'm almost certain of it. Growth takes place so slowly in the natural world. When we find the evidence, it will be elegantly evolved.'

'Will I draw them in the water?' Was I to be allowed inside the rooms alone?

'I'll have Barker bring them to the library, they can stay out of the saline for a while. They might smell. I'll leave some alum with them.' He put my wings into a pile, tucked them under his arm and patted my shoulder on the way past. 'Try to get an early night.'

Overstimulated by thoughts of how the drawings might work, I settled myself to start some sketching again and realised I was also down to the last inch of ink. I could hardly go alone to buy materials. I'd have to see Caroline. Would two of us looking this way attract attention? Since my shape had become obvious, I'd mostly stayed indoors. Lucius had stopped taking me to dinners. In some ways London circles were more worldly than home – women drinking, discussing the fallen, openly flirting with others at dinner. And yet I wouldn't be welcome in my altered dresses and soft boots. My belly was a stark reminder of mortal weakness.

While my mind wandered, my hand moved across the page, accompanied by the soothing sound of a scratching nib. Lines followed lines, for once not copying intricate detail but sweeping across the paper. Bells rang downstairs. Carriage wheels came and went. I silently wished Lucius luck with his new group. When I looked down at the page, I had imagined and drawn a creature coming out of the ocean, growing the feet and hands it needed to move in a world without water.

I must have new materials if I was to draw, and I enlisted Tizzy's help with concealing my shape so I could venture outside.

'You must be carrying twins in there.' Tizzy laughed at her own joke and re-rolled the tape measure, dropping one of the pins she held gripped between her teeth.

'You'll swallow those if you're not careful,' I pretended to scold, but I could never be cross with Tizzy for long. 'I don't think I

199

can be. Wouldn't I know?' Twins featured in the Everley family, according to Lucius, every other generation. Edmond had half strangled his twin. The same thing had happened to his great-uncles, one of whom didn't survive. Pushing into the wall of my belly, I tried to feel for discernible limbs.

'Don't know. Not always, I suppose. Your little one certainly moves around a lot. I'm not sure he'd have room if there were more with him.' Tizzy lifted the dress back over my head, taking care not to scratch me with the line of pins she'd used to mark the area to cut and insert new material. 'I can feel him now.' She put her hand on my bump, laughing as a fierce kick moved it up and down.

'Thank you, Tizzy. You've been so kind. The material couldn't be a better match and your sewing is beautiful. Much better than mine.' It was as much as I could say without tears.

'It's my job, Mrs Everley.'

'Do call me Maddie.'

'You know Mrs B don't like it.'

'Mrs Barker isn't here.'

'No. But don't you sometimes think she has spyholes about the place?'

Hard to laugh when it could so easily be true. 'She's just very particular about things being done right. She's managed this house a long time.'

'Don't we know it.' Tizzy tutted and a spray of pins flew from one side of her mouth onto the floor. I tried to bend to help pick them up and she put out a hand to stay me. Warmth from her fingers shocked my skin. 'Don't you dare. You'll do yourself a mischief like that.'

Her concern was touching. 'Thank you for looking after me.' If only I could keep her here with me. Curl on her lap. Be held like a child. I felt still with Tizzy, as though the Everleys didn't matter. As though everything would turn out as it should.

'Someone's got to.' She shook her head, but I could see that she was smiling. 'This bodice is a real job, though. It'll take me hours to get it looking just right. Probably going to grow a lot more as well.'

'Really?' My breasts were already twice their usual size; the idea they would grow more was alarming. Hopefully Tizzy was exaggerating. Suddenly it struck me that she would know better than anyone. 'Isn't it . . . hard for you? After everything?' Her face fell, and I kicked myself. 'I'm sorry. I shouldn't have said anything. I just wanted you to know that I realise it isn't easy for you to be around me, around this, after everything that . . .'

'You can say it, it's alright.' Tizzy's eyes were bright, her chin jutted forward. 'I was going to keep her though. I wouldn't have let them take her to the Foundling Hospital.'

'I assumed . . . please, if you don't want to talk about it?' She batted her hands impatiently. Perhaps it would do her good not to bottle things up. 'I assumed that your child was adopted, like the others.'

'She didn't survive. Didn't even see her. They said it would upset me too much. Never even got to hold her.'

'I'm so sorry, Tizzy.'

'There's a shop on Marlborough Crescent, photography studio, where you can take them to get a photograph done. I would have liked that. Don't have anything now to remember. Just this.' She held up a beautifully embroidered rose, sewn in different pinks, surrounded by a ring of spiked leaves. 'They said I'd need a token for the Foundling, so I played along, sewed this for her. I was never going to take her though. I would have run if I'd had to. Then in the end there was no need. Just this. Rose was going to be her name.'

Tizzy sat down on the bed and I moved to comfort her, though I was the one who cried. Her slight body was surprisingly muscular beneath my arm. 'Rose *is* her name,' I said, 'she's watching you from above, at peace.'

'Couldn't understand it. She was such a lively thing. Always kicking me, like yours. They made me stop work at Evergreen. I'd have carried on. Working never hurt Ma. But they was all "rest in the afternoon" and "good for the baby" like I was ill or something.'

'I'm sure they meant well.'

'I wanted to see her though. They could have let me see her.' She leant against me and sighed deeply. I felt the warmth of her skin beneath the thin cotton dress, breathed the laundry scent of her pinafore. 'Happens all the time, doesn't it? Mrs Atherton said I should think myself lucky. Said it would have been hard for me to bring up a child on my own.'

'Did she?' Such coldness. Grace spoke like Lucius, practical, clinical. Necessary in his profession, but I would have thought some compassion could help at Evergreen. 'Mrs Atherton doesn't know everything.'

'Don't know where we'd have lived. I couldn't go home, could I? Everyone knowing. Couldn't go back to work anyway.'

Tizzy had told me before about The Green Man, the pub by the market in her hometown where the traders ate breakfast and returned after closing if business was good. Her eyes shone when she talked about it, how she'd loved serving drinks and cleaning tables, how the landlord liked her to be nice to the customers. It seemed that some of the customers didn't know how to be nice in return. If she'd gone back it would have happened again probably. She was better off here in some ways, though she hated blacking grates almost as much as she hated Mrs Barker. And she was too good for us, anyway. In a fine dress, with her beautiful hair loose, she could have society eating from her elegant hands.

'I'm sad for Rose, and you, Tizzy. But I'm glad to have you here. I don't know what I'd do without you.'

'You wouldn't have much to wear at the moment.' Tizzy's good spirits returned quickly. *No point in being gloomy*, she'd said before, *only brings the gloom to everyone else.* She was right too. The more I sank into myself the less company I became. I should stir myself to visit Caroline.

Insistent bells began to ring on the ground floor. 'Almost time for lunch.' Tizzy folded the dress, deftly slotted the last of the pins into a needle case. 'I'll finish this later. What do you think you could manage today?'

'Could you do it? Something light, some fish perhaps.' I couldn't face one of Mrs Barker's dishes. I shifted my weight and the baby pushed itself up under my ribs until the thought of eating made me feel nauseous. Standing made me sigh; I had to sit again to put on my shoes, forcing my swollen feet inside them. It was hard to recognise myself in the glass. I was changing. Like Lucius's creature leaving the ocean, slowly morphing into something unrecognisable from its former self.

I was left to myself all afternoon, too tired to leave the house. I dined alone and retired early but was woken by the sound of voices. I wasn't imagining things, whatever Lucius thought. Clear voices shouting to one another. Short, intermittent wails. Ariadne scratched at the door as though she worried too, but I didn't want her coming with me. Bending awkwardly, I patted her bed and she curled round in it, propping her head on her front paws and staring up at me with her huge sorrowful eyes. 'I'm not scolding you. Good girl. I'll be back in a moment.' Trying to sound braver than I felt. Usually we were both too drowsy to venture out at this time of night, but I'd stopped drinking the cocoa because I worried for the baby. Instead I poured it into the drainpipe by the window. There was so much rain it would have washed clean away.

The floorboards were ice to my bare feet, little slivers of cold air pushing up between them. I reached for the letter opener on the dresser, holding it stiffly out in front of me, and opened my bedroom door. Footsteps along the corridor, a flash of light. I followed, eyes adjusting to the dark, my own breath heavy and loud. I couldn't move quickly. The baby sat high and pushed against my ribs, his weight awkward unless I shuffled with a rolling gait. Just as I reached Lucius's rooms, I saw a figure. Pale skin, loose red hair. Layers of white petticoats like a ghost in a story. Old Mrs Everley, it must be. All the time I'd thought the house was haunted by their father, it was *she* who stalked the night. I screamed, dropped the paperknife; it clattered to the floor. The ghost disappeared and suddenly Lucius was there.

I crouched to the floor, covering my face with my hands. My heart beat so fast that the baby began to kick. I breathed slowly, deeply. When I opened my eyes, Lucius was edging towards me, his left hand out with palm raised, as though fending off a wild creature. He moved slowly to where the knife lay on the floor, keeping eye contact, reaching for it with his right hand.

'I wasn't going to hurt anyone.'

His fingers closed around the blade and drew it towards him. 'What did you think you were doing?'

'I heard voices.'

'I'm the only one here. I was working. The Barkers and Tizzy are long asleep, as we thought you were.'

We? Did he talk to his mother's ghost? His shirt was loose over his breeches, as though he'd thrown it on quickly. 'I saw someone . . . something. Here in the corridor. A woman wearing white. She had . . . she looked like . . .' I didn't want to upset him. Was I really the only one who felt the things in this house? She looked like his mother, like Grace.

'Do you think this is good for the baby, Maddie? This nonsense?' He put the letter opener carefully into his top pocket, as though the blade might attack him of its own accord, and leant back on his heels. 'You're becoming hysterical. I don't know what's wrong with you.'

Surely he didn't think I meant him harm? I hung my head.

'I think it's high time you talked to someone other than Venables.'

Sighting the ghost left me weakened and fearful. I knew what I'd seen. It couldn't have been Grace, why would she wander the corridors half dressed? Why would Lucius claim to be alone? My husband apparently worried for my sanity and I barely trusted my own senses. When Dr Venables prescribed rest, I wrote to Caroline, asking for art materials, and she arrived two days later in a Hatchards delivery wagon with a large parcel of papers, charcoal and paint.

'What are you reading?' Caroline looked pretty, blue eyes set off by a dress the colour of the irises that grew by the Lynton pond, her cheeks flushed by the chill. The sickness that plagued her early pregnancy had gone and she appeared full of energy, moving around as gracefully as before. As I watched her, I felt my own discomfort keenly. I held up the book.

'Why would you read that!' She gave a cry of dismay that surprised me for a moment.

I turned the book to face me. Below the title, *Medical Freaks*, was a delicate woodcut illustration of a conjoined foetus, two skulls on curved necks protruding from a single torso.

'Something Tizzy said, about having twins. I thought I'd better read up. They're common in the Everley family, apparently.'

'Doesn't Grace have twins?'

I nodded.

'Do you think it's likely?'

'Not sure. Tizzy thinks not.' A sudden movement from the baby made me shift uncomfortably. 'I'm an awful lot bigger than you, Caro.'

'You would *know*.'

'It does feel like one.'

Caroline's eyes travelled from my bump along my legs to where my feet were soaking in a mustard bath, my swollen ankles veined purple-blue.

'I wasn't expecting visitors.' I began to remove my feet and wipe them, wrapping them in the towel-cloth for warmth.

She took the book from me and flicked through its pages, her face a picture of disgust. 'Are you worried about having twins?'

'I'm worried about having a baby at all. Are you not? It seems so strange. I have no idea how to care for one, and as for two, even if both survived, how could they be held together? Or nursed?'

'But you'll have help with all of that.'

A brief flash of envy rose at Caroline's careless tone. The Fairlys' household was full of staff, and she'd already told me they'd added nursemaid to the list. Her family lived close by, in Highgate. Who would help *me*? Mother was days away, Isabel would not tear herself from the chance of marriage. How could I lean too hard on poor Tizzy after everything she'd suffered? I didn't answer.

Caroline closed the book with a look of distaste. 'No wonder you're worried. Let's find you something else to read.'

I made a note of where she replaced it. Fascination for the illustrations would bring me back to the book later. Though the images were gruesome, there was a gentle appreciation in the way the artists had sketched them, beautifully rendered drawings of deformed bodies and freaks as well as twins or even litters of three or four. Four! How could that happen? Research to keep to myself. I wriggled my feet and looked around for my stockings.

'Really I would like some fresh air.'

'I can take you in the carriage?'

'Lucius says I'm to stay indoors.'

Caroline gave me a questioning look. Obeying one's husband wasn't something she felt should be a rule of law.

'He's just concerned. The last time I went out I returned feeling quite unwell.'

'Where were you?'

'Saying goodbye to Mother and Isabel.'

'But that was ages ago.'

Caroline leant towards me, then seemed to think better of her question. It must seem strange, to have remained inside for so long, but the time had passed quickly. I had my drawing, and Tizzy, and I wasn't feeling strong. 'I haven't felt especially well. I almost fainted there. It was so noisy and there was . . .' I didn't want to talk about the puppets and the beaten baby's dirty flat gown. Nor could I mention the ghost of Mrs Everley. Suddenly I felt I had little to say. 'I'll ask Lucius about a drive. It can't hurt if I feel well enough.'

'A mothers' meeting. How cosy. I do hope you're not planning to go against your doctor's advice, Madeleine.' Grace swept into the library and stood by the window. Sunlight burnt her hair in streaks of orange. She flashed a smile that didn't reach her eyes.

'Good afternoon.' Caroline, who'd been pacing around the room ever since she arrived, sat down in what I saw as deliberate defiance, as though she knew she may be asked to leave. Grace made no secret of her hatred for Dr Stepwood and contempt for Ambrose.

'I'm charmed today, two visitors, neither of whom I was expecting. We'll be quite the party for afternoon tea.' I tried to stand, thinking of refreshments, but she reached the bell before me. When Tizzy arrived, Grace asked pointedly whether Caroline planned to stay. 'Please do,' I replied quickly for her, 'it's so long since I've seen you.'

'Very well, Harriet, tea for three. Bring the fruitcake.' Anyone would mistake her for the lady of the house. A wonder she didn't just move in. Room was something we didn't lack. By Caroline's face, I imagined she had the same thoughts. 'What have you been doing, you're not fit for upstairs. Have you forgotten everything we taught you?'

Tizzy scowled and hid her dirty hands below her apron. It looked as though she'd been blacking the grates again. Mrs Barker seemed to enjoy the sight of her on hands and knees. If it wasn't the grates, it was the back steps. More than anything I wanted Tizzy to join me for afternoon tea with Caroline – it would have been cosy to see my favourites together and I wanted Caroline to like her. It was important they were friends.

'Thank you,' I said. She nodded and flounced back through the door. I would have to tell Lucius we needed more help. When the baby came I'd need her with me. 'Please don't speak to Tizzy like that,' I bravely squared up to Grace. 'She's managing everything herself. It won't do when the baby comes and I need help.'

'Her name is Harriet – it's not proper to call her that, no wonder she's forgetting her place. You're very unlikely to need any help,' said Grace. 'Besides, I will be here.' Unbuttoning her jacket, she came to my chair. My heart sank. It seemed that she planned to stay and my afternoon with Caroline was over. Grace drew a shawl around my shoulders. 'Madeleine needs rest, she is not to be excited. There'll be no more talk of carriage rides for today.' She squeezed my shoulders, and I felt her rings dig into my flesh. 'This baby is more important than anything.'

Had I judged too harshly? Perhaps all she wanted was for her brother to be happy, for our family to be happy. A new life and a new story for the house. Hope for the Everley future. I wanted it too. It seemed the one thing I could do for Lucius was to give him a family of his own. A loving place to support him against the relentless push of his profession and his pride. As if it knew, the life inside my stomach kicked and turned. My baby would be loved so much; he would change all of our lives, even Tizzy's. A baby was all that we needed.

24

The Marlborough Assizes

'You missed today's session.' Maddie looked grey and weary, as though every ounce of fight had been taken from her. 'I thought you might be ill.' I took some soup from the flask in my pack and poured it into a dirty wooden bowl I found on the floor. 'You need to keep up your strength.'

'It seems to make little difference what I say. Why listen to me when they have a dozen doctors to confirm my madness?' She looked up at me with bloodshot eyes. 'I begin to wonder whether they're right.'

Soup splashed onto her filthy dress as I pushed the bowl into her hands and urged her to drink it. 'I made it myself.' I'd forgotten the spoon. It didn't matter, her hands shook too much to eat that way. I nudged the bowl upwards to show she should drink from it and watched while she took a sip. 'Of course they're not right. They're trying to silence you and they're winning.'

'They were always going to win.' She handed back the empty bowl. At least she had eaten something. 'If I didn't end up here, I'd be in St Margary's with Annie or . . . like Tizzy.'

'What happened to Tizzy?'

Maddie wrung her hands together. She looked desperate, wild. If anyone saw her that way they'd agree with the court in an instant.

Everything about her appearance and gestures indicated madness.

'Grace sent word to the guards to tell me she was dead. It was my fault, Caro, I should never have asked her to help. She was used all her life and I was just as bad as everyone else.'

That didn't sound right. I thought for a moment. Why would Grace be sending notes to Maddie's cell? She'd disowned and condemned her. What reason could she have to bring her news? Unless it was to undermine her completely.

'You don't know that it's true. What if she just said that to make things worse?' I knelt down by the mattress, gagging at the smell, and placed my hands on Maddie's shoulders. 'Grace lied to you about everything. Why would this be different?' Was it fair of me to give her false hope? If I was wrong and Grace told the truth, it would simply be prolonging Maddie's pain. But it might give her enough hope to fight. I could see in her eyes that she wanted to believe me.

'Who spoke today?'

'They used your sketchbooks. No-one was there except Barker, who said he'd found them in the library and thought they should be seen.' The gathered crowds had enjoyed passing them along, crowing over the contents. *Unnatural, that's what it is.* Even the magistrate had suggested bones and relics were unusual subjects for young ladies, asking if Maddie ever bothered herself to draw flowers or landscapes. Barker, obsequious with his bowed head and shiny morning suit, took miserable pleasure in confirming her only interest lay in things that were dead.

'All my sketches?'

'Two books. Mostly filled with wings, bones and relics.'

'I bet they enjoyed those.'

'They're just drawings.'

'Drawings that will help me hang. I should have listened to

Mother. If I hadn't been so insistent that he let me . . .'

'Nonsense. You have an incredible talent that you were selfless enough to want to use to help your husband. Why should women be prevented from working?' The complaint was dear to my heart. Ambrose's clinic was doing well, and yet he turned away patients because he was hopeless at managing the paperwork. I could help him. And his pride refused to let me. I understood Maddie's longing only too well and I had not half her talent.

'You're braver than I am.'

When this was over, I determined to ask Ambrose again. No, I wouldn't ask him, I would draw up a system of managing his patients and I would tell him. 'I'm not brave at all, Maddie. You make me brave.'

She lifted her head and I saw tear tracks streaked with dirt. A deep-red weal on her left cheek. She mustn't give up. Along the corridor a faint clanging noise started, growing louder, like something metal being banged against the metal doors.

'Five minutes or I'm coming in,' the guard shouted through the door.

'What can I do? Maddie, tell me what I can do.' I threw my hands up in despair. 'I know you didn't do this. I won't let you give up.'

'There's a chance . . .' Maddie started as metal clanged against the wall.

'What! We will take it. Just tell me and I will take it for you.'

Maddie held out her left hand, placing her right finger on her lips to tell me to be quiet before miming writing. She wanted to write something. I rummaged in my pack for the notebook I kept in court, handed it over with a short lead pencil. With one eye on the door, she took the pad and scribbled furiously, thrusting it back to me just before the door opened and the guard called me out.

'You need to feed your prisoners properly,' I said, covering the paper with my pack. 'She's not well.'

'Should have thought of that before she went murdering babies, shouldn't she?' The guard twirled his right hand around his ear. 'Loopy. Like they said. Threw her dinner at the wall yesterday, half of it went all over me.'

I covered a smile. There was hope for Maddie yet. Though it might explain the mark on her cheek. The guards wouldn't care that she was a woman.

Outside, I walked to the end of the street before opening the paper, hoping for some proof or confession. But she'd written:

Search garden. Find Stoneham the fossil hunter. Charmouth.

Exhibit 25

Bone tongue depressor. Early surgical. c. 1720.

Lucius disappeared as soon as he'd announced Dr Threlfall, 'to leave us to get acquainted'. An awkward silence grew. Why send another doctor to interrogate me? I had little enough to say to Venables. This one seemed barely old enough to be qualified. His jacket was lavender, his shirt a froth of lace. Why should I put him at ease? I waited, silent. Threlfall cleared his throat with a cough.

'May I sit?' he asked.

I didn't care if he stood on his head. He took the chair next to mine and I turned towards the window.

'Has your husband explained why I'm here?'

'He's concerned that I grow nervous.'

'Do you agree with him?'

Be careful. All the things I wanted to say could hurt me. I tried to make my face less sullen. 'I don't know. He's kind to be worried.'

'Are you troubled by anything in particular?'

A house filled with ghosts and spirits. The smell of death that followed me everywhere. Ravens in the garden and dead crows in the house. The stain of murder on the Everley crest.

'I *have* grown more sensitive, I suppose.' His pen remained poised; he wanted my darkest fears.

'Lucius explained that you've been hearing . . . seeing . . . things that are not there?'

I did not reply. Pointless to protest. He wouldn't believe me either and I wouldn't give him the satisfaction of describing it.

'These things, voices and so on, do they accompany physical feelings?'

'Such as?'

'Headaches, perhaps? Pains?'

It seemed a good idea to put him off the scent. 'Sometimes. I do suffer from headaches. Often I hear voices when my headaches wake me at night.'

'We call those auditory hallucinations.'

'Unless they are really there,' I said sharply and instantly regretted it. Threlfall scribbled it down in his notebook.

'They can seem very real to the person hearing them.' Maybe I *should* tell him. All of it. Might wipe the smirk from his face. 'Do the voices usually say the same things? Do you hear them use your name?'

The voices were always raised, arguing, sometimes screaming. I remembered every word I'd heard, and my name was never used, though I was certain they spoke about me. How could I say that? It sounded mad. It was mad.

'No.'

'They don't talk directly to you?' He sounded disappointed.

'No.'

'They don't ask you to do things?'

'No.' What did he imagine?

He stroked his clean-shaven chin, then wrote a line or two in his book. 'You seem not to want to answer my questions.'

'I *am* answering.'

'But not elaborating.'

'I wasn't aware that was the request.'

Threlfall sighed. 'Do you enjoy games, Mrs Everley?'

Was he about to claim that I imagined it all for attention? Who was he to come here and pretend that he knew about me? I fixed him with what I hoped was a hard stare. 'No, I do not.'

'Did you hear voices on the night you were found with a knife?'

'Yes. That's why I left my room.'

'Why did you feel you needed a knife?'

A good question. For my protection. Would I have used it? Probably not. It didn't even make me feel safe. And what good would it be against a spirit? I should be honest with myself and admit that ghosts were what I feared in this house. The spirits that came to my room and moved things around, took things from me. If I said that out loud, then Lucius and this foolish young man would have me sent to St Margary's. But I *did* hear voices. And I *had* seen Lucius's mother walk the corridors, pale as moonlight.

'It wasn't a knife. A letter opener.'

'A blade nevertheless.' Threlfall walked over to the fireplace. He stood with his back to me, warming his hands. 'Did you intend to harm somebody with it?'

A brief vision of myself stabbing him hard through his lavender jacket made me gasp. I drew my hand across my mouth. Such violent thoughts. Where did they come from? 'I could never harm anyone.' Oh, but I could. And by the look on his face Threlfall knew it. What was to become of me in this house of nightmare?

After Threlfall's visit I felt even less safe. If they wanted, Lucius and Grace could have me disappear at any moment, and I determined to see Caroline's baby before I lost the chance.

'Come with me.' My fingers gripped Tizzy's hand tightly, but she shook her head.

'Mrs B will miss me in an instant. Go on with you if you're going, or you'll be missed 'n all.'

I tucked a stray curl back under Tizzy's cap, resisting the urge to hold her face in my hands. I'd have to be brave alone. 'Thank you.' She'd already put herself at risk to chase out and stop the carriage, paying a child to hold the reins three doors down. Avoiding suspicion. I was still required to rest, prohibited excitement of any kind. Anything likely to cause merriment was banned. Since Caroline was my only other friend, such rules seemed deliberately designed to keep us apart. We'd written most days, sharing stories of our changing bodies, our hopes for the next few months, our dreams for our children. They'd be friends, of course, though she hoped for a girl and I was certain I carried a boy. I'd taken to calling him Arthur. There was talk of them sharing a governess, jokes that Ambrose might get ideas. But we hadn't visited in weeks, and I had to see her child before my own confinement. For courage. And for comfort. I felt close to tears most of the time and more than anything I needed affection.

The driver, half asleep under heavy-lidded eyes, helped me heave myself in. Tizzy must have gone to the rank to wake him, making the most of the few hours I had free during nap time. What would he look like, Mortimer Fairly? Caro had given birth to a boy after all. Ambrose came to tell me himself. A gesture so touching that I wept on his shoulder until Barker asked him to leave, implying that he'd upset me.

The carriage wheels spun on frost, spattering Tizzy as she stood waving, still shouting instruction. Poor Tizzy. She'd be in trouble over her apron again. Fingers crossed Mrs Barker wouldn't notice, though the old woman constantly watched for opportunities to scold.

* * *

Caro and Ambrose were in the nursery when I arrived, sitting on the low sofa with fingers entwined, watching Mortimer sleep. They looked happy, rested. She wore a dress so cinched that I marvelled at a woman's ability to shapeshift in such a short space of time. The baby was barely a month old. The same time before my own would arrive. So many questions came to mind that I wished Ambrose would leave us to talk freely. It wasn't for men to hear. Even doctors.

'Lovely as it is to see you, shouldn't you be lying-in by now?' Ambrose greeted me with a kiss; his warm skin was freshly shaved and smooth, damp with cologne. My own husband never gave me such a welcome.

'I feel well, better than I have for a while, and I so wanted to see Mortimer in case . . . something happened to prevent me visiting.'

'Try not to worry. It unsettles the baby.'

Easy for a man to say. Was Ambrose there for the birth? He wasn't a general doctor like Lucius, who'd delivered his own sister's children. I couldn't imagine any of it. Was it worse to have my husband there, or even Grace if she tried to attend? She'd told me that they delivered Evergreen babies together. No-one had told me what to expect, and the only person I felt able to ask was Caro.

'May I see him?' Caro stayed on the seat. Was it still hard for her to move? Ambrose indicated the vast wooden bed with its caged sides, and I peeped inside. My heart melted at the sight of his new-ancient face, a tiny mummy wrapped in swaddling bands. Smooth and peaceful, blue-veined eyes closed, a pearl-white sheen on his skin. Such abundant hair. Sticky tufts covered the pillow. One hand, free of swaddling, waved creased fingers through the air as though hoping to catch dreams. A sweet milk smell surrounded him. 'He's beautiful,' I breathed. 'Not a girl after all. Lucky you had readied a name.'

'My father's,' said Ambrose proudly.

'We'll save "Charlotte" for the next time,' said Caroline, smiling at Ambrose. Perhaps there was my answer. Birth can't have been so terrible if she was already planning the next.

One eye popped open as though he felt me leaning over his crib, and Mortimer set to wailing loudly, his face crumpled and red with effort. Startled, I jumped back, and Ambrose laughed.

'They do that. Like little alarms. Something else to get used to.' He reached in and scooped him up. Almost immediately the noise stopped. I held out my arms. 'Heavier than he looks. You'll need to sit.'

Caroline shifted along to make room and, when I was settled, I took the baby on my lap like a parcel. Heavy and hot to the touch, hair stuck with sweat and back arching with the effort of escape from the cloths that held him. After a few moments of gentle rocking, he quietened and began to stare at my face, quick eyes searching.

'You'll have yours before long.' Caroline reached over to smooth his hair. 'And the boys will have each other, just like we do. We'll sit together while they play, and we will all grow old together.'

For a moment I allowed myself to picture the scene, enjoying the warmth of close friendship, though I knew well that plans could change. A family's fortune might turn on a hairpin.

'They will be lifelong friends,' I said, and Mortimer began to wail again, even more loudly than before.

'He's hungry.' Caroline rang the bell at her side. 'Always hungry.'

A plump girl with a matronly body and the fresh face of a child answered the call. Nodding at each of us in turn, she took the baby and threw him up on her shoulder, turning in the same movement, and closing the door gently as she left. Presently the crying ceased. So, Caro didn't feed him herself. Another difference between the drawing rooms of London and the families of Cheshire. Another of my questions answered, and another raised. What did Lucius expect? If he, or Grace, were to hire a nursemaid then I wished to meet her, to choose her, if possible, even if that meant a visit to Evergreen House. She would spend as much time with Arthur as I did.

'How is Lucius?' asked Ambrose. 'I missed the last few meetings to be here, with everything going on.'

'You've been such a dear,' said Caroline.

'He's well.' What could I tell them? He still spent an hour or so with me each day, made sure I ate what he prescribed, checked my pulse. Sometimes he brought me things to draw, strange things with joints that pushed through skin in unusual places. In return I sketched them, increasingly adding the creatures of my imagination, trying to show him what he sought from stone as proof for his theories. It was the oddest marriage, I realised, looking at my friends. 'His research progresses. He's in Dorset now for a week and has another trip planned soon.'

'Babies don't always wait for convenience,' said Caroline, brow furrowed in concern. 'You don't want him so far away at the moment.'

If he weren't away, I'd never have managed this visit. 'I believe he's close to finding what he seeks.' What we had might not be conventional. It wasn't a house full of flowers but, in our work, we managed a certain level of trust. Caro would be pleased he let me help and besides, it was all we had, and I must try to make the best of it. 'I've been assisting Lucius, too, as you suggested. With the sketches and drawings. I can show you, when you visit.'

Caroline turned to Ambrose. 'Maddie has such a talent. We

should ask you to draw Mortimer for us. Would you? They grow so quickly.'

She wouldn't like the last sketches I'd done. Perhaps it would be nice, after all, to draw something pleasant. 'I'd be delighted. But I need to get back before . . .' I checked myself. No-one would understand my fear of upsetting the Barkers. 'Tizzy booked the carriage to wait. She'll worry if I don't return soon.'

Ambrose had to shake the driver awake. He slept hunched down in his greatcoat, hands tightly gripping the reins as though someone might try to steal his cob from under him. As he woke, his arms jerked up, pulling the reins, causing the horse to stamp its giant fringed feet. The carriage rocked as I climbed in and I fell back against the seat, struggling to pull down my skirts before we sped away. Ambrose waved in the distance and I could not stop my tears. He was a good man, a good husband. He'd go back inside and sit with Caro, tell her stories, ask her opinion. When they held dinners again, they'd choose the guests together, she'd select the service she preferred, and he would compliment her taste. I saw it plainly. When things were settled it would do us good to spend more time with them. Lucius could learn from Ambrose, he'd spent too many years with his ghosts.

Frost still rimed the road, crunching under our wheels and showering the pavements with a fine ice dust. The streets were busy. A hawker shouted, peddling chestnuts from a huge iron pan that hung from his neck on a bridle strap. At his strident call, the horse reared again, throwing me hard against the seat. Sudden pain gripped my middle. Worse on the left side. My stomach felt seized by huge unseen hands. Gasping for breath, I braced myself against the carriage, calling to the driver to slow down. He didn't listen and the rest of the journey passed in a blur, doubled over against the pain, holding my breath and exhaling with such force I could not hear anything else.

I didn't notice the cab draw up. Didn't notice Tizzy until she climbed up beside me and pulled me upright with her strong arms. 'Mrs B's on the hunt. She knows you left. Mrs Everley, Maddie, can you look at me? Oh sweet Mary, he's coming. We have to get you inside. Can you walk? Maddie, can you walk?' I leant on her, breathing heavily, suddenly frightened. I didn't want to be scolded by Mrs Barker. Lucius was away. Who would help me deliver this child? I clung to Tizzy.

'Gently,' Tizzy admonished the driver as he helped to lift me down. 'Bring her this way.' She threw the reins at a gawking child and promised him a penny if he held them tightly. Half of one trouser leg was missing. Just one. Why? I imagined him in a fight with a younger child, or an animal. My head swam.

'Why we going round the back?' grumbled the driver.

Tizzy gave him a coin. A grand lady, and I had to let my servants pay my way. I must remember and get it back to her somehow. I owed her so much and all I did was bring her trouble. 'You can pay the boy from that.' She turned to face me as he set me down at the back door. 'You're going to have to be strong now. The quicker we can get you upstairs the sooner I can make you comfortable.'

Taking a deep breath, I threw myself at the stairs and began to pull myself up on all fours. Slowly and painfully, I reached the bedroom where Tizzy began to take off my boots and loosen my dress, spreading a blanket for me to lie on. 'You're safe now,' she soothed, 'I'll fetch a hot pan for you to hold.'

Warm and comfortable at last, propped on pillows in my own room. The stomach pains diminished and I found that I could breathe again. 'You'll be tired,' said Tizzy, 'takes it out of you, all that huffing and puffing. We'll send for Lucius. Have a sleep if you can. You might have a long night ahead.'

Sharp pains woke me. As I struggled to focus in the dark room, strong hands pulled my wet hair back so roughly it could only have been Mrs Barker. She had bruised poor Annie easily and I was frightened by her vicious grip. I did not want her here. Where was my husband? He was there at his nephews' birth, though much good it had done them. Had Grace been treated like this? Or was difficult childbirth the Everley curse? I thought of the books in the library – those hideous images of babies born deformed or damaged in the process. And of Amelia, who had not survived. I should have asked why.

Where was Tizzy? She would calm my nerves. I tried to call for her and a hand clamped over my mouth. I wanted to bite down hard but the hand was firm. Sweat poured from my brow, stinging my eyes and blurring my vision. It ran down my neck in clammy rivulets, sticking to the nightdress Tizzy had fetched. My skin crawled. I clawed at the cotton, trying to rip it off, and the hands that had fastened my hair gripped tightly to my wrists, bent my arms behind me. I took the chance to scream and another figure loomed in, pushed a rag into my mouth. The scent of lime and chemicals clung to his fingers, faint cigar smoke on his clothes. Lucius. Perhaps now I would be treated kindly?

The rag was powerfully scented and my head began to swim. Flashes of pain swept from my stomach, across my chest; my arms ached in their unnatural position. I heard voices. Snatches of speech in low urgent whispers.

'She was unprepared.'

'Racing all over town.'

'A higher dose.'

'May not be another chance.'

I screamed again. Loudly this time, in the hope I would bring Tizzy to my aid. The hands pulled at my arms and I felt someone lift me from the bed, then another unseen person grabbed at my legs and pushed them into something cold and hard like leather. Straps were tightened, buckles fastened. My wrists were restrained to the bedposts. As I opened my mouth to scream again, a metal bar was wedged between my teeth and something pulled over my head.

'She can bite on the bridle.'

'Hysterical.'

'Won't be long now.'

The voices became faint and I closed my eyes, slumped back against the pillows. I felt feverish, cold sweat on burning skin, my head pounding. I swam in and out of nightmares. Visions of half-formed babies and lizard creatures merged together with the Barkers, armed with kitchen knives, bearing down upon my bed. Lucius began to roar in anger. Annie returned, still screaming. I felt water thrown across my legs, and a fish-like creature with clammy fins slipped out of my body and lay gasping on the bedroom floor.

It was dawn when I woke, feeling as though weeks had passed. My head pounded, nausea rose and the room smelt strange and sour. Three figures stood in the corner, impossible to identify in the dim light. As I struggled to sit up, they dispersed; two disappeared and one moved towards the bed. So Lucius had returned. He must have travelled through the night. I was touched by his concern, but when I opened my mouth to tell him so I found I couldn't speak.

'Shh, Maddie. You've had chloroform. Don't worry about the baby, you need to rest.'

Why did he insist on saying 'the baby'? His name was Arthur. And where was Tizzy? It wasn't her in the corner, they were all too tall. More doctors? Was something wrong? Inside me felt still. Perhaps the chloroform had affected Arthur too. I moved my hands across my stomach. It felt flat, squashed – the bump was gone. 'Where is he?' I cried.

Lucius took an object from his bag, something I recognised from the small museum. A tongue depressor. Could it be the same one? Both made of bone with wide, splayed ends. He pushed it into my mouth and held it in place with one hand while he turned to speak with the figures in the corner. The bone tasted earthy. I couldn't swallow. The questions that welled in my throat were silenced. Only when they'd finished talking and the other figures had left did he remove it.

Lucius took a blue bottle from his pocket and shook a few drops of liquid onto his handkerchief. As he held it over my mouth and nose, I caught another scent beneath the sickly sweetness. Something acrid and sour. The smell of the lime room clung to his hands.

When I woke again the room was dark, but they were all still there. I must remain calm, or I knew Lucius wouldn't hesitate to use his blue bottle. 'I heard him. I *know* I did.' The way they looked at each other, the pity in their eyes. I wanted to scream at them.

'Not from this house, Maddie.' Grace sat gingerly on the counterpane and patted my hand. Why was she in my room? Why were any of them there? Lucius, the Barkers. Crowded around the bed like pall-bearers.

'Yes. From downstairs. A baby crying. I heard it several times throughout the night, but I was too tired to fully wake and I slept again.'

'A dream. It's understandable, of course. But you must let go now.'

'Grace is right, Madeleine.' Lucius stood close enough to touch but his voice was distant.

'My child isn't dead! I know it. I can *feel* it.' And I heard a child cry. My child. Arthur was full of life, he never stopped moving. If only I could remember. I tried to pull my thoughts back. I remembered pushing, someone gripping my hands. Straining so hard the room became red, my body red-hot, muscles taut. How long was I like that? How long since? I had no idea of the time, or the day. But I was certain he lived. 'Where's Tizzy?' She would help me.

'Fetching a warming pan. We'll need to move you and change these sheets,' said Mrs Barker, a fold of linen over her arm. Shaming in front of Grace, however many children of her own she had. I tried to pull the counterpane over my arms and the sudden movement caused a searing pain between my legs. Everything felt hollow; my stomach folded in on itself, my heart was empty. I should be holding Arthur, wreathed in smiles, Lucius playing the proud father beside me. Tears welled.

Tizzy clattered through the door, holding a pan that was almost her size and struggling not to turn its contents all over the rug. She seemed surprised to see me awake. All I wanted was to feel her strong arms around me, for us to share our pain in long ragged howls. Her eyes shone as though she'd been crying. Was it for me? I wanted her tears, yet I felt guilty for causing her pain.

'Will you give poor Mrs Everley some space?' Tizzy was braver than me, looking pointedly at Grace until she rose to move away, her dress lifting to reveal delicate boots made of deep-green leather. They seemed to reach to her knees. I couldn't imagine her having the patience to wait while someone fastened all those buttons.

'Come, Lucius, while they make her comfortable. She's not going anywhere.' Had she forgotten my name?

I reached for my husband's hand and clasped it. 'What happened?' His face was serious, but he could not meet my eye. 'Where is he?'

'He's gone, Madeleine. Stillborn. It was not God's choice for us this time.'

Why would he speak of God now? I knew well he did not believe. 'Then *where* is he? I want to see him. Hold him.' Stillborn. A stone baby. I imagined his little arms held stiff like a garden statue.

'It will do you no good at all.'

'Worse not to see him.' Tizzy spoke quietly and I understood the truth of it. Her own stone baby never left her thoughts because she couldn't picture her properly. Rather the shock of reality than a haunting. Rose and Arthur would never leave us.

'I forbid it,' said Lucius. His mouth became a thin line and he pulled away his hands and disappeared with Grace. The scent of lime clung to my fingers.

Tizzy helped me into the chair by the window and my eyes watered. All I wanted was to be held. But how could I ask? I'd have to be strong. She'd done this already, alone. I would have to do the same. The barrow on the corner was setting out flowers – colourful carnations and huge red poinsettias in the colours of Christmas. If I had any coins I would fill the house with them, just to see something happy. I watched Tizzy move around the room, changing the sheets and plumping the cushions, making things pleasant in a way that left me maudlin to think someone cared so much for my comfort. She set my sketchbooks on the dresser, moving things to make space, and I noticed the locket box was returned.

'Did you find it, Tizzy?'

She shook her head, picked it up and turned it in her hands. She looked at the initials on the bottom. Could she read them? It wouldn't surprise me. She was too good for us. 'This? Is it the one you lost?'

I didn't lose it. Someone removed it deliberately and now that person had put it back. But I didn't dare say so, even to Tizzy. Because in my heart of hearts I felt it was the ghost. Who else would want it? It was Old Mrs Everley. Could she have taken Arthur too? The thought chilled me, and I knew I could never speak it out loud. It would be the end of my dignity. Perhaps the end of my freedom. Grace and Lucius watched carefully for the first sign that I'd be better off at St Margary's.

Tizzy handed over the box. It felt smooth and shiny with polish. Cold against my skin. I held it a few moments before opening it carefully. The locket was inside, resting on its velvet, gleaming as though it, too, had been cleaned. Could a spirit do such a thing?

'It's pretty,' said Tizzy. 'I'm not surprised you missed it.'

'It was Lucius's mother's.'

'The initials?'

Holding the chain, I lifted it out and laid it on my lap. Pale stone, the colour of Threlfall's jacket. The clasp was looser, it opened easily, and it was no longer empty. Inside was a tiny lock of dark brown hair, tied with a thread of purple embroidery silk. Arthur's. I shut it quickly before Tizzy asked questions. I needed to think. It was definitely empty before. And a ghost could hardly do that, could it?

'Do you believe me about the noise?' I asked. 'Did you hear it?'

'A baby crying?' Tizzy bundled the used linen and secured it with an expert knot before throwing it towards the door, ready to carry down. 'There's not a night goes by when I don't.'

Exhibit 26

Wooden pole with bone hook. Boatman's tool. c. 1820.

Tizzy finished winding the long cloth tightly across my breasts and fixed it in place with a pin before handing over my chemise. It was hard to breathe. Wads of cotton under the bindings made my chest even larger and I struggled to pull down the slip. It caught under my arms and made me feel trapped. Who had shown her how to stop her milk from coming? Grace? Whoever else helped at Evergreen, I hoped it was someone more kind. Hard to put a child from your mind when your body still wanted him there. Feeling full and empty at the same time. Milk for a missing child. At least the crying had stopped. Though every now and then the urge to search the house was too strong and I found myself wandering the corridors, opening doors, surprised to find silence. The guest rooms were all covered in dustsheets, as though visitors would never be expected. They wouldn't allow me to cover the mirrors. 'Superstitious nonsense,' Mrs Barker said smartly, pulling the shawl from my bedroom mirror. As soon as she left, I'd heaved myself up to replace it, lest Arthur's soul was stuck there for ever.

Tizzy looked careworn, older. Hopefully I wasn't the cause. Suddenly the idea of another day shut up indoors, with only Ariadne for company, was too much to bear. 'Stay with me.'

'You know I can't. The dragon's already calling and there's always so much to do.'

'I will ask for some help for you.'

Tizzy gave a sad half-smile. 'Mrs Atherton's been asked. She says there's no-one else at Evergreen we could trust, though I scarce believe that. There were some good girls there when I left. And they won't get help from anywhere else.'

'Why not?' Poor Tizzy must be as lonely as me. Worse for her after living in a house full of women and an inn full of men.

'All she says is that they're too flighty to be trusted in service.'

As I seemed to be excluded from discussions about my own staff, it appeared I wasn't to be trusted either. At some point I would need to find the strength to confront Grace. For now, I just wanted to sit with a friend.

'What will they do?'

Tizzy shrugged. 'They don't stay. They must go somewhere. Mrs Atherton says there's little use in saving anyone if she can't put them to work.'

Would she put them to other work? A sudden image of Rebecca in a yellow dress came to mind. Was she ever with Grace? Was she forced onto the streets, too flighty for service? I would drive myself mad with such thoughts and no means of escape. I must find company.

'Could you bring my writing things, please?' I imagined that Caroline had enquired, and been told to stay away. I would invite her to see me. Whether or not she brought Mortimer would be her choice. He'd be changed already, growing fast while Arthur's shadow stayed behind him.

Tizzy put the writing slope on my lap and arranged the paper and pens, as well as my stack of pressed flowers and ribbons. 'Don't tell Dr Everley I brought you those. He says you're not to be stimulated. And don't sit up for too long. You need rest.'

'Did you? Rest?'

She folded her arms. For protection, or battle. 'A little. A day or two, perhaps.'

'And then?'

'I don't know, I suppose there was work,' she shrugged, 'and it was boring with nothing to do but lie there and think about things. Wondering what she looked like. If she looked like me. I hope so. Though her pa was a real charmer.'

Of course. How else would he get away with it? Was he somewhere wondering what his child would have looked like? Was Lucius? No. It struck me suddenly that he knew, and I didn't. Had he seen something in the child that would frighten me? I could drive myself mad imagining Arthur's face.

'You agree, then, that it will do me good to have something to do. And some company.' I'd have to write to Mother too. The thought of home brought a flood of self-pitying tears. Tizzy patted my shoulder, but even as I tried to take her hand she was pulling away.

'I'll come back as soon as I can.' She clapped her hands and Ariadne padded across to her. 'She'll be needing to go out, she can slip out the back door for a bit.'

'Thank you. Keep an eye on her, please. Barker doesn't like her in the garden.'

Tizzy rolled her eyes. Ariadne looked at me for approval, head cocked to one side. The door closed behind them and my tears fell freely onto the paper. They'd blamed me, Grace and Lucius, speaking together. Not openly, but they mentioned my visit to the Fairlys', the bumping carriage, the early birth. Arthur was with me the whole time, I knew that much, I could feel him moving. I knew he was alive, but Lucius would hear no more of it. Wouldn't listen when I told him how I heard a baby crying. *You have developed a nervous disposition, Madeleine. It's not uncommon, but you mustn't dwell on things. It won't help you to recuperate.* He warned me of the madness that sets in after a difficult birth, the hysteria. Insisted Dr Threlfall should help. As he patted my blankets with his elegant hands, I fought an overwhelming urge to bite hard through his skin. More violence. I must be careful not to give myself away. I might be angry, but I wasn't going mad. I felt my baby and I heard him crying.

Writing to Caroline raised my spirits enough to dress properly and sit by the window. Over the following days I began to move more easily, though I still felt pain and was desperately lonely. Tizzy stayed away and I worried it was my fault. Had I pushed her too hard to remember? Or was she simply busy with the festive preparations, held downstairs at Mrs Barker's bidding? Christmas drew closer and I could not stay hidden for ever. Even if it made Lucius cross, I was determined to be well enough to attend church, and to please him I agreed to greet the friends he invited for supper.

For once the house looked warm and I was pleased that I'd left my room to join the others. Barker had brought in a tree that Tizzy and I spent a happy afternoon covering with paperchains and stars, while Mrs Barker baked downstairs. Candles twinkled on every table and sill, and the scents of pine and cinnamon masked the sweet-rotten smell of the house. Lucius seemed content, holding court with a group of his peers. It was good to see life in the house, the only people we had entertained since Mother left. But as soon as he saw me, Lucius tried to push me towards Threlfall.

'It's Christmas Eve,' I tried not to plead.

'I'm afraid illness doesn't care for the time of year. We're all worried for your behaviour, and we think it will help.'

'Do as Lucius asks, dear, he's only thinking of you. And you've been so very strange.' Grace took a sugared plum from the basket Mother had sent with the shortest note.

Start again soon. Merry Christmas. Isabel is to be married in spring.

She bared her teeth and bit into it slowly. Clotted juice ran to the corners of her mouth.

Threlfall stood with one hand in his trouser pocket, the other on the mantel, staring across at the group by the piano who were laughing and clinking glasses.

'He looks as though he'd rather join the fun,' I mumbled.

'You can both join us later, should you feel like it.' Lucius steered me towards the doctor, and we stood awkwardly for a moment. I felt the eyes of the party on me. 'The library is quiet, you can talk more comfortably there.'

We walked in silence, and I fought the urge to cry like a scolded child. For once I'd decided to leave my room, hoping to feel better, wanting to feel festive. It was too much. Wasn't it natural to hide away when you were sad? I'd done nothing but grieve for my child, so how could I be punished for it? And why wait until this evening? To be sure I wouldn't protest or to ensure people witnessed it? I had my suspicions. Lucius usually hated parties.

Threlfall closed the door behind us in an exaggerated gesture, holding its weight so it didn't slam or creak. Why bother? Everyone knew we were here. He brushed a piece of lint from his jacket, flicked the tails of his coat behind him and drew up a chair. He even sat ostentatiously, legs wide apart, curled either side of the seat. Dressed for a party in his velvet and lace; perhaps Lucius had sprung this on *him* too.

There was nowhere for me to sit but the sofa, facing him but much lower down. Immediately uncomfortable.

'You didn't want to speak with me this evening?' The chair creaked as he shifted his weight, and he flexed his legs to balance. Muscles bulged obscenely through his tight velvet breeches and I pictured them in cross section, hatched and stretched, stuck to the bone at either end by a knot of tendon. Would Lucius ever allow me to make such sketches again? I covered my face with my hands.

'Mrs Everley, if you're fretting about something then it's best to talk to me. Lucius is deeply worried. He says you spend all day asleep and wander at night. That you imagine babies crying.'

'I hear cries.'

'There are no babies. You remember our discussion before? When people have nervous dispositions, they can sometimes hallucinate. They see or hear things that aren't really there. Such visions can worsen when you're upset.'

Something scrabbled at the door and Threlfall turned, startled. Perhaps this very house caused nervousness. I rose to open it and Ariadne ran in, body wagging. She must have escaped from my room. Clever of her to find me. Seated again, I cuddled her on my lap. 'Lucius has told me he believes I invent things.' After he found me on the floor in the hallway, exhausted with wandering to find the source of the cries, he'd insisted I needed sedating. Apparently, it was better for me not to think at all.

'You don't agree?'

I pressed my face into Ariadne's fur. How could I answer? If I spoke my mind I'd be disagreeing with my husband.

'I want to hear how *you* are feeling,' said Threlfall.

He wouldn't want to hear the raw emptiness I felt, the fear of sleeping in case something evil found me. How did any of them think I was feeling? 'It's Christmas Eve, Dr Threlfall, I had felt that a more sociable evening might lighten my spirits.'

'Have your spirits been heavy?'

'I have lost a child.' He was young and naïve. And a man. Whatever happened to him in life, he would never know the hollow emptiness that dragged inside. His fingers began to drum on his thigh. I wanted him to understand me. 'Father once treated a man, a soldier, who fought in the Crimea . . .' I waited for him to stop drumming. 'He lost a leg, probably had it roughly amputated at the side of a battlefield and he was definitely lucky to survive. He came to see Father because of a pain in his missing leg. It was agony, he said, this pain in the leg that wasn't there. Nobody could understand it. I understand it now.'

Threlfall leant towards me, and I leant back involuntarily. 'Did he recover?'

'No. There was nothing Father could do to treat flesh that didn't exist. His soldier started drinking heavily, to numb the feeling. And he fell under a train.'

'Is that how you see your future?'

'I don't think of it. All I see when I close my eyes is the imagined face of my child.'

'Imaginary?'

'I wasn't permitted to see him. Or hold him.' Threlfall opened his eyes in what seemed like surprise. 'I was told that was the usual way.'

'It depends. I suppose if the doctor felt it might be more upsetting for the mother, then . . .'

'Why would they think that?'

'If the child was . . .' Threlfall pushed his hands together, struggling for the words.

'If it was deformed?'

He flinched. 'Perhaps, or if the mother was particularly nervous.'

A good job Ariadne sat on my lap, or I'd have flown at him and what would Lucius have to say about that? But I felt that if I heard that word again, I would scream the house down. Such terrible violence welled inside me.

We sat in silence for a few moments. Threlfall still leant forward expectantly, though I could tell he strained to hear the party downstairs. There was no way I could join them now – what awkward silences and stilted questions would arise? How much would Grace delight in my discomfort? Threlfall tapped his pointed leather shoes and their showy buckles banged against the chair legs. He didn't deserve any more answers from me.

Suddenly the door burst open, and Tizzy rushed in. 'Excuse me, I didn't know anyone was in here! I'm looking for Ariadne, she's missing.'

'It's quite alright. She's here, safe and sound, see?' I held her up around Threlfall. 'It's so kind of you to look out for her.'

'Sorry to disturb you.' She bobbed a curtsey towards us and turned as if to go.

'Dr Threlfall was just leaving,' I said. 'Could I ask you something, please?'

Tizzy stayed by the wall, hands folded before her. Invisible and patient.

'Thank you for your concern, Doctor. I hope you got everything you needed? You can see your way back downstairs I think?' He rose, hesitated. 'Tell Lucius I'll join you directly.'

As he left Ariadne scampered after him and Tizzy seized her deftly, beaming at me. 'No you don't! We'll have to get you a cage, you little monkey.'

'Thank you.' I half suspected that Tizzy was rescuing me. She seemed always to be in the right place. 'Is everyone still downstairs?'

'I think so.'

'Mrs Atherton?'

She pulled a face. 'She'll be the last to go. I had to hide your plums from her, she'd have gone through the lot.'

'Thank you.' I hadn't the heart to tell her I didn't much like them. They were Isabel's favourites. How like Mother to forget. Christmas always threw her out with its frenzy of activity and people. Such fun while it lasted, especially cooking with Ellen, my favourite part. It felt like a lifetime ago. This year would be even busier. Isabel's engagement would require appropriate celebration. I tried not to mind that they hadn't invited me back.

'Don't you miss being with your family at Christmas?'

'That life's gone now. Been gone for a long time,' said Tizzy firmly.

I fought the urge to embrace her. It was as though she knew me from the inside. A place without words or explanations. Something I'd imagined from a husband, not a maid. I could not have been more wrong. As she wrestled with Ariadne, I watched the elegant turn of Tizzy's wrist, the curve and line of her slender neck. I could watch her for hours. She wasn't made to clean grates. She was made to be loved. What could her life have been? What could our lives be together? I should not allow myself to think such things, but my heart was hard to ignore.

Christmas passed in a haze. After the party I rallied to draw gifts – a faery for Eloise and a boat for Edmond – wrestling frames from the prints in my room to hang them in. I tied them in material cut from an old wrap. If Lucius was surprised, he didn't say. Neither did he show me anything he had bought them, though I saw Edmond had new soldiers. I was touched to receive an empty diary from Grace, something I wrote in most evenings, but I hid it carefully in different places. Within its pages were thoughts I wouldn't want to get into the wrong hands. Lucius gave me another piece of his mother's jewellery, a pretty emerald ring, asking me to be careful when I wore it, which I assumed meant not in front of Grace. It remained unworn. Lucius alone was delighted with his gift, a drawing that took days and sapped my energies. It showed how I imagined his sea creature, pulling itself from water on thick muscled arms, finned tail swishing a spray of water behind it. Lucius proclaimed that I'd realised his deepest imagination. *This is your very own mammoth drawing.* Such praise should have pleased me, but thoughts of the creature left my spirits low, and I was pleased when he removed it to his workshop.

Grace and the children stayed for two days, taking trips they said I would not enjoy. They were probably right. How could I enjoy skating, or theatre? I was glad when they left and Lucius returned to his patients. At the first opportunity I decided to walk to Evergreen House, to see the place for myself. I entertained vague thoughts of meeting Rebecca, or talking to some of the residents. In reality, I did not know what I sought, but I was restless. I wanted the company of women, to talk to them about their own lost children, and I felt sure that the house would have answers for me, if only I could find it.

When I walked out onto the street, I felt brave. No-one had noticed me leave and there wasn't much left for me to fear. I had lost Arthur and spent long weeks with my emptiness – filled with a darkness that even the Barkers couldn't worsen. I began my quest by following the direction of the river – wide and grey, edged with silt beaches, littered with debris and many times the size of the clear streams at home. I walked stone-flagged pathways, following its course, stopping occasionally to rest and catch my breath. The tide walls were slicked green, studded with mooring rings. Every now and then an iron ladder was set into the brick, rungs reaching down to the water, and I imagined climbing over, descending below the surface, finding Tom and the other lost souls beneath. The weight of water closing over me. Would it wash me clean?

Damp crept through my clothes as I leant across the wall to watch the boats, trying to guess what they carried. Rare spices and silks, perhaps, tobacco and flour. They jostled to pass under the bridge struts, dropping boxes as they swayed. Precious flotsam soon spotted by the Thamesmen in their rowboats who hurried after it, fishing it into their holds. They picked up all the debris on the river with their long, hooked poles, their only wage being what they collected. But they couldn't keep everything. Some things had to be taken to the mortuary, and sometimes they were tipped off as to where those might be found. Could that really have happened? Just as Caroline said? I couldn't imagine Lucius and his father talking to these men with their huge forearms and rough wool jackets. They wore peaked woollen caps pulled down over their foreheads, giving them a look of menace. Tough men. If the stories were to be believed, they fished bodies from the water every week. Their real work, the price they paid for being allowed to keep the rest of it. Would they ask questions over one or two more?

The nearest boatman looked up, caught my eye, called something that was caught by the wind. Unnerved, I stepped back and began to walk again, more quickly this time. Dank mud smells rose from the river and filled the narrow streets. Houses were different here – snaking terraces of skinny cottages, untidy shops on the corners where they met, factories belching behind them. How long had I been walking? It was tiring to be outdoors after so long inside. I'd headed in the direction of Evergreen House, not really expecting to find it. I didn't even have an address. When Tizzy had asked me where I was going, I'd been vague enough, though I'd thrown so many questions about the place I'm sure she could have guessed. I'd heard her speak of Putney before, between the water and the heath. She said the common reminded her of home. If I could get there, I could find Evergreen.

How much further? No grass in sight, just terraces and narrow streets beginning to fill with factory workers on their way to and from shifts. Men with glassy eyes sharing tobacco. Women wearing shirts rolled at the sleeves, their arms and hands stained purple-yellow with chemicals, dragging children behind them. I had been foolish to venture so far from the familiar on my first unaccompanied outing. What was I thinking? That I would stumble across Evergreen like a scene in a story? That I would find Rebecca in the shadows? I started at every figure with a passing resemblance, every pale face with dark hair. Ariadne whimpered, sensing my anxiety. We were lost. In my head I practised asking for help. 'Would you be so kind as to direct me to the heath, where I understand I may be able to find a house for fallen women?' Could Rebecca live like that? What work had they put her to? She was even less domesticated than Tizzy. I was so sure it was her in the carriage with Grace. And there was Eloise's rabbit. Rebecca was an uncommon name, she must have heard it somewhere. But if it *was* Rebecca, then what coincidence had brought her to the care of my own husband's family? All this way from home?

A man in a tattered coat and hobnailed boots approached, leading a large white dog on a piece of rope. The man doffed his hat and smiled, baring a mouthful of blackened stumps. The dog turned its long head towards Ariadne and growled, drawing its nose up over its teeth. She darted back and, before I realised, had slipped her lead and was running along the road.

'Want me to let Cromwell chase it?' the man leered. ''Ee'll catch it for ya.'

Before he could try, I ran after Ariadne myself, feeling foolish as I called her name. I couldn't let her get lost here, I'd never find her. The streets were like warrens, twisted and turning, littered with cut-throughs and blind alleys. Why had I come? There was nothing for me here. 'Ariadne! Ari!' My own voice echoed back to me. I ran from street to street, stumbling on kerbsides, tripping over rubbish. Overhead the sky began to darken and drizzle. Mist rose in clouds from what I thought was the river but when I neared, I realised it was the heath itself. Tall brick buildings flanked two sides of the open common. Even supposing I found Evergreen, how could I visit in such a state? My face was smeared. I'd lost my hat and my hair clung to my face and neck in long wet clumps.

How could I go home without Ariadne? If I left the heath, I'd never find her. Overcome with weariness, I sat down on the sodden grass and wept. Rainwater soaked through to my underskirts and the skin on my legs began to chafe beneath my wet stockings. Rebecca was the only one in our family who liked such weather. Mother used to find her outside every time it rained, chasing puddles. When she was older, she would dance on the lawn in storms, and we would laugh watching Mother try to catch her and bring her home. Did she feel so free now? I hoped with all my heart that I was wrong, and that the woman I had seen with Grace was someone else's sister.

A lamplighter walked along the street that edged the heath, whistling tunelessly, stopping to drop his bag and lift the lighter at every post. Yellow glow warmed the drizzle, showed the lines of rain in relief. Buildings loomed. If I walked past now, I could read any signs without having to go to the door. I heaved myself from the ground, reaching round to brush wet mud and grass from my skirt, when I heard a series of short, sharp barks. Ariadne! It was hard to tell the direction, but they were coming closer. Had she found me? All the time I was looking for her, should I have stayed put? I whirled about, searching, and in the distance spotted her bounding across the heath, chased by a tall figure. 'Ari! Come here, good girl.'

'I'm not trying to steal her,' said the figure.

As he stepped from the shadows, I recognised Lucius. How could I run to him, soaked and dirty? What could I say to explain my escape? 'What are you doing here?'

'Helping Grace with a new girl. I think the real question is what are *you* doing here?'

'I decided to take a walk, to get some air. I followed the river and then I was here.'

His eyes narrowed. I was awfully far from home. It would be hard to believe as coincidence.

'You're lucky I found you, and that foolish dog. She was shivering in the doorway of Evergreen as I left.' His eyes looked directly right as he spoke. A wide brick building with ornate stone balconies, stone mullions around the windows and what looked like bars across them. 'Ran off when I tried to pick her up. She should be properly trained. A dog that won't do as it's told isn't worth the food it eats.' He handed me Ariadne's lead. 'You're soaked. You'll catch a chill.' He removed his greatcoat and hung it around my shoulders like a blanket. An unexpectedly kind gesture that made me want to weep all over again.

'Ariadne *is* good. She was startled by a bigger dog and I didn't want to leave without her.'

Lucius shook his head. 'You're not strong yet. And it's not suitable for you to be here. There are places behind the busiest streets that aren't safe for you.'

What was the difference? Why were such streets safe enough for people like Tizzy, and maybe Rebecca, to walk in? 'What about

243

the women who live here, the ones Grace *rescues*. They're women too, must they live in streets that are not safe?'

'They're not women like you.'

'They *are*. They're women just like me.'

Lucius gave a deep sigh. Why was he always so sure he was right?

'You're not well, Madeleine. This business with the child has brought on the worst of your nervous disposition. I go to Charmouth the day after tomorrow. To conclude the last visit which was cut somewhat short. If air is what you want, you may accompany me this time. It would be useful, in any case, to have someone who could draw what I uncover.'

Exhibit 27

Scallop shell, family Pectinidae. Dorset.
Catalogued Wilkes, 1810.

'We was beginning to think Dr Everley was making it up about his wife. "Won't believe it 'til we sees it," I says to Tom. Didn't I Tom?' Sarah's husband stopped splitting logs and feeding them into the stove to hold up his enormous hand in agreement. 'Been coming here so long on his own he has. We never thought he'd take a wife at all. I dare say a lot of these doctors don't. Always working. Always got to look after someone else. Not much of a life is it, waiting round for them to come home?'

'He's very considerate,' I answered like a dutiful wife. Yet even here, where I'd been brought to recover, I was awaiting his return while I stayed at our lodgings, watching the landlady prepare dinner.

'Well, we're very pleased to have you. Aren't we, Tom? Don't get many young ladies stay here. And I miss my daughter now she's gone over to Bridport. Only married a fisherman. Why she couldn't have found a local one and stayed in Charmouth is a mystery to me.' Sarah threw a handful of flour directly onto the kitchen table and began to roll a great ball of pastry with a wooden pin. 'Did you stay near your family, dear?'

'I've only seen Mother once since I married.'

'You'll be the death of us, you girls. I bet she misses you.'

Perhaps. But she sent me away. Exchanged my freedom for her reputation – and my siblings' chances in life. Her last letter was full of them. A few lines of solace about Arthur, encouragement to try again, and then pages of Isabel's wedding plans. She was due to be wed in May, and suddenly almost three months wasn't long enough for the preparations. It was as much as I could do not to remind them that I'd barely had two weeks to get used to the idea of my own before it happened.

'Are you sure I can't help with anything?'

Four huge dishes lined with pastry sat in a line on the table. Sarah turned to pull a pot of rich beef stew from the stove and started ladling portions into them. 'You just sit there. Your husband says you should be resting. Have you been unwell?'

Tom took his cue to lumber out the back door and I considered sharing our news. Sarah seemed kind, in the unsentimental way of country folk. Though she was twice her size, she reminded me a little of Grandmother. She would tell things as they were.

'Slightly unwell. Lucius thought that the sea air would do me good.' He hadn't actually said that we should go away and take some time to be together to get over the loss of our child. I'd just assumed that was what he intended. Unless he wanted me out of trouble? Better for him to have me walking on the beach in Dorset than asking questions at Evergreen House.

'Sea air will *always* do you good, don't worry about that. Get him to take you for a nice long walk tomorrow. Or a boat ride if it's not too choppy. Beautiful time of year for a little trip around the headland.'

'I'm not so sure about a boat.' My first glimpse of the sea as we arrived wasn't inviting. Dark grey water at high tide, churned and swirling, spraying peaks of foam across the cliff. 'I've only ever taken a rowboat on a quiet river before.'

'Sea's changeable.' Sarah crimped the edges of the pies, spinning them round with one hand. They were lidded in basket weave that would look beautiful when baked. 'Rough today. But it might be calm as a millpond tomorrow. You'll see. You get that husband of yours to take you. It's a beautiful bay.'

'I expect he will.' I should have gone today. Our first day. After making such a fuss about me coming to draw the specimens, I didn't want him to just bring them back to the lodging house for me to examine. I couldn't be stuck inside for a week. I'd spent so long imagining what Lucius's creatures were like, picturing them embedded in the rock face, that I wanted to see for myself.

Sarah dipped a small brush into milk and swept it across the pastry, humming softly to herself. There was happiness to be found in simple tasks, concentration that left no room for thinking. No wonder dark thoughts constantly crowded me, idle as I was. Even Tizzy, fearful of the Barkers, never let me do anything. The lodging house kitchen was cosy compared to the formal rooms, similar in style to the kitchens at Lynton. Warm from the huge stove and the light from the long picture windows that looked onto the vegetable garden. Farmhouse chairs painted apple green. A row of photographs stood along the huge carved mantel, some faded by sunlight. Children or young men and women in stiff collars and hats, dozens of eyes staring solemnly out into the room.

'Are these your children?'

Sarah stopped humming as she looked up. 'Most of them. Some are their sweethearts, though they're nearly all married now. These two on the end are my grandchildren, Ewan and Annie. Dear little things they are, trouble though. Much naughtier than mine ever were.'

'A lot of children.' I counted along, trying to work out which ones were the same faces. 'Four sons as well as your daughter?'

'Five sons and two daughters.' Sarah's face took on a wistful expression. Wiping her floury hands across the front of her apron, she moved over to the mantelpiece and drew down two cards, edged in black and tied with black curled ribbons. 'Horace and Hilda. Taken by God on the day they arrived.'

She passed me the cards and I took them, pulling open one of the ribbons to find a hollow that contained a small lock of light-brown hair, tied with thread like the hair in the locket. Like Arthur's hair. At least I knew the colour of that.

'Did you see them?'

'Course I did. Held them both for a long time. Still see them now when I close my eyes. So different when they're first born.'

'Why?'

'Soft, like faery creatures. Ma used to say the soul escapes from that little spot on the top of their heads sometimes, I suppose that's what happened to those two. Makes me feel better to think it.'

There didn't seem to be anything wrong with these two, they looked like perfect babies. 'What does that mean?'

'How did you think they grew inside you and made it out? Newborns have a little soft spot in the centre, where the sides of the skull meets. Fontanelle they call it, funny medical word. Closes up after a bit, but they're delicate 'til then.'

I passed her back the cards and she set them on the mantel, nestled in between their brothers and sisters. 'Special to me, they are, because they never grew up to give me any trouble like the rest of them. Little angels. And they stayed angels, didn't they?'

'They did.'

Sarah straightened the cards and turned back to the table.

'Is that usual? That you would hold the child and have a

keepsake? I had understood that doctors didn't think it did the mother good to see their child if it was . . .'

Sarah gave me a curious look. 'I don't know about London ways,' she said finally. 'But we always do here. Have a proper send-off. They're people, aren't they? With souls. It's only right.'

I envied Sarah's conviction. She carried those children with her in the same way she carried the others. Comfortably. With a sense of order. She understood what it was to know, and lose, a child. All I had was an image in my head. Lucius may have his reasons. But I would always be wondering if I'd carried a monster, something he couldn't bear me to see. It would be hard to forgive him. Harder still to carry another.

There were seven other guests at the boarding house. Three single men – two fossil seekers and a pale youth visiting family – and two married pairs. Both couples were older than us and there for their health. A squire and his lady, very amenable but almost completely deaf, so that conversation with them was impossible. It was hard to warm to the other couple, a retired clergyman and his wife, Arabella, who did nothing but criticise the food or complain about the prices and the hardness of the beds. I wondered if a life of the cloth would do the same to Isabel. They made grace last for five full minutes before each meal, including breakfast, making Lucius positively growl with impatience.

'They will hear you,' I whispered, keeping my head bowed. Lucius grumbled and continued to knock his egg spoon against the table. The dining room was small, and though we sat at separate tables they were easily close enough for every conversation to be overheard.

'Nobody says grace at breakfast,' he muttered. An audible *tsk* of reproval rose from Arabella, who looked far too stern for her girlish name. Her husband finished but kept his head bowed, hands on his lap, as though still considering the effect of his words.

Our table was littered with all the implements and dishes of a hearty breakfast, and it was hard to eat without our hands coming into constant contact. It was also small enough for our knees to brush beneath it. I was unused to eating with Lucius and found it unnerving.

'I've missed tea. In the mornings.' I indicated the rose-painted pot. Lucius stopped, his fork midway to his mouth.

'Ask for it then.'

'I have. Mrs Barker says your father preferred coffee.'

'So he did.' He ate in silence for a few moments. 'He was a good man. The best of men. The Barkers served him a lifetime, you know. Habits can be very hard to break.'

I didn't mention the marmalade. I would have liked that too. Mrs Barker would curl her lip and put it down to my weakness for sugar. Perhaps, when we returned, I would make a point of requesting tea in Lucius's presence. They could hardly deny me then.

'What will you do today?'

Lucius wiped his mouth with a napkin and dropped it onto the floor, surveying the pile of used dishes with distaste. 'Don't they have anyone to clear this?' A timid girl of about thirteen scurried forward and began to stack things. I smiled at her and tried again.

'Will you be at the beach?'

'This morning. There's a low tide at ten. Should be useful. There's a new seam of lime exposed that's throwing up the right conditions.'

The dining room had almost emptied. Before I could reply,

one of the fossil hunters leant across from his table. 'Couldn't help hearing. Jack Stoneham.' He reached out a hand to Lucius and nodded in my direction as though I couldn't interest him less. 'We've been working that seam all week. What are you looking for?'

Lucius eyed him with suspicion. 'An ichthyosaur,' he said. 'A type of ancient fish.' It certainly wasn't what he'd explained of his research to me. He was clearly trying to put them off the scent, very different to the way he paraded his research in London.

'Same here! We found a snout yesterday. I can show you if you like?'

'Fascinating,' said Lucius. 'Perhaps later. I really need to catch the tide.'

'We should look together.' Stoneham stood and fastened his jacket as though waiting for a friend. I saw my chance.

'Lucius, I thought we were going together today? I so wanted to take a walk together and hear more about the fish.'

Stoneham's face fell. Lucius stood and offered me his arm. 'I'm afraid my time is already promised to my wife.'

He barely waited for me to dress in his haste to reach the beach, and I knew he'd have left me behind if it hadn't been for Stoneham's interest. When we got to the seam, he put on long waders, fastened by a belt at the top of his thighs, to help him walk to the furthest ends. He examined it, taking his time, walking this way and that along the exposed ridge of limestone. I waited on the dry sand, wondering what he saw. Had he found his creature? A part of his creature? Did he carry my drawings in his head as he searched? For the first time in months my thoughts were focused on something other than Arthur. Salt spray on my cheeks made me feel more alive than I could remember. The air tasted fresh. I wanted waders too, so I could be in the water. Perhaps I should take a boat, as Sarah suggested.

A damp chill settled in the small of my back, urging me to move to keep warm. I walked slowly towards the headland, missing the company of Ariadne. She would have loved it; water was her favourite. I pictured her running in the soft white foam, criss-crossing the shallows. Pets were not permitted at our lodgings and so Tizzy had promised to look after her until we came back. She was probably curled in the hallway, getting fat on all the treats Tizzy stole from the kitchens and not missing me at all.

In the distance Stoneham and his friend were striding along the sand, still dressed in their formal black suits, pointing at the cliffs. Shading my eyes against the pale sunlight, I tried to see some sort of pattern in the striated rock. Long stripes of yellow and orange, like a sunset fixed in stone. I could see nothing in it but colours. Nothing to warrant excitement. Stoneham turned and raised a hand in greeting. I responded and he looked back towards the ridge where Lucius bent down, the water rising slowly around his feet. No doubt he was wondering why neither of us had been permitted to join in the end.

When the tide had risen to Lucius's calves I turned and walked back, following the crust of shells and pebbles that marked the high-tide line. Different shapes appeared, long twisted cones as striped as the cliffs and pure white rounds like ancient snails. I bent to collect them as I walked, rubbing their smooth edges between my fingers and, when I reached the wooden jetty, I tipped them from my muffler and began to sort them into types. Scallops with round bodies, with flat sides, red stripes, or white shot through with one line of greenish-grey, the colour of the sea. Layered oysters lined with dazzling mother-of-pearl. Tiny whelks, black or bright yellow. It was absorbing work and

I didn't notice Lucius return until he was beside me, unbuckling his waders.

'Starting a collection?'

'Passing time. I've seen shells before, but never on a beach. I was interested to see how they were found together, all the different types.'

'That's how collecting starts.' He folded the oilskin waders and placed them under the jetty. The boots he wore underneath were perfectly dry. 'Interesting how you've put these together.'

'Probably wrong.'

'Quite the opposite. You've matched the bivalves by the shape of their auricles, rather than by colour or pattern.' He held up a scallop shell and pointed to the nubs that jutted from either side of the bottom edge. 'A natural taxonomist. You should draw these.'

My cheeks warmed with such unexpected praise. My things were safely stowed in the bottom of our trunk. It would be good to practise. Some of the patterns were complex, challenging. 'I plan to. Did you find anything interesting for me to draw on your ridge?'

'Not there. But the conditions are exactly right. There's clear evidence of backbones that end in shapes like rib structures, raised at the fore-edge. It indicates front fins that were incredibly well developed, perhaps almost muscular.'

'They could have walked on such fins?'

'Dragged themselves forward at least. We're close now.'

Close to discovering merfolk. Standing by this vast expanse of water, the taste of salt in the air and the litter of shells on the beach, it felt like the most natural thing in the world to hear.

'You didn't want to talk to Mr Stoneham about it?' Surprising considering he'd been so keen, in London, to convince his peers.

Lucius pulled an incredulous expression. 'Why would I want *these* people knowing? Amateurs with hammers. So they can find it before me after all these years of research?'

'Wouldn't it help to have more people looking?'

Lucius turned his head to look out over the waves, and the outline of his features seemed chiselled in stone. 'All that matters is to be the one who found the perfect specimen.'

Exhibit 28

Human infant skullcap with overlapped cranial bones.
Decorative tooling. c. 1873

Several days passed so pleasantly at Charmouth that I began to find hope for our marriage. I slept, without waking to voices or screams, and dark thoughts seemed far away in the bright salt air. We walked the shoreline, talking of Lucius's research and the plans he had for the time when his reputation was fully restored. I understood the devastation of a family without a mother, the fear of his father. It seemed that everything he did was to please the spectre of Old Dr Everley. Arlington Crescent was full of ghosts. I felt so different by the coast that it was clear the house was the cause of my nervousness.

When Lucius was engaged in his digging, standing waist-high in the wet rocks, or aiming a huge magnifying glass at the cliffs, I wandered alone, finding shells for my collection or sketching. He brought me a little folding chair from the guest house to sit on and another on which to rest my materials. A small act of kindness. If the future didn't hold happiness for us, at least we might find mutual respect. He brought me fragments he found, impressions of ancient bodies sculpted into rock, and I rendered them faithfully on paper. Later, imagining them all together, I drew faerytale creatures that writhed across the page in skin and scales. Mer-folk with human eyes and faces. Fish with strong forearms that pulled them out of the sea, dragging their tails behind them.

Lucius seemed to approve. Over unhurried dinners we spoke endlessly of what he hoped to find. He wasn't distracted by societies or dominated by his sister, and I began to enjoy his company. It felt as though he enjoyed mine and it came as a surprise when I awoke one morning to find he had already left. Thin curtains and a west-facing room meant I rose with the sun and saw the best of the day. He must have risen early. I'd grown used to our routines and was slightly put out not to walk to breakfast on his arm.

The room was chilly and I dressed quickly, adding extra layers for warmth, before sitting at the boudoir table with its frill of cotton. The brush and mirror sat on linen cloths, sewn roughly with roses and other flowers in bright embroidery silks, as though a child had made them. The walls were painted in similar flowers. It all lifted the heavy dark furniture and made the room seem cosy. I was becoming fond of it.

Holding the mirror in my left hand, I began to brush with the right, stopping frequently to empty hair from the bristles. Mine was still falling out in handfuls, something Tizzy said was natural after a birth; for some reason it thickens in abundance over months of carrying a child and then loosens all at once. It looked alarming. I wanted to clean the brush properly and remembered I'd brought my own set with a comb. It must still be in the trunk. With some effort I pulled open the heavy wardrobe doors to find our enormous travelling case. It was necessary to pull it forward slightly, in order to hold the lid high enough to rest without it falling on my fingers. Behind, tucked into the back of the wardrobe, was a much smaller trunk, the kind a travelling book salesman might use to carry his wares. I couldn't recall having seen it before and I pulled, lifting it up to rest on the wooden lid.

The box was heavy for its size. It was also locked. What could be inside? Something precious for Lucius's research, a weapon perhaps or a large sum of money? What reason could Lucius have for needing to hide something in a locked box at the back of a wardrobe? I placed it on the floor and opened the trunk again to look for the pretty silver-backed brush and comb, a wedding gift from Father. It had fallen from its strap on the wooden shelf right to the bottom and I had to lean over slightly to reach. As I closed my hand around it something cold and metal brushed my skin. A key. Antique, with an oversized bow and tied to a long blue ribbon.

It was a different prospect from merely opening a box that happened to be in the closet where my clothes were kept. To use a key would mean breaking a trust, risking the relationship I was beginning to value. Everyone knew what happened to Pandora. I held it in my hands for a long time, kneeling on the rug until my knees were numb. Eventually I convinced myself that living with questions would change things between us anyway. If I didn't at least peek, I certainly wouldn't forget it was there and the secret would eat away at our conversations until I spoke of it, the outcome of which may well be worse.

The bit turned easily in the lock, as though it had been oiled, and I raised the lid, almost dropping it again in shock. Nestled inside, on a pad of deep-blue velvet, was a tiny human skullcap, bowed and concave in the centre, as though it had been pushed together, with neat edges where a delicate saw had ground the bone around. It may have been cut by Lucius himself; that wasn't hard to imagine. Underneath the skull part was a separate roll of velvet full of tools. They lay neat and precise in shaped holders. Highly polished, like cutlery. Some were slim and elegant, made for delicate design, scrolled marks perhaps on a bone or shell.

Then a row of mysterious deep cutters, gougers, their tops blunt and thick for gripping, squat and ugly, their practical business unhidden. I imagined them scraping at flesh.

Carefully, slowly, I re-rolled and fastened the tools, settled the sculpted skullcap back in its place, and closed the lid. When I was certain the box was locked, I pushed it back behind the trunk and dropped the key where I'd found it. Something told me to replace my brush and comb as well. I didn't want Lucius to know I'd touched anything. He may be waiting for me downstairs. But all the questions that rose and choked in my throat would have to remain unasked until I could think more clearly.

Lucius wasn't at breakfast. By the time I'd composed myself enough to walk downstairs, Sarah and her granddaughter were beginning to clear the plates. Stoneham was the only other guest still at table, poring over the pages of a newspaper, and he barely acknowledged me as I entered the room.

'Morning, slugabed. All this fresh air's fair worn you out. I'll fetch you some eggs if you like?' Sarah stood with a stack of dishes in one hand, the other on her hip.

'Just toast and marmalade, thank you.'

'Got to keep your appetite up, young marrieds.' She winked and I tried my best to smile in response. I didn't want to answer any questions about Arthur or be told I should be trying again by now. Enough that the room I slept in had an adjoining door with Lucius's own; that was close enough for the time being. Until that morning I had thought it was bringing us closer. But I couldn't put his secret box from my mind. Why would he need it? And what else had he hidden?

'I'm not hungry, thank you. Sleeping late doesn't really agree with me.' Sarah shook her head and turned to stack the crockery onto a wooden trolley. As she was about to push it into the kitchen, I called her back. 'Did Dr Everley breakfast this morning?'

'He was off early. We hadn't got anything ready, it was barely daylight. Just stopped for his coffee. Wouldn't eat anything. I offered to pack him up some lunch, but he said he'd be fine. Won't be anywhere in Charmouth open at this time, I said, but he went off anyway.'

'That's right, I remember now. He said he wanted to catch the right tide.'

Once Sarah had left the room, Stoneham folded his newspaper and rose from his chair. 'No low tide early today.' He narrowed his eyes.

'Good morning, Mr Stoneham, I hardly noticed you there.'

He passed the newspaper over. It was folded to the nautical charts, printed in tables for fishermen. 'No low tide at Charmouth until late morning,' he repeated.

I gave him a tight-lipped smile. 'He didn't mention low tide, just said he wanted to catch it right.'

'He'll be at the cliffs then.'

'I really couldn't say.'

'I know what he's looking for. He'll need my help to find it.'

'You should explain. I'm sure he'd be interested to hear.'

Stoneham pushed his newspaper under his arm and left the room without another word. I hoped for his sake that he didn't speak to Lucius in the same manner.

By then I was brave enough to walk down to the shore alone and, as the morning was pleasantly warm and dry, I strolled the length of the bay before walking up the steep steps cut into the rock to reach the very top of the cliff. Lost in thought, I didn't realise how far I'd climbed until I reached the summit and found myself on the edge, my knees buckling at the sight of the drop. Lucius was nowhere to be found. From such a vantage I would have seen him in the bay or, indeed, on the bays at either side of the headland. But the only figures I could make out were Stoneham and his companion, attempting to climb the striped cliffs at the other end of the beach. The climb back down was more difficult, and I arrived at the guest house late and tired, my clothes slicked with green from the rocks. When Lucius didn't return for dinner, I asked Sarah to bring supper to our rooms, leaving his in a covered dish on the table when I retired. She seemed concerned, but I reassured her that men of science didn't keep normal hours. This pattern was more what I was used to, and his absence didn't keep me from sleep, although I missed the warmth of Ariadne as comfort.

Next morning, I could see that the food had been eaten, and there was evidence that things in the room had been moved but, although it was early, there was still no sign of Lucius himself. His bed had not been slept in and a blanket was thrown across the armchair. Doctors were used to resting in such an uncomfortable manner at the bedsides of gravely ill patients. I didn't worry for him, though it was an inconvenience to be left. It was different to London, where I might retire without questions or spend time with Tizzy or Caroline. In Charmouth, I was at the mercy of questions from Stoneham and Sarah and I felt unable, or unwilling, to engage in conversation about Lucius.

I breakfasted early, a hearty meal of eggs with ham from Sarah's small stock of pigs. She seemed to approve. Conversation was easier when she wasn't trying to fuss over me; she didn't mention Lucius and I didn't ask. Afterwards I borrowed some huge shells she had on display in the dining room, intending to spend the day sketching. It was drizzling with rain. Whatever Lucius had found to occupy himself, he was welcome to the weather. A day with my drawing seemed to better suit my mood.

Upstairs, though, away from the cosy bustle of the dining room, it was hard to settle. Some of the shells were ugly and bulbous on one side. *Devil's toenails,* Sarah had called them, and I wondered why the common names of shells must be so filled with horror. On the inside they were smooth, pearlescent, shot with tiny rainbows against the creamy-white. Only watercolours could do them justice and I hadn't remembered to pack paints. It made me irritable and restless. My mind returned to the box. How could it hurt to take another look? Lucius had clearly found something he couldn't leave and was unlikely to be back early.

Locking the door in case Sarah came to tidy, I opened the wardrobe again, throwing the doors back boldly, as if to show I wasn't frightened, though there was no-one to convince but myself. The trunk scraped on the wardrobe floor as I pulled it forward, and I stopped to listen in case I was overheard. Nothing else stirred upstairs. I finished moving it, but when I looked inside for the key it was gone. Flustered and worried in case I'd been responsible for losing it, I removed everything from the trunk and searched through each item of clothing. It wasn't there. Perhaps it was in the box itself? I lifted it up. It was still locked, but so light in comparison to the day before that it must be empty. The skull had been removed.

Later that afternoon, Lucius burst into the sitting room, carrying a large box. I'd been pretending to read, deterring conversation from Stoneham and his companion who sat with their newspapers, griping about the rain as though it were somebody's fault. My thoughts had wandered to questioning whether I would be better off returning to London and leaving Lucius to his foraging, and I was pleased to see him. At least I could ask him for his plans.

'It is done.' He placed the box on the floor and took the chair next to mine. His face was flushed as though he'd been running.

'What is?' I asked quietly, keen not to be overheard. The fossil hunters held their newspapers silently.

'I have it. Here. It's been cleaned and brushed. Ready for showing at the Society.' His eyes shone, though not with the excitement I'd expected on hearing such news. He seemed on edge and feverish. At the same time I wanted, and did not want, to see inside the box. What if his transitional creature looked nothing like either of us had imagined? I dreaded seeing something ugly and primeval. Equally I dreaded seeing a lump of rock that I couldn't decipher form in at all. He had plenty of finds like that. Things I didn't understand. The merfolk were supposed to be something we did together, something that brought us together.

'We should take it upstairs, Lucius, you don't wish for it to be damaged. Not after searching for so long.'

'No reason to hide it. Before long, the entire collecting world will know.'

I wanted to ask where he'd been for days, whether he realised I'd been lonely. I wanted to ask why we couldn't have looked together, why he had to disappear like that. 'Where did you manage to find it? Was it your seam?'

He shook his head. 'There's a quarryman along the coast, nearer Seatown, his name's James Harrison. You might remember he was credited with finding a particular large lizard?' I didn't recall ever discussing such a thing. Stoneham had put down his paper and turned his chair to face us.

'Scelidosaurus,' said Stoneham. 'Really it was discovered by Sir Richard Owen. Had to separate all of the bones and bits and pieces from the quarry and estimate what it would truly have looked like.'

I expected Lucius to ignore him, but he whirled round, nodding his head in excited encouragement. 'Yes. That's the one. The first bone he found was a knee joint. Did you know that?' Stoneham did not. 'He didn't know what it was, but he knew it didn't belong to any animal he'd seen. Imagine that. Self-taught. Remarkable man. You're right about Owen in a way. Owen encouraged him to look for the rest of the beast. He did too. And what he discovered in his quarry was quite remarkable.'

'Owen called it a dinosaur. A great lizard. Extraordinary to think they walked the same ground as us.' Stoneham shook his head in wonder. 'One femur could be as tall as a man!'

'So I'm told,' said Lucius.

'I thought you were here to look for the giant fish? Not lizards.' Stoneham could barely take his eyes from the box.

'I don't understand how you found it in a quarry. So far from water.' I steeled myself for disappointment, for some sort of giant knee bone to be hidden inside; on a cushion, perhaps, like the section of skull.

'I didn't. Not in the quarry. I just went to talk with him. I estimated that no-one would know more about local stone than the owner of a quarry. And I was right.' Lucius patted his jacket, reached inside his pocket, and pulled out a lump of near-white stone. 'Limestone, yes, but not the kind you find on the cliffs or by the sea. That's perfect for finding shelled creatures. But creatures with scales, bone, skin, they need to be found in the kind of sedimentary rock that gets covered in mud, that preserves them over time. And where can we find such stone?'

I thought for a moment. The rivers at home were full of mud. It got stuck between your toes when you were wading. Full of grit and silt, impossible to dry off, and it smelt bad too. 'In a river?'

'Yes! Clever Madeleine. Why didn't we talk of it before?'

Stoneham glared across at me. It pleased me almost as much as Lucius's praise. 'Yes, a river. And it made perfect sense to me that these creatures . . . of course they wouldn't fight their way out of the sea. They would climb across the mud, take their time, without being crashed by the waves.'

More like water babies than crocodiles. In which case my drawings would be correct. Lucius slid back the box lid and dropped it onto the floorboards with a loud crash. He took out a roll of velvet, worn in patches, wrapped over at either end. It was about the size of a large dog, or a child. Sarah came in, wiping her hands on a kitchen cloth. She stopped short at the sight of it and her hands flew to her chest.

'Whatever is that, Mr Everley? I heard the commotion and thought I'd better see for myself. What have you got there? Something you found on the beach.'

'A great discovery, Sarah, something that will put the name of Everley up there with the greatest of discoveries. A find that will draw together the theories of all the taxonomists and evolutionary theorists to prove our human history.' He unwrapped the velvet and held aloft his creature, suspended in air, the cloth hanging down over his hands.

Sarah peered in closer. 'What is it then?'

'A water baby,' I breathed. It was almost beautiful. An elongated ribcage, muscular back fins and stout shoulders that jutted from either side of its body, ending in long, handless arms. A small human-shaped skull crushed at the dome like the one in the box, the sides of its face pushed together as though it had a long snout, like a seahorse. Bright white bones. 'Did you clean it with lime? I didn't know you brought any with you.'

'I took it to the apothecary. It needed alum anyway, the silt I broke it out from smelt appalling. They let me clean it there.'

'Jones's? Can't imagine him helping anyone,' said Sarah.

Lucius frowned and looked down at his feet, as though questions were not welcome. 'No, a gentleman in Seatown. Recommended by Harrison.'

Stoneham had risen and was edging closer to Lucius, holding up his hands to touch the creature. Lucius raised it slightly higher, as though fearful of damage. 'What did you say you called it?' he asked, leaning forward so that his nose almost touched the left shoulder.

'I didn't say. And I'm still unsure. A land-fish, perhaps. An ichthyopod.'

'It's a chimera,' said Stoneham. I couldn't be sure, but I thought that Lucius flinched at the word.

'What's that?' I asked. I'd heard the word, of course, in old stories. A mythical thing, a faerytale beast. It seemed right for this creature. Why would Lucius dislike it?

'A creature made of parts,' said Stoneham, still staring. 'Sometimes the head of a lion and the tail of a snake. This is more like a large eel with a seal's head and the fin of a dogfish; not sure about the front fins, or are they arms?'.

Lucius began to wrap his find in the velvet, with slow deliberate movements.

'Are they arms? Did you find it like that, or did you have to put the pieces together? If you found them separately, you'd really need to know they were from the same creature.' Stoneham tried to stay his hand and the edge of the velvet caught. Lucius almost dropped his bundle. He made a sound like a snarl and Stoneham jumped back as if bitten.

'So many questions,' said Lucius with a sneer. 'Perhaps you should read a few more books before you take another climb along the cliffs. If you leave me your home address, I'll be sure to send a copy of my paper when it's published. I intend to present this to the societies next week.' He turned to me. 'We leave early in the morning. It might be best to start packing.'

I nodded, taking a last look at the ichthyopod's head before the velvet was replaced. A fine line surrounded the skullcap, and the jaws looked wrong somehow, the lower jutting forward in a way I would never have imagined a water creature to look. Wouldn't such things have longer upper jaws and noses, to aid breathing as they swam? Had I read too many storybooks and not enough of the books Lucius wanted me to read? Either way the skull looked just like the one in the box upstairs, the box that was now empty. A tiny human skull, the size of a baby's.

29

Back Lane, Limehouse

Stoneham lived in a part of London that was unfamiliar to me, and by the time I reached his lodgings it was late afternoon. On the south bank the streets formed a dank tangle, soured by the stench of the river and filled with characters I was quite sure Ambrose would not like me to meet. Though he had asked me to wait for his return from Charmouth, there was no time to lose. I regretted my clothes. In my haste to save Maddie I had rushed out immediately his letter arrived, confirming the address, without a second thought as to where I was going, and I stood out like a fool, a gentlewoman waiting to be robbed.

Pulling my cloak tighter, I took a wide step to avoid a man slumped against the railings and began to climb the steep stone stairs, trying to ignore the animal noises coming from the basement rooms. Student lodgings, Ambrose wrote, and I'd imagined a respectable place for men of science to live together. But these were common lodgings, cheap single rooms with shared facilities and few questions asked if the rent was paid.

Ambrose should have been with me. He hadn't hesitated to travel to Charmouth, abandoning his patients to find the boarding house where Maddie and Lucius stayed, writing to me as soon as he found Stoneham's name in the visitor's book.

A student of nature, according to Sarah, the landlady, who
vouches for his character though she expressed concern that
he and the Everleys did not seem friends. She talks a lot but
seems kind and the lodgings are sweet. I have been made to
promise we will visit together in the summer.

Such pleasant plans seemed pointless without Maddie, and
I'd lost no time in rushing to meet the man she hoped could
help. Why hadn't I waited?

Finally, the door was opened by an angry-looking woman in a
brown serge dress and a grey apron smeared in what appeared to
be soot. 'Is Mr Stoneham at home?'

'Depends on who's asking,' she replied, hands pushed into her
substantial hips. 'We don't allow *lady callers* for our gentlemen.'

'I wish to speak with him about his research.'

'What research?' Her tone was suspicious, her eyes narrowed to
currants in her doughy face.

I considered my response. He was a fossil hunter, an
evolutionist. His landlady did not strike me as learned, and too
much explanation of the things he studied could end with a
closed door. Could even get him evicted. I tried a smile. 'I am not
personally acquainted with Mr Stoneham, but I have been asked
by a good friend to deliver a most important message.'

'I can give him a letter.'

'The message is too important to write down.' And if she could
read at all, it would most certainly not remain private.

'He's not in.'

'Then I will wait.'

'Fine. But you can wait out there.'

Before I could protest, the landlady slammed the door shut,
leaving me on the top step with little choice but to walk down to

street level or stand foolishly in the way.

Instinctively I gripped my reticule, pushing it into the hidden pocket of my skirt. Curtains were being drawn across windows, lamps lit inside. The slumped man muttered something vicious to himself and I had never felt so out of place, though I knew I couldn't leave. I thought of Maddie's face, the pleading in her eyes as she pushed the slip of paper into my hand. Who else could help? She had no-one. And she trusted me. Opposite the building was a high brick wall, greening with damp, and I pushed myself into the corner of one of its struts. Shrinking from the street, I pulled my hood over my face and waited. Swirls of mist appeared at the end of the alley like the ghosts of sailors, and the damp air hung heavy on my chest.

Though a steady stream of people came and left the house, none looked young enough to be Stoneham. As darkness fell I realised I must leave for my own safety and find a hansom on the riverbank. I would return in the morning, ask the driver to wait. What else could I do? *Search garden. Find Stoneham the fossil hunter. Charmouth.* I could hardly search the garden at Arlington Crescent. I was terrified. And the Everleys would take great delight in sending me to join Maddie in the dock. No – Ambrose had been to Charmouth, we had Stoneham's address. I had to see this through.

Morning brought sulphur skies, a late sunrise of factory chemicals and river damp. Strange light, only slightly less menacing than the dark. It cost more than usual to convince the hansom to wait, especially as I had no idea how long my visit would take. How would I even recognise Stoneham? What Ambrose gleaned from Sarah and outlined in his letter could describe any studious young man. Must I call across the street to each one? I felt unable to ring the bell, unwilling to face the landlady, and I skulked in the rear seat, watching the sickly-coloured sky fade to the grey of a prison dress.

I needn't have worried. The youth that hurried down the worn stone steps could be no-one else. His fringe flopped over one eye, papers bulged from his pocket and he still carried his hat in one hand, as though, deep in thought, he had dressed and eaten breakfast at the same time.

'Mr Stoneham!' I called from the carriage before throwing open the door, and he whirled around as though frightened. Who could be after him? The sudden thought that Dr Everley might be near made me fearful. Had Lucius planned to get to him first?

'Mr Stoneham, do wait, please.'

He seemed astonished that I was attempting to catch his attention, perhaps unused to the company of women.

'I am late for a lecture.' His eyes were weary and bloodshot, his skin pale, though whether from an unsuitably late night out or an evening poring over research was hard to tell. He was certainly in want of looking after; a good meal, a quiet room. There was much Ambrose and I could offer for his assistance.

'I wish to speak with you about the Everleys. You met them in Charmouth. Dr Everley is . . .'

'An extremely rude man,' he interrupted. A look of anger flashed across his face. Had he been slighted? It would not surprise me; Lucius could be brutal to those he considered inferior.

'Indeed. I think we may agree on that point.'

To my relief, his expression softened. I would have liked to find somewhere more private for our conversation, but I did not want to enter his lodgings and I could hardly offer my carriage. I lowered my voice, and began to speak plainly. There was no time for delicacy. 'Mrs Everley is currently on trial.' His eyebrows shot up under his fringe but he made no comment and I was glad. 'She is wrongfully and miserably imprisoned and seems to be under the impression that you may be able to help.'

'I am not sure how. I knew the Everleys only briefly and in truth they seemed keen to avoid my company. Dr Everley is opposed to what he believes to be amateur collectors but did not care to find out what I know.'

'You are a student of the natural sciences?'

'I am. Though my family's business has failed,' he gestured around him at the squalor of the damp-chewed street, 'and without a patron I will be forced to find work before I graduate.'

'Did something happen while you were all at Charmouth? Mrs Everley was particularly keen for me to find you.'

'The chimera,' he whispered.

An imaginary monster? I waited for him to explain.

'He insisted he had found a missing link, showed us a collection of bones. Something about it did not seem right to me, but they left soon after and I assume he took it to one of the societies, though I'm still waiting to see the promised paper.'

His fish with feet. Of course. I was filled with horror at what that could mean, and a sudden light-headedness caused me to fall against Stoneham's chest. 'I'm sorry. An early start without breakfast.' Embarrassed, I pulled myself away.

'It is cold, Mrs . . .' He showed concern and I was glad he did not match his dwelling. He was a gentleman underneath.

'Fairly.'

'I can see you are a good friend, but you should be somewhere warm.'

'Will you help? I believe that if you could examine this . . . creature, you would understand what to do. I know Mrs Everley thinks so.'

'I am not permitted to enter the societies.'

I was as powerless as a woman. But I had my means. 'My father is. If we go to him now, he will take you there, I am sure of it. He is no supporter of Lucius Everley himself.'

Stoneham hesitated. 'May I ask what is alleged to be her crime?'

I took a deep breath. 'Murder. And we do not have much time to save her.'

Exhibit 30

Set of taxidermy tools, with sharpening stone,
in green baize roll. English. c. 1830.

'Come back soon, won't you?' Sarah waved her enormous handkerchief at the carriage as Tom helped the driver to stack our trunks behind. He flinched as the set of tools I had found unrolled from its baize, sharp blades glinting in the clear coastal light. There was no sign of the empty skull box. I could speak with Tizzy before she unpacked, but what would I say? It would sound as though I disbelieved my husband, something I could never discuss with staff.

'I'll miss you, Sarah, and your pies!' I called. She waved again, pretending to dry her eyes on her apron. I would miss her too. Such kindly wisdom would be welcome in London. 'I'll write.'

'I won't have time to write back! Not with all these mouths to feed.'

'Don't worry about that.'

'And we'll be famous after Dr Everley's discovery! Don't forget to mention us, will you? We'll be mobbed with guests.'

'For goodness' sake, she's not your mother.' Lucius climbed into the carriage and took the facing seat, settling his arm on the box as though he feared it may be stolen. 'You're embarrassing yourself.'

I withdrew from the window and stared at my lap as the carriage pulled away. Already things were different. Without our breakfasts and morning walks we would go back to a life of strangers. Lucius couldn't wait to get back to share his find with people who mattered.

'I will miss it. I hope I am to be permitted to accompany you on your next visit?'

'I'm not likely to stay there again.' Lucius's face had settled into its familiar expression of displeasure.

'I thought you always stayed there?'

'Before they filled the place with hobby fossil hunters. All those questions!'

'You usually like talking about your work.'

'To my peers, yes, not to amateurs like Stoneham. Besides, it seems that Seatown has more to offer than Charmouth. I only wish I'd realised it sooner.'

So many questions and none I dared to ask. Lucius's mood seemed to turn on the edge of a knife. As we left, Stoneham had waited for Lucius to walk outside and then grabbed my arm. 'I'll be visiting London soon. I want a closer look at that chimera.' Not a word Lucius liked and one that I found deeply unsettling. What did Stoneham mean by it? He seemed to imply some impropriety, though his own manner left much to be desired. I shook myself free, my spirits sinking. The anticipation I'd felt for new beginnings when we arrived, the excitement of lodgings and seaside, felt a hundred days ago.

Scenery passed. Bare and budding trees, mud-slicked fields and staring sheep. Birds flew in and out of the hedges edging the sides of the road, bringing twigs and tufts of lambswool to line nests ready for young. As we travelled, neither Lucius nor I could find anything more to say. We fell silent in the way of people who know each other, or who have no need to know. My questions remained unasked. My hopes for a new phase of our marriage felt dashed like waves on rocks.

When we returned, Lucius spent each day writing, closeted in his study. There was only one way for me to get a closer look at the creature: I had to draw it. On the third day of asking it was permitted, but he insisted on joining me as I worked and it was hard to focus with him there. I imagined his eyes boring into me, though every time I looked up he was writing, head bent low over the desk in concentration.

Lucius had set his find on a block of wood, like a statue, and placed it in the centre of the large library table. Even if I stretched, I couldn't reach to touch it. Light from the window made the bones glow ghostly white. Lucius said the mud had preserved them. Thick river silt, full of oxygen, combined with lime rock, was perfect for fossils and bones. Whatever fell into it remained unchanged. All that was missing from the creature was its flesh. Once I'd drawn the bones in various ways, I planned to draw it as it would have been, with smooth-scaled skin and trailing fins. A nightmare water baby. It was the image in which I was most interested, but I had to complete these first. Lucius planned to show at the Society two days later, and everything must be ready.

'It is *vital*, Madeleine.' Vital for scientific understanding or the Everleys' reputation?

After I finished the first sketch, in long charcoal lines, I leant back and rested the sticks on the table. Reaching down absent-mindedly, I was momentarily surprised to find that Ariadne wasn't in her usual spot curled by my feet. She was still locked in my room, because when we'd first set up to draw, she'd prowled around the central table growling up at the creature from underneath, unable to settle or leave me alone. When Tizzy was called to fetch her, Lucius prevented her from entering the room.

'I have no wish to lose another housemaid to superstition and fear.' Would she baulk at the creature? It was certainly a strange object, but Tizzy wasn't timid and I'd hoped for her to see it. We'd have to talk about the drawings instead. I wanted to make several versions, inks and lead lines as well as charcoals. It was going to be a long day and Lucius showed no sign of stopping.

I took the paper that I'd prepared with a light watercolour wash, ready for using inks. The wash stopped them bleeding in the paper's pitted surface, creating the clean lines of true anatomical sketches. Important to prove their worth and lend an air of authority to such extraordinary ideas. My version would need to be intricate and accurate, showing the mechanics of each joint, the possibility of each movement, and I was glad of the practice I'd had.

Easy to draw the lines of the body, the shape of the ribcage. Not much difference between the breathing of a fish and a human, except one breathes water. What did this one breathe? Both? The ribcage itself was wide. The creature would have had a bulbous chest, probably strong with muscle too, enabling it to pull itself free of the mud. Its rear end was weaker, the structure thinner, three nubs of bone where tail and dorsal fins attached. I would need to choose the right colour for the watercolour version. Much as I wanted to paint a faery-sheen on the fins, I couldn't imagine a bright pretty creature in the mud.

Perhaps I should first have drawn the head. It was hard, much harder than the rest, to visualise as a living thing. By the time I reached it, the light from the window was dimming and Lucius had lit a gas lamp by his desk. Flickering flame threw shadowed fingers, changing the shape of the head. It could have been human. The plates at the top seemed pushed together, like the skull I found in the locked box. There were no cheekbones and the sides of the skull were collapsed, unnatural. No teeth remained, which was surprising to see. All the skulls in Lucius's study, animal and human, had at least a few teeth intact. They didn't rot like other tissue, so the mud should have preserved at least a few. What would this creature's teeth have been like? Was it a predator? A forager? Did it eat seaweed? It was big enough to look as though it needed more than plants to live. Other fish perhaps? Then what happened when it left the water? What would it eat then? Could it live on water and land at the same time? Lucius was still angered by questions. Instead, I kept a list of them, waiting for the right time to ask. I was curious to know the size of its brain. Could a fully developed brain live in such an odd-shaped skull?

The longer I drew, the more questions appeared on the pad. If Lucius would let me read his research, perhaps some of them would be answered. If I could get close enough to see the creature properly, I may well be able to answer the most pressing questions for myself.

'Shall I ask for supper to be brought here?' I asked. Lucius looked up, dazed, woken from a dream of words.

'If you like. Shall I ring?' He knew it was better for him to ask. The bell would be answered by the Barkers at such an hour, and requests from Lucius were performed with better grace than they were for me.

'You should rest, Lucius, you've been writing for hours.'

'This is the cusp of brilliance. Don't you feel it?'

'I do.' I pushed the drawings across the table. He rose, stretching, took a last look at his papers and moved to see.

'Extraordinary. A likeness and cross section at the same time. My paper will be perfect.'

My fingers itched to seize the list of questions.

'I'd like to start the next. My imagination of the creature as it was when alive.' I leant back in the chair, feigning more weariness than I felt. 'Refreshment would be welcome though. Did you find the bell?' It was tucked beneath my chair, where I'd placed it earlier.

Lucius looked from his creature to his papers and then my drawings. 'I'll go down. It'll be quicker.'

I thanked him, pushed the list of questions below the pad of paper and began to set out the small easel and paints. As soon as the door closed, I rose and walked to the edge of the table, crouching down to see the creature at eye level. From such an angle it was easier to understand. The chimera that Stoneham had intimated. The skull looked unnatural because it was. A pointed head, too narrow to breathe either air or water. I couldn't forget Sarah's words. The skull of a human child was malleable at birth. Weak enough to be pushed through a birth passage. Soft enough to be taken and pushed again. To make the shape of a demon. I knew then that Lucius's creature was a lie. Bile rose in my throat, and I doubled over as though punched in the stomach. How could I have been so blind? All along I'd felt violent horror in his house, and I'd pushed it aside. Worried what Mother would say, feeling like a foolish girl with an overactive imagination. Lucius placed everything below his need for fame and notoriety, and he had sacrificed our child for his game. I would not throw up, I could not. He would be back at any moment. If he noticed something wrong, I would follow Annie to St Margary's. Now it was clear. Dr Threlfall, my 'nervousness'. At the first sign of trouble, I'd be locked out of sight.

Gripping the table, I took a huge intake of breath and held it until the sickness subsided and I felt strong enough to stand. I could never look at the creature again. What could I do? There was no-one to help. If I ran, I'd be found, brought back. Father liked Lucius, he would never believe me. Mother would do anything to prevent scandal. Isabel would insist I was spoiling her chances, selfish as always. I must keep Caroline and Ambrose as far from this as I could; I would never forgive myself if I dragged friends into such horror. Where would I even begin? I knew Lucius's creature was a lie. What I did not know was how to fix it.

Tizzy was the only person in the house I felt I could trust and, at the first chance, I attempted to draw her into conversation, trying hard to be patient.

'You must find us quiet here, Tizzy. Don't you miss the girls at Evergreen?' I pulled at the thread with which I was attempting to sew a pattern of forget-me-nots around my embroidered Spaniel. Some of the flowers were too big, out of all proportion with the dog. But something must steady my hands and focus my mind. The conversation I needed was difficult and dangerous.

'Worse when you were away. It's nice to have you back.' Tizzy was arranging the dresses in my wardrobe, having washed and dried the beach from the hems of the clothes I took with me. 'What was it like?'

My mind was so preoccupied that for a moment I thought she meant the creature. 'The trip?'

'Charmouth is nice, isn't it? I miss it. You've been hiding in the library with Dr Everley since you've been back. I want to hear about it.'

'The weather was good,' I began slowly.

Tizzy rolled her eyes. 'What about the people? I hear no end of people go on their holidays to Dorset now, looking for rocks and bones and goodness knows what else besides.'

I clasped my hands together on my lap, nails digging into skin.

Pain felt like relief, something to focus on. 'There were a couple of them in our guest house, much to Lucius's disgust. "Hobby collectors". They asked him a lot of questions and annoyed him daily. I saw them climbing the cliffs in their morning suits.'

'Glad you didn't try any of that. You must have sat down on the sand though. Your blue dress was full of it.'

'I tried not to. The only other guests were a clergyman and his wife, and a pair of very old, very deaf aristocrats who also seemed to irritate Lucius. They couldn't hear a thing anyone said. It made for some rather amusing conversations at breakfast.'

'What about the food?' She jerked her head in the direction of the kitchen. 'Her ladyship's been reheating rabbit stew all week.'

'Sarah, the landlady, is a lovely woman, you'd like her.' Horace and Hilda; I saw the cards, heard her voice: *the top of their heads is soft, how else do you think they come out?* 'She's a wonderful pastry cook. We ate well.' I patted my waist. 'You'll have to work a bit harder with the stays.'

'You look well on it.' Tizzy stepped back to consider me. 'Got some colour in your cheeks. Got a serious face on though. You seem a bit . . . far away.'

Where should I begin? Straight in with accusations? Linking the loss of my baby with Lucius's research was likely to raise questions about her own child. She'd never seen Rose either. Such anger could be dangerous. It was hard enough to repress my own, a cycle of dark thoughts that raged and pushed and left me feeling as though madness could approach at any moment. And I wasn't sure. I needed to know more before I could bear to believe it. A familiar sickness settled in the pit of my stomach.

'Arthur is much on my mind. I find that I can speak with you, Tizzy, because I know you will understand. But if you'd rather I didn't . . .'

Tizzy's eyes grew bright. She pushed out her jaw and folded her arms. 'It's my opinion that we *must* talk about them. They all hushed me up as soon as it was over. Mustn't see her, mustn't speak her name. Best to forget it all. I'm not a doctor but I don't think that's best.'

'Neither do I.' I thought of Sarah's mantelpiece, with her children honoured together. A part of her family. 'I want to remember. But I'm finding it hard. My thoughts return again and again and there's an empty space where his face should be. It's impossible for me to stop.'

Tizzy was nodding eagerly, encouraging. 'Me too. I tried to tell them, but they wouldn't listen.'

'Is it usual, do you think? Is it for the best? Lucius was very clear that he didn't want me to "dwell" on it. That's the word he used. But it seems to me that it only makes things worse.'

She thought for a moment, a frown of concentration that made her look even younger. I wanted to comfort her, and I would, but I needed her to talk first.

'It's what always happened, at Evergreen. The girls that were due stayed in a separate part of the house. Afterwards they separated us, to get over it, in rooms on our own. They didn't want us to upset the others, they said, and run the risk that something would go wrong with theirs too.'

'What happened afterwards? Did you never get to meet any of the babies?'

Tizzy shook her head. 'I always assumed they went on to another place to be looked after. There weren't any babies at Evergreen.'

There weren't any. Then where were they? At the Society? In the small museum? I breathed deeply, forced myself calm. 'You didn't ask?'

'Like I said, they didn't like us to talk about it. Bad for our recovery and all that.'

'Did lots of the girls return, though?'

'Most of them. Mrs Atherton said it wasn't surprising that we couldn't keep our children, said we weren't healthy. She sometimes said it was good they didn't survive and have to face a life of poverty.'

Coldness slithered the length of my spine.

'She said it was good for us as well. A chance to live more normal lives.'

'Did she.' I could hear her speaking like that, taking pleasure in their relative status. Before, I would have assumed that to be the entire reason for her work at Evergreen, to enjoy looking down on unfortunates. But I was starting to consider the distinct possibility that her role was more sinister. I took a deep breath. 'What if . . . they didn't die?' Tizzy said nothing but her eyes widened, fearful. 'What if they were taken? I don't believe Arthur wasn't born properly, and I don't think you do either.'

'You think Dr Everley sold them?'

'I'm not sure. Nothing makes sense. Sometimes I wonder whether Lucius and Grace are right and I'm losing my mind. I want to show you something. You must promise not to tell.' And once she'd seen it, would I know then? It would, at least, be easier to speak of. I held her gaze, willing her to understand. She was the only person I trusted, the only person in my life I felt I truly loved. Could I be absolutely sure she wouldn't let me down? Her eyes were extraordinary, blue-green like a water faery's. A good faery. I moved to embrace her, but Ariadne jumped from her basket and the moment passed.

'Not this time, girl.' I picked her up and put her back, ignoring the protesting whimper.

'Where we going?' Tizzy knew I hated to leave Ariadne behind.

'She'll give us away. She's been quite naughty since I returned.' I tried to lighten the atmosphere. 'Someone must have been spoiling her.'

'I don't want to go somewhere I shouldn't be.' A note of fear crept into Tizzy's voice. Was I expecting too much? She'd always seemed so brave to me. Perhaps it was just show.

'Mrs B keeps telling me I'm on final warnings.'

'What for?'

'What *not* for. Can't do anything properly.' Tizzy looked glum.

'You work for me and Dr Everley, not Mrs Barker.' I was trying to convince myself as much as Tizzy. She looked doubtful but she followed me anyway. Through the door, past Lucius's rooms, down the corridor and to the stairs. The strange, sweet-rotten smell was overpowering and sickness rose again. I had to stay strong. We descended the stairs, but at the door of the library I heard a noise on the ground floor. I leant over the bannisters just in time to see Lucius leaving the house. Barker walked behind him carrying a long wooden box. I'd missed him. And missed my chance to show the creature to Tizzy. He must be taking it to the Society, but which one?

We went to the library anyway. As I'd suspected, the creature wasn't there. Lucius had taken most of his papers too, though his desk was messy, and his jacket hung on the back of his chair, his slippers below, as though he'd jumped up to leave in a hurry. If I missed this chance to speak to someone, there wouldn't be another. Tizzy wouldn't follow me again.

'He's moved it.' I tried to keep my voice steady as I marched to the desk and began to leaf through his papers. 'No matter. Tizzy, how would you like to come with me to Evergreen House?'

'I don't want to go back there. Mrs Atherton is worse than the Barkers.' Tizzy looked doubtful.

'Just to visit. I promise you won't be in trouble.' I could promise nothing of the sort. More likely I'd end up in trouble myself. But I had to find answers to the questions that wouldn't die. Was Rebecca living in London, at Evergreen? Did my baby survive? It would help me understand if I was really living with a monster, as I suspected, or if I was slowly going mad like everyone claimed.

Exhibit 31

Stonemason's chipping hammer. Double-ended.
Wrought iron and oak. c. 1730.

T he name was half hidden. Covered in a branch of creeper,
only visible from the top of the steps. The worn stone curve
was deep on each tread, as though the feet that climbed them
weighed heavy. Everything about the house was weary. Mullions
reached far into the walls, creeper gathered and draped across the
windows, shading light. No lamps or fires glowed through the
panes, though the curtains were open and the afternoon beginning
to darken. I pulled hard on the bell-rope, feigning courage, and a
deep rumble echoed inside. Two sheets of newspaper chased down
the street, blown by the wind.

Nobody answered. Grace always claimed that Evergreen was a
lively place, full of people and colour. I'd imagined rooms full of
women, all with different stories, helping each other to heal and
find new lives. That was how she described it sometimes and it
was the version I preferred. Sometimes she just dwelt on their sins,
the lives they deserved. Lucius barely mentioned Evergreen at all,
though when he did it was dismissive, something to keep his sister
occupied.

A faded sign leant against the glass of the right bay window.
Unsolicited traders and other trespassers will be dealt with accordingly.

According to what? Clearly, they didn't respond to the bell. I wasn't leaving without something. An indication that I was correct in my assumptions, or something to tell me I'd got everything wrong. I didn't know what the sign would be, but I knew I'd understand when it appeared. I wasn't leaving without answers. Flakes of paint from the handrail stuck to my gloves. The pavements were uneven on the street in front of the house, lifted by tree roots, dark earth exposed beneath the white stone. I sat on a nearby bench and counted the broken slabs, all the time watching the front door as though something would happen.

A raven perched on the Evergreen gatepost, tilted its head, pecked at the sign and flew away. Threatening clouds gathered in bunches. How long could Tizzy cover my absence? Headaches sometimes kept me from dinner, though Mrs Barker usually checked afterwards, bringing something to help me sleep. I couldn't risk anyone thinking Tizzy had lied for me. She'd lose her place and then I'd have no-one. But I couldn't risk nothing happening either. I was unable to make a second journey. With no sign of an allowance from Lucius and the last of Father's money spent, I'd been forced to ask Tizzy to sell a butter knife to pay the hackney. I had to stop putting her in harm's way.

The chill from the stone bench seeped through my clothes to my skin. Watching the place was pointless. I decided to try the back, to see if I could enter through the garden. As I reached the wall, I noticed stones missing and bent down to peer through the gap. Clearly visible in the gloom were columns twisted with vines and two tall stone greyhounds. Instantly I recognised the garden from the photographs in Lucius's room. Those horrible images swam before my eyes. They were taken here, at Evergreen. Poor girls. How had I not thought of it before? Did Grace man the cameras or Lucius? Perhaps they both enjoyed humiliating the models, and I had found cameras in his room, but I could not imagine him wielding such machines. He was more at home slicing inanimate creatures, more tender with cadavers than flesh, and he had never seemed to enjoy looking at me. His night-time visits were brief, rough, perfunctory. Something told me the photographer was more likely Grace. I could imagine her selling the images to collectors. She was fond of money and she certainly coveted beautiful things, always dressed in such fine clothes and jewels and without a husband to be seen. I had heard nothing of him in all this time. No letters or news, and she never spoke of him. Neither did Lucius.

As I swayed on my feet, not knowing what to do next, a small hatch at the side of the main entrance opened. Next to the grandeur of the front door, I hadn't noticed it before. A low-arched doorway in the same pinkish stone that edged the windows. Its wooden door made it look like a storage room. An entrance to sneak from.

Still standing, I watched the figure look up and down the street before opening the side gate and hurrying through. For want of a better idea, I followed, legs awkward and stiff from the cold and so slow that it took several minutes to catch up and realise the figure was Rebecca. At least it was the woman I had *thought* to be Rebecca, though she had thrown a dark cloak over the yellow dress. When we were far enough from Evergreen, I called out and the sound of her name caught in my throat because Mother prevented us from discussing her, as though in disgracing us she'd disappeared from memory. Three times I called, willing my suspicion to be correct, before she stopped and whirled around to face me. Beautiful still, though hardness touched her features and anger flashed in her eyes. I was keeping her from something important.

'You're after the wrong woman. Whoever you want, it's not me.

My name's Anne.' She tossed her black curls. Anne. That was why Tizzy hadn't heard of Rebecca at Evergreen. I should have thought of that before.

'I would know my own sister anywhere,' I said softly.

For a horrible moment I thought she would deny me. Her eyes narrowed and her expression grew wary, as though she weighed up the chance to escape. Nine long years had passed. I was a child when she left and I'd lived much since. Lack of sleep and grief for Arthur gathered under my eyes and my girlish figure was gone.

'Maddie,' she whispered. 'I hardly knew you.'

We looked at each other for a long time. 'I've missed you. We all have.' I threw my arms around her, and our tears mixed on each other's skin. When we pulled apart, we still wept.

'How long have you lived there?' I asked at the same time as she said, 'Why are you here?'

'I know them,' I said. 'Mrs Atherton and her brother.'

Her face clouded at the mention of their names. 'Have they hurt you?'

'No. Yes. To be honest I'm not sure. I need to talk to you, to find out more about this house. Tizzy . . . Harriet came to work for us and . . .'

'Is she safe? We were worried. Mrs Atherton said that . . . and what do you mean she came to work for you?'

'She's safe. For now. Rebecca, there's so much I need to know. About you.' I needed her to tell me everything so I could understand if my suspicions about the Everleys had any foundation. It was one thing knowing they took advantage of girls who had lost their way. Quite another to accuse them of murder. If I knew Rebecca's story, knew more about Evergreen House, I might find enough certainty to involve the magistrates and make my escape. There would be time enough for Rebecca to hear my own story later.

'Not here.' Her eyes darted along the street, and she pulled us both nearer to the wall. 'I'm not going back there. Not ever. Walk with me to George's house and we can talk there.'

Her face hardened again. I didn't ask who George was, or where he lived. I would go with her anywhere. The sun had still not set, and I had a few hours before my absence would be noted. A few coins in my pocket to get me home. Finally, I was getting somewhere. Rebecca linked her arm in mine and began to hurry us along the street. We walked in silence until we reached the end of a long, twisting alleyway and she seemed to relax.

'I don't know how you know Mrs Atherton but you can't trust her. At first, she seemed nice. Father brought me to her at Evergreen House when he found out I was in the workhouse.'

'The workhouse?'

Rebecca frowned. 'There aren't many places a girl can go. Not once it begins to show.' She patted her stomach. So she had a child too. Of course. No wonder she couldn't come home. I wanted to ask about the man she left with, but the words were falling from her fast. I had to let her tell her story.

'He left me. I should have known, but you don't think when you love someone. You think they love you back. They don't always.'

An image of Tizzy came to mind, strong and beautiful. Would she think of me? I'd brought her nothing but trouble and she had proved herself true. If I told her what I really felt, would she love me back? My stomach twisted at the thought she would not, and I pushed it from my mind. Such imaginings couldn't help us now.

'Who was he?'

Rebecca turned her head, but not before I saw tears gather in her eyes. Hard to dismiss love once it came, despite how things may turn out. I waited.

'Marrick's nephew.'

'The stonemason?'

She nodded. Marrick was the blacksmith, and his nephew Bran had come to stay with him the summer before she left. He was training to be a stonemason, still apprenticed, barely older than Rebecca herself. While he worked on the church he drew plenty of attention from the village, foolish girls with new ribbons, trailing wildflowers in the brims of their hats. Isabel and I used to laugh at them on Sundays. I had not thought Rebecca would compete for such a man, with his easy charm and his blond curls, though I had once caught her and Mother staring at the muscles of his arms as he worked in shirtsleeves.

'There was no-one like him in the village. Writing poems and bringing them to the house in broad daylight. He didn't care who knew he liked me. And his words were beautiful. He wrote all the time he wasn't working or waiting outside our house.'

I had never noticed. A child, blissfully unaware, absorbed in the gardens at Lynton, my sketching, the dogs. Mother must have seen it coming. No wonder she was so distraught. The whole village must have known.

'We *were* to be married. I knew Mother would never agree and it was my idea to leave, to elope and be married where we weren't known. We planned to return with the good news, when we could not be parted. But none of the churches in Cheshire would help and we didn't know what else to do. It was hard to be so close, when we loved each other, and it wasn't long before we lay together.'

I felt my cheeks redden at the thought. What must it be like to love so much, without care for anything in the world? All I had to compare was the angry, resentful coupling of my husband. Who had never cared for me at all.

'At first we were happy. Bran found work and a place to rent. But I soon fell with child and I began to fret. He worked long hours, without time to write, and he blamed me for his missed chances. We quarrelled. And one day he just didn't come home.'

It was not the tale of seduction I'd expected, but the cruelty was there nonetheless. To leave a young woman to her fate in such circumstances. He must have loved himself more. Why must men hold such pride in their talents?

'I walked to the workhouse at Handbridge, didn't know where else to go. I was showing, disgraced, and no-one would give me work. I was put to the laundry, then the sewing rooms when I could no longer stand all day.'

'What was it like?' I whispered. The workhouse. The very word struck fear. I had only heard it mentioned once at home, when Father lost his last patients and Mother said we would be ruined.

'Cold. I was freezing cold and hungry the whole time. Even in the laundry. And I shared a bed with two others, who hit my legs when I turned in the bed to ease my discomfort. Father came to fetch me after a while, and I was so pleased to see him. I thought I was forgiven.'

Tears welled as I thought of her there, so close to Lynton, yet so far from her family. I drew her towards me, clung tightly to her arm. Whatever happened now, we would not lose each other again. I looked around to see the alleys had narrowed still further; grand houses had changed to rows of rough cottages and the air smelt of chamber pots. How far had we walked?

'Are we nearly at George's?' I asked.

'Not far. By the river. He's a boatman.' She threw me a look of defiance, perhaps expecting shock. The Thames boatmen were rough creatures, their work dirty. They paddled up and down the reeking river all day, paid to fish all kinds of horrors from the water, and many had reputations for fighting and drink.

'You will find no judgement from me, Rebecca.' When she heard my story, she would understand why, but I needed her to finish first. So I could understand what evil really dwelt in that house. 'Did Father take you to Evergreen House?'

'He did. Said he'd met another doctor whose sister could help me, who ran a house for unmarried women. It was alright, at first. I didn't like the way they called us all "fallen", as though it was our fault, like we chose to be left.' Rebecca frowned and I realised it was true, it was only women who were blamed. 'But they fed us, and we rested. The company was nice, the other girls.'

'There didn't seem to be anyone home when I knocked.'

'No-one would answer. Visitors aren't allowed. You have to agree to that before you move in. Anyway, the girls come and go all the time. Doesn't do to get too friendly with anyone or you miss them too much when they're gone.'

'I followed you before, into the market. Did you see me? Where were you going?'

'To work, Maddie.' Her face hardened again. 'We were given no choice. First the photographs and then the threat of sending prints to our families . . . do not look like that, I can't bear it. You haven't lived enough to understand.'

Exhibit 32

Scrimshaw nightstick with concealed dagger.
Whalebone and pewter. c. 1780.

George scolded Rebecca for leading me to his house. 'Dressed like a rich woman. She'll bring eyes to the place just when you need to hide.' While Rebecca moved a stack of clothes from the only chair, he set a fire and banged around by the sink, washing cracked cups for tea. He wore the Thames boatman waistcoat and oilskin breeches, striped shirtsleeves rolled to the elbow as though cold couldn't affect him. Good-looking and dark-skinned, he wore his cap pulled down over his black hair, piercing eyes staring out underneath. I couldn't hold his gaze for long and I felt uncomfortable perched on a low wooden stool in his one-roomed house. Everything felt as intensely male as Lucius's rooms, somewhere we shouldn't really be. Or somewhere *I* shouldn't be anyway – it was clear from the way George looked at Rebecca that they were more than friends. Even so I did not like to ask questions, in case he was unaware of the full story. I sat awkwardly, arranging the folds of my dress, until Rebecca sat down on the small bed and patted my hand.

'It's alright. George knows everything. He's been trying to get me to leave for a long time.'

'I'm glad you finally saw sense.' George spoke with a broad

accent. He brought mugs of scalding tea and as there was no table, set them on the floor.

Was it sense for Rebecca? Though I hated to think of her working for Grace, she would be missed, and searched for. And what of the photographs? Would they be posted home? Mother would never recover.

'Do you think they will look for you? Where will you go?'

'She'll stay here.' George's chin jutted as he spoke. I had no doubt he would protect her as far as he could, but she couldn't hide for ever, and she could hardly come to Arlington Crescent.

'If you wrote to Father . . .'

'Father! When he came to find me in the sheets room at Handbridge, I thought he'd come to take me home,' she said bitterly.

Would he? Perhaps. But Mother would never have allowed it. Poor Rebecca, so close by. 'What's a sheets room?'

She frowned, as though my ignorance was irritating. 'Where they sew linen, for fancy stores and grand homes. At least I could sit down. But Father said he'd been told of a place that was better for me and we went straight to London. He didn't even talk to me on the way. Just held onto me every time we stopped, like he thought I was going to run. Where would I have run to? I was near my time.' Tears welled in her eyes. 'It was better, too, at first. There was food for a start.'

'Isn't there food at the workhouse?'

A snort from George showed he was listening, disapproving.

'Leave her, George, why would she know about it?' Rebecca pulled her shawl tighter across her shoulders. Strips of cotton were pinned across the broken glass in the window frames and, despite the fire, it was no warmer in the room than outside. George lifted her mug of tea, and she took it in both hands. As he looked at her his face changed, his expression pure tenderness. Whatever Bran had been, she had someone who loved her now. 'She's not had that kind of life. And anyway, she's just a child.'

Why did everyone insist on calling me that? 'I'm a married woman.'

'Isn't your fancy husband going to miss you, then?' George's face was stony again.

'He won't notice I've gone,' I replied. Others would, though, if I wasn't careful.

Rebecca looked down at the rough blanket covering the bed. She picked up the patchwork cushion, the only colour in the room, and began to knead it. 'Some of us aren't fortunate enough to have been allowed husbands.'

I bit my tongue. I wanted to scream that she'd abandoned us, that she'd left me to use my life to make her amends. But her eyes were sad and tired. She'd paid the price a thousand times over.

'Do you know who my husband is?'

She shook her head, eyes down, as though it was of no consequence.

'Lucius Everley. Grace Atherton's brother.'

Rebecca's mouth dropped open. 'How . . . what did . . .'

'He came to stay with Father. Was he there? When Father took you to Evergreen?'

She chewed her lip, like she always did when thinking, and I saw a flash of my Rebecca.

'Yes. Yes, he was there. They both greeted us, and Father stayed downstairs when she took me up to the room. I didn't see him again. They gave me something that made me sleepy.'

They were fond of that. Did Lucius and Father come up with the plan to pass me off as penance that afternoon, or did Lucius think of it on his own? Wasn't it enough that they had a whole house full of women with babies to be taken? There was no need for him to take so many. The small museum was full of bones. Small bones, white from the lime room. Such greed. Although suspicions had been forming in my mind for some time, it suddenly became clear why Lucius needed to marry me. His fake creature. He'd already tried with others and realised he couldn't wait to transport the little things. He needed a wife because the baby had to be born in his house for its skull to be soft enough. Just a stone's throw from his workshop. Hideous even to imagine a fellow human as capable of such a deed. *The devil's work.* Is that what Annie saw? No wonder the poor girl was hysterical. She would never be believed in St Margary's. I shivered, and took a sip of tea from the chipped enamel mug. It was bent, as though it had been thrown against the wall, but the tea was good and strong.

'Does he know you came to find me? Maddie, your husband . . . I don't think he is a good man. His sister is hard, cruel. What they do at Evergreen is not natural and they pretend it is philanthropy. We had ordinary clothes that we were made to wear when the charity board came, good food that was laid out and sewing brought so we looked occupied. As soon as they were gone it was swept away and we were put to work we could not talk about, even with one another. Some of the girls weren't strong enough and they were sent away.'

'Where? Where did the other girls go after Evergreen?'

Rebecca shook her head and her beautiful curls cascaded across her shoulders. 'Don't know. Into service. Out to work.'

'What about . . .' I struggled to ask the question. 'What happened to their babies?'

Rebecca shrugged. Easier not to think about it. How could I begin to say what I thought? George glared as if daring me to upset her again.

'Maybe they took them to the Foundling, maybe they farmed them, I don't know. They weren't at Evergreen. My daughter didn't survive the birth.'

'Neither did Tizzy's – Hattie's – apparently,' I said softly. 'Neither did mine. His name would have been Arthur.'

'You had a child?' Rebecca's eyes widened.

'No. I didn't. But that's the point. My husband, Lucius, delivered them all. Were you allowed to hold yours? To keep a lock of hair? An image of her face to remember?'

She shook her head.

'No-one ever saw their child? So many didn't survive? It's surprising, that's all.'

Rebecca's face was white, anxious. Her hands plucked at the bedcover, twisting it between her fingers. 'I wanted . . . first of all I was glad. No. Relieved. Easier to manage without a child. That's what Mrs Atherton said, too, when she came to ask how I'd pay my way. Then it hit me hard. By the time I asked to see her, it was too late. They wouldn't tell me where she was buried, said it couldn't be . . . because I wasn't married . . . it couldn't be in the churchyard. I don't even know where she is.'

Tiny bones in the cloth-wrapped mummy, the arms of the faery child, the little skull and shrunken head. I knew what he was doing. Had suspected long enough and still the thought brought nausea, choked my throat. How could I describe it to anyone else? I placed my hand over Rebecca's on the bedcover and she stilled. 'As far as I can see, it's only his sister's children that he was able to deliver safely.'

George, who was leaning against the wall, suddenly straightened and walked over to us. 'What are you suggesting? That he killed the babies? That he's a murderer like his father?'

Like his father? I had heard some things from Caroline about

Old Dr Everley, were those rumours true? 'I don't know what to think.' But the words came anyway, tumbling from me in a waterfall of relief. The small museum, the lime room, the skullcap and the sea creature. When I'd finished George was changed, his handsome features concerned. He no longer glared as though I'd come to hurt Rebecca, but his jaw was set, his expression determined. Perhaps I could rely on him for help.

'He can try all he likes to save his family name. Everyone knows what Everley did. It doesn't surprise me to hear his son's the same.'

George put his arm around my shoulder, and I felt the hardness of his muscles. Someone to lean on. After everything, that must be what Rebecca needed. I pushed thoughts of Mother's disapproval to the back of my mind. If all this was true, she'd never want me or Rebecca near the family again.

'What did he do?' asked Rebecca in a quiet voice.

'Him or his hired thugs. Amounts to the same thing. Grabbed a couple of men on their way home from the alehouse, stoved their heads in at the back and pushed them in the river. Didn't look right when they got fished out of the water, but the peelers didn't want to know, never do when it's that sort. Saves them a job. We knew it was him soon as we saw him in the morning. Eager, he was. He knew the bodies would be there. "Just seeing if anything arrived overnight?" he said. As if anyone would be there on the off-chance at six in the morning.' George's arm tightened on my shoulder, almost hurting. 'I'll never forget the look on him. "Good," he said when he saw them, rubbing his hands. "Those injuries don't matter." They did, though. Couldn't understand it, I had to ask the gaffer what it meant. Then he explained that they wouldn't show on the operating table, when they'd be on their backs. Everley took them straight off, still wet, had the boxes all ready for them.'

'Why wasn't it reported to the magistrate?' I asked.

'I'd only been in the job a few months, hadn't seen a body before. Seen plenty now, of course. But even then, I knew a bluebottle wouldn't side with someone like me over him. Those men . . . coming from there, they were likely already known to the magistrates for all the wrong reasons. Wasn't going to waste his time on that, was he? Besides, he paid us well for them. So we couldn't tell, because we're not supposed to take anything for bodies except from the authorities, the shilling for hooking them out. I know that now, but I was a boy.' George's chin pushed out defensively and he moved away. I wasn't sure quite how long ago it was, but he must have been young and new in the job. He seemed a decent man.

'She's just asking,' said Rebecca. 'No-one did anything to you, did they?'

'Mr Atherton did. Grace's husband. He used to run Evergreen for Old Dr Everley, but everyone knew it was her who did it really. He wasn't hard enough for the job but he was a big man. Word among the boatmen was he was made to hit those men and push them in, and he took fright from it. He tried to get the magistrates involved and then he disappeared.'

'So where is he now?'

George gave me a look that said, *Where do you think?* What did I think? If the rest of it was true, then they could have dispatched him as easily as sent him to work abroad. Lucius would know how. His drawers full of tools. I felt suddenly faint.

'Mrs Atherton used to talk about it, "The stain on the family name". Something stuck to them, didn't it?' Rebecca believed it. Already. She had spent time with them, and she believed it too. 'She was always talking about how her brother was going to make the family name great again.'

Hiding the stain with another. Unwanted babies. Were they the same as underworld villains – dispensable and easy to hide? How long had the Everleys been getting away with it? And what on earth did I think I could do? George was right. Neither police nor magistrate would care about such stories. I'd been foolish to think anyone would. How would it help me now, or Rebecca, or Tizzy?

The colour had returned to Rebecca's face. 'I should never have run away.'

'No going back there,' said George grimly.

'But it will mean trouble for Maddie.'

If Tizzy wasn't back at the house, I would run away too. I would stay with Rebecca and never return. But how could I leave my dear friend?

'There are girls at Evergreen now, they don't have long. If we don't do something they'll go through the same thing. I can't let that happen,' Rebecca cried.

'We can get proof,' I said, trying not to show how scared the very idea was making me. 'But I'll need help.'

'I'll do it. Not you, Rebecca – if that woman sees you . . .' George clenched his fists. 'Her father was a murderer, and it sounds to me like a family trait.'

George fetched a man called Albert from the rooms next door. A tall man dressed in the same boatsman's cap and jacket, but stockier than George, less handsome, with the florid complexion of one who spends most of his time outdoors. We travelled to Arlington Crescent in virtual silence once I'd explained my plan, and I wasn't sure if that was a good sign or not. I knew they believed me; but did they believe it would work?

We crept along the passage to the garden and I paused to turn, to check they were behind me. Albert carried a nightstick and a length of metal pipe, one in each hand. The sight of them, grim and serious, made my knees buckle. What did we think we were doing? Above the high wind I thought I heard the sound of Tizzy howling, and I cringed at the thought of the Barkers holding her down. It was all I could do not to break in and rescue her instead. But that wouldn't solve everything, and we didn't have long; we had to get to work. We could save her when we had proof. I unbolted the kitchen door, tiptoed on the gravel to the garden gate and opened it slowly. Tizzy's screams had set my nerves on edge, and I was flustered, no longer certain of answers.

I brought my finger to my lips, though the men knew the need for silence, and held the gate as they passed through, closing it softly, flinching at the squeak of the hinge. Part of the gate was broken, as though something heavy had been thrown against it, and I wondered again what Barker did out there for so long each day. So much needed repairing. The toolshed door hung loose, the grass was long.

We needed proof. We'd all agreed on that, but Rebecca was the most adamant. She'd seen a side to Grace that was unbreakable, untouchable. If I was going to put myself at such great risk, it had to be a foolproof plan. Something the magistrate could not dispute. Ideally, we needed the creature, which was still at the Society while Lucius enjoyed his fame. But the others would do, the things with bones. If we showed those, they would at least have cause to seize the creature. First, we had to get into the locked rooms, and the only way to do that was from the outside. George said Albert had experience in scaling walls and opening windows. Neither of us commented on why that might be, because such skill was exactly what we needed. From memory, I'd drawn several pictures of the things we needed to find. These drawings I thrust into George's hand.

As I turned to indicate the third-floor window he'd need to scale and enter, Tizzy screamed again and I fell to the ground as though it were me being struck. My wrists still bore the scars of restraint. Would this be worth Tizzy's pain? It had been her idea, which she'd shared before I left for Evergreen House, and she was right – nothing would have convinced the Barkers to leave the house. They had to be kept occupied. Remembering my story about Annie, she would pretend to have found something that terrified her, knowing they would respond as before. She was the bravest person I'd ever met and I wouldn't let her down. We had to move quickly before she too was taken away to St Margary's. If they took her, it would be hard to get her out and I couldn't let that happen. I felt already that to live without her would be like living without air.

George held out a hand to help me and, as I pushed away from the ground, I touched freshly dug earth. I felt around in the gloom. A small mound at the edge of the border, newly piled, the size of a dog, or a child. Nausea rose in my chest, the air too thick to breathe. It couldn't be. Suspicions were one thing, but this could mean we didn't have to enter the house at all. I began to scrabble with both hands and George dropped to the ground beside me. Small white bones glinted silver in the light of the moon.

'This is it,' whispered George. 'Enough. Push the earth back and we'll leave. There's no point in anyone but you talking to the magistrate, he'll just ignore us. He'll ignore anyone at this time of night, but especially us. You'll have to sit tight until the morning.'

'Tizzy . . .' How could I leave her to that? How could I listen and wait until morning? Wouldn't the Barkers bring Grace and Lucius back? How could I face them?

George put his hands on my shoulders. 'You don't have a

choice. For Rebecca. For you and Tizzy too.'

'So this is the truth of it.' Mrs Barker's voice startled all of us; her footsteps had made no sound. 'Stand back.' She walked towards us, her face grim set. 'I knew you were mad. Lucius was too soft on you, he should never have removed your straps. Look what you've done. Your own child. How could you?'

Earth clung to my hands, my dress. The moon shone across the half-dug border. The screams had stopped. All was quiet as a churchyard. Mrs Barker's fingers dug into my arms. I jerked my head towards the gate and George and his friend ran just as Barker reached the garden and pushed a cloth into my mouth.

33

The Marlborough Assizes

'Taking account of the evidence of Dr Venables, it's easy to understand how things may have simply spiralled out of control. A sudden wedding, a new home, the weight of responsibility that comes with being a wife, then a mother.'

The magistrate paused to drink from a wine glass filled with what looked like water. After everything he'd heard, it may well have been gin. Two women leant further over the gallery rail. Such bated breath for the summing up, it would have been easy to hear a hatpin fall to the floor. Even the gentlemen from the news-sheets, who'd talked through the rest of the hearing, were quiet for a change. They, too, leant forward from their places at the back of the room.

'Such responsibility often proves too much for young women. We have heard that you had a tendency towards melancholy, to nervousness. And we have heard that your nervous disposition was worsened by situations beyond your control – the loss of your sister at a young age, your father's difficulties, and then being apart from your family. Members of your household – your husband and his sister, your housekeepers – have explained the trouble you had adjusting.'

Though his words addressed her directly, the magistrate's eyes avoided Maddie and travelled around the court as he spoke. He seemed not to have seen her at all. I had to lean to the right to check she was still in the dock. Sitting on the bench, her bowed head barely reached the top of the wooden sides. She was miserable, crushed. They had not let me visit with the news that I'd found Tizzy. Not dead, as Grace had cruelly insisted, but in St Margary's, which wasn't much better. Poor Maddie looked as small as a child. She'd placed her faith in me to help and, though I'd done as she asked, I seemed to have failed. A miracle was needed. I held my breath and listened.

'I have absorbed the advice of Dr Threlfall, who maintains that you were not in your right mind. He has recommended internment with a course of treatment using cold baths and electricity.' Furious scribbling from the newsmen. Loud tutting from the women leaning over the gallery rail. They were there for the hanging and nothing else would do. 'However, I remain to be convinced of the efficacy of these modern treatments, or the work of the alienists. It is my considered opinion that a murderer, or murderess, is by nature not in their right mind and yet they must face appropriate punishment for the crime they have committed. All right-thinking members of society must wish for that to be the case.'

'Hear hear,' shouted a red-faced man at the end of my row. His arms flew above his head and his eyes bulged as though his cravat was too tightly fastened. The woman next to him, with whom he'd been sharing a bottle of gin, pushed him down again, although she also seemed excited over the unfolding drama. She wore a huge pair of men's hobnail boots that stuck out from under her skirts like warnings.

The magistrate took another draught from his glass, wiped his mouth with satisfaction. 'I must ask visitors to the court to remain calm.' He allowed the noise to abate before continuing. 'Considering the evidence I have heard, and seen, it is my understanding that you, Mrs Madeleine Everley, lost control of your thoughts and actions and in a moment of blind madness, murdered your own child.'

Amid the gasps I finally turned to look at the far rows, where Lucius sat with Grace. His face was buried in his hands. Grace wore a look of absolute triumph and placed an arm around her brother, patting his shoulder. A spike of light from her diamond bracelet reached the dock where Maddie sat, unmoving. Why did he not just finish? We knew what he'd say. Maddie would be hanged by the neck until dead. While crowds ate toffee apples and applauded. Barbaric that such punishment should still be public.

I felt numb. Why hadn't I allowed Ambrose to come with me? He'd wanted to. Probably knew what would happen. Deep down, perhaps, so did I, though I'd hoped against hope that what she had asked me to do would work. That Stoneham doubted Lucius was clear. I took him out of his pitiful boarding house, gave him a room and decent meals, and he drafted pages of reasons why Lucius's 'finds' could be proved to be fakes. Ambrose took them straight to the Society. It was not, he said, his place to take them to the court. Men! What place had such pride when a life was at stake! And what could we do with the evidence now that judgement had passed? Surely it proved his motive? Perhaps it was all too late. Once the magistrate gave his order for punishment, could anything change his mind? What was taking him so long?

Murmurs began, rippling like rings from rocks thrown in water. Over by the Chair, two clerks furiously waved papers and pointed to the entrance. Grace watched intently. The magistrate held up a hand to silence the clerks and motioned for them to open the door. A tall figure walked in, dressed in a wide-collared jacket and neatly pressed striped trousers. He looked familiar and my mind raced through possibilities. Where had I seen him before? His face was serious, framed with wiry grey hair curled just under the ears. Eyes shining behind a small pair of spectacles. Why had he arrived at such a late hour? Had he come to rescue Maddie?

A clerk led the tall man to the dock. People were openly talking now, all attempts to stay calm thwarted. A theatrical interruption, right at the point of verdict. It was too good to be true. I tried to focus amid the noise. Surely this must be good news. Why else would they allow the intrusion? Not to hear more of the same evidence, that would be pointless.

Maddie's head was still lowered; Lucius looked pale, though he and the stranger had nodded towards each other in recognition. The magistrate read carefully through every paper in the pile before removing his glasses and rubbing his eyes, dragging his open palms down his face as though infinitely weary. He contemplated the court, gestured the clerks to move to the doors, then seized his wooden mallet and banged hard upon the desk.

'This is most unconventional,' he muttered, 'but I am urged to consider late-submitted evidence that appears to undermine the assumptions made in my assessment of this case. I am not so narrow-minded as to ignore it.' He threw a meaningful look at the clerks by the door. Evidently, they hadn't wanted him to listen. Was he reading Stoneham's notes? If so, were they enough? A pungent scent of gin, a scrabbling under chairs and in pockets. I was tempted to ask for some myself. It was hard to stop my legs from shaking.

'Please swear yourself in, Dr John Henry Wilson.'

Of course. Chair of the Society of Collectors. He'd been at Father's once or twice, but I'd never spoken to him. He did not, I was told, think highly of women with questions, and Father kept us apart in case of 'upsets'. A pity. He looked nice enough and it might have been useful to know him. Dr Wilson stood with legs apart, hands clasped together, as though he could wait things out all day. A Society man, with all the patience of endless meetings.

'Thank you for bringing these papers.'

Dr Wilson inclined his head. Grace tried to rise but Lucius stayed her, a fixed smile on his face. He appeared to have every faith in his mentor.

'They are authored by yourself and by a Mr Jack Stoneham.'

'That is correct.'

'A student?'

'Indeed, but an astute one.'

At the mention of Stoneham's name Lucius's face grew ashen. My heart began to soar. Clever Maddie, had she really known what she was doing all along?

'Contained within these papers is a description of a fossil creature that Dr Everley submitted to the Society.'

'That is correct.'

'A creature he claims to have found in Dorset . . . but you assert otherwise?'

'Dr Everley's creature is a sham.' Wilson spoke clearly and slowly. 'A chimera, as Stoneham rightly asserts. The various bone parts of the creature we have identified as belonging to a dog and a pasture animal, perhaps a sheep. But the skull is undoubtedly that of a newborn human child. As are the shoulder joints.'

Gasps of shock. A woman screamed. The newsmen pushed forwards to better hear his words. All I could think of was Maddie. Poor, brave, tortured Maddie. Her Arthur. She knew. She wouldn't have asked me to find Stoneham if she didn't. All that time she kept it to herself and it would have eaten her alive. Enough to send anyone mad. Surely they must release her now?

'Is it your belief that the skull of this . . . creature belongs to the child that Mrs Everley stands accused of murdering?'

'It certainly appears to belong to a child.'

Lucius jumped from his seat and was restrained by the clerks at the door. Grace took her chance. She hit one of them hard with her umbrella and he jumped back; she ran and he took after her in pursuit. I willed him to catch her. It should have been easy with the dress she was wearing.

'Your letter asserts that Dr Everley himself had the most to gain from such a crime, given his . . . submission. But the evidence does not prove, one way or another, which of them carried out the deed. We have heard of Mrs Everley's descent into madness. Perhaps . . . perhaps this was a husband's attempt to cover a heinous crime?'

'I do not know Mrs Everley. And that would, perhaps, be one view.' Wilson breathed in deeply, like a doctor who doesn't want to share his diagnosis but knows he must. 'Were it not for the fact that there were many others. Mrs Everley's sister alerted the authorities as I read these papers and I believe Dr Everley's garden is still being searched. As I understand it, the constabulary already believe the number of bodies is significant.'

Exhibit 34

A horn grown from a human forehead.
Origin unknown.

'We therefore commit this body to the ground, earth to earth, ashes to ashes, dust to dust; in sure and certain hope of the Resurrection to eternal life . . .' The reverend intoned from memory, as he had on my wedding day. He looked older, his robes plainer. It must have been hard for him to make sense of things. Hearing everything that had happened would shake anyone's beliefs. When we arrived for the funeral he'd apologised, taking me to one side and speaking in hushed tones as he welcomed me into his fold. Why bother with such secrecy with only six of us there? My story was well known and, finally, I was among friends.

Lifting his right arm high, he sprinkled earth into the grave. Dull thuds rained on the coffin lid. He gestured for us all to do the same and I moved forward, fearful of slipping on the wet earth. Finally, the drizzle had stopped. The sky was clear blue, but the ground was still soaked and my boots were caked in mud. Tizzy took my arm as I leant in to drop a single white rose on top of the earth, holding me tightly to keep me safe. As I hoped she always would.

Rebecca and George came forward together to place their

flower and the one passed to them by Ambrose, who held Caroline back. Kind of them all to come. They hadn't known Annie, but Rebecca had and she insisted everyone pay their respects.

'It could so easily have been me, or Tizzy, or even you, Maddie. They would have stopped at nothing to get what they wanted. Nobody's life was important.' Rebecca was right, too. They could have killed us all. Perhaps they had planned to. The thought still haunted my sleep.

Caroline, as good as her word, had gone to St Margary's to find out the truth. Sensibly, she'd taken Ambrose, knowing they wouldn't refuse admission to him, and they'd been permitted to remove Tizzy the same afternoon. Dazed and weak from sedatives and vicious beatings, it had taken several days for Tizzy to recover her senses under their care. When she did, she insisted they go back for Annie, bravely offering to go herself. It was too late. Annie was never the strongest of the Evergreen girls and by the time they returned she was already dead, starved and heavily battered. Ambrose was furious enough to start proceedings to close them down. It was, he said, a fitting legacy for Annie and one from which I should take comfort. I did. It still hurt that I'd been powerless to stop it earlier.

After Annie's funeral, Caroline insisted that we return to Arlington Crescent for a final visit. Just once, before the house and contents were sold, because Ambrose said it would help to close the memories and allow me to start living without fear.

'I don't know if I can.' My hand trembled, shaking the heavy key in the lock. It struck me that I'd never held the key before, never been allowed such free access to my own house. There was nothing I wanted to take; even my clothes would remind me of Lucius. When I'd regained some weight and felt more like myself,

I would take pleasure in replacing them, enjoying Rebecca's company as I chose the dresses I'd always wanted.

'You can,' said Tizzy firmly, covering my hand with hers so that we both twisted the key at the same time. Caroline pushed me gently in the small of the back and we entered the hallway together. The smell of decay was fainter, but still there, cloying and sweet-rotten like dead flowers in water. No-one spoke of it.

We passed through the rooms in a daze. Uncleared plates lay on the breakfast table. The rug in the dining room was caught up at one corner, as though someone had tripped on it. Drawers were open and some of the silver cutlery lay scattered on the floor. Had the Barkers planned to run? They hadn't managed it. Both of them were in a cell like mine, already tried for their part in assisting and covering up murders, awaiting the noose. Lucius and Grace would be too. I pushed the thought from my mind. Tizzy planned to watch each hanging, *to make sure it's done*. But I couldn't face it. I would have to take her word and let her be brave on my behalf again. So much for me to thank her for. It had been easy, in the end, to tell her how I felt. All the weeks and months of worrying had been a waste of time. She had, she said, loved me first, and she laughed as she rolled her eyes at how long it had taken me to catch up.

Caroline picked up a knife, traced a finger over the scrolling on its handle. 'These are old.' She weighed it in her hand. 'Heavy. They'll be valuable. Don't you want to keep anything?'

How could I ever use them without thinking of evil? Everything in the house was filled with it like the ghost of Old Dr Everley. 'No. I don't.' I opened up the chiffonier to show the rest of the silverware, candlesticks and mustard pots, gravy boats and sugar-tongs, all studded with thin silver bees and lined up along the shelves like trophies. 'These can be auctioned, or melted. I doubt whether anyone would want to own them.'

'Collectors will want them. They always do. Might even drive the price up.' Caroline winced as she caught my eye. 'Sorry. But you'll need the money.'

'I'll be fine.' I glanced at Tizzy. We'd both be fine. 'I know we can't stay with you for ever but—'

'I didn't mean that at all . . .' she interrupted. I held up my hand to silence her.

'I know. And you've been very generous. Tizzy and I are grateful, but we'll need our own place to live. With the money from the sale of the house and effects, we'll be able to find one.'

'Where will you go?'

I shrugged, though I knew where I wanted. A house near Alice's was for sale and I'd already written to the owner to ask for patience while I arranged the sale of Arlington Crescent. A sweet mews cottage, with room for both of us as well as a maid. It had a large bright studio for my work. I wouldn't need to sell my paintings to live but I wanted to try. To live there, in a community of like-minded women and artists – it seemed like the thing that might save me. A future I could imagine. 'We have some plans.'

'You're not about to follow Eloise?'

I swallowed hard. It hadn't been easy to say goodbye and for a while I'd entertained hopes of raising her as my own. But Tizzy was right, she'd never escape the family stain. Better for her to grow up in a country that knew nothing of her story. We'd already waved goodbye to the boat that would take her to the colonies. A family had been found to take her in, a couple with a huge farm in Australia – a country big enough for her story to be lost in. By the time she arrived, her own family home would have been sold and the money divided between her and her brothers in their private nursing home. It was quickly arranged. Once the gardens were fully exhumed there was little point in continuing the pretence that her father was still working in India. The decomposed corpse of a man that matched his height and wore his ring was unearthed among the many smaller bones in the garden.

'Don't worry, we'll stay close. Near to Alice hopefully. I shall be a bohemian yet.'

'And I'll be around to keep you straight and proper,' said Tizzy. 'Can't have you swigging sherry all afternoon with those artists.'

'You're the one that will need keeping on the straight and narrow,' I laughed. 'If you have your way, you'll be running riot with a houseful of fallen women.'

'I thought you agreed? Anyway, I won't be there the whole time. We'll need to find someone to run it. I haven't got the first clue about things like that.'

Caroline looked at us, puzzled.

'Evergreen House,' I said. 'We talked about selling that, too, but Tizzy's right – women who can't go back to their families need somewhere to go.'

'Might as well give them somewhere nice.' Tizzy's face was serious. 'Don't know how it would work. We talked about selling some of it, but we want to help as many as we can.'

'Why doesn't Maddie teach them to paint?' Caroline asked. 'There are all kinds of cottage industries. You could sell painted wallpaper, or baskets, or . . .'

'Yes, yes,' Tizzy agreed in excitement. 'Couldn't they keep the babies with them then? We don't want them having to give them up so they can go into service. Or worse.' She scowled at the thought.

Rebecca would want to help. She'd be good at it too. Much as she'd convinced me she was happy living in George's place, I didn't like to think of her there, in the thick of the river's damp and stench. We could make them a neat home at Evergreen, a proper home. George deserved it after what he'd faced to help me. Going back to the house and digging for evidence in the dead of night, alone. When I thought of what he'd seen, what he'd uncovered. I hoped our plans would lay such ghosts to rest.

Though I didn't want to look, I forced myself to walk through the kitchen. Bowls were strewn across the table, a rotten smell came from the larder. I turned away. The auctioneers could deal with it. Through the window I caught sight of the garden and my stomach lurched. What would we find? Shallow graves, untended? But the flowerbeds were empty. Freshly dug over. All evidence removed. Fourteen babies they said, all with missing or damaged skulls. He'd been trying his creature for years without success. What he needed was a baby to be born in his workshop. Arthur. Now I was glad I'd never seen his face. But he'd have a proper funeral, I'd see to that. They all would.

'Come on.' Caroline tugged my arm. 'We don't want to be here all day.'

We walked up the back stairs to the bedrooms, moved through them one at a time, Tizzy holding up things she thought I'd want. The locket was there, Arthur's curl still inside. His hair was red-brown, the same as Lucius's. The curl was dried and stiff, but it was all there was. It gave me some comfort to think that Lucius had bothered to put it there. Somehow it made me feel that he was not all evil, that some shred of humanity remained. I pushed the locket into Tizzy's hands. I couldn't trust myself with it. All I took was Ariadne's lead. Brave girl. Throwing herself at the Barkers as they caught me. She didn't stand a chance. We'd have another dog when the time was right, more than one perhaps. I imagined us walking a dozen Spaniels in the park, leads clasped in both hands. There'd be no more children. Not ours anyway. We'd have enough to care for at Evergreen.

All the doors were open, and the lime room and workshop were exposed. We stood in the doorway and I wondered how many of the newsmen would attempt to pay their way in here when the house went up for sale. They'd tried with me already. Trying to wheedle Ambrose into letting them in, offering bills that could feed an army of girls at Evergreen. Maybe I'd tell them one day. But if they got in here now, they wouldn't think much of it. All the equipment was gone, Lucius's tools, the vats, his skeletonising equipment. The magistrate's men had cleared it all. What would they do with it?

The small museum was stripped of almost everything. The jars and mummies taken, even the mammoth tooth. All that remained on a single shelf was a handful of animal parts. A small lump of bone, labelled as human though it was horn-like; an armadillo skin, nubbed and shiny; a severed monkey's paw, the fingers curled in on themselves like a baby's fist. And my seahorse with the terrible, beautiful face. I stared at it for a long time before slipping it into my pocket. When I could, I would find it a box and keep it to remind me of what I'd lost, and what I'd found. It could become the face of the unknown thing that still swam through my dreams.

Acknowledgements

Though writing a book is a brutally solitary process, bringing it to publication requires the dedication and enthusiasm of many. Wholehearted thanks to Wendy Bough, the firepower behind The Caledonia Novel Award, an important platform for new writers and without which this story may still lie dormant. Huge gratitude for the patience, care and love of literature from my wonderful agent, Charlotte Seymour. I'm also grateful for the enthusiasm and experience of Susie Dunlop, Publishing Director at Allison & Busby and for the skill of her team of copy editors, designers and proofreaders. It's been a great pleasure to work with all of you.

I will forever be indebted to the support and love of my sister, Jacqui, and dear friend, Becky, both of whom loved this story from the outset and encouraged me through the self-doubt. For my husband, Matt, and sons, Ben and Ted: just know that you three are everything.

JODY COOKSLEY studied literature at Oxford Brookes University and has a Masters in Victorian Poetry. Her debut novel *The Glass House* is a fictional account of the life of nineteenth-century photographer, Julia Margaret Cameron. *The Small Museum*, Jody's third novel, won the 2023 Caledonia Novel Award. Jody is originally from Norwich and now lives in Cranleigh.

jrcbooks.co.uk
@jcooksleyauthor
@jodycooksleyauthor